BLUE BLOODED

LORD & LADY HETHERIDGE MYSTERY SERIES BOOK #5

EMMA JAMESON

For my dear friend and fellow mystery author Cyn Mackley, who held my hand every step of the way. Thanks, Cyn!

CHAPTER ONE

$\mathcal{A}$nthony Hetheridge, ninth baron of Wellegrave and former chief superintendent for New Scotland Yard, welcomed the spring. In January, he'd been forced out of his distinguished career by old enemies who'd long been sharpening their knives. In February, he'd returned to the Yard as a consultant, a role that allowed him to do things heretofore only dreamt of: bill by the hour, ignore internal politics, and go home each day at five o'clock. In March, as daffodils sprang up all over London and pink camellia trees spilled over wrought iron fences, Tony had paid the £300 fee, took the "Fit and Proper Person" test, and passed the competency exam necessary to receive his private investigator's license. Now it was April—warm, sunnier than usual, and full of surprises.

On April fifth, his brother-in-law, Ritchie Wakefield, had modified the shape of a Lego brick by heating it with a cigarette lighter. In the process, he'd set ablaze a two-hundred-year-old French mahogany sofa. This had caught the nearby Italian silk brocade curtains on fire, which went up like tissue paper. Half of Tony's ancestral London home, Wellegrave House, had been burned out.

Thankfully, no one was injured. As his wife Kate raged, his assistant Mrs. Snell tutted, and his manservant Harvey wept, Tony decided that he, too, would abandon British reserve and vent his true feelings on the matter. Specifically: relief. Ringing up an interior design company recommended by his friend Lady Margaret Knolls, he'd authorized its head decorator to chuck out what was ruined, sell what remained, and chase away the ghosts of Hetheridges past.

No more living in a museum, he thought, smiling as he poured himself a cup of tea. He was still a newlywed, in the process of adopting a son, and "only" sixty, as he'd begun to think of it. Once, he'd viewed sixty as the beginning of the end. Now he saw it as the end of the beginning. This second volume of his life was like a sequel that surpassed the original: higher stakes, deeper valleys, and the capacity to surprise him.

On April twelfth, Tony and Kate had moved into Westminster's newest high rise, One Hundred and One Leadenhall. Its kitchen, all quartz and stainless steel and web-connected mod-cons, flowed like mercury into the slate blue living room, which was both comfortable and elegantly modern. Tony felt like it was designed especially for him. He spent each morning there. Sometimes he missed his view into Wellegrave House's walled garden, but living in the city center had its compensations. These included the living room's floor-to-ceiling views of London: impressive by day and breathtaking by night.

Lady Margaret had found the condo, which boasted three levels, five bedrooms, underground parking, and 24-hour porterage. Her friend, a prince based in Dubai, had purchased the townhouse as a wedding gift for his son and future daughter-in-law, only to be stuck with the fully-furnished, professionally-decorated property when the nuptials were nixed. The prince had been looking to sell at a profit, but by leaning on him, Lady Margaret had secured the Hetheridges a three-month sublet agreement instead. There was even an option for going month-to-month thereafter if the renovation of Wellegrave House, a Grade II listed building, dragged on due to strict regulations about approved materials. At over 6,000 square feet, the condo was far more than Tony and Kate required, but after the fire and all its attendant drama, the convenience of moving into a home they didn't have to wait for was too good to resist.

Within five minutes of entering the condo, Tony had felt at home. Kate had hated it on sight, and hated it still. Her under-privileged childhood had rendered her frugal, and not just with money. Tony's former subordinate, Detective Sergeant Deepal "Paul" Bhar, called her condition "psychologically skint." This he defined as the belief there wasn't enough cash, trust, praise, or security to go around, inducing the sufferer to dig in her finger-nails and cling to those things for dear life.

There was some truth in Paul's playful diagnosis, Tony thought, but it didn't tell the whole story. No one was more generous with her time than Kate; no one was more willing to help those who couldn't possibly return the favor. Many a career woman, after a decade of looking after her mentally disabled brother, would have given up after the fire and put him in an institution. Not Kate. And it wasn't as if she hadn't been offered the chance. Recently a pair of social workers, sent round to inquire how Ritchie got access to a cigarette lighter, had suggested she do just that, arguing that a professionally-managed clinical environment would better suit his needs.

Kate had sent the social workers packing, kindly but firmly. According to her will, she'd named Tony as Ritchie's primary guardian, should she die or become unable to make decisions for him. In the event Ritchie survived both Kate and Tony, he would likely spend his golden years in a group home. His childlike, semi-unresponsive nature made solo living impossible. But until death or illness separated them, Kate wanted Ritchie with her. Who could do a better job of looking after him? She knew him better than she knew herself.

Ritchie had been rescued from the Wellegrave House fire without burns or significant smoke inhalation, but the conflagration had thrown him into what the family called "meltdown mode." The social workers, after meeting Ritchie for the first time and watching him vacillate between sobbing, hiding, and pacing in circles, had suggested new meds and a week of residential care. Kate, who'd spent a lifetime witnessing those meltdowns, had ignored their suggestion in favor of her own treatment plan: Burger King, ice cream, doughnuts, and a full day at LEGOLAND Windsor. It had worked brilliantly; Ritchie was back to normal, the fire forgotten. But Kate still checked the smoke alarms twice daily and woke up gasping from nightmares about a second fire, one from which there was no escape.

Maybe she finds this condo as stressful as the fire itself, Tony thought, cup and saucer in hand as he surveyed the view. He liked to get right alongside the picture window, so close that his wingtips tapped the glass. From such a vantage point, it was rather like hovering above London.

He suspected Kate found living at "One-oh-One," as the residents called it, a blow to her cherished self-image as a scrapyard dog among pedigreed poodles. After years of mocking exclusive communities for adverts promising "grandeur and prestige," not to mention refuge from the rabble, she'd wound up sleeping with the enemy. It was tough to trot like a rawboned mutt while taking a private lift from living room to master bedroom.

She also worried that Ritchie and Henry might do serious damage to their temporary surroundings. If not by another fire, by their usual bag of tricks: Sharpies, unwashed hands, ground-in crisps, melted Cornettos, and vomit. These concerns had led Kate to consign most of the owner's fine possessions to a storage unit. Now the condo's walls were bare, its shelves bereft of knick-knacks, its rooms furnished with wobbly particleboard furniture from IKEA.

Assembling those modernist pieces had turned out to be a

pleasant way to spend a family weekend. Kate had partnered with Ritchie, who was a natural. Their finished tables and chairs were the strongest and best-looking by far. Tony had worked with Henry, who did well when he focused and made ruinous mistakes when he didn't. The wardrobe they'd assembled for his bedroom was cracked in two places where he'd overtightened the screws. After Tony's warning fell on deaf ears, he'd allowed the boy to err without intervening. Why? For the same reason he'd occasionally let his detectives blunder forth unto the breach after ignoring his expert counsel. Henry would learn a lesson about following directions, Tony hoped, from putting up with a lopsided wardrobe that didn't close properly. Or maybe he wouldn't. But at least he'd receive the opportunity. No child could learn from a mistake an adult corrected ahead of the consequences.

Harvey and Mrs. Snell had also participated in the mass furniture assembly, though they had declined to work as a team. Harvey had invented reasons why he needed to go it alone, all of them calculated to make him sound selfless. Mrs. Snell had done a slow burn, throwing the manservant occasional contemptuous looks through her thick magnifying specs. Harvey, who'd worked for Tony for more than twenty years, believed his territory had been invaded. Mrs. Snell, who'd worked for Tony at Scotland Yard for over thirty years, believed she was rubbing elbows with a rank amateur. Some men, finding themselves the object of a loyalty pissing contest, would be flattered. Tony wanted to knock their heads together. He suspected he would, if they didn't achieve *détente* soon.

This morning, April twenty-fourth, Tony had the condo almost entirely to himself. Kate was at work, Henry was at school, and Ritchie was off with his paid carer, taking in the sun at Regent Park's bandstand. Harvey was at Wellegrave House, as he was every day, micromanaging the rebuild. Even Paul had texted only once, which was an improvement. Apparently, he found the loss of his old guv difficult to accept. Texting Tony was his chief coping mechanism.

Poor Paul, Tony thought. Over the years he'd had many subordinates, but with the notable exception of the one he'd married, Paul was his favorite. He'd had a rocky time of it at the Yard. Golden in his didactics and brilliant in his first months on the job, Paul had made several ethical lapses during the Sir Duncan Godington triple murder case. In the process, he'd lost the girl of his dreams, Tessa Chilcott, and the Crown had lost the case.

Tony had saved him from the sack, though he'd never admitted as much, and never would. He still believed Paul could right the ship and become the fine detective he was meant to be. But first he needed to regain his confidence, to bury the past once and for all. It hadn't happened yet.

Today, only Mrs. Snell was present. She occupied the condo's first-floor reception room, which they'd rearranged slightly to serve as his temporary office.

He was calling the agency "Hetheridge's." Kate didn't like it. She thought Hetheridge's sounded like a haberdasher or a bespoke chocolates shop. She was pushing him to adopt a stern industry-standard name like "Vigilant Investigations" or "Encompass Intelligence Ltd." When Tony had remarked that calling anything "Intelligence Limited" was asking for trouble, Kate had cordially invited him to do two things, one of which was think up something better.

On the day they moved into One-oh-One, Tony had believed he could call his agency "Manky Monkey on a Stick" and it would have done just fine. At the Yard, he'd routinely shaved in his office, answered his phone in the men's room, and spent Christmas Day catching up on paperwork. The job never stopped. But as April dragged on and Mrs. Snell sat alone at her reception room desk, fielding those rare phone calls that led to nothing, he'd realized that life in the private sector would be altogether different. If he wanted to attract clients, rechristening his agency would be a good first step. The only thing holding him back was the knowledge that Kate was smugly awaiting his capitulation.

I could still prove her wrong, he thought, crossing to the picture window's opposite end. From there, he had a better view of a new Westminster skyscraper. This one would alter the London skyline and even obscure 30 St. Mary Axe, better known as the Gherkin. After an all-too-brief run, the beloved landmark was being eclipsed.

I know how it feels. I need a case before I disappear, too.

Recently, Tony had visited two PIs he knew slightly, infrequent snouts for the Yard, to see how they approached the business. Both operations were one-man hole-in-the-wall affairs; windowless offices with peeling paint, lino floors, and electric fans instead of air conditioning. PI number one owned a cheap metal desk, a laptop, and a mobile. PI number two had that, plus a well-worn *London A-Z* map, a bottle of Maalox, and a pile of empty takeout boxes. Neither had adopted the stereotypical fedora or trench coat, but chain-smoking was apparently still in fashion in the gumshoe world, as was informality. Both men had swilled coffee and snacked behind their desks while Tony quizzed them.

"You're hung up on hands-on investigating, but it's all databases now, innit? Databases and mobile records and CCTV footage until it's all I dream about, guv," PI number one, a pasty man called Dennis, had said between spoonfuls of curry. "I used to get out and about. Knocking on doors. Ringing up tossers and saying they'd won a prize so they'd cough up their current address. Back in the day I'd mix it up a little, too. Get in a lad's face or crack heads."

Still chewing, Dennis had mimed a left hook. "Now all the debtors and missing daddies got mobile video. They scream 'I know my rights,' don't they, while their mates film the dust-up. A poor bugger like me is as much at risk of being banged up for brutality as you wankers at the Met. No offense."

Tony had taken none, which was good preparation for his chat with PI number two.

"Save yourself, mate," PI number two, a sad-eyed man called Raj, had said. He was working his way through a packet of Tim Tams, and unlike his colleague, saw no reason to speak only between bites.

"Preserve what faith in humanity you have left. This is a job for people who like to be the bearer of bad news." Demolishing a Tim Tam in two bites, he said around a chocolate-colored mouthful, "'Oh, yes, Mr. Jones. About that charming young man you'd like to hire. He faked his references and he's spying for your competitor. What's that, Ms. Smith? Your new boyfriend? He's got a wife and kiddies. Another girlfriend, too.'

"Last week," Raj had continued, "a geezer engaged my professional services. Wanted the name and whereabouts of the miscreant who robbed his daughter's flat and made off with his cash gifts to her. I had to break the news that she robbed herself to pay her dealer. Figured her old dad was thick enough to give her the cash all over again. Bloody wanker cried. Then he paid me. Then he cried again and asked for his money back. I said I had my own problems and beat it. It's a dirty business, mate. Life's too short. Especially for a bloke with one foot in the grave. No offense."

Once again, Tony had taken none. It was hard to resent a PI who mainlined Tim Tams just to make it through the day. Perhaps one-man agencies were especially stressful? Tony had quite literally never worked alone in his professional life. He'd always had a partner, a guv, a department, or a staff of his own, ready and willing to take orders 24/7. In addition to Mrs. Snell, he expected to someday take on at least one junior detective, possibly two. Perhaps interviewing someone at a bigger agency would yield more pertinent information?

He'd picked one, Wheelwright's, via Google. A black cab had whisked him to a smartly-decorated office on Earls Court Road. There was no sign or marquee, only the name painted on the glass door. At the reception desk sat a black woman with a cool, assessing gaze.

"Booking?" Her tone was neither friendly nor unfriendly.

"No. I'd like to speak to the person in charge, if he or she can spare a moment. My name is Anthony Hetheridge. Ninth Baron, Wellegrave. New Scotland Yard, retired."

That was what Henry called his "shock and awe" line, the bomb Tony dropped when he wanted something done quickly, with as little inconvenience as possible. The receptionist scanned him with her acute gaze, no longer quite so cool, and apparently decided he was the real deal. Without demanding credentials, she'd invited him to take a seat while she had a word with the boss. In less than two minutes, she was back, offering a professional smile so perfectly calibrated, she might have purchased it from Staples.

She'd led him deeper into Wheelwright's, which looked as stodgy as any Edwardian men's club: oak-paneled walls, brass sconces, and oil paintings of the industrious-peasant variety. Given the office's pronounced air of masculinity, Tony had been surprised when PI number three turned out to be a middle-aged woman with bobbed hair and lips as red as a banker's power tie.

"You came to the right place," she said, rising to shake his hand as he entered the office. "I'm Cecelia Wheelwright."

There were no more niceties. She'd launched straight into answering his questions. "There's no comparison between my agency and the pair you talked to. Independent operators pluck the low-hanging fruit. Your public records searches. Your who's-the-daddy cases. Agencies like mine operate in a different universe. We offer a full menu of services. One menu for the typical English nuclear family. Infidelity, divorce, hidden assets, child on drugs. Another for businesses. Bug sweeping, corporate espionage, employee fraud. And one menu for in-depth investigations. Missing persons. Lost heirs. Even a cold case homicide, once in a blue moon.

"But those are to be avoided at all costs," she'd added with a smile as hard as her blood-red fingernails. "I'd rather tangle with a paranoid off his meds who thinks Prince Charles bugged his bog than grapple with eternal grievers. You know the type? Their kid went backpacking through Somerset and turned up dead in a hostel. It's been twenty years and they're still looking for justice. To an efficient organization, eternal grievers are like Kryptonite. No offense."

In Cecelia's case, the casual "no offense" had been helpful, as Tony had indeed been on the brink of a sharp retort. At the Yard, he'd never permitted subordinates to speak unkindly about the families of victims, or to broadly suggest that their grief should come with a sell-by date. But his days of cracking the whip over younger detectives were done. And rather than dress down PI number three, he'd passed her his card, deciding to take an altogether different tack.

"Bugged bogs don't play to my strengths. Cold homicides do. By all means, direct your eternal grievers to me."

Cecilia had flipped over the card and raised an eyebrow. "Not even a number?"

Per Paul's recommendation, the card was plain white with nothing on it but the words ANTHONY HETHERIDGE in bold black ink.

"The casually interested can Google my name," he'd replied. "For the rest...." He recited his mobile number, which she'd dutifully jotted onto the card. It was impossible to tell if she was humoring him or if she was intended to subcontract his services at some future date.

"You know, I worked for the Met when I was young and clueless," Cecilia had said, giving Tony a long appraising look. "Dinosaurs like you at the top ran me off. Best thing for me. I ought to send you flowers. You seem pretty hale and hearty for a recent retiree. What drove you into the private sector?"

"An approaching meteorite," Tony had said lightly. "Thank you for your time, Ms. Wheelwright. Remember me to the eternal grievers."

Now a massive crane lifted a steel beam into place. The Gherkin was half-obscured. Tony watched the construction for awhile, then remembered his tea. It had gone cold. He wasn't surprised.

At the Yard, teatime consisted of stolen moments between emails, phone calls, emergencies, and meetings. At One Hundred and One Leadenhall, alone with his living room view, teatime was peaceful and uninterrupted. It was ghastly. Self-reflection wasn't his strong suit. He hadn't been brought up to indulge in such things. Wasn't that the entire point of work, to drown out the beastly voices of one's internal committee?

Returning to the kitchen to pour out his cold tea, Tony chuckled over the only private case he'd had to date. A dog-napping he'd solved in one day—in two and a half hours, to be precise.

He wouldn't have accepted it, only the young woman who engaged his services, a referral from his adult daughter Jules, had made it sound like her child was missing. She'd referred to the dog as "Jeremy," mentioned his gluten sensitivity, his penchant for trusting strangers, and his favorite T-shirt, white with blue piping. Only when Tony arrived at the self-styled "jewel of the coveted E14 postcode," a luxury condominium called the Madison in Canary Wharf, did he learn he'd been engaged to locate a Chihuahua.

Fortunately, Tony's long career in what was unaffectionately known around Scotland Yard as "the Toff Squad," had prepared him to deal with all sorts of indignities. The twenty-three-year-old mistress of an influential Labour crusader presented no challenge. She'd opened the door wearing nothing but earrings and a string bikini, and Tony hadn't batted an eye. It was mid-April, and it was 9 AM, but as Tony frequently misquoted F. Scott Fitzgerald, the rich were indifferent.

Once he'd realized it was a dog-napping, not a missing persons case, Tony had tried to back out. "But you're the best! I want only the best," the Labour crusader's mistress had insisted. Jeremy was her "entire life" (which might have come as news to her bigwig boyfriend) and only a former Scotland Yard detective was good enough to find him.

At least locating Jeremy had required more than logging onto a database. After interviewing the twenty-three-year-old mistress, which was wearisome, and her best mate, which was worse, Tony had knocked on the door of her only neighbor on the Madison's thirty-third floor. Interviewing that young man, a fourth-generation denizen of the indifferent class, had completed Tony's journey into idiocy. Irritated by pop-eyed, shivery little Jeremy's constant overtures of friendship, the young man had scooped up the Chihuahua, blue-piped T-shirt and all, binned his collar, and dumped him at the nearest dog-rehoming center. Fortunately, adoptions had been slow that week. Tony had popped round to the center, collected Jeremy, and returned him to the Labour crusader's mistress, who'd squealed with delight.

Of course, all this could have been discovered, perhaps even averted, by a five-minute conversation between neighbors. Jeremy's owner believed she had a right to let the dog roam freely on "his" floor; her neighbor believed he had a right to seize and dispose of unattended animals. Tony had left the pair to fight it out, probably via lawsuit and countersuit. He'd thought he'd at least enjoy receiving his fee, which he'd impulsively tripled on the spot. But the mistress was happy to pay. She'd called her lover to request an advance on her allowance while Tony paced her living room, checking his watch. In the end, he wished he'd simply plopped the dog in her arms and walked away. Kate, as it turned out, felt the same way.

"Triple? You charged her *triple?*" she'd demanded later the same night.

That had been during their after-dinner summit. That was the time when Kate revealed everything he wasn't meant to know about the Yard, and he confided everything happening in his world. Revealing his actual thoughts and emotions was still difficult for Tony. Half the time he couldn't classify those emotions, or even say what had inspired them. Maybe he was too old, or as Henry would say, too "old-school," to become entirely comfortable with the process. But it meant everything to his wife, so he persisted.

"It's unethical," Kate had continued. "Reminds me of that plumber. The one who heard my voice and quoted me one fee, then took one look at Wellegrave House and doubled it. I told him he'd get a reputation as a shakedown artist. The same will happen to you."

"Heaven forfend," Tony had said. "You saved us fifty quid. You also intimidated the poor sod so thoroughly, the bog ended up in worse shape than when he started. Not to mention he promised to report you for verbal abuse."

"Do me a favor," Kate had scoffed. "I was gentle as a baby lamb with him. And listen to you. 'Bog,' eh? I'm rubbing off. What'll come out of your mouth next? 'You're nicked, sunshine?'"

"You didn't teach me the word bog. In fact, I defy you to cite even one occasion when I said 'loo' in the company of hardened detectives. That sort of poncy talk torpedoes careers. Especially in the days when we were a police force, not a police service."

"Oh, the days when we were a force," Kate had laughed. "A manly, snow-white, un-PC, dead of a heart attack at fifty and bloody well grateful for it *force,* and not a weak, womanly, criminal-coddling *service* full of people like me."

"You would've loved it."

"Would I?"

"In those days, there was such a thing as five minutes alone with a suspect to 'encourage' them to come clean. Not to mention *carte blanche* to issue threats as needed. Even dole out bribes, within reason, when innocent lives hung in the balance."

"Where exactly did that bribe money come from?" asked Kate, who knew.

"I'll never tell."

"You know if I'd been around back in the day, you blokes wouldn't have let me play your reindeer games. Still. It would have been lovely, taking the gloves off when the moment was right." Smiling at the idea, Kate had smacked her fist into her palm. It was the sort of unselfconsciously ballsy move that bypassed Tony's cerebrum, arousing his most primitive instincts. No wonder so many of their after-dinner summits ended behind a locked door. Even after a few months of marriage, Kate still crackled with an aura of invincibility. He'd never been a man who could resist a challenge.

Later, when they were in bed with the lights off and the television news muted, Kate had picked up that conversational thread rather abruptly. "So. What's your take on it now?"

"On what? Brexit?" Tony asked, thinking she referred to the muted argument between TV talking heads.

Kate recoiled. Mentioning Brexit, Britain's withdrawal from the European Union, was breaking a Hetheridge family rule, as the topic had become an unprecedented bone of contention in Tony's expanded household. He'd taken one position. Kate had taken another. Meanwhile, Mrs. Snell was ardently in favor of leaving the EU. Harvey was actively campaigning for a legislative escape hatch that would permit Britain to remain. And Henry found the adults' passion on the topic so upsetting, the mere hint of another row put him in tears. In the end, everyone had agreed to stick to less tricky subjects, like how to achieve peace in the Middle East, or which religious faith was superior to all the rest.

"Ugh. Never," Kate had said, turning off the TV. "I'm talking about your PI career. You can't go on as the finder of lost pups, bilking obnoxious clients who are too loaded to care. I know billing is new to you. You never had to deal with fees at the Yard. Probably never gave a thought to your salary...."

"Except to ensure it was appropriate. Not an insult, and not some sort of sycophantic tribute."

"Oh, to be the man whose only financial concern is the elimination of sycophantic tributes." Grinning up at him wickedly, Kate had played with the stiff silver hair in the center of his chest. "Here's a thought. Take cases according to merit only. Walk away from anything that isn't worth your time. Accept payment on a sliding scale."

"I've been thinking along those lines," he'd admitted. "I didn't expect you to approve."

"Why? Did you think I married you for your earning potential?" she'd asked, folding herself into his embrace. "You're a workaholic. So am I, but you're worse. There's no twelve-step program that'll turn you into an allotment gardener or a chat show watcher. Work for free if you have to, but work for people you respect."

She was right, Tony thought. Rather than refill his teacup, he left it in the sink. *I can't enjoy my cuppa unless I'm on the job.*

* * *

"You again, right on cue. It's like you read my mind."

Cecilia Wheelwright ushered Tony into her office right away, which he hadn't expected. All signs pointed to an unhappy day in her ultra-traditional, climate-controlled realm. She was smoking unfiltered Camels at her desk and finishing a Red Bull. A mug of coffee, brought in by an assistant on tiptoes, steamed in readiness nearby.

"Here's the thing. These people I'm giving you will test your patience. They're beyond angry. They're incandescent." Cecelia took a deep drag on her cigarette. "They lost two children, young adults, in two weeks — one dead, one to the streets. Mariah threw herself off a building. Ten days later, her twin brother Mark went missing. He's troubled. Probably an addict. No one was surprised that a kid like that would ditch his family in their time of need. Well. No one except his parents.

"A week after I took the case, one of my old friends at the Met gave me a tip. He said Mark was living in a C of E homeless shelter. I sent an agent, but by the time she got there, he'd legged it. This keeps happening. Somebody sees Mark waiting to buy drugs or loitering by a free clinic. We try to make contact, set up a family reunion. He pulls another disappearing act and his parents hold my agency responsible.

"Now, I sympathize with their grief. Sincerely. So help me God," Cecelia said in the tone of one asking a waiter for salt for the third time. She blew out a plume of smoke. "But I'm running a business, not a charity, and these people," she said, seemingly substituting "people" for some other term, "expect me to focus all my resources on Mark, week in and week out, to earn a retainer that doesn't cover a month's manicures. They think Mariah was driven to suicide by a shadowy Svengali. They think the same Svengali got Mark hooked on drugs and convinced him to leave home. They want me to aggressively dig into the man's life and history. But he's—"

"He's Sir Duncan Godington. And the parents are Peter and Hannah Keene. The Earl and Countess of Brompton."

"You know them." Cecelia sighed in relief.

"Less well than I know Sir Duncan, but yes." It took all of Tony's self-control not to look as interested as he felt. "Tell me more."

CHAPTER TWO

*T*he Earl and Countess of Brompton resided in a modest house in Shepherd's Bush. The shrubbery wanted pruning; a fifteen-year-old BMW sat by the curb. For so many English families, this was a dream increasingly out of reach—old house, new roof, bit of green, bit of shade. In his thirties and forties, Tony had rejected such a life. Now he saw its appeal: marriage, two kiddies, two careers, and a comfortable London home. But the title "Earl" conjured higher expectations. Many would have looked on Peter and Hannah Keene's lifestyle with pity, even contempt.

Peter Keene's father had been a gambler, like his father before him. When the grandfather humiliated his family and faced prison for his financial misadventures, he'd done what men of his era did — locked himself in his study and shot himself in the head. But Peter's father belonged to a new day, one in which public requests for absolution were common and disgraced public figures occasionally regained their former standing, even after a stint behind bars. Therefore, when he was sued by his creditors for fraudulent dealings meant to fund his gambling habit, he'd chosen one last roll of the dice: hiring the best lawyers and fighting like hell. This had ended in bankruptcy, loss of the family home, and incarceration. After five years in HM Pentonville, Peter's father had died, passing the title of Earl to his son.

He's done well for himself, Tony thought, looking around the tidy home with admiration as he awaited the cup of tea that Hannah Keene had promised him. Plenty of men would've spent their lives trying to rebuild the family fortune by hook or by crook: risky investments, product endorsements, some sort of reality TV show. Peter Keene had married a scientist, used what little inheritance he had left to purchase a four-bedroom detached house, and worked his way up through the rough-and-tumble world of English politics. They'd been blessed with twins, Mark and Mariah, and enjoyed peaceful, useful lives until tragedy struck their children.

"It's green tea," Hannah Keene announced, entering the front room with a tray. She placed it on the coffee table in front of Tony. The service—Japanese, off-white with a subtle lotus design —resembled his favorite service at home. "Will you drink it?"

Something in her tone suggested Hannah didn't want him to agree; that she would have liked nothing better than to spark a refusal. Maybe she was spoiling for a fight.

"Green tea is fine. One of my employees swears by it. Because of flavonoids or antioxidants or possibly both," Tony said mildly. "I don't have to keep up with the latest nutritional edicts. Harvey reads the health news compulsively. He does his best to keep me alive."

"It's useless. Sorry. Journalists turn health studies into rubbish stories with clickbait headlines." Hannah seated herself across from Tony. Tall and slender, she had broad shoulders, trim hips, and a flat chest. Her rose-patterned maxi dress hung on her beautifully, giving her the appearance of a mature model rather than a chemist. Her features were strong but well-balanced, the lines around her eyes and mouth hinting at a lively woman who smiled often. But now those lines were deepened by sorrow and animated by narrowly contained rage.

"Doesn't matter what the study is," Hannah continued, pouring for Tony. "I've spent my life in a lab coat, writing research grants and analyzing human trial data. Take it from me: if you read it in a newspaper, the data has been dumbed-down, stretched beyond reason, and framed as a life-extender or a life-ender. That's all people want to know. Will avoiding fizzy soda let me live forever? Does eating meat condemn me to an early grave?"

"I think perhaps you're right." Tony tasted the green tea. Fragrant as well as flavorful, it required no sweetener. Nodding his appreciation, he added, "There's an almost supernatural aspect to Harvey's interest in these things. We all want assurances. Once, I suppose the medicine man gave them, or the priest. Now we expect science to tell us what's a virtue and what's a sin."

"Which isn't science's place at all. As for sins—don't get me started." Hannah's laugh was bitter. "When Cecelia called to say she was sending over a retired Scotland Yard detective, I nearly came unhinged. As far as I'm concerned, the Met has proven, through word and through deed, they have no interest in finding Mark or getting justice for Mariah. Cecelia insisted I shouldn't hold that against you. She tried to soften me up by reminding me that we've been introduced."

"Yes, I remember."

"I don't." Hannah studied him over the rim of her teacup. "Perhaps you made no impression on me."

"Small talk at a charity gala. Ten years ago. Easily forgotten," Tony said. Again, he sensed she was determined to get a rise out of him, which only made him calmer.

"Yes, well, my husband might remember. You're both seated on the board of some foundation. Meets twice a year."

"Thrice a year. It's called the Bootstrap Stratagem. And you're right, our connection is gossamer-thin," Tony admitted. "I'm pleased you decided to meet with me anyway."

"I didn't want to. But Cecelia left me no choice," Hannah said. "Told me if I didn't accept her advice and meet with you, she was firing me and blocking my number."

"Knowing Ms. Wheelwright only a fraction better than I know you, that seems entirely in keeping with her character," Tony said. "But she strikes me as the sort who issues threats only to serve the greater good. I doubt she meant to sound unreasonable."

"You miss the point. I'm the one who's become unreasonable. Now I must be threatened to act in my own best interests. And it's the Met that's driven me to this sorry state." Hannah's low voice turned mannish. "Your function at Scotland Yard was to head up murder investigations that intersected with titled or famous individuals. Wasn't the Earl of Brompton worthy of your attention? Were we too poor? Too ordinary?"

Tony put down his teacup. He knew what he wanted to say; that required no contemplation. But it didn't take a board-certified psychiatrist to realize that Hannah Keene was adrift in a world mostly indifferent to her and her lost children. For her to hear his reply, she first had to watch him digest her accusation, to be satisfied that it was duly considered. Several seconds ticked by.

"Though I'm retired, I maintain a certain loyalty toward the MPS, and in particular, to my colleagues at the Yard," he said at last. "I offer that in the spirit of full disclosure. Now. I can answer your question. If you'll forgive me for answering it truthfully."

Hannah nodded.

"I understand that your daughter, Mariah, was associated with Sir Duncan Godington. That she became close to him, perhaps romantically, in the final months of her life."

"Yes."

"I agree, it's possible he bears some culpability in her death. At the very least, he may have information that will answer questions and provide closure. As a private investigator, I look forward to exploring that avenue with you. Having said that, I know why Scotland Yard declined to take up the matter. I was the man who reviewed your family's complaint and put it aside. Not a supervisor or some faceless committee. Me."

Hannah went rigid.

"Why did I do so? Because I saw no evidence whatsoever that your daughter was murdered. Nor could I find anything in the statements and preliminary data to indicate that your son was kidnapped."

"If you'd bothered to ask—" Hannah began.

"I didn't have to. I read your complaint. It was based on feelings. Hunches. Parental intuition. All of which I respect. But there was no evidence. Absolutely no testimony, no physical clues, nothing which would allow the Met to go forward. Scotland Yard can only pursue investigations that can be legally defended. Especially, and it pains me to say this, against a person like Sir Duncan."

"So it *was* about money," Hannah said.

"In part. He can afford the finest legal counsel, the sort that makes mincemeat of weak circumstantial cases. But his history with the Met is also key. His acquittal in his triple murder case left some, if not most, of the public convinced he'd been fitted up, as it were, by the powers that be. To try and connect him to an apparent suicide would have been insupportable without hard evidence."

"Mariah did not commit suicide." Hannah's tone was granite.

"Forgive me. I did say, apparent. The circumstances of Mariah's death look cut-and-dried to disinterested observers. Surely you accept that?"

She blew out her breath. "Dear God. Are you lying about reading the report, or just terminally thick? No one who knew the details would call it cut-and dried."

"I do know those details. And more besides," Tony said serenely. In this case, the soft answer might not turn away wrath, but he'd try it all the same.

"Tell me."

"On the night of January the second, at approximately three in the morning, Mariah entered the construction zone of the Leadenhall building. To do this, she climbed two fences and cut the padlock on a door. She also set off a silent alarm that went unanswered," Tony said. "The security firm apologized for the breach and paid a fine. They blamed the failure on extended New Year's holiday-making.

"Inside the building, which was nothing but girders from the twentieth floor up, Mariah traveled by lift as far as she could go. Then she used scaffolding to reach the top, or close to the top—about thirty stories up. She jumped to her death. The body was discovered on the street below at around half-four by a homeless man and confirmed by officers on the scene at half-five. She was preliminarily identified by her medical alert bracelet, which signaled her severe peanut allergy. Her mobile, handbag, and other personal belongings were not recovered."

"And you, a detective, consider what you've just described an open-and-shut case, do you?" Hannah laughed harshly. "Is it typical for twenty-one-year-old university students to break into construction sites?"

"No. But risky behavior of all types is most common in that age bracket. Moreover, Mariah was fit and athletic. She ran track, jumped hurdles, and so on. She was certainly capable of the act."

"Godington might have forced her to break into the site. Threatened her with a gun or knife."

"There's no evidence of that."

"But is there evidence he didn't?" Hannah shot back. "People tell me he was in London for all of January and most of February. Can you prove he didn't?"

Rather than lecture a grieving woman on the impossibility of proving a negative, Tony decided to share a privileged detail instead.

"The alarm Mariah set off was a motion detector. The system is sophisticated. It can differentiate between a small animal, like a cat, and a human being, or multiple human beings. Only one person trespassed on the site."

"I'm expected to trust the device installed by a company too incompetent to monitor its own alarm?" Hannah scoffed. "How ridic—" She stopped. "They never told me it was a motion detector. In fact, the company refused to tell me anything at all. Said disclosure was against their policy."

"That's not unusual. But in preparing to meet with you, I made some off-the-record inquiries," Tony said. "Being a retired lawman helps. So does subletting a condominium in the building Mariah jumped from."

Hannah flinched. "What?"

"There was a fire at my family home in Mayfair," Tony said. "No one was hurt, but renovations proceed at one of two speeds: slow and stop. A friend located a condo for us in One-oh-One. We accepted long before I had any idea of offering my services to Ms. Wheelwright. Rather a morbid coincidence, certainly."

"I'm not sure I believe in coincidence anymore," Hannah said. "From a scientist, that's tantamount to heresy. Have you heard of the Law of Truly Large Numbers?"

"I don't think so."

"It's an adage, really. Not a true mathematical law. In science, we use it to help folks understand that in a world of seven billion human beings, the sample for any given occurrence is so enormous, statistically improbable things happen every day." Hannah seemed to remember her tea. She picked it up, tasted it, scowled, and set it down again. "Ice cold. Anyway. As a scientist, I'm meant to believe that events are random. Any apparent coincidence— any highly improbable event that seems ironic or reinforcing of some idea—is an illusion. Just our minds' attempt to impose meaning on the meaningless."

"We are pattern-seekers," Tony said. "Some of us more than others."

"Yes. For you, it's a way of life, clearly." Hannah sighed. "Same with Mariah. She was one of those crafty young people. When I was twenty-one, I would have sooner been stood up against a wall and shot than so much as hold a pair of knitting needles. That was a symbol of the bad old days. But Mariah and her friends thought all those homey skills were wonderful: knitting, crocheting, needlepoint. She would knit the most complex patterns. Mark, being a computer gamer, was even more keen on discerning patterns. Almost religious about it. There's another concept. Sacred geometry...." She trailed off. "My God. I just referred to him in the past tense. What does that mean?"

"Nothing," Tony said. Contentious as Lady Brompton was, he instinctively wanted to give her comfort, even if the only comfort he could offer was closure. "Before you decide whether to hire me, permit me to make one final point. What I couldn't do as a policeman, I can do as a private investigator. Of course, there are other detectives in London. Ones who had nothing to do with Scotland Yard's decision not to pursue a criminal inquiry. But I may be the only PI at your disposal who's actually met Sir Duncan. Who knows beyond a shadow of a doubt what he's capable of."

Hannah sighed, folded her arms across her chest, and said nothing.

She needs time, Tony thought. This was new to him—pitching his abilities and waiting for a client to ponder his fitness in real time. It didn't particularly discomfit him, so long as he conducted himself with dignity. He'd made the case. To keep talking would descend to the level of salesmanship, and that he could not abide.

As Hannah considered it, he rose and took a turn around the living room. It was "lived-in," as Kate liked to say, without spendy designer pieces or ostentatious heirlooms. On the mantelpiece, a row of pictures in silver frames, round, square, and rectangle, told the family's story. Peter Keene grinning next to a campaign poster; Hannah in a white lab coat, hugely pregnant with the twins; Mariah and Mark as infants, then toddlers, then first-formers, and so on. Mariah was usually smiling at the camera, her dark hair often in twin braids. Mark didn't seem to appreciate being photographed, and never smiled.

"There's more recent ones. Just there," Hannah said, pointing to a console table across the room.

Tony stepped over for a look. Mariah hadn't changed much from tween to teen, except to bob her hair and attain her full height of about six feet. She was a capable-looking young woman, shoulders squared, chin down, feet planted confidently. It was easy to imagine her running track, jumping hurdles, breaking into a construction site, or knitting the complicated shawl draped around her shoulders. It was hard to imagine her taking her own life.

Mark's photos between age twelve to twenty documented more of a transformation. The slender, camera-shy child became a spotty young man with thick specs who stared intently at the photographer but never smiled. In the end, a boy seemingly constructed entirely from acne eruptions, elbows, and knees resolved into the mirror image of his twin. Same height, same deep-set brown eyes, same large nose and firm chin. Only the stance was different. Mark kept his head down, shoulders slouched, as if willing himself smaller. Perhaps invisible.

"Thank you for allowing me time to collect my thoughts," Hannah said at last. "Now. If we're to work together, there's one thing you must understand, and understand completely.

"Mariah did not commit suicide. I can't bear to hear the word spoken in conjunction with my daughter. She *loved* her life. She made a terrible mistake, cozying up to that lunatic. She wasn't a perfect child, far from it, but I'm telling you as her mother, she didn't want to die. Now, Mark… Mark is the image of his great-grandfather. He's bone china. Easily hurt and easily led astray. Losing his sister threw him over the cliff. I think that's why I referred to him in the past tense. I know that if I don't find him, he might —might—"

She dissolved into tears. Tony cast about for a box of tissues. Finding none, he reached inside his jacket and withdrew a silk handkerchief. He was never without one. He had a long history of making women cry. As for their tears, he was immune to them, unless they were Kate's.

Pressing the silk handkerchief against her face, Hannah wept with abandon. As Tony waited, unwilling to press her until she was ready, he heard the front door open.

"It's only me," a man called from the foyer. He sounded hesitant.

Tony turned. He expected a trespasser; an intrusive social worker, perhaps, or a nosy neighbor who'd already been warned off. Instead, he saw the Earl of Brompton, Peter Keene.

Judging by his suit, tie, and leather briefcase, he'd come from the House of Lords. He looked from Tony to Lady Brompton, still sobbing brokenly into that white handkerchief, and rounded on Tony.

"What the ruddy hell is going on? Who are you?"

Before Tony could remind him that they'd met before, Peter went rigid. His briefcase slipped from his fingers, struck the floor, and burst open on impact. Out spilled the tools of the bureaucrat's trade onto the red Turkish rug: papers, folders, letters, a couple of jump drives. He seemed not to notice.

"It's Mark," he whispered, eyes wide. "You've come to say he's dead."

"Nothing of the sort." Tony stood up. "Forgive me, Lord Brompton, for blindsiding you with my presence. I'm not the bearer of tragic news. Or indeed, any news at all."

"Oh. Well. Only…." Peter closed his eyes, pinched the bridge of his nose, and started over. "Who *are* you? And what have you done to my wife? Darling—"

"Don't," Hannah interrupted. The word was a cut; an amputation. "Why are you here?"

"I—I still live here."

"Why are you here *in the middle of the day*," she boomed in that mannish voice.

This was an unseemly display. The typical Englishman would've perhaps cringed, mumbled an excuse, and departed, or at least ducked into the front garden to hide while husband and wife sorted things out. The typical detective, including Tony, couldn't have been persuaded to leave at gunpoint. Now was the moment when people told the truth, if asked the right questions.

"Again, forgive me," he said, interposing himself between Peter and Hannah. "As for who the ruddy hell I am, I'm Tony Hetheridge. Baron Wellegrave and all that. From the board of the Bootstrap Stratagem. How do you do?"

"Er. Um. How do you do?" Peter mumbled automatically. They shook hands.

"Now to explain." Tony pivoted to include Hannah in the discussion. "Countess Brompton was telling me about how the MPS declined to investigate your daughter's death as a murder, or your son's disappearance as a kidnapping. Naturally, things became a bit fraught. Making this the perfect time for you to help put me in the picture."

"What picture?" The light dawned. "Oh. You're the detective Cecelia mentioned. No offense, mate, but piss off. Sorry you got the sack. But you won't revive your career at the expense of my children." Still boyish at almost fifty, Peter's anger made him look sulky rather than dangerous.

"How bracing," Hannah said. "The man of the house takes charge. This isn't a flag of surrender." She tossed Tony's white handkerchief on the table. "Who are you to tell anyone to piss off? You're unasked. Unwanted. Unfit to offer an opinion."

"I do live here. *Still,*" Peter insisted, looking and sounding all the more like a boy resisting his comeuppance. "Listen to me. I happen to know this is no reputable detective. Forgive me, Lord Hetheridge—"

"Of course," Tony inserted dryly.

"—but if you find my daughter's suicide worth investigating—"

"It wasn't a suicide," Hannah shouted.

"—you might've done so in your professional capacity," Peter continued inexorably. "And please don't try to sell us on your supposed connection to Sir Duncan. You've never done anything but let him slip away. The police are impotent enough. We don't need their rejects."

Casting a look at Hannah, Peter swallowed hard before continuing. "Unlike my wife, I accept that our daughter took her own life. That doesn't mean Sir Duncan isn't partially responsible. There's such a thing as a pernicious influence. Words can be deadly weapons." A tear spilled onto his cheek.

"Oh, yes. There it is," Hannah said savagely. "Metrosexual daddy brought to tears."

"You weren't there for her." Peter dashed the tear away. "You weren't even there for Mark. And we all know he was your favorite."

"Is that so?" Hannah stood up. Like her husband, she was over six feet tall, and her heels gave her a slight advantage.

"Someone had to balance the scales, given the way you mooned over Mariah, always making cow's eyes at her. Do you know," she told Tony, "around Whitehall, Mariah was often mistaken for Peter's bit of stuff? I used to laugh about it. How I didn't have to worry about my husband taking up with a younger woman because he'd done it already, the day Mariah was born. When he started an actual affair, I missed the signs. I heard the rumors, but I assumed people had mistaken our daughter for his lover once again."

Peter's shoulders sagged. "It wasn't an affair."

Hannah didn't seem to hear. "I've done my due diligence on Sir Duncan Godington. They say he sleeps with his sister, Lady Isabel Bartlow. A normal young woman would've been repulsed. Perhaps given her father's not-so-subtle behavior, Mariah was drawn to someone a bit more upfront with his proclivities."

Peter swore under his breath. "Hannah. Torturing me won't bring them back."

"I simply want Lord Hetheridge to know everything. Perhaps that's where we went wrong. We weren't honest in our family life. We weren't honest with anyone," Hannah said. "Now I'll shout it from the rooftops. I was an absentee mother. My career consumed me. Our twins were raised by au pairs and tutors. You were an inappropriate father. You treated Mariah like your child bride. And Mark? Mark was a burden to you. I once overheard you tell a neighbor, 'The boy's a retard. Pretend you don't see him and he'll go away.'"

Tony expected Peter to defend himself, but the man hung his head and said nothing.

"Our son is different, no one disputes that, but he isn't mentally challenged," Hannah continued. "I was on point of explaining that to you, Lord Hetheridge, when my husband burst in. Mark's IQ is actually rather higher than average. He's on the spectrum, as we say now. And to give Peter his due, once the official diagnosis was made, he began to treat Mark with the bare minimum of consideration. I suspect someone on his re-election campaign advised him that plenty of individuals on the spectrum are voters."

Peter still said nothing.

"When Mariah found a Uni boyfriend, Peter went through a sort of crisis," Hannah said. "I was relieved. I thought, 'Right. Brilliant. Mariah's finished playing daddy's girl and Peter's fallen back to earth. We can have another go at making our marriage work.' But Peter didn't turn to me. He burrowed into his secretary's arms. Excuse me. Administrative assistant. She doesn't like to be called a secretary. I wouldn't, either, if my job duties were as onerous as hers."

"You've spent long nights at the lab over the years," Peter retorted feebly. "How do I know you weren't carrying on with Dr. Millet?"

"Because Dr. Millet and I professionals trying to cure leukemia."

"Yes. Well. Twenty years and you haven't put forth a single drug that made it through clinical trials. Missed the cancer at home, too."

Time to intervene, Tony thought. Peter shook with half-suppressed shame; Hannah looked dangerously energized by her screed. Either might say anything now.

"How were Mark and Mariah introduced to Sir Duncan?" he asked. "Who initiated the relationship?"

"We don't know," Peter said.

"No one knows." Hannah laughed bitterly. "No one admits to having seen a thing. Of course, Mariah was passionate about ecological issues and Peter's first position in government was at DEFRA. He met Godington several times over the years. No doubt that's just a coincidence. Except I don't believe in those."

Peter's cheeks, already bright pink, grew pinker. Tony didn't have to ask if the accusation was true. Clearly, Peter had played some role in initiating his twins' relationship with Sir Duncan. Yet he refused to admit it, even now.

"How was your relationship with Mariah at the end? In November or December of last year?"

"Strained."

"Ask him why," Hannah said.

"I shall. But first," Tony turned to her. "How was your relationship with Mariah? Did you have a happy Christmas?"

"I worked that day. Monitoring a critical test at the lab."

"New Year's?"

Hannah shook her head.

"She hadn't spoken to Mariah since Bonfire Night," Peter announced triumphantly. "Mark, either. Poor Mariah suffered two months like that, her mother refusing to speak to her, before she killed herself."

"Mariah didn't kill herself," Hannah bellowed. "And I didn't refuse to speak to her. Or Mark. I simply waited for one of them to make the first move. I was well within my rights. They owed me an apology."

"For what?" Tony asked.

"For speaking disrespectfully."

"For speaking truthfully," Peter said. "Mariah told Hannah she was a terrible mother. Mark stood by and nodded. Hannah can't bear to be challenged. So she gave our children the keys to the street. And we haven't seen them since."

CHAPTER THREE

"Get out," Hannah told Peter.

"Gladly. I'll be gone within the hour." Redness suffused his face; even his ears were scarlet.

"Don't make promises you can't keep. You've slept in Mariah's bedroom for three months. You can sleep there another night if that's what it takes to get you out for good. I don't mean an overnight bag. Take everything you've ever touched," she said. "Whatever of yours I find after you've gone, I'll burn in the front garden for the neighbors to see."

"May I suggest an armistice for the remainder of the afternoon?" Tony interrupted mildly. Here his long-perfected rhetorical device, the patrician tone of command, was useless. Not only because he addressed blue bloods who occupied a higher place on the aristocratic food chain, but because it was a warring couple. Only imbeciles took on embattled spouses on their own turf.

"That is," he continued, "if you've decided to allow me to take over the case as Ms. Wheelwright proposed. Assuming you have, I'd quite like to interview each of you separately, in greater detail. Also, to view the twins' bedrooms, if you've maintained them."

"She's already boxed up Mark's things," Peter accused.

"Because I'm not a ghoul. Wait till you see Mariah's room. Kept up like a bloody shrine," Hannah said.

I'll take that as acceptance of my professional services, Tony thought. He'd expected his first real case to begin with fee negotiations, a contract, perhaps a nondisclosure agreement. A hard-nosed career woman like Kate would have insisted on all three, plus twenty-four hours to read the fine print. The Earl and Countess of Brompton, by contrast, seemed willing to proceed as Peers of the Realm so often did—by a verbal contract. It wasn't because they were more honorable than the hoi polloi. It was because the law had great difficulty proving, or disproving, an unwritten agreement after the fact.

Hannah regarded Tony tiredly. She looked drained of all emotion, as if she might never weep again. "Which of us will you interview first?"

"Lord Brompton," Tony said. He always wanted a go at the psychologically weaker person first. Also, statistically speaking, the father of a dead or missing child was the most obvious person of interest. Followed by the mother, the second most obvious.

"Very well," Hannah said. "I'll be upstairs. Ring my mobile when you're ready for me." Gathering the tea-things onto the tray, she made as if to exit, then turned back.

"Lord Hetheridge. Remember what I said. We were never honest in our family life. I'm convinced my husband—my soon-to-be ex-husband—has secret knowledge of Mariah's final days. Knowledge he's never disclosed to anyone. Do try and carve it out of him. Even if it's something ghastly. Something you might imagine a mother couldn't bear to hear. At this point, any pain is preferable to the hell of not knowing."

* * *

AFTER HANNAH CLOSED the door behind her, Peter covered his

face with his hands. A full minute passed before he took a deep breath, removed his hands, and shot Tony an embarrassed glance. "Right. Lovely. So good to have a witness for all that. Are you married?"

"Yes."

"Still got your balls?"

Tony glanced down at himself as if to check. Peter chuckled.

"You know what? You're all right. Tony, is it? Sorry I was an arse. Who knows, maybe you can help us. Get to the bottom of why Mariah did it." He knelt to retrieve the mass of papers that had burst out of his briefcase. "How many years?"

"Married? Five months. Well—nearly five."

"Still counting, eh? Those were the days. Wait, didn't I read something about it? I did. Your first marriage?"

"Better late than never."

"Can I make a friendly observation? One married man to another?"

Tony nodded.

"When it comes to marriage, you'll never hit bottom. No matter how far you fall. Even the blackest pit has a trapdoor."

"Lord Brompton. I wonder if—"

"Leave off the Debrett's rubbish. I'm Peter." He looked up from his hastily re-stuffed briefcase. "Shall I show you Mariah's room?"

"Please."

* * *

HANNAH HADN'T EXAGGERATED. The room was grotesque. Tony, who'd had the unhappy duty of viewing many carefully-preserved rooms over the years, wasn't easily surprised. But the sight of Mariah Keene's bedroom, and her father's evident pleasure in revealing it, startled him. The man was smiling. Grinning like a politician at a ribbon-cutting ceremony.

"This is my sanctuary, now," he said.

Fortunately, Tony never had to wonder if his facial expression gave him away. He'd been born poker-faced. When it suited an investigation, he retreated instinctively behind that wall. Sometimes he had difficulty emerging.

Affecting a cough, he made a show of studying the room. "Remind me of Mariah's age again?"

"Twenty-one."

"Yes, of course. Twenty-one." Folding his arms across his chest, he looked up at the ceiling. "Are those bits of crystal I see? Forming the rings of Saturn?"

"Yes," Peter said proudly. "An artist friend painted the ceiling. Hannah and I asked for a celestial fantasy—signs of the Zodiac and all that. The artist took it upon herself to paint our solar system instead. The overhead light serves as the sun, you see. Crystal embellishments for the planets came later. Hand-glued. Countless hours on the ladder. A literal pain in the neck, if I'm being honest."

"You did it yourself?"

"Yes."

"Would you mind if I took pictures? Bit of video?" Tony pulled out his iPhone.

"How will that help?"

"I don't know yet. Sometimes photo documentation reveals little or nothing. But in my last official case for the Yard, it was everything. Better to waste time looking too closely than to neglect even the smallest clue."

"Yes, of course. Only...." Now it was Peter's turn to employ that time-honored transition, the manufactured cough. "There's something we have to get straight. I'll need your assurance that the pictures, video, etc., will stay with you. Or, if need be, the authorities. It can never be published or made available to the public in any way."

So he isn't totally round the bend, Tony thought. *He's still suffi-*

ciently cognizant of parental norms to understand how all this would look to the world. Or at least, his voters.

"I don't foresee a circumstance where your privacy would be violated," Tony said. "Unless I uncover evidence compelling enough to open a criminal case. In that event, the relevant images would become evidence."

Peter didn't look convinced. Rather, he looked very much like a man formulating an excuse to refuse. Or at least put it off long enough to give the room a private once-over first. Time for a distraction.

"May I suggest you ring your family solicitor?" Tony asked. "I'm happy to sign an NDA governing my use of such photos."

Peter brightened. "Yes. I should've thought of that. There's a bloke on my staff—we call him Dr. Optics. His real name is Aaron. He started as an IT consultant. Now he helps me safeguard my political image. He's a genius. Indispensable. I intend to stand for PM in a few years, you know. Others have let 'optics,' if you will, muck up their campaigns before they begin. I'm determined not to make that mistake."

Tony nodded. Peter's assertion, anodyne to most people's ears, triggered a thrill along his secondary nervous system, the one detectives grew. How many murders had happened because someone with a prized public image sought to erase a mistake?

As Peter went off to ring his counsel, Tony worked quickly to document the room: pictures, video, and even video in the round, which a detective with a standard smart phone could now perform on the fly. At a fresh crime scene, formalities mattered. Where there was blood spatter or a chance of touch DNA, CSIs were indispensable. Here, a PI with an iPhone could do the job nicely.

Mariah's furniture was white with gold-leaf accents: bed, desk, bookshelf, chair, and doll-sized tea set. The bed had a canopy, but it wasn't supported by four posters like the canopies Tony had glimpsed in so many homes. Rather, it was a massive, curtained affair, with a bower made of gauzy purple netting. Accented by white fairy lights, the bower hung suspended from the ceiling, trembling faintly.

The duvet was pink with white daisies. Atop a mound of assorted pillows sat a stuffed unicorn, its mad plastic gaze made all the madder by glittery purple eyes. Only in the last year or so had Tony noticed soft toys on offer with that style of plastic eyes. Had Mariah been a collector, even into adulthood?

The pillows were all in similar vein, fuzzy lightweight yarn or glitzy silver finishes. He dug into them, feeling within the shams. Nothing was stashed inside. On impulse, he sniffed them. Again, nothing, apart from the chemical-fix that textiles received before being shipped to the high street.

Undeterred, Tony searched deeper. Some clichés sprang out of truth. He'd always found that adult children living at home really did stash valuables where their younger selves had: in or around the bed.

The sheets were pristine, but the mattresses weren't—far from it. The top mattress, stained and bearing evidence of frequent spot-cleaning, looked thirty or forty years old.

The covering on the old-fashioned box spring was torn in spots. Working his fingers under the fabric, Tony snagged something. He pulled it free. It was a small plastic bag. Inside was roughly an ounce of brownish-green stuff.

Tony sniffed. It smelled powerfully of cloves. This wasn't weed. It was the synthetic version of marijuana known as K2, or Spice.

He tucked it into his coat pocket. In theory, K2/Spice and its most famous varieties, like Black Mamba, were illegal in the UK and most of the western world. However, declaring a substance illegal meant outlawing its precise chemical composition. Each time that drowsy Leviathan, Law, bestirred itself to declare a variety of Spice illegal, chemists would simply tweak the outlawed formula, adding or subtracting to produce a brand-new substance.

This exploitation of the legal loophole had been so successful, health and safety advocates had shifted to public education to quell the "lawful" high's demand. Like any street drug, Spice carried the usual risks: contamination, combination with a highly addictive opioid like Fentanyl, and unsavory dealers. Moreover, there was growing evidence that certain varieties of Spice triggered psychiatric disorders, including psychosis.

Reminds me of "Angel Dust," back in the day, Tony thought. *Individuals on PCP did terrible things. Some even jumped off buildings, trying to fly. Could that be why Mariah jumped?*

Under the bed, Tony found two storage boxes. One was stuffed with ladies' shoes, British size 8.5. Definitely the province of a grown woman between 5'9" and 6 feet tall. Most of the shoes were strappy sandals or four-inch pumps, black, taupe, and red. No little girl styles or colors.

The other storage box was more interesting: a cache of personal belongings. Tony sorted through them swiftly, aware that Peter might return at any moment. Although he'd given permission for Tony to search the room, he was likely to balk at the sight of a near-stranger touching his dead daughter's things. Especially if he had something to hide.

The box contained, in no order: Sharpies, a 1937 threepenny bit, bangle bracelets, a cube of yellow Post-Its, sunglasses, Boots No. 7 waterproof mascara, a student ID from Cardiff University, a bottle of essential oil labeled Geranium, a box of colored pencils, bras, knickers, and knit socks. The socks were novelty items, probably gifts. One set had a phrase beginning on the sole of one and concluded on its mate.

IF YOU CAN READ THIS
BRING ME WINE

Another sock bulged, concealing something heavy. Tony shook it out. It was a palm-sized, silicone rubber-coated item with a shape that suggested nothing to him. He saw no visible switch, only a USB charging port. As he pondered the item, he spied a near-imperceptible divot. He pressed.

The device vibrated exuberantly, continuing till he thumbed the divot again.

Mystery solved. Tony slipped the personal massager back in its sock. He had no intention of telling Kate such an item had momentarily flummoxed him. Maybe he'd mention it to Paul someday, over a pint. It was good to occasionally compare notes with a younger man.

Next, he searched Mariah's desk. Stuffed teddy bears occupied most of the bookshelf real estate, apart from an illustrated children's Bible and a couple of Harry Potters. The soft toys were beautifully constructed and, like the unicorn with the glittery eyes, apparently never touched by sticky childish hands.

Inside the desk drawers, which had pink glass rosebuds for pulls, he found childhood mementos. An old diary full of complaints about the burden of a twin brother, written in messy block print; photo albums; a couple of half-dressed Barbies; report cards; a stack of letters written by Mariah to her parents from camp when she was ten years old. These were sorted by date, tucked into their original envelopes, and tied with a pink ribbon.

"Revolting, isn't it?"

Tony turned. Hannah stood in the doorway, a glass of white wine in hand.

"It seems to have been redone. Is any part of this room unchanged from when Mariah was alive?"

"What do you think?" Hannah stuck to the corridor, as if stepping over the threshold into her daughter's room constituted some form of violation. "I suppose the bed is still hers, under all that airy-fairy froufrou. The mattress and box spring, I mean. But it's no good searching that desk for clues to anything other than Peter's madness. He bought it, dragged it up here, and decorated it with props to remind him of his perfect child's perfect childhood." She laughed.

"Was there a specific incident?"

Hannah studied him for a moment. "No," she said at last, without conviction. "Mariah could be grasping and greedy, like any child. She was disciplined in school for drugs—marijuana. She lied sometimes, and pulled Mark into those lies. His worst mistakes were always at her urging."

As Tony took that in, Hannah continued, "The original desk might have helped you, but it's gone. Along with everything in it, I suppose." Something about the way she swirled her wine right to the very rim of the glass suggested she was on the brink of inebriation. Either she'd consumed plenty of alcohol since the end of their interview, or she was mixing wine with prescription tranquilizers.

"You should've seen it," she continued. "Peter up on a ladder, hanging that purple monstrosity over the bed, hot-gluing bits of crystal to the ceiling. Two things Mariah wanted as a child that we said was too expensive, or too much bother. Now that she's dead, nothing is too much."

"Did you keep all of Mark's things?" Tony asked.

"Yes. Boxed up, like Peter said."

"Why boxed up? Don't you think that after he's found, he'll be willing to return home?"

Hannah shook her head. "We put the ultimate burden on him. Drove him away. Even if he forgives us, I can't imagine he'll live here ever again. Perhaps after you find him, he'll allow me to set him up in a cozy flat somewhere close. That's the most I can hope for."

"What do you mean, the ultimate burden?"

Hannah took another sip. "When they told us that Mariah fell thirty stories to her death, Peter didn't believe it. He insisted it was a case of mistaken identity. He was half out the door, coat over his pajamas, ranting about incompetent cops and how it must be some poor Jane Doe. I told him we needed to send someone else. That I couldn't do it and neither should he. He wouldn't listen."

"But then you said two words. 'Smashed watermelon.'" Peter appeared beside her on the landing. "Gave me nightmares for months. Our daughter, dead on the pavement, with the head of an exploded gourd."

Hannah shrugged. "Maybe when you stop sleeping in here, you won't dream of her."

"That's all you have left to take from me, isn't it? My access to the place where I feel closest to Mariah's spirit." Defiantly, Peter plopped down on the elephant in the room: his sleeping cot, which was pushed up against the foot of Mariah's bed.

The cot was unmade and messy. Its blue tick mattress peeked out; the sheets and pillows were tangled. Under the cot, Peter had stashed his nighttime effects: carpet slippers, a John Grisham novel, a prescription bottle, and a glass tumbler. Tony had already noted the name of the prescription, Haldol, but hadn't been able to Google it yet.

Could it be an antipsychotic? he wondered. Given all the times he'd been privy to the medical records of disturbed individuals, his working knowledge of psychiatric meds should have been better. As good as his knowledge of poisons and street drugs, anyway.

Perhaps he was just reacting to the uncomfortable juxtaposition of Mariah's twin bed under its gauzy purple bower and a grown man's flop-spot shoved up against it. The way Peter sat atop it, smiling from ear to ear as if the recipient of some cosmic comfort, gave Tony another chill along the detective's nerve apparatus.

"You ghoul," Hannah said, speaking Tony's thoughts aloud. "You killed her. You did. Didn't you?"

"Right! Well done, you." Peter's laugh was high and unhinged. "I drove her to a construction site in the middle of the night. I accompanied her up to the highest beam and gave her the push. Of course I did. Never mind that I slept beside you in our own bed the entire night. Never mind that heights make me so wobbly I won't even walk across the Millennium Bridge. And when I was done killing my daughter, whom I loved more than I ever loved you, I put on a show of not believing she was dead. I was all set to burst into the Wapping morgue until *you* told me she was broken open like a dropped jack-o-lantern. And what did I do when your words sunk in? I fainted. Because that's the sort of diabolical killer I am."

"I mean you drove her to jump," Hannah shrieked. "What did you do to her? What was happening in this room that I didn't see?"

"Everything," Peter roared. "Her entire life! You were too busy with Petrie dishes and gene splicing and your precious Mark to see anything at all."

"*Forgive me*," Tony said in a tone that sounded remarkably like two other words. Hannah and Peter goggled at him as if he'd interrupted their row with profanity instead of an apology. He seized on the silence.

"Lord and Lady Brompton, I understand you were frustrated by what you perceived as a lack of hands-on attention from Cecelia Wheelwright. I assure you, I will be available to a far greater degree. In return for my undivided attention, I must ask you to avoid one another, and this sort of unseemly display, during my investigation. If I want to interview you simultaneously, I'll say so. Otherwise, separate is best. That means you, Lady Brompton, should remove to some other room while I discuss matters with your husband."

"Fine." Hannah knocked back the remainder of her wine. A drop slipped down her chin. She didn't seem to notice. "I'm tired. Insomnia. Maybe I'm ready to sleep. Never mind today. We'll crack on tomorrow."

"Sorry about her," Peter said after his wife had gone. "We've had this screaming match a dozen times already, but she doesn't remember. She mixes horse tranqs and Sauvignon Blanc until she's reeling, screams at me, sleeps through dinner time, then stays up all night Googling Sir Duncan and other serial killers. I can always tell when she's close to passing out. She accuses me of driving Mariah to jump. It's the only time she admits Mariah actually took her own life."

"May I ask you an unpleasant question, Peter?"

"What? Don't tell me you're going to accuse me, too. If not of murder, of being a paedo?"

"No. It's about this room. Why did you tear it down to mattress and box spring, then rebuild it this way?" Tony asked. "Complete with toys she never played with and children's books she never read?"

"She read the Harry Potters," Peter muttered. "As ebooks. I bought the hardcovers so I could see them on the shelf." His gaze wandered to the floor and stayed there.

Tony allowed him a minute's silence. Then: "Are you ashamed to tell me?"

"Of course I'm ashamed." Peter's eyes shone. "Hannah was never around. But neither was I, when it counted. I loved Mariah, I encouraged her, but I'm still guilty. She wanted a canopy bed and I said no. She wanted sparkles on the ceiling and I called her spoiled. She asked for soft toys and I lectured her about not playing with the ones she already had. Remaking this room was therapy to me. Just like packing up Mark's room and fantasizing about moving him into a flat was therapy for Hannah."

"If you'll forgive me, Lord Brompton — Peter. I sense what you're holding back is something you fear no one will understand." Tony pinned his client with his gaze. "Something you suspect is relevant to the case. Perhaps even crucial. Yet at the same time, something you fear being found out. Even though you've hired me to dig up everything I can."

Peter looked like he wanted to run away. Tony expected him to do just that. Instead, he squared his shoulders and spoke.

"I introduced Sir Duncan to Mark and Mariah. Encouraged the friendship. When she had a falling out with him, I told her she was being ridiculous. That was the last time I spoke to Mariah," Peter said. "She rang me in my office to say she thought Sir Duncan was abnormal. I told her his friendship was worth putting up with a bit of eccentricity."

"What sort of eccentricity?"

"A religion, of sorts. Sacred Geometry." Peter sighed. "It's all over my head. Not sure if it's a cult like Scientology or just a woolly notion, like in that book *The Secret*. Anyway, Mariah said she thought it was bad for Mark. That Sir Duncan kept obsessing over their friendship. Said they formed a triangle. Or a triptych. Something like that. Looking back, it makes my skin crawl. But...."

"But what?"

"I was cross with her. Cross with Mark, too. I was expecting Sir Duncan to speak on my behalf during my reelection campaign and I didn't want to rock that boat," Peter said. "But mostly, I could sense that Mariah wanted permission to tell Sir Duncan to go to hell. So instead I told her, stick it out, be a friend, and encourage Mark to do the same. Once I was reelected, they could pull the plug if they wanted."

Tony waited. Peter didn't look like he was finished. Nor did he seem willing to go on.

"Tell me," Tony said.

"I've said all there is to say." Peter lifted his chin and stared, unblinking, at Tony. The liar's stare.

I will find out, Tony thought. But aloud he said, "Explain this business about sacred geometry, then."

CHAPTER FOUR

*D*eadenfall, Kate thought. How could she be expected to feel at home at a place nicknamed Deadenfall?

Of course, her discomfort with living at One Hundred and One Leadenhall wasn't literally about the death of Mariah Keene. That was sad, but such things happened. No one could have expected the builders to abandon the project simply because an apparently disturbed young woman died on the site.

Nor was her discomfort superstitious in nature. There probably wasn't a square foot of London that hadn't been baptized in blood or used as a burial ground at some point. As recently as 1811, a murderer had been staked through the heart and buried at the crossroads of Oxford Street and Tottenham Cross Road. At last count, a third of all Londoners believed in ghosts. Sometimes, Kate counted herself among them. New building or old, ghosts came with the territory in the city of her birth.

No—Kate disliked the name Deadenfall for more personal reasons. When she was thirteen years old, she'd suffered a traumatic fall from a building in which she, like Mariah Keene, had been trespassing. And the night before they moved into their sublet condo, Kate had dreamed of that near-miss.

Like most dreams, it had unfolded not as pure memory, but rather as a series of impossibilities. She'd been all grown up, alone, and standing atop the Leadenhall building, fifty-one stories high. Her friend and colleague, Paul Bhar, had been rappelling down the side of the Walkie-Talkie building, shouting her name, imploring her not to jump. At the same time, a menacing presence behind her crept closer.

The soft crunching sound of his footsteps, like trainers on pebbles or grit, had been eerily real. Whirling, dream-Kate had performed a roundhouse kick at her unseen attacker. In waking life, it was a move she'd twice used on the job, and executed perfectly. In the dream, she'd lost her balance and tumbled, shrieking, over the building's edge.

It was absurd for a grown woman to connect a universal nightmare, falling, with the fate of Mariah Keene and that not-so-clever nickname, Deadenfall. Much less allow that association to follow her around like a personal raincloud. But Kate had always taken her dreams seriously. In the real world, she chased clues for a living. In her dreams, clues sometimes chased her.

In their five short months of marriage, Kate had been surprised by how easily she and Tony had combined two wildly different lives into one. He deserved most of the credit. He'd entered marriage with the philosophy that nothing could be held back. In his mind, Wellegrave House was no longer his alone. All its contents—the heirloom/Gilded Age/baronial folderol that had delighted her when they were dating and made her feel like a fraud once they were wed—was fully hers as well as his.

His calm in the face of catastrophic property damage was no stiff upper lip routine, she knew. As he saw it, guardianship of his brother-in-law, Ritchie, was now fully his as well as hers. This included meltdowns, Lego pieces strewn like caltrops across the living room floor, and the occasional million dollars in irreplaceable antiques. Many men, after forty years or so of serene bachelorhood, would moan, grumble, or collect pamphlets about care homes and drop them in strategic places around the house. He didn't. There were numerous reasons why his character did not permit him to pursue matrimony so single-mindedly, then complain after the fact about the baggage that came with it. Kate preferred to collect all these reasons into one simple phrase: Tony Hetheridge was a real man.

He has an easier time seeing the big picture than I do. She was sitting in the lobby on the ground floor, a vodka martini with three colossal olives positioned at her elbow on the illuminated Lucite bar top. Staying at One-oh-One meant never having to venture out into the wind or rain for a drink. One-oh-One boasted several pubs — eight, to be exact – but the lobby pub, Archie's, was the poshest.

Leave it to a place like this to make me long for a hole in the wall.

Viewed from thirty thousand feet, subletting a condo at the Leadenhall building was an experience most people in London (or England, or the world) would relish. Until Wellegrave House was restored, the Hetheridges would dwell in the very heart of the city. They would order meals up when the fancy took them. Take the lift down when they wanted a little light shopping. Savor breathtaking views of London whenever they pleased, night or day. Kate felt sure that if she, too, could ascend above the clouds, she'd see their temporary residence at One-oh-One as the privilege it was. Perhaps even a vacation. But she was too accustomed to the view from six inches, otherwise known as "in the thick of it."

Archie's was ultra-modern. The light-up bar top pulsed along with canned dance music. Every spot at the bar included a recharging port. There was no bartender. Drinks were ordered via touchscreen menus and dropped off by nameless rotating servers. Most of them tasted watered down. Kate had discovered they were injected into glasses via a computer-brained liquor dispenser. Bartenders who poured by eye tended to splash a little humanity into their drinks. An extra jigger of vermouth, a juniper garnish, a double shot for a regular's big day, etc. Drink-dispensing robots never gave up an extra drop. Which was one reason why Kate, a lover of pale lager, had ordered a vodka martini at five o'clock in the afternoon. It was only marginally stronger. The other reason was to aggravate her older sister, Maura Wakefield.

Kate and Maura had spent their adult lives at war. Not always a shooting war. Sometimes they went months without speaking, a sort of East Germany-West Germany situation, separated by miles of psychological bricks and mortar. Sometimes promising diplomatic talks occurred. Other times military maneuvers were carried out in the DMZ, night and day.

After Kate married Tony, the Wakefield war had heated up again. Kate had predicted this during their short engagement. It had been one of the many reasons, along with her own insecurity, she'd been reluctant to accept Tony's proposal. Kate's mother, Louise, still very much a part of Maura's life, was a bad influence. The two women shared a knack for acquiring dosh under shifty conditions and making it go *poof.* Kate called them grifters. They called her a stooge.

Soon after Kate said, "I do," Louise and Maura swooped in demanding payouts. First came the guilt trip. How could Kate live in luxury while her own people dwelt in penury? Very well, as it turned out.

Second, attempts at flattery. Kate had chosen a remarkable groom. Tony was so dashing, so distinguished, so eminently capable of supporting his in-laws. Wouldn't Kate like to intervene with him on their behalf? Nope.

Last came threats. So Kate liked playing mommy to her nephew, Henry? Couldn't have babies of her own so she'd nicked someone else's? Well, if she wouldn't see her way clear to prop up dear old mum and down-on-her-luck sis, she'd better kiss the boy goodbye. Was Kate willing to put Henry through a custody lawsuit? She was, as it turned out.

That was better than committing to a decade of picking up Louise and Maura's tabs. So now Maura was suing for full custody of Henry, the son she'd abandoned when he was four years old.

Kate sipped her drink. An aggressively average libation, as generic as Archie's dance beat. But to Maura, it would be as tempting as a double portion of cheesecake to a slimmer.

That's the best thing about family, Kate thought, munching an olive. *No need guessing which buttons to push. They're all clearly labeled.*

The Leadenhall building's lobby was public, according to its glossy brochures. Nevertheless, uniformed doormen alerted the security desk if someone not quite fit and proper entered. While awaiting the weekly hand-off—when Maura brought Henry back after her legally-mandated visitation—Kate had observed the workings of One-oh-One's lobby. Professionals who looked the part (suits, laptops, self-important frowns) were permitted to get on with it. So were the tea room customers awaiting their table in the Leadenhall building's neo-Victorian tourist magnet. Residents like Kate were never disturbed unless they raised a hand or glanced around in an imperious manner, in which case one or two employees fell over themselves to respond.

Sometimes people wandered in from the street. Within seconds, they were subjected to the sort of "service" that only the very naïve consider welcoming. Under the stare of an Impressive Concierge asking questions in an Impressive Tone ("How might I assist you today, sir?") those interlopers got themselves to the bar or turned around and left. That was the desired effect: a force field of courtesy to drive out those who didn't belong.

The Courtesy Force Field didn't always work on the homeless. The uniformed doormen generally kept them out, sometimes with a threatening gesture or unkind word. Kate had never seen any of the doormen cross the line, but she found herself watching nonetheless.

Once, a ragged man laden with overfilled Tesco bags and wearing his entire wardrobe had somehow evaded the doormen and entered the lobby while Kate was there. On cue, the Impressive Concierge had sailed up and made a show of offering the man help. Specifically, a prepackaged sandwich, bottle of juice, and printed directions to the nearest shelter. The ragged man had rejected that. He'd plopped down on a sofa, saying he just wanted to sit down. The concierge had withdrawn, rang up the City of London police, and had him escorted out.

That memory stuck in Kate's craw. She wasn't sure why. Luxury high-rises catered to the wealthy. Such people valued privacy and well-kept surroundings, and why wouldn't they?

Of course, it was no good living someplace enviable without permitting others to envy it. That's why they allowed well-groomed tourists to play Jane Austen in the tea room and take selfies in front of the Twombly. But homeless people? Bathing in the lavatory sinks and napping under the potted ficus trees? Never. Not even Kate, who wanted to be inclusive and progressive and a lot of other "ives," liked the thought of that. Not if she was being honest. So why did the memory sting?

Because of the Kabuki theater. The sandwich and juice and list of resources. It isn't meant to spare the homeless person's feelings. It's meant to spare my feelings. Mine, and every other resident or guest who has a "right" to be here. So we don't feel bad when the doormen show them out, or the City of London police take them away.

She checked her phone. Maura was fifteen minutes late. It wasn't surprising, given the hour. Nevertheless, Kate resented it. A responsible adult would expect the evening rush and take steps to compensate. But complaining about small infractions would do no good. In Family Court, the judge had insisted that Maura be permitted weekly visitation, usually from Friday after school until five o'clock Saturday evening. Kate had ranted and raved until their solicitor, whom Tony had selected from a top-drawer firm near London Bridge, set her straight about what adoption would and wouldn't do.

Even if Kate and Tony prevailed in adopting Henry over Maura's wishes, she would still be permitted into Henry's life. The courts would never deny her visitation unless she relapsed back into drugs and alcohol. Even then, visitation would only be suspended even if she was arrested, sectioned, and re-incarcerated. As long as Maura took her meds, saw her psychiatrist, and checked in with her social worker, the law would permit her to see her son.

Kate thought that made about as much sense as allowing a bank robber to work as a security guard, so long as he kept his uniform razor-creased and didn't nick any chained pens. Why did the law favor the birth mum no matter what? It wasn't like Maura was an unknown quantity. Why didn't Kate's testimony on Maura's maternal fitness count for anything?

Maura had never intended to get pregnant. At the time, she'd been alcoholic, often coked-up, and on the game, which meant Henry's unknown father was quite likely one of her clients. The pregnancy had progressed because she'd been in denial until around the sixth month. Then she'd decided it would be easier to go forward with motherhood than to try and arrange an adoption. Immediately after the birth, she'd elected for surgical sterilization, telling Kate, then a twenty-five-year-old police constable, "One nipper is already one too many."

As far as Kate was concerned, Henry had survived his infancy only because she and her mother took an interest. Louise, who'd given up drugs but would never throw over her one true love, gin, had watched the baby by day. Kate had looked after him on nights and weekends, as her schedule permitted. She hardly slept, but time with baby Henry was its own reward. And in her mid-twenties, she didn't need much sleep. At least not compared to how much she needed it now.

While Louise and Kate changed nappies, washed bottles,

oversaw vaccinations, and bought clothes, Maura got on with her life: booze, coke, men. Sometimes she cooed over Henry, sometimes she seemed to forget he existed. When he was four, she cleaned up, moved into her own tiny Council flat, freaked out, and disappeared, leaving him alone for days.

That was the nadir of Kate and Maura's relationship. Kate, by then a trainee detective, had worked forty-eight hours straight on the assumption that Louise would drop in. But Louise had run off to Manchester with a boyfriend on the assumption that Maura was "cured" and taking responsibility at long last. When Kate, exhausted, daunted by the rigors of becoming a detective, and eager for a personal life outside the Met, discovered the truth —Henry had been abandoned in a filthy apartment to scream himself hoarse—she'd wanted to strangle Maura. Instead, she'd made a snap decision: to take Henry in.

Sometimes people assumed she'd done it to be a martyr. To pass herself off as a modern-day saint, the one good Wakefield. After all, she'd already brought her elder brother Ritchie into her home, an act that required both personal sacrifice and lots of help from the NHS like paid carers. Taking in Henry was supposed to be temporary. But six years had deepened their bond to something very like mother and son.

Over that time, Kate had gradually kindled some sympathy for Maura. She should have been diagnosed with schizophrenia around twenty-two, but in those days she'd been considered a bad apple; just another brawling, light-fingered East End slag. She'd treated her paranoia with alcohol; she'd drowned out the voices with a variety of street drugs. Ironically, sobering up was what forced the crisis that led to her abandoning her son. After five years in state custody, she was ready to have another go at life.

She was dealt a bum hand. But there ought to be some consideration for my feelings. Why should Maura be allowed to treat Henry like a baby doll she dropped behind the bed, then turn up when he's nine and take over as his mum? Why do I have to prove myself to the court after looking after for him for so long?

Kate glanced at her phone. Half-five and no apologies. Not even an excuse re: crowded tube stations or clogged roads. Right. It wasn't as if she had anything better to do. Tony would be home soon. He'd been on his first real PI case for three days. This was her first chance to discuss it with him. Paul Bhar would be joining them for dinner, partly to hear about Tony's case, and partly to make some announcement he'd been hinting at all week. She suspected it had to do with his complicated love life. Maybe he was throwing over brunette Kyla, whom Kate had never liked, and settling down with blonde Emmeline at long last?

And though she looked forward to an evening with her husband and colleague, that didn't mean she wasn't knackered from work and longing for some Kate-time. Ideally, a long soak in the tub with lit candles and soft music. Instead, she was stuck in One-oh-One's lobby, listening to stale electronica and waiting on someone who always left her holding the bag.

I ought to chug it, Kate thought, contemplating her weak martini. Instead she limited herself to a sip. The cocktail had to look enticing when Maura arrived. Yes, tempting a newly-sober person was cruel and inappropriate. That was the point. For those keeping score at home, Kate trailed her big sis in "Cruel and Inappropriate" plays by double digits.

The lobby, always full of chatter, quieted suddenly. Men in pinstriped suits stopped barking into their mobiles. A group of business women networking amongst the ficus trees paused to stare at One Hundred and One Leadenhall's grand entrance. There, a woman in a grotty old donkey jacket and high-waisted jeans was having words with the doorman. Her gray hair was loose and wild. Her hands gripped overstuffed Tesco bags.

"I don't need *help*, mate. I need to crack on," Maura said in her loud East End bray. "Sorry I don't look the part. Forgot my Chanel coat and Manolo Blancs. But I'm here with this here young man. He lives—bloody hell. Where'd the little eel slip off to?"

She looked left. Looked right. Spun in a circle and boomed at the top of her lungs, "*Henry*! Get back here! These tossers want to arrest me for breathing their air."

The doorman, handsome and impeccably groomed, must have had enough. He lifted a white-gloved hand—index finger up, as if summoning a waiter. Instantly, that shift's Impressive Concierge, a Frenchman with flared nostrils, sprang into action. Out of the cupboard under his computer came a sandwich in a plastic clamshell and a little bottle of orange juice. Kate hopped off her barstool.

"Put that away," she said, intercepting him. "That woman's not a vagrant. She's my sister. Here to drop off my nephew. He lives with me in 4400."

The concierge regarded Kate as if she'd materialized from a dimension where everything smelled like dirty socks. It would have been infuriating, except he looked that way all the time.

"Madam, is there a problem with your cocktail? Shall I direct a server to assist?"

This misunderstanding of her statement would also have been infuriating, except the French concierge misunderstood every sentence directed to him the first time around. If asked, "Which floor for your tea room?" he might respond, "The tea room of the Marriott near the Houses of Parliament comes highly recommended, I think you'll find." If told, "I need the number of a good optometrist," he might say, "Apparently, the National Health has a useful website." Because of his thick accent, Kate had initially believed his command of English was subpar. Now she suspected it was pure passive aggression.

"You heard me," Kate bawled, every bit as loud as Maura. In moments like these, her Received Pronunciation disappeared altogether. "She's my big sis, innit? And look, there he is, the man of the hour. My nephew, Henry, who I just mentioned. Hey?

Remember our Henry? The boy who says hello to you or mentions it's a lovely day while you stare back like one of them potted trees piped up?"

"Of course." The concierge cleared his throat. "I apologize, madam, for your misinterpretation of my innocent query. I am always pleased to exchange greetings with small children. That is the privilege of my position, to mix with all sorts. But I see no vagrant," he insisted. "I intended these refreshments for a colleague. Did you imagine it was charity for the lady at the door? Never mind. It's easy to jump to conclusions."

His tone, one of narrowly-suppressed rage, delighted Kate. She plucked the prepackaged sandwich and bottled orange juice from his grasp. "Cheers. Bit peckish, I am."

As the concierge retreated to the safety of his enclosed box, Maura and Henry reached Kate at last. Henry was scowling like he didn't want to be seen with either of them. Maura was huffing and puffing like she'd been training for a 5K.

"What the bloody hell is that you've got there? Late lunch?"

"Never mind. Why are you breathless?"

"Why aren't I breathless? This kiddie had me at sixes and sevens all day." Maura grinned down at Henry. He rolled his eyes.

"He wanted to visit the Museum of Natural History. I said all right, thinking it would be like Madame Tussaud's. Or the London Dungeon—bit of trivia, bit of fun, exit through the gift shop and get on with your life," Maura said. "Hah! It's big as bloody Heathrow in there. Lord, I never knew there was so much of it. Not just the museum. History. My brain is full. I came out feeling stupider than I did going in."

"What about you? Learn anything?" Kate asked Henry.

"What do you think?" he huffed.

"I think you'd better mind your manners. Especially if you hope to lay a finger on your Xbox anytime soon," she snapped. "I've been sitting here awaiting your pleasure. No call, no text, not a word. Just me parked in this fishbowl, bone-tired, feet aching, while you trundle up in your own good time. Then I ask a civil question and get a snotty answer. Not fair, is it?"

Henry, a moon-faced boy with owlish specs, pale skin, and medium brown hair, did that thing with his mouth. The particular twist of his lips that indicated he was poised equidistant between shouting and weeping.

Kate didn't care. She had no problem with Henry challenging her on a factual basis. She had a very large problem with ungrateful backtalk after a Saturday spent catering to his interests.

"I said, not fair, is it?"

He looked at his feet and muttered something.

"Louder."

"If I had a mobile, I could've texted you that we were running late."

"Really? The mobile again?"

"Actually...." Maura said, but Kate held up a hand.

"Look. I accept you're his mother. You make recommendations. But I'm his guardian. I make decisions. Nine-year-olds don't need mobiles. It's madness."

"It's modern life," Maura countered. "I know he doesn't need any more screens. And I don't want to see him spoilt. But you don't have to buy him a smart phone. What about a burner? No-frills. Just for safety."

"I can't—" Kate began.

"You can! You *can* afford it," Henry roared. "You have money now. Stop pretending you don't!"

Human sounds in the lobby ceased. For three excruciating seconds, Kate felt all eyes on her. The canned beat emanating from Archie's went on. Behind the concierge desk, the Frenchman smiled.

"Henry. Straight up to your room. Sharpish," Kate said.

"But it's true!" Henry cried, turning red. "You could buy me a mobile. You could buy Mum a mobile. Hers is rubbish! The screen is cracked. Its texts won't go through. Have you seen where she lives? The roof leaks. She flushes the bog with a bucket. You have *everything* and Mum has nothing."

Mum?

Kate sucked in her breath. The substance of Henry's tirade didn't shock her. It had been building for a while, ever since he came back from his first visit to Maura's bleak bedsit in Norbiton. He was the kind of kid who shared freely—lunch, toys, and opinions. At nine years old, he was a veteran of public housing: unresponsive Councils, leaking pipes, and rats in the walls. Now he enjoyed the kind of luxury he'd once assumed existed only on telly. With only a vague idea of Maura's history and track record, it was natural for him to want to help.

But he called her Mum, Kate thought. That three-letter word pricked her all out of proportion, like a sliver of glass underfoot. Henry had long been in the habit of calling Kate by her Christian name and Maura by hers. In conversation outside the family, he referred to Maura as "my mum" for simplicity's sake. But in her presence he never accorded her that title. Kate had been patiently-impatiently waiting for him to bestow it on her.

"I said, straight up to your room," she said stiffly. "No Xbox. No computer. I'll be up when I'm up. If I catch you on either, you'll regret it."

"Don't change the subject." Henry's eyes shone with tears of rage. "You have money now. You could solve all Mum's problems by writing a check."

"Henry, love. That's enough, innit," Maura said. "Kate doesn't owe me a payoff. And this isn't the time or place for a family throw-down. Do as you're told. I'll give you a ring tomorrow." She tried to kiss his cheek, but Henry wasn't having it.

"It's no use hoping, Mum. Tony says if you want something, you have to ask for it straight out. Tell Kate what you told me. Tell her you need—"

"Never mind," Maura cut across him. "We had a lovely day

out. Don't wreck it at the end. Go up to your room. Don't forget these," she added, handing him the overfilled Tesco bags.

"What is all that?" Kate asked. The insufferable French concierge wanted to know, too, judging by his intent stare.

"Marvel Infinity War sheets. Mum bought them for me. She's *generous*," Henry added. "They're my favorite now. I hate the sheets you bought me after the fire. So Mum let me take these off the cot and bring them here."

"Fine. I don't care. Just take them up to your room and stay there," Kate said. "No computer. No Xbox."

"No shit." Henry turned toward the residents' bank of private lifts.

"I heard that!"

"I hope so!"

When he was out of sight, Kate glared at Maura. "Nice."

"Too right. He learnt to swear like that from you, didn't he?"

Maura had a point. Kate had grown up cursing freely around her mother, Louise, who could scarcely complete a sentence without at least one expletive. Kate wasn't quite that bad, but colorful phraseology came with her chosen profession. At the Met, profanity was as much an art form as a safety valve. Only when Henry was sent home from school at age seven (for suggesting a schoolyard bully do something physically improbable) did Kate realize he really did absorb and repeat everything she said. Since then, she'd cleaned up her act, but the damage was done.

Kate tried another line of attack. "What was that he said to you? 'It's no good hoping?' Did you ask Henry to convince me to buy you a new mobile? Maybe a new place to live?"

"No. Well. Yes. More or less," Maura muttered. "Not my finest hour. I was upset at my sponsor. She says working the twelve steps means making amends, and that includes paying back what I nicked from Phil. You remember Phil? My boyfriend, before I was sectioned. I stole a couple of hundred from him back in the Stone Age and my sponsor says she'll sack me if I don't contact him with a payment plan." She shrugged. "Recovery problems. Never mind. I shouldn't have vented to Henry. He's such a sympathetic soul. Sometimes I forget I'm meant to be the rock, not him." Clearing her throat, she said, "I'm sorry."

Kate was too surprised to reply. Rather than lie, Maura had admitted she was wrong. Admitted she was wrong *and* apologized. Maybe the combination of the correct psychiatric meds, an absence of alcohol and street drugs, and her twelve-step work was doing her some good. Or maybe it was just another con.

"We don't have to be at each other's throats," Maura said earnestly, as if emboldened by something she'd glimpsed in Kate's eyes. "I'm getting too old for it."

"Then drop the suit. Tony and I will adopt Henry. You'll still get regular visitation. Everybody wins," Kate said.

"You know I can't do that. I'm his mother. If I sign away my rights, I walk away from the best thing I ever done. Maybe the only thing I ever done that weren't a crime or a delusion." Tears welled in her eyes. "Crikey hell. My meds have me bawling over yogurt commercials. All I mean to say is, people who are disagreeing don't have to be disagreeable. That's my sponsor's motto." Digging in her handbag, Maura produced a crumpled tissue and dabbed at her eyes. "What's all that, then?"

"What? Oh." Kate had forgotten she was holding the sandwich and juice. "That bloke there," she said, pointing at the concierge. "He reckoned you were homeless. Meant to give you some food and tell you to piss off."

"Oh. Well. I am a bit windblown, if I'm being honest." Maura, an admirer of men in all their varieties, looked the Frenchman over approvingly. "Dead handsome, innit? I'm not homeless," she called to him, waving. "Bad hair day! Not homeless."

"Let's go to the bar and tuck in," Kate said. "That'll take the mickey." But then she remembered her vodka martini, waiting seductively on its cocktail napkin, to tempt and torment her big sister.

"Scratch that. There's a better bet." Grinning, Kate led Maura to the plush sofas and overstuffed armchairs where business-people were pretending to be masters of the universe via laptops and mobiles. There, they split the sandwich (chicken salad) and the orange juice (from concentrate) and soaked up the mass disapproval like a tonic.

* * *

BACK IN THE CONDO, Kate paused to check her phone for voice-mails and texts before taking the lift up to Henry's room. She was stalling. They needed to clear the air, but first Kate had to decide what she felt. Taking sides with Maura against an admittedly easy target, a crowd of upwardly mobile tossers, had brought a lot of old emotions to the surface. Once upon a time, Kate had admired her older sister, even idolized her. When they worked in tandem to embarrass a bully or regale a crowd with taboo behavior, young Kate had felt like Maura was her a soulmate.

But then she started using. I couldn't count on her anymore. And after that night....

Kate pushed the memory away. She was all grown up and she knew the pattern. Maura would let her down again. She always did.

The lift dropped whisked her to the condo's second floor, which was divided into two outrageously large bedrooms, each with a full en suite bath. Ritchie's door was open. He was listening to the radio while disassembling a Lego project.

Kate stopped to watch, untroubled by his failure to acknowl-edge her. He was pulling apart one of his mysterious creations. When that was done, he'd sort the plastic bricks into piles, assign each group to its own compartment in his Lego box, close the box, and stare at it. Sometimes he stared at his closed Lego box for hours. Maybe he was meditating on the completion of the cycle. Maybe he was envisioning what form those bricks would assume next.

Henry's door was closed. A whiteboard hung on it. Its message, in crowded block print, varied daily. Sometimes it was an announcement; sometimes it was a doodle, or a cinema quote. Tonight it was a declaration.

YOU COULD LEARN TO SHARE KATE NOW COULDN'T YOU

Kate knocked. She was careful to always knock and announce herself before entering. Her mum had taken a different approach, breaking in whenever she pleased and taking anything that sparked her fancy, especially items she could swap for gear. Kate wanted Henry to know she was in charge and what she said was law. But she didn't want him to feel besieged in his own space, with not even a corner to call his own.

"What?" Henry bellowed from behind the locked door.

"Pax."

Henry didn't answer.

"I'm invoking the Pax Wakefield. I have three. This is my first one this year. Let me in."

Henry opened the door. He hadn't been crying, which was good. He regarded her suspiciously. "When you use the Pax, the row never happened. No punishment. No discussion."

"I know." Kate stuck out her hand.

Henry shook it. "So I can play Xbox? Or get on the computer?"

"Is your homework finished?"

He nodded.

"Did Tony look at it?"

"He looked at the maths. I repeated the problems he marked.

He doesn't look at my English or Science anymore," the boy said proudly. "He says it's unnecessary."

"Then Xbox or the computer is fine. Can I come in?"

Henry stepped back to allow it. "I put the sheets on the bed. Aren't they cool?"

"Yeah. But you've got a corner bollixed up," Kate said, automatically smoothing the bottom sheet and tucking it securely. "Right. Now it won't spring loose in the middle of the night." She fluffed one pillow, which featured Thor, then the other, which depicted a hunky Captain America. "Listen. Henry. About Maura…."

"You used the Pax. You have to drop it!"

"I'm not arguing. I'm just saying. You and me and Tony need to have a discussion before too much longer," she said carefully. "I know you think her problems could be solved with money. And maybe some could. But it's more complicated than that. For adults, it's not just about paying off debts and having nice things. It's about self-respect, and feeling beholden. There's a power dynamic," she finished lamely, wondering if a nine-year-old could possibly understand.

Henry looked thoughtful. "So you think she'd resent help?"

"She might."

"Nobody likes charity. But sometimes people need it. Mum's been sick. She's still sick, really, even with her meds," Henry said. "She needs a hand up. If we need to talk about it, why can't we do it now? Tony will be home any minute."

"I know. But Paul's coming, too." Kate, who'd inwardly winced when Henry again referred to Maura as 'Mum,' hoped her face hadn't given her away. "Tony's on a case that touches on crimes the three of us worked on at Scotland Yard. We're going to discuss it over dinner."

Henry brightened. He'd grown very fond of Paul, whom he seemed to view more as an older brother than an authority figure. Whenever Paul joined the Hetheridges for a meal, Henry inserted himself in the occasion, often trying to stick around even after the conversation turned to murder.

"Can I come down and join you? I'll be quiet as a mouse, I promise," he said, shifting quickly from query to outright begging. "I won't ask questions. I won't make a sound at all. I just want to be there."

"Nope. You can eat up here," Kate said. "Here you have your choice of Xbox. Computer. Your new book about Greek myths. You can even play with Ritchie, if he isn't too wrapped up in his Legos. Much more fun up here, I promise."

"But I'd rather be with you guys. Family time. And it would be educational!"

Smiling, Kate shook her head no, closing the door behind her. When she was almost to the lift, something occurred to her. Returning to the whiteboard, she erased Henry's challenge, replacing it with one of her own.

What new chores will you do to earn yourself a mobile?

Beneath that, she drew a heart, signed it with a giant K, and went downstairs to await Tony and Paul.

CHAPTER FIVE

$\mathcal{H}$enry Wakefield loved living at One-oh-One. He loved Wellegrave House, too. Together they were like Betty and Veronica—both too good to be true, but in completely different ways.

Wellegrave House was wonderful because it was creaky, cozy, and packed with curiosities. Curled up by the Regency-era fireplace with a book and a cup of tea, he liked to imagine himself as one of the Pevensie children, on the brink of discovering a magical wardrobe. Or a student at Hogwarts School of Witchcraft and Wizardry, studying in Ravencroft's common room.

An agreeable amount of danger lurked around Wellegrave House's every corner. Bogs that overflowed if you asked too much of them. A splendid antique lift that sometimes failed, trapping the rider between floors. A guest bedroom with an unpleasant odor that someone had probably died in. Moreover, there was Harvey, always watching and waiting. Mrs. Snell also seemed to materialize at will, appearing just as Henry reached for a vase or pried open a locked drawer, but at least she liked boys. She understood his thirst for adventure. Harvey was determined to squash it. But there was no Harvey at One-oh-One.

In the condo, Henry felt independent, even grown up. At Wellegrave House, he wasn't allowed to cook for himself, not even a snack. Henry had been cooking as long as he could remember, but he wasn't permitted to use a single appliance in Wellegrave House's cavernous kitchen, lest Harvey's combover braid itself. In the manservant's eyes, nine-year-old boys were such babies, apparently, they couldn't spread jam on toast without stabbing themselves, or heat up leftover curry without breaking a bowl.

In the condo, Henry could stroll into the mod-con kitchen and go nuts. Scramble eggs. Boil pasta. Even use the cooker to warm some milk, crumble in chocolate and cinnamon, and voila —a mug of Café Diablo. He'd often seen Tony make himself a cup of tea and drink it alone in the living room, contemplating the cityscape. After school, Henry liked to make his own spicy hot chocolate and sip it while he, too, looked out over London. He felt very much like Tony in such moments, an experience as sweet as the drink itself.

Moreover, at One-oh-One, there was room to explore. And not just the interior of their overlarge condo. Henry's resident key card allowed him almost full access. And where he wasn't meant to be, he went anyway, often with great success. A quiet, self-possessed boy could lurk on the periphery of several adult spheres without raising suspicion for a surprisingly long time.

Take the fifth-floor pub, Skittles. It was what Paul called a "gastropub corporate nibbles monstrosity." As near as Henry could tell, that meant it was clean and well-lit, with wall-mounted tellys and a standardized menu. Skittles wasn't meant to entice the residents, except on quiz nights, when it was packed. It was designed as a hub for conventioneers networking or having a break between seminars. Because One-oh-One hosted so many conferences and corporate retreats, Skittles was always packed with grownups identified by lanyard name tags, the way cows are tagged by ear. A nine-year-old boy should have stuck out like a sore thumb. But Henry had discovered that bothering no one and studiously keeping his nose in a book was as good as a wizard's invisibility cloak. And invisibility was key, because it meant hearing the truth at last.

Adults always accused kids of lying, but as far as Henry was concerned, they were the ones who wouldn't know the truth if it bit them. Harvey talked down to him. Mrs. Snell, although friendly, talked at him. Kate bossed him, Tony bossed him, and even Paul bossed him, or tried to. They only spoke freely while bossing. The rest of the time, they were on guard. How often had one of them looked up from a conversation, seen him coming, and clammed up?

At Skittles, the adults talked and talked. Sitting in a mini-booth with an open maths book, pencil, and paper, Henry could monitor unfiltered grown-up communiques until his head hurt. They nattered on about everything. Who was getting the sack. Who ought to get the sack. Which supervisor was shagging which subordinate. Plenty of it was incomprehensible, but Henry nevertheless sat and absorbed it. He felt sure that one day it would all come clear, like a string of arcane symbols resolving themselves into words.

Skittles wasn't the only place he could turn invisible. He went lots of places no one, including garden-variety grownups, were meant to go. At One-oh-One there were so many possibilities. You just had to look beyond the obvious. The lobby was a prime example.

Everyone knew there were public lifts for visitors and private lifts for residents. But behind an unlocked door was a private lift for staff. It needed no code, went everywhere, and moved like a rocket. Henry suspected there was supposed to be a code, but harried housekeepers, servers, and janitors kept it disabled for their own convenience.

Then there was the lobby-level bar, Archie's. From four o'clock in the afternoon until midnight, Archie's served drinks and starters. But from six o'clock in the morning until ten, Archie's served coffees, teas, pastries, and fresh fruit. Coffees were highly individual, right down to the temperature or the number of syrup shots. A robot barista couldn't handle such complexity. So for four hours every morning, human beings staffed Archie's. And that meant the system had multiple vulnerabilities. Purely for sport, Henry had nicked pastries from the bell jar, slipped behind the bar to help himself to a bottled Pepsi, and rifled one of the barista's backpacks to see what the hip young man was reading. (*The Two Towers* by J.R.R. Tolkien.) He didn't consider himself a thief or a snoop. He was simply honing his spy skills.

One-oh-One's lobby even had direct access to the alley behind the tower, an unloading dock. Henry had been thrilled to discover an ingress/egress that didn't require the use of his key card. It was like being off-the-grid. If Kate ever got her knickers bunched, she could literally track his movements by pulling the key card's swipe data. Except when he wafted like a ghost through an open door, in which case the trip was logged on someone else's account.

Alas, the unloading dock, where lorries dropped off newspapers, crates of liquor, coffee supplies, etc., wasn't a realm of high adventure. It wasn't even dodgy, like an alley in Batman's Gotham city. It was clean and dull. The industrial-style rubbish bin smelled halfway decent. And there was no nosing around on a lorry. The overall-clad workers who drove them, the sort who clomped about in reinforced-toe boots while unloading them, saw straight through Henry's invisibility cloak.

"What's all this, then?" the woman delivering the *Independent* and other daily tabloids had demanded the moment she set eyes on Henry, sitting quietly on the curb pretending to do his homework.

"Waiting on my dad," he'd said. Henry's First Law of Boy Spies: when parked in a strange place, it's no good saying you're waiting on mum. No one will believe it. But he could sit smack in the middle of Skittles, a nine-year-old surrounded by grownups sipping pints, claim his dad had dropped him there for an unspecified duration, and have everyone take it on faith.

"Waiting on my dad," the woman had repeated. "Am I a mental defective? Am I all on my own without the sense God gave a llama?"

"Naw, he's Oliver Twist, innit?" A little black man, dressed in a uniform identical to the skeptical woman's, had snatched Henry's purported homework out of his hands.

"Oh-ho! A spy," the little black man had crowed. "'Sunday concierge shift change at seven am. Door to his booth open today. Locked last week.' You casing the joint?"

Mortified, Henry had snatched his notes back as the man added, "That's not how you spell concierge. I before e, my lad. I before e."

"A real spy writes in code, I reckon," the woman announced, slinging around twenty-pound tabloid bundles like they were cotton balls. "Piss off, phony spy. Go on, or I'll report you. Piss off."

The experience had taught Henry two things. (Three, if one counted the proper spelling of concierge.) First, to make his notes illegible through strange abbreviations. It wasn't exactly a code per se, but close enough. Second, to think up a plausible excuse for his presence whenever somewhere that working-class people might turn up. They were more aware of their surroundings and less likely to write off anyone, even a child, as automatically harmless. He respected that.

But despite the occasional roadblock, Henry's explorations in and around One-oh-One were a cracking success. Kate was a detective. Tony was a detective. Paul was a detective. Henry would make a fine detective, too. Or an agent for MI-6. Possibly both.

Tony will be so impressed when I show him all the data I've gathered, Henry thought. He was sitting on the floor of his room, a half-eaten plate of chicken tikka masala abandoned nearby. Now he wanted something sweet, but his stash of lemon sherbets was long gone.

The only reason he hadn't yet shown Tony was, of course, Kate. Kate would overreact to everything, as always.

Even if she doesn't shout at me for eavesdropping, she'll say it's dangerous. Tell me I'm nine years old. Jeez. She always says that. Does she really think I don't know how old I am?

Whenever he returned from visitation with Maura, he found Kate's ways more irritating than usual. When he grew up, he wouldn't waste time carping over the distant past. Imagine that— being twenty or thirty and still cross with Ritchie for burning down the house. It was stupid.

Yes, the fire was terrible. They all could've been hurt or killed. Tony had lost countless estate doodads; Kate had lost coats, suits, shoes, and a box of keepsakes from her late teens. So what? Henry had lost more personal items than the two of them put together. Everything in his room had been destroyed. Toys, books, school papers that earned top marks, his favorite trainers, his old photographs. Including the only baby picture of him that ever existed, a snap taken of him in Maura's arms when he was three days old.

I could have scanned it into my phone. If I had a ruddy phone, he thought. The picture, once safely tucked in his sock drawer, had long been his private link with eternity. Once, he'd been a tiny baby and his mum had been young, pretty, and happy, at least in that snap. He had no father, not even in theory; no name, age, or occupation. Virtually all Henry's memories revolved around Kate, Ritchie, and their old flat in South London. But that snap had been proof that once upon a time, he'd been an ordinary kid with an ordinary mum cuddling him in her arms as if she'd never let go. Thanks to Ritchie and his blinking Lego obsession, the picture was ash. If he was willing to let that go by the time he was, say, twenty-eight, why couldn't Kate let go of her grudge against Maura?

She thinks she's in competition with Maura to be my mum. And she is. Kind of.

It was hard to suss out how he felt about the situation. For ages he'd toyed with the idea of calling Kate "Mum." Other kids had mums. Other kids didn't have to frequently launch into a short speech: no, she's my aunt, yes, my "real" mum is alive, no, I don't live with her, no, it's really not very interesting and let's talk about something else, thank you very much. Next, people invariably asked, "But what about your dad, then?" It took superheroic self-control to answer politely instead of kicking the questioner in the shins.

So yes, calling Kate "Mum" would be neat and easy. It would eliminate questions from nosy parkers and make Kate happy. But calling her "Mum" wasn't just a case of substituting one noun for another. Words were important. Names, even more so. In ancient Britain, the Celts had believed if you knew a person's true name, you could control them. If he named Kate "Mum," he was choosing her as his mother. He was closing the door on that young, pretty, happy version of Maura with the blue-swaddled baby in her arms. He was saying Maura didn't matter, and he came from someone who hadn't wanted him.

That was tough to think about. When Maura first announced she was suing for full restoration of her parental rights, Henry had gone sick with dread. He'd wanted to be adopted by Tony and Kate; the proposal felt like a dream come true. But then came the fire, incinerating so much that he treasured, including that baby picture. Was it a sign? Was God punishing him for wanting to become Tony and Kate's son?

Maura had never said anything of the sort. But she and her solicitor, a reedy man with square spectacles and no hair whatsoever, not even eyebrows, seemed eager for him to take their side. After the fire, they'd amended Maura's original petition, citing it as proof that Henry was unsafe in Tony and Kate's care. That, plus Kate's round-the-clock work schedule and her and Tony's run-ins with criminals, often murderers, constituted a good case, according to the solicitor. What would make it even better was testimony from Henry stating a desire to live only with his mother.

One day Maura and the solicitor had sat him down at his favorite restaurant, McDonald's, and suggested over a Happy Meal that he make a video statement to that effect. Henry had lost his appetite. Then he'd snapped the head off the accompanying toy, a transforming robot. While the solicitor droned on, he'd squirted ketchup on the tabletop, placed the head and the body in the red mess, and changed the subject to decapitation.

That was the last time Maura asked him to meet with the solicitor. But after she bought him the Marvel Infinity War bedsheets, she'd asked him to stop calling her Maura and start calling her Mum. So he had. And he'd called her that in front of Kate, who'd looked hurt.

Good people don't hurt people. Henry wanted to think of himself as a good person. Probably he was, apart from eavesdropping, occasional lies, a few fights at school, and looking up some forbidden stuff on the Internet. But he was being positioned to hurt someone. Maura and Kate couldn't both be winners. Each wanted him to choose one over the other. And each said a lot about his welfare and his happiness and never word about the ropes and pulleys creaking between them. Maybe they thought he was too thick to hear.

The chicken tikka masala tasted like bug spray. A big clump was still on his plate. He'd ignored it as long as he dared; Kate's rules on leftovers were ironclad. Take them downstairs, scrape them into a Tupperware, and stick them in the fridge. Waste not, want not.

Why does she pretend we're not rich? So other people won't ask her for money?

Maybe she was afraid too much ready cash would turn him into a bloody wanker. Maura had said as much, in those words. She'd thought if Tony became Henry's adopted father, Henry would one day be Lord Hetheridge, in possession of Wellegrave House and the Devon estate called Briarshaw. "One of them bastards," as she put it. Apparently, hereditary peerages and the writs governing their succession had never been on Maura's radar. It was Henry who'd explained that only "sons of the body" (or in the case of a few peerages, daughters) could take up the mantle of the hereditary peer. But after adoption, Henry *would* receive a courtesy title: the Hon. Henry Hetheridge.

Maura had been transparently relieved to hear it. She'd feared that if she erased his chance to become Baron Wellegrave, he'd hate her forever. With that concern put to bed, she'd gone full steam ahead, oblivious to how important Tony was to him.

From the moment Kate accepted Tony's ring, Henry had begun thinking of him as Dad. He just hadn't screwed up the courage to say it yet. Suppose it went wrong? Kids that grew up taking a dad for granted were luckier than they knew.

The chicken tikka masala was transforming itself into paste. Snatching up the plate, he took it into the lavatory, scraped it into the bog, and flushed the whole sorry mess.

Of course, bossy Kate had rules about dirty dishes, too. Henry was meant to promptly take them downstairs, prewash them with a little Fairy soap, and place them in the dishwasher. He was still irritated enough with her to toy with the notion of "accidentally" smashing the plate. But that would be in direct violation of Pax Wakefield. Besides, Tony, Kate, and Paul had probably finished eating by now and settled into talking shop. If Henry played his cards right, he might be able to listen in.

In his stocking feet, he padded into the hall. Spying Kate's question on his message board, he erased her query with quick, vengeful strokes. Then he wrote,

THIS IS MY PRIVATE BOARD!!!!!

If he was going to try and creep up on the adults downstairs, step one was to silence the lift. Its bell dinged every time the doors open. Not unbearably loud, but unmistakable, at least in a house full of detectives. Luckily, the lift had a touchpad control panel. By tapping in the family's global code, which Henry had acquired via application of what he called his "methods," he could access the lift's preferences menu and shut off the bell.

The lift whisked him down to the living room. The doors opened onto darkness.

Henry had expected that. The room's stunning view of London was best enjoyed with the lamps switched off. Tony, Kate, and Paul had indeed moved into the living room to talk. As soon as he set foot off the lift, Henry heard Paul, who always spoke at a fair clip and tended to get louder when making a point.

"Of course, I double-checked it. The man is evil," he said. "Heathrow confirms that he flew out of the UK on his Syberjet Sj30 at approximately two pm on 24 December. No other passengers, just him and the pilot. Brunei confirms Godington flew out of BWN at an unspecified time on or around 8 January."

"You can always count on Brunei to be vague," Kate said.

"For a fee," Tony agreed. "But for Christmas with the orang-utans, Godington usually flies directly to Borneo. Instead, he's seen celebrating the holiday in and around Bandar Seri Begawan...."

"Which is under Sharia law, last I checked," Paul interjected.

"...and going here and there like a camera-hungry socialite," Tony said. "I made a few inquiries at the British High Commission and got several hits. I expected nothing. When Godington goes abroad, he typically disappears."

Henry crept closer, eyes adjusting to the gloom. The hall was pitch dark; he had no fear of being seen. The adults, however, were backlit by London's glittering skyline. Paul was on the sofa. Tony had his usual spot, the overstuffed armchair brought over from Wellegrave House. Kate stood by the window, wine glass in hand.

"Not to contradict the BHC," she said. "But Lady Margaret and Lady Vivian feel certain Sir Duncan *was* in London between 24 December and 8 January. He was invited to all the best parties. Black Tie in Bloomsbury. Christmas Jumpers at the Blue Fin. You get the idea."

"All for charity, old stick. Widows and orphans," Paul said.

"More like a yearly excuse to take those Greubel Forsey wrist-watches and Chopard necklaces out of the vault and flaunt them in front of people who can price them at a glance," Kate said. "Buy a car and some of that money goes into the economy. Buy a watch that costs more than a plane and you're keeping it all in the family."

"Railing against the one percent doesn't change the fact you're one of them now. By choice," Paul said. "But yeah, it's a dirty trick."

"Wearable wealth is the oldest trick in the book," Tony said. "But we digress. So despite the difference of opinion on Godington's whereabouts, I think it's reasonable to assume he was out of the country during the time Mariah Keene jumped to her death."

Henry, who'd been dismayed by talk of countries he'd never heard of and a detour into wristwatches, of all things, sank to the floor and settled in to listen. If one of the grownups went into the kitchen to refill a drink, he'd be invisible. If they started down the hall for the bog, he'd dash to the lift and pretend he'd just arrived.

"I know the bloody monster's a magnet for bright young things," Paul said. "He's always had young people as accomplices. Sometimes he doesn't even have to recruit them. They recruit themselves, like what's-his-name...."

"Jeremy Bentham," Kate said. "Who topped himself in prison when Sir Duncan froze him out."

"I know." Paul sounded slightly peeved. "He stabbed me in the shoulder. I remember his name, I just don't like to say it. My point is, if Lady Brompton thinks Mariah and Mark were victims rather than willing accomplices, she's as unhinged as she sounds."

"I don't think it's a clinical issue," Tony said. "Just grief, resentment, and too much white wine. She'd feel equally vindicated if I turn up proof that either Godington pushed Mariah to her death, or if her husband did it. But I pulled the neighborhood CCTV camera footage. He never left their house that night, and woke up when she did, to the news about Mariah. The housekeeper corroborates what he said—that he took it harder than his wife. She was shocked when Lady Brompton announced that Mariah's head would look like a smashed watermelon."

Henry caught his breath. This was why he eavesdropped. Tonight might be the motherlode.

"Maybe I should feel sorry for Lord Brompton, but I don't," Kate said. "He sounds like a creep. And creeps with dead daughters usually stuck a finger in the pie, didn't they? Probably drove her to suicide. That's why he ditched her stuff and replaced it with paedo fantasy props. I don't know why else a poshie girl would have broken into a construction site over a holiday."

"I had friends from good families who did stuff like that." Paul, who never sat still for long, was up and pacing. "BASE Jumpers. They didn't want to end it all. Did it just for kicks."

"BASE jumping?" Tony sounded intrigued. "Is that an acronym?"

"Yeah. About the things they jump off," Paul said. "Buildings, obviously. Antennae. Not sure about the S, but the E is probably for edifices."

Kate made a sound like a quiz show buzzer. Trading wineglass for phone, she'd already found the answer. "Wrong. According to this, S is for span, as in a bridge or catwalk. E is for Earth."

"Reliance on Google makes you stupid," Paul said.

"Says who?"

"People on telly. They're none too keen on being eclipsed."

"This sounds a bit like the Urbex people," Tony said. "But assuming Mariah was one of them—do Urbex or BASE jumpers attempt stunts alone?"

"Nope. They have a healthy respect for how dangerous it is," Kate said. "As do I. Maura and I broke into a no-trespassing site when I was thirteen."

"That doesn't sound like you." There was no censure in Tony's voice, only interest. Henry was interested, too. Everyone—Maura, Louise, even Kate herself—agreed that Kate had been born a wet blanket who lived to uphold the law.

"I knew it was wrong," Kate replied. "But in those days I worshipped Maura. She could have asked me to pop round to Hell with her and I would've said 'Yes, please.'"

"Did you get hurt? One of my BASE jumper mates cut himself on a bit of metal and needed twenty stitches," Paul said. "Tetanus shot, too. That's why I wouldn't go. That, and I was already sort of a mini-plod by my teens."

"So was I," Tony said.

"So was I, after Maura took me into a burned-out Council block. Bloody cow tried to kill me."

CHAPTER SIX

*H*enry's breath caught. Heart speeding up, he peeked around the corner as much as he dared, the better to try and see Kate's expression. Was she exaggerating? She had to be exaggerating.

"Kill you? You've never told me about this," Tony said.

"What happened?" Paul sounded equally taken aback.

"Oh, it was probably an accident. But I've never forgiven her for it." Kate emitted a mirthless laugh. "Thing is, when I was small, Maura took care of me more than Louise. Made toad-in-the-hole for me on Saturday mornings. Walked me to school. Braided my hair. I looked up to her. Thought she painted the sky."

Henry had never heard Kate talk that way. Not like the family lawgiver. Like someone who didn't have it all figured out.

"It couldn't last," Kate continued. "By the time I was thirteen, she was a grown woman, really. Tired of being followed around by a kiddie. She kept ditching me, and I kept refusing to take the hint. Then one day she says to me, 'My mates are having a peek inside the Capslow block. Want to tag along?'"

"Was that a tower block?" Paul asked.

"Yes. Burnt down," Tony said. "Quite the scandal. Fire exits fell off the walls with evacuees on them. Some residents died in their beds because the alarms didn't sound. Turned out they were only for show. Never wired. The public was appalled."

"No one I knew was surprised," Kate said. "Anyhow, as far as Maura's invitation, I should have known she was taking the piss. Her mates didn't want a kid around. They reckoned I would grass. But of course, I was so bloody needy, I couldn't see the scrawl on the wall.

"We met up after sundown and broke into Capslow. It was easy. No security. No floodlights. If anyone on the Council cared about kids getting hurt on the premises, they couldn't be arsed to do anything to stop it."

"It was a shooting gallery, if memory serves," Tony said.

"Yeah. We came in waving torches around," Kate said. "First thing I saw was a half-naked boy, passed out on the floor. At least, I thought he was passed out. Maura and her bloody awful mates tried to convince me he was dead. That he'd been murdered. That nuisance little wankers like me disappeared into Capslow and were never seen again. I should have pissed off straight away."

"What? And look like a pious little bint?" Paul flopped onto the sofa, full-length, feet up, like he owned the place. "Even at thirteen you had your pride. You had to stick it out."

Kate chuckled softly. "Yeah. I thought if I showed I was game, and not a snot-nosed little baby, Maura would like me again. Her mates kept trying to scare me, every step of the way. Most of the stairs were blocked, but we found some that got us up to the seventh floor.

"Our torches had gone dead. Rubbish batteries. But it was light enough because the Capslow was missing a wall. I was working my way to the edge to peer over it when I heard Maura say, 'Dare me?' I looked over my shoulder. Her mates were all,

'Yeah, that's right, do it.' Maura came at me. Shoved me right over the edge."

Henry's chest felt tight. He realized it was because he'd been holding his breath. He forced himself to inhale.

Paul swore. "Seven floors up? Really?"

"Yeah. Lucky me, there was a construction container just below," Kate said. "A huge one crammed with carpet rolls, drywall, glass wool and all that. I fell on the pile. Climbed out on my own steam, bruises and soot all over me. I reckon I'd be dead or crippled if I'd hit the side of the container. Much less the pavement."

Henry closed his eyes and held them shut, thumb and forefingers on his lids. He was too old to cry all the time. He bloody well wouldn't cry over this. It was an old story, something that happened before he was born. Maybe Maura had been drunk, or high, or both.

"I assume your sister was under the influence?" Tony asked in the neutral tone he always used when discussing Maura. Henry loved him for that. It would have been so easy for a man like Tony to look down on his mum, to speak of her as a disposable person, to be binned and replaced without a second thought. But he didn't, even when he had no idea Henry was listening.

"I don't know. She was hearing voices by then," Kate said. "I didn't find out till later, but she was. Anyhow. All I heard when I climbed out of the rubbish heap was cheering and clapping. Bunch of tossers. I took off running. All Maura did was shout, 'Tell Mum and you're dead.' So I didn't tell Louise. And I never had anything to do with Maura again. Not till Henry was born."

"Even the toughest family connections have silver linings," Paul said.

"Spoken like someone who's never met my nephew, Roddy." Tony, still in his overstuffed armchair, reached out to Kate. Catching her by the hand, he pulled her onto his lap. She folded herself against him.

Something tight inside Henry relaxed. Seeing them together like that, outlined by the glow of the city lights, made him feel like everything would come out all right in the end.

"So I accept the possibility that a young woman of Mariah Keene's age and background might participate in these urban explorations," Tony said. "Yet her parents knew nothing about it. I interviewed her friends, too. They were all mystified that she died in a construction site."

"Was she the type who told her parents everything?" Paul asked.

"A good question." Tony seemed to ponder it. "If she was, I don't think Peter and Hannah listened. Peter still saw her as a little girl. Hannah was more interested in the twin brother, Mark, and her career. But surely Mariah's friends would have known."

"Did the parents supply the friends list?" Kate asked pointedly.

Tony gave a pleased little rumble deep in his throat. "Ah. Yes. I'll need to dig deeper to uncover the real friends, won't I? All three of the women suggested by Hannah said they'd long ago stopped hearing from Mariah."

"What about her computer? Her mobile?" Paul asked.

"Mobile is gone. BT turned on the GPS but there was no response. Possibly smashed to bits in the fall and missed by the coroner's team," Tony said. "Her laptop was removed from her bedroom and stored in the attic. Peter brought it down for me to examine. It booted up with no data. Nothing but factory settings. He claimed it must have got a virus. Not very convincingly, I might add."

"You did say he was hiding something. Maybe that was it," Paul said. "What about a boyfriend? Ordinarily I'd say, track down her last boyfriend and if he's an Urbex guy, there you have it. But if Godington is the last boyfriend, all bets are off."

"Do you think Sir Duncan was dating Mariah? Honestly?"

Kate slipped off Tony's lap. "Wine's never good the second day. I'm finishing the bottle. You lads?"

"I'm fine," Tony said.

"I'll have a Stella, thanks," Paul said.

Henry scuttled deeper into the hall, all the way back to the bog. If he was caught in there, it wouldn't look good—he had a lavatory all to himself upstairs—but ducking into the lift wasn't an option. Light would spill out when the doors opened, and from the kitchen, Kate might see. All he could do was lurk in the bog and pray no one needed it.

He heard Kate's glass clink against the quartz countertop, then the *glug* of wine. Footsteps, and then Kate's voice, safely back in the living room. Creeping back to his place where the hall and living room intersected, Henry saw that Paul, now sitting upright so as to drink his Stella Artois, looked angry. Usually he was good-natured, smiling, up for a laugh, not like a harried grownup at all. His grim adult side only emerged, as far as Henry could tell, when Sir Duncan Godington came up.

"Seriously," Kate said. "About Sir Duncan and Mariah. It sounds off. He's meant to be this incorrigible playboy with a supermodel on each arm. Never seen without a woman who isn't a knockout, and semi-famous to boot. Was Mariah in that league?"

"She wouldn't have been mistaken for a model," Tony replied. "Then again, I've never quite believed Godington's *haute couture* dates were anything other than protective coloration. He's obsessed with his sister."

"And Kate," Paul said.

"And Kate," Tony agreed, still in that calm, neutral tone.

What Kate? Henry wondered. *Is there another Kate?*

He wasn't supposed to know about Sir Duncan, so of course he'd made it his business to find out everything he could. Half of Britain seemed to think him an innocent man fitted up by government hacks. The other half thought he'd got away with murder many times over.

"I don't think he's actually obsessed with me," Kate said. "He's just the sort who can't resist making a conquest. Every time he flirts with me, I have the feeling he's laughing inside."

Henry squinted at Kate's silhouette. It was impossible to make out her expression. But clearly *she* was the Kate. The one a serial killer's eye had fell upon.

"Yes, well, it's all fun and games until he stops me in the street and threatens to kill you," Tony said. "He wasn't laughing. And he wasn't bluffing."

Henry went cold. Suddenly he needed the toilet, badly. He'd always known Kate's job was dangerous. But not that she might die. Not that London's upper crust boogeyman might kill her.

"In the street?" Paul repeated. "When?"

"Around the same time he was tormenting you with the attack dog. The appropriately named Kaiser," Tony said. "He just so happened to be walking the dog along our street in Mayfair, timed perfectly to cross my path. He said killing me wouldn't be nearly as fun as killing Kate and watching my reaction."

Paul set down his bottle hard. "Why didn't you tell me?"

"Because this is how you react," Tony said. "It serves no purpose."

"Fine. I don't like death threats. Silly me," Paul spluttered. "What did you do?"

"Told him I'd kill him first."

"How?"

"How do you think?"

The discussion veered off into densely garbled adult-speak: references to old cases, retired MI5 agents, Arifs, and Brindles. It made no sense to Henry. Besides, if he didn't get to the bog soon, he'd have an accident.

The lift seemed to take forever. He rushed to his room's en

suite, used the toilet, and rushed back to the lift to re-enable the floor chime. Then it hit him again, harder than it had downstairs.

Kate could die. Kate could *die*.

* * *

HE WAS LYING in bed under his new *Avengers Infinity War* sheets and staring at the ceiling when Kate rapped lightly on his door.

"It's only me."

"Come in." He sat up and switched on the bedside lamp.

"Oh. Look at you, snug as a bug. What's the occasion?"

"I got sleepy," he lied. He couldn't tell her he was too scared to do anything, even play on the Xbox. If he did, he'd have to say why. And if he pleaded guilty to eavesdropping, the grownups would take precautions, and he'd never, ever hear anything important again.

"Seem wide awake to me." Kate sat on the edge of the bed. She was already in her sleep uniform—striped socks and an oversized T-shirt that fell to her knees. She smelled like lilac moisturizer. "Thinking deep thoughts?"

"No. I, um… had a bad dream. That you died," Henry blurted.

"Yikes. Hope it was death by chocolate." Kate smiled at him. "Just because I turned thirty-four doesn't mean the Grim Reaper's on my trail."

"You didn't die like that. Natural, I mean. Someone killed you." Realizing himself on the brink of tears, Henry reached for his specs and put them on. Usually he could stuff down his emotions if he gave himself a few seconds' breathing room. He wanted to sound neutral, like Tony. "You were after a murderer but he got to you first."

"Oh. Well." Kate nodded. "Lot of optimistic statistics on the web about stuff like that."

"I know." Henry had the sites bookmarked. "It's more dangerous to be a bin man or a builder than a detective. But you deal with murderers. There's no statistics on detectives who run about chatting up murderers all day."

"All day? Is that what you think my job is? I wish," Kate said. "If only I could sneak you into the Yard to see all the paperwork. The conference calls. The mandatory seminars." She accentuated each duty with a little huff. "Interviewing the murderer is the icing on the cupcake. The rest is bureaucratic boondoggles with a double handful of wank."

Henry giggled.

"Forget I said that. At least don't go about repeating it." Kate wagged a finger at him. "Every time you say something rude in public, I get labeled a bad—" She cut herself off. The unspoken word, "mum," hung between them.

Henry didn't want to go down that rabbit hole. All he could think about was Sir Duncan telling Tony—Tony!—that he'd murder Kate.

"If I tell you a secret," Henry said, watching her face, "will you answer me one question? Honestly," he added. Making a deal with a grownup was often like asking a genie for something. Failure to use the correct words could result in a wish that turned bad.

"Well. Sure." Kate sounded a little nervous. Nevertheless, she leaned closer, brushed a lock of his hair into place, and said, "Fire away."

"I know how Ritchie got the lighter."

She blinked. "Is that so? Did he tell you?"

"No. I think he's forgotten the whole thing. I know *some people*," he huffed, "think it was mine, like I'm Mr. Fags-on-the-sly, and Ritchie took it out of my school bag or something. Which is profoundly *stupid* because I hate smoking."

"'Profoundly,' eh? Where'd you get that one?"

"Comic book. Anyway, I knew it wasn't mine. And I didn't think it was my mum's, either, because she knows Ritchie as well as we do. But I asked her anyhow."

"What'd she say?"

"She said only a bleeding muppet would put a lighter in Ritchie's path. And she showed me the one she bought when she got out. Flameless," Henry said. "The only kind her halfway house allowed."

"I should get one of those," Kate said. "Not sure how they work, mind you."

"It's an electrical arc. Between two ceramic points. With a lithium battery," Henry supplied impatiently. "I told you about it after the fire. You weren't listening. *Again.* Anyway. I knew I was innocent. I eliminated Maura as a suspect. So I expanded my investigation."

"Did you now?" Kate sounded pleased.

"Yeah. Tony quit smoking twenty years ago. Did you know that? He has an old lighter in his valet case, but it's out of butane," Henry said. "You don't carry a lighter. Harvey does, but it's always on him. And it's cool—a square Zippo that clicks. The one Ritchie had was rubbish plastic. It melted away. Fire inspectors only found the flint wheel."

Kate looked impressed, which made Henry's next words tumble out excitedly.

"Mrs. Snell doesn't carry a lighter. And none of Ritchie's assistants bring lighters or sharp objects into their clients' houses. So by process of elimination," he said, savoring the phrase, "we arrive at Paul. Who once told me he always carries a lighter for birds and perps. I saw him take it out of his Armani coat. Rubbish plastic from Bugden. Last week, I asked him why he never wore that coat anymore, and he said he forgot it at Wellegrave House. That it burned up in the fire," Henry said triumphantly. "Maybe the lighter fell out. Maybe Ritchie poked around in the coat's pockets and pulled it out. It doesn't matter. That's where the lighter came from. Case closed."

Kate slow-clapped him. Henry's chest swelled. Then he

remembered why he'd kept his investigatory findings under wraps.

"But now that you know, you can't tell him. Paul will be gutted if he realizes it was his lighter. It was an accident. And it's not like telling him will change what happened."

"Well done, you. I quite agree."

Henry basked in that for a few seconds. This was true happiness. He was snug in his warm flannel pjs under Avengers sheets, Kate was impressed, and life was perfect. Then it hit him. "You worked it out already, didn't you?"

"Yeah. Well. It's my job, isn't it? Not only to solve mysteries, but to protect Ritchie. I'm his guardian, just like I'm your guardian."

"Does Tony know?"

"I haven't brought it up. Paul admires him so much, and Paul would die if he knew he was technically at fault. If he knew *Tony* knew—I guess he'd die twice. Paul needs a win," Kate said firmly. "He's been losing for too long."

Henry thought about that. "But... Maura's solicitor said the fire was a win for them. Since you and Tony can't even say where the lighter came from. He said it's proof you provide an unsafe home environment."

"Whereas a flat with a semi-functional toilet in Norbiton is ideal." The bed creaked as Kate shifted slightly. "I'm not worried about it. So. What did you want to ask me?"

Henry took a deep breath. "If you were in danger... in real danger... would you tell me?"

"No."

"Just—no?"

Kate folded her arms against her chest. "If I were in real danger, I'd sort it, thank you very much. Or more likely, Tony and I would sort it. It would be done and dusted and forgot without the slightest interruption to your homework, or your hot dinner. Feel better?"

"No," Henry shot back, astonished that even a grownup could be so thick. "Nobody's invincible in real life. You can't sort everything. I don't like being afraid. I want to know when it's absolutely necessary."

"Don't we all, kiddo. Don't we all."

CHAPTER SEVEN

"Wotcha," said an attractive blonde woman to Paul Bhar as she passed. She was walking her dog along the Victoria Embankment, home of what he called the *new* New Scotland Yard. In the short time that London's Metropolitan Police had been headquartered there, Paul had learned many things about the Embankment. Not the least of which was the time when the smartest, most enticing women passed through—half-seven, Monday through Friday.

"Pretty." He grinned at her.

"Fresh."

"I meant the Maltese," he said, nodding at the little white dog with its bejeweled collar and pink leather lead.

"No, you didn't." She passed him, hips swinging, and peeked over her shoulder. Her long hair and trim figure reminded him of Emmeline Wardell.

The thought of Emmeline gave him a pang. He'd meant to bring up the topic last night at the Hetheridges'—how he'd finally made a decision between Kyla and Emmeline. He was determined to surf the wave of change sweeping through his life, rather than find himself underwater once again.

That wave had begun with Kate's arrival on the Toff Squad. Even good change was still change, and while Kate had rapidly become Paul's best mate, her presence had shaken up everything. Until her arrival, Paul had believed his professional redemption was just around the corner. Tony was a generous boss with nothing to prove, willing to share credit and let subordinates shine. And Kate had shone from the start. She'd solved two huge cases, made key contributions to two more, and after a rocky start, become a rising star.

Paul wasn't envious—he refused to be envious—but he'd longed for more time in the spotlight. Then Tony was forced out, DCI Vic Jackson had taken the helm, and Paul's chances at professional reinvention suddenly looked shakier. Jackson was less of an irritant now that he'd put the plug in the jug, but like Kate, he had plenty to prove. Hoping for DCI Jackson to share credit was probably a fantasy.

Paul's personal life had been roiled, too. While working a case, he'd visited Tessa Chilcott in the secure mental facility to which she was confined, probably for life. He'd hoped it would be an opportunity to finally get her out of his head. Instead, it had reminded him of everything he'd lost.

Unlike his mum, Sharada, a successful romance novelist who wrote about predestined loves, Paul believed relationships formed out of chance, were dependent on chemistry, and faded with time; no magic or mystery required. At least on paper, he believed that. In truth, he'd gone through his teens and twenties without a serious girlfriend, just a series of one-offs and short-timers, only to meet Tessa at age thirty-three and fall arse over teakettle. With Tessa, it had been a say-anything, do-anything kind of love. Now that she was gone, he'd done his best to shake it, to ignore it, to deny it, to reframe his memories of their affair in the coldest possible light. Dating Emmeline Wardle had helped. She was the anti-Tessa: sure of herself, quick to anger, quick to forgive, never blue for long and ever up for a laugh.

Then there was Kyla. One had only to glimpse her to guess she was a model. She was tall with a cloud of dark hair, big eyes, pouting lips, high cheekbones, and a prominent collar-bone sharp enough to slice bread. Pre-shoot, no makeup, hair pinned back, in trackies bottoms and a loose T-shirt, she looked forlorn, a rag doll in need of fresh stuffing. After the makeup artist and the hairdresser, sewn into a couture gown too snug to sit down in and balanced on stiletto heels, Kyla strode down the runway like a demigoddess. Paul loved watching her work. He was proud of demigoddess-Kyla in a way that he wasn't quite proud of, if that made sense. Something about the intensity of his pride was off. He couldn't say why.

At home, things were different. He always felt vaguely thwarted by Kyla, simultaneously drawn closer and pushed away. Since they'd become exclusive, she'd withdrawn, little by little. If Paul suggested they pop round to Chinatown for dim sum, she agreed, though according to the dictates of her profession, she didn't eat enough to nourish a child. If he tried to spark a spirited discussion—giant West End productions like *Hamilton* vs. tiny fringe shows at the Hen & Chickens—Kyla shrugged and said she couldn't decide. If he lingered over a kiss goodnight, she matched his ardor precisely. No more, no less. She never froze him out or made excuses, but she never made the first move. Ever.

Tessa had been the same. Maybe it wasn't surprising, since Kyla was Tessa's younger sister.

There was nothing wrong with that. There was no law against dating sisters. Moreover, it wasn't as if Paul had known Kyla when she was a teen. Early in their acquaintance, he hadn't even realized she was related to Tessa. He'd never brought up the connection to anyone, although Kate and Tony knew. He'd even put off introducing Kyla to his mum, Sharada, for fear she would guess the truth. Sharada had never liked Tessa, even before her final betrayal. She would see the shadow of Tessa in Kyla: the flutter of her lashes, the curve of her lips, the cascade of dark curls.

There's nothing wrong with dating sisters, Paul told himself for the thousandth time as he veered for Pret A Manger. There was nothing new under the sun. Probably it had happened before. Boy meets girl. Boy plans to propose. Girl returns to her serial killer boyfriend, loses her mind, gets sectioned for life. Boy swears off serious relationships for a few years, meets girl's sister, and again haunts jewelry shops for the perfect engagement ring.

Mum will come around when she sees I'm serious. She wants grandchildren. She hasn't exactly been subtle about it.

The line at Pret was fifteen deep. Londoners ordered in precise bursts and passed over the money before they were asked; tourists read the menu aloud, asked each other what sounded good, and fussed with their pound notes and coins. Such was life on the Embankment. Outside Pret, Paul glimpsed the blonde dog walker again. Again, he was reminded of Emmeline. She'd taken the breakup a bit harder than expected, drunk-dialing him later the same night to comprehensively detail his flaws and bad habits. After vowing never to speak to him again, she'd rung back twice with additional slander. Paul had been touched. He'd never guessed he meant that much to her.

But if he was ready to settle down—and at thirty-six, shouldn't a man be ready to settle down?—he had to be realistic. Marrying Emmeline wasn't even in the realm of possibility. Her parents hated him. Her friends were just young enough to consider him boring and middle-aged, a term he couldn't bear to hear applied to himself. Emmy herself was married to her new career as an estate agent, and making a go of it against all odds. It was the perfect job for a brash, flash blonde who was intimidated by nothing and no one. Would she want to put that on the back-burner to marry him, make nice with Sharada, and start a family? Not bloody likely.

"Flat white. Large one," Paul told the barista, handing over two coins. He dropped his change in the tip jar and shuffled aside to wait.

Last night, he'd assumed he'd have impressive news for Tony and Kate: that he'd asked Kyla to move in, and she'd said yes. But instead, she'd smiled and said she was flattered.

"Only my career's taking off," she'd said. "I've wanted this since I was twelve. It's finally breaking open, Paul. I'll probably be in Paris come September. It wouldn't be fair to you, saying yes to the next step in a relationship while I'm so busy."

Paul didn't know how to translate that to his best friends, given that they were cynical, suspicious types, just like him. Kate would hoot at the term "flattered." Tony would frown at the phrase "it wouldn't be fair to you," which virtually every man from the Pliocene Epoch to the present had used while escaping a relationship. Kate and Tony would think Kyla was initiating the process of letting him down easy, and that was ludicrous. Better to skip the discussion until there was something concrete to report, like a ring on her finger.

Large flat white in hand at last, Paul skipped Pret's bright red dining room in favor of the great outdoors. It was a pretty morning: blue skies with delicate mackerel clouds and a brisk wind off the Thames. The new HQ had been designed without internal gathering spots, to force Scotland Yard's officers, detectives, supervisors, and support staff to get out in the community and mix with the public they served. Thus, it had no break rooms and no canteen.

The old guard, most of whom hadn't been consulted, was predictably up in arms. To them, the old canteen had been a sacred place. Those two day-old sandwiches and vending machine coffees were copper comfort food. Paul, who'd despised the canteen, thought the new scheme was brill. Why would anyone yearn for a sullen, windowless dining room when they could do this: get out in the fresh air, sit down at a cast-iron table, watch the boats navigate the river, and soak up the sunshine?

"Oi! There he is," Kate called, emerging from an Embankment shop. She advanced on him rapidly, shaking a greasy paper bag. "I have mini doughnuts."

"After all that food and Chardonnay, I figured you'd be slimming this morning." He, too, had overindulged last night, but that didn't stop him from digging into the bag. A fair proportion of the Met now overindulged in the mini doughnuts daily. According to MPS PR flacks, the *new* New Scotland Yard's design would contribute to the health of public servants by getting them out of the office and walking along the Embankment. But many walked no farther than the bakery. There'd been a time, ten or twenty years ago, where many Brits had felt comfortably superior to their rotund American cousins. Recent public health trends suggested the glory days of laughing at Yank fatties was done.

"Told you. I'm off slimming for good." Kate bit defiantly into a mini doughnut. "After the fire I went through my wardrobe, plucked out the itsy-bitsies and packed them off to Oxfam. I'm not fat. I'm just not as thin as I used to be. It's fine."

"You're a liar."

"I'm at peace. No more starvation diets. More cardio, more weight training, and more veg with every meal. Except this one." Finishing her doughnut, Kate plucked another out of the bag. "You've inspired me. Look at that skunk streak. It's getting bigger and I don't see you fighting it."

"I'm dyeing my hair next week."

"Get out!"

"I am." He resisted the urge to run his fingers through the streak, which started at his temple and zigzagged toward his crown. According to experts—his mum, his aunts, Kyla, his neighbors, two pensioners in Tesco and a full-regalia Morris Dancer on the underground—concealing the white streak would be a commitment. Once he started, he'd have to color it every two to three weeks.

"It's not that I'm vain," he said, wishing there was a reflective surface nearby for him to check himself in. "If my hair was going salt-and-pepper, or even full-on gray like Tony's, I could live with it. Maybe. But it's snow white. Mendelsohn's calling me Pepé Le Pew."

"Mendelsohn in the Vetting Bureau?" Kate asked scornfully. "Tell him to shut it. He's a big girl's blouse."

"Mendelsohn in SCO19."

"Oh. Well. In that case, if you don't like the nickname, you'd better dye it quick. Speaking of big girl's blouses...." Kate narrowed her eyes at him.

Paul groaned. He knew what she was getting at. He'd been postponing it for months. Six months, to be exact.

"I'm still up for training. I had to heal," he said, referring to an injury that had sidelined him around the previous Halloween. "Then we had another big public case and you and Tony got married and it was Christmas, then it was New Year's. Next thing I knew, Wellegrave House burned down and you were busy with the move...."

"Apart from the four month gap in that narrative, you're quite right. Look. If you don't want to improve your CQB skills, that's your business," Kate said, referring to Close Quarter Battle, a martial arts discipline in which she excelled. "But before you know it, you'll be up for review. A poor score won't serve your dream of becoming DI Bhar anytime soon."

That was true. Paul exercised daily, but not like Kate, who set goals and took classes, or like Tony, who followed roughly the same routine of fencing, weight training, and boxing he'd done for the last thirty-five years. Paul's notion of a great workout was to pop in the ear buds, run a couple of miles, have a coffee, check his Sky Sports fantasy football stats, and run home. For him, it was all about fresh air and music. For Tony, it was a deeply ingrained habit. For Kate, it was a competitive sport.

"DI Bhar does have that magical ring to it," he said. "Maybe if I master your signature move—the roundhouse kick—and wow the reviewers, I'll finally change my S to an I."

"360-degree roundhouse kick," Kate corrected. "Right. Time and date TBA. But soon. Don't expect me to go easy."

They polished off the rest of the mini doughnuts while watching the river. According to the *Daily Mail,* a London version of the Loch Ness monster had been sighted recently. That was bollocks, of course. But if any body of water on earth might actually contain a cryptozoological beast, it was the Thames. All manner of things had been pulled out of it: Roman swords, bullet-riddled crime bosses, and the occasional BMW, parked too long on a slipway and taken out by the tide. Paul was watching a rusty old fishing boat chug by when Kate said,

"Think we ought to go in? I've got Gulls."

"Sounds like a diagnosis. 'Why so blue?' 'I've got Gulls.'"

"And there's no cure. Just an endless stream of rainbows and unicorns."

"Some would say taking on a trainee detective constable was an honor," Paul said, meaning it not in the least.

"Pull the other one. I think my number came up because I'm female. Meant to be nurturing."

"I reckoned it's because you're prickly. Payback for one of your gobby moments. Besides. I overheard you with Gulls the other day. Admit it. You're a mother hen. I think you're starting to like her."

"She did good work on our last case. Off-the-record, weekend work," Kate agreed. "Dedication isn't the issue. Neither is competence. She's just so... chipper."

"Another six weeks with you should cure her of that." Rising, Paul gathered up the empty doughnut bag and napkins, pitching them into a nearby receptacle that said, "Do the right thing! Bin it for a cleaner Thames." The notion was about three hundred years overdue, but better late than never.

"I was only taking the mickey, by the way," Kate said, rummaging in her bag for her sunglasses. She popped them on and fell into step with him as they headed for the new HQ.

"About what?"

"You hopping back on the promotion obsession. And if you did, you'd better hop back off. You passed the exam. You went out for drinks and lunches with the top brass. Now all you can do is wait for the stars to line up. A higher rating at CQB won't make the wheels turn any faster. Might save your life, though."

"I was never obsessed with making DI," Paul lied. "You're the one who paid someone to prep you for the written exam."

"Money well spent. I'm hopeless when it comes to tests. My A-levels were the worst experience of my life."

"Yes, well, one thing I learned from three years in the wilderness. People love an underdog," he said, hoping it was true. "I mucked up and everyone knows it. Had a few hiccups getting back on my feet. Now I've proven I can take my lumps. I chased a cat through an entire borough to secure an eyewitness, for heaven's sake. Now I'm sidling into the chief's good graces by volunteering for his scut work."

"Right. This has to stop," Kate said, stopping dead in the middle of the thoroughfare as fast-walking Londoners fell over themselves to evade her. "DCI Jackson is our guv now. It's been months. You have to start calling him that."

"No. You're married to the guv. Jackson's our boss. The chief."

"Jackson's the guv. I'm married to Tony. Two syllables. Toe-nee. Say it."

"I won't. It's not natural."

"Tony is now a private investigator. Say it. Or I'll stand rooted to the spot till you die of shame," Kate said.

Dying of shame was a possibility. The Embankment had plenty of foot traffic on sunny afternoons; Londoners didn't appreciate a hold-up. Passers-by were glaring at them, tutting at them, or both. On a nearby bench, an old lady with tightly permed hair sat, handbag clutched to her chest and shaking her head.

"Fine. *Tony* is a private investigator," Paul forced himself to say. "Maybe I'll call him Lord Tony. I know it's incorrect, but it sounds better, somehow."

"This isn't right. You can do better, you know." It was the bench-sitter. She'd risen to approach them, vinyl bag still melded to her bosom.

"Right. Yes. Sorry," Paul said automatically, like every Englishman ever. "We'll clear out of the way."

"I mean her." The old lady drew closer to Kate. "You're a pretty thing. Still young enough to find a proper bloke. One that won't break your dad's heart." To Paul she said, "We had a vote, you know. You have to get out."

Kate groaned. "Shove off, you mad bat."

"We had a vote. We have borders now." Trembling with emotion, the old woman stared at Paul, watery eyes wide.

He said, *"Hab SoSlI' Quch."*

She gave a little cry, apparently shocked he would even address her. "Don't you curse at me, you ruddy Paki. How dare you!"

"Tera'ngan Soj lujab'a'."

"Do you hear that, Lizzy? He's cursing me in his heathen tongue!" the woman cried.

On cue, Lizzy, a middle-aged lady with a matching face but looser curls, turned up. She slid a protective arm around what could only be her mum.

"What's all this, then?" Lizzy demanded.

"I should be asking you," Kate snapped. "Are you meant to be minding her? She strolled up, bold as brass, and unloaded a lot of racist remarks."

"All I said was we voted Leave and he cursed me in his

heathen tongue!" the old woman wailed.

The daughter looked gobsmacked. Paul felt a little ashamed. "Actually, I wished her a happy birthday. In Klingon."

"Are you mad? Why would you frighten her that way?"

"Why would she tell a man she's never met to bugger out of the country?" Kate was turning red.

"Well, because we had a vote. We're taking back our country. And besides, you should have respect for your elders." Lizzy lifted her chin as if seizing the moral high ground. "Scotland Yard is just there, you know," she added, pointing at the iconic revolving sign. "I should report you for abuse."

"Oh. Please. *Do.*" Kate whipped off her sunglasses. "Take note of my face. I'm Detective Sergeant Kate Hetheridge. H-e-t-h-e-r-i-d-g-e. This here's my colleague, Detective Sergeant Paul Bhar. He's as English as Dickens and he grew up in Clerkenwell, not that it's any of your damn business. And not that we're likely to get a thank-you, but we work to keep the public safe."

"And you're doing a bang-up job, aren't you?" Lizzy cried. "Foreigners driving vans into crowds of people. Blokes that look like *him* beheading soldiers in broad daylight. No one's safe."

"Where's MI6?" her mother added. "Where's the ring of steel? We don't need the likes of you two! We need good English men to clean up our country before it's too late."

Kate looked ready to deck the pair of them. Paul tugged on her arm, hard. "Walk away."

She shot him a mutinous look. He tugged harder. "Come on."

She relented. Paul was relieved the mother-daughter duo didn't follow them. The mother was probably satisfied by her outburst, and Lizzy didn't strike him as a shout-remarks-in-the-public-square kind of gal. She seemed more like the sort who would shuffle away quietly, write to her MP, write to the editors of all the London papers, complain on Facebook, rant on Twitter, and bitterly recount the confrontation for years to come, framing it as a moment when she'd bravely spoken out and been insulted for her trouble.

"Did you really tell that mad bat happy birthday in Klingon?" Kate asked as they passed the new HQ's reflecting pool.

"Yeah. It's one of two phrases I know. The other is sort of an insult."

"Let's hear it, then."

"Tera'ngan Soj lujab'a.' It means, your mother has a smooth forehead."

"Huh?"

"Klingons are aliens. Their skulls are meant to be bumpy."

She still looked blank. He took out his iPhone to Google a photo of the *Star Trek* characters, eyed his push notifications, and snapped to attention.

"What is it?"

"The ch—the guv wants us upstairs. Now."

"Why?"

"'Somebody blew up a politician,'" Paul read aloud. "'10 D wants a preliminary report in two hours. You and KH better get up here.'"

CHAPTER EIGHT

*T*he HQ designers never saw a hoarder like the guv coming, Kate thought as she and Paul entered DCI Vic Jackson's new office.

It was less than half the square footage of his old one. The furnishings chosen by the design team were almost cruel to a man like Jackson, who never discarded anything. The minimalist desk was a slab of blond wood on a slender iron frame. The lightweight wire bookcase was clearly ceremonial, meant to display one or two symbolic volumes. Even the chairs were more of a statement than functional items: uncomfortable-looking, as if to signal a culture where public servants were too busy to ever sit down.

Water always finds a way, Kate thought. *So does the hoard.*

The desk's slender iron frame was mostly obscured by Jackson's beloved cardboard file boxes, which he collected and filled obsessively. He'd stacked them up so they seemed to support the desktop, which Kate supposed was still there, though she couldn't prove it. That minimalist desk, designed for a world of digital memos, digital case files, and endless Cloud storage, had disappeared under Jackson's pile of dog-eared folders, three-ring binders, and piles of loose paper. Kate, who'd begun her detective career as Jackson's subordinate, back in the days when they couldn't so much as share a lift without going for one another's jugulars, knew for a fact that 90% of Jackson's data hoard was months, nay, years out of date.

Now that they'd achieved a polite, and at times almost cordial working relationship, she looked upon his piles more kindly. The information Jackson kept put her in mind of a furtive mammal's lair, filled with picked-dry bones, shiny buttons, and bits of reflective rubbish. Jackson couldn't see a relevant, or potentially relevant, fact without wanting to physically possess it.

The appropriately-named Joy, their guv's friendly, upbeat new administrative assistant, announced Kate and Paul's arrival.

"Come through," he shouted. He was a shouty fellow, even when in a peaceable mood. As Kate had expected, they found Jackson behind his invisible desk, down-at-heel loafers on a three-ring binder, a bottle of Cherry Coke Zero Sugar in hand. It was an open secret around the Yard that Jackson had given up the drink. Now his vice was fizzy soda. His mini fridge was always stocked with bottles, which Joy packed in by the case.

"Hello, Chief," Paul said, reverting back to his forbidden nomenclature.

"Hiya, Guv," Kate said. Since his promotion, she'd decided to address him with the same general warmth she'd accorded Tony. He repaid her by being slightly less shouty.

"Hiya yourself, Hetheridge. Is this what you call bright and early? Never mind. I don't want to hear about your struggles getting little Wally off to Wally Academy or wherever." His tone was amiable. "Ears burning? First thing I did this morning was sit through a conference call about you."

"Is it about the Trout case? Maybe I shouldn't have let Gulls do the interview. Rough start, sure, but she sorted it by the end, don't you think?" Kate said, launching into a rebuttal she'd mentally rehearsed during her Underground commute. "Newbies have to make their own mistakes, that's what I always say. But in future I suppose I might —"

"In future I suppose you might let me squeeze a word in," Jackson cut across her. He fiddled with his tie, a relic of some crumbled civilization that favored 100% polyester in shades of brown and cream. "Gulls *did* start like a mealy-mouthed prat, but who's to say that's not a strategy? Old Trout didn't lawyer up because he thought he could steamroll her. Now he's confessed to hiding his sister in the deep freeze. Been sectioned, too, which from a PR standpoint is the ideal outcome. Or so I'm told by people whose purpose in life is to decide how things look. The top brass are happy."

"That's down to Gulls, sir."

"That's down to you." Jackson cleared his throat. "Well done."

Kate didn't know what to say. She tried to think of something gracious, but she had difficulty with soppy moments.

"Well done," Paul concurred. He sounded sincere, but looked guarded. What she'd told Henry the night before was true. Paul had been losing too long.

"Moving on," Jackson said. "What does the name Ford Fabian mean to you two?"

"Midsize sedan. Boxy," Paul said.

"Bargain Chardonnay. Pairs well with a cold burrito," Kate said.

"Wrong and wronger." Jackson scraped at a spot on his tie. "At least you weren't fans of the bloody loon. He was a fringe candidate for PM. Backed by the Scottish Greens, all ten of 'em. Entirely on account of his wife."

"Alfalfa Fabian," Paul said. "Her, I remember. Silly name, but she seemed pretty common sense. Clean water, protecting the Green Belt and all that."

"Come to think of it, I saw her on telly around New Year's," Kate said. "Sounded a bit radical."

"Oh, yeah, I saw that. No nukes, no oil, no fracking, no GMO foods," Paul agreed. "No meat, no dairy, no captive animals – cows, horses, house cats. That's where I thought she took a hard left into Crazytown. Her son was there, pumping his fist and shouting, 'Back to Nature.' I think he meant all the way back."

"That wasn't her son," Jackson said. "That was Ford Fabian. Thirty years younger than Alfalfa. Took her last name when they married." He rolled his eyes, then appeared to check himself, glancing sideways at Kate as if to gauge her reaction.

She wasn't surprised. Older women and younger men tended to still be tut-tutted in public discourse, though surprisingly few people brought up the age difference between her and Tony, at least to her face. When the woman was much older, some people spoke of her as unnaturally lustful, while assuming the man to be entirely mercenary. As for men taking their wife's surname, instead of the other way around, this was also generally regarded as an affront to something. Kate had opinions. But when there was a murder to discuss, it superseded trivia.

"You're past-tensing Fabian. He's dead, then. How? Put us in the picture." She settled into one of the bucket-style chairs that had come with the desk. Paul did the same.

"Car bomb," Jackson said with satisfaction. "How long's it been since we had a good, old-fashioned car bombing, I ask you? Sick of knifings and double-sick of murder vans. Time was, a car bomb got everyone's juices flowing. But this is a little frou-frou, of course, because Millennial thugs are as frou-frou as all the rest of them. Where's the bloody file?"

Jackson started rooting in his desk-detritus like a pig sniffing for truffles. Paul, apparently unable to help himself, ventured, "Maybe on the computer...?"

Jackson grunted. He didn't care about data he could locate quickly, Kate knew. He cared about data he could crumple, rip into bits, or wave threateningly under someone's nose.

"Right. Here it is," Jackson said, seizing a tranche of printed-out emails, official statements, and photos, held together with a binder clip. Kate looked sidelong at Paul, who acknowledged her with a flick of his lashes. If "Back to Nature" Ford Fabian's shade knew the chief investigator of his murder was requiring subordinates to print out hard copies on reams and reams of dead trees, a haunting would surely follow.

"PC Kincaid brought this to me," Jackson said. "You remember him? Gobby but clever with research. Like you, Bhar."

Paul looked pleased. In public service, the further you progressed up the food chain, the more arse-kissing was required. Why else had her supremely talented husband reached the rank of Chief Superintendent and settled in for the long haul? But Paul always overdid it slightly for Kate's taste.

"Here we are. From the official statement, made around half-six this morning by Mr. Fabian's personal assistant," Jackson said, holding the page out at arm's length. He read aloud,

"'The accident happened around half-three. The Fabians were due at Television Centre for a daybreak interview on *This Morning*. They were running late, and I was struggling to get them back on schedule. If anyone was lurking about, neighbor or stranger, I took no notice...'" Jackson skipped to the next relevant detail. "'Their car was a Mercedes Benz C-class coupe, purchased last year. I saw no sign of tampering. But naturally, I never peeked under the bonnet or did any special inspection.'

"'As I said, we were running late. Mrs. Fabian became indisposed. She kept requesting a few more minutes to compose herself before departing. Mr. Fabian was in a state. Finally, he said he would do the interview solo, and perhaps it was better that way. Mrs. Fabian went back into the house. I remained outside to watch Mr. Fabian drive away....'" Jackson hummed tunelessly as he flipped pages. "Here's the specs on the C-class. Keyless entry and an ignition button. Now, back to the assistant." He read,

"'From where I stood, the car started up normally. I turned and went up the steps. As I grasped the door handle, it happened.

Squealing tires. Peeling rubber, I think you say. Mr. Fabian was accelerating straight toward the intersection at the end of our street. In the wee hours, there's no traffic, but you must go left or right. Straight ahead is only a curb, a patch of green, and a brick wall with a hornbeam behind it.

"'I don't think Mr. Fabian hit the brakes. If anything, he sped up. And he was screaming, I think. Perhaps it was me. Right before my eyes his car jumped the curb and slammed into the wall. I ran to help. It was ghastly. The airbag didn't deploy. He was dead. He must have been dead. I hardly got a look at him when I got a strong whiff of petrol. I ran back to the house to ring 999 and that's when the car exploded.'"

"I don't get it," Kate said, wondering if they were meant to believe Fabian's brake lines were cut.

"Neither do I," Paul said. "What's a neo-agrarian fringe candidate for PM doing in a 240 horsepower coupe?"

"You poor sentimental bastard." Jackson shook his head. "I don't like to be the one to tell you. But some of these pols say one thing and do another."

"Convenient that Mrs. Fabian took a powder at the last second," Kate said. "And the assistant is the only witness on a deserted street. His story's bollocks, unless the car was hacked. Which is still theoretical, isn't it?"

"Hacked." Paul gave a low whistle. "Wait till we get self-driving cars. We'll need a new murder squad. A new kidnapping squad, too."

"You two are savvy to this stuff?" Jackson sounded relieved. "When I asked Kincaid if the car's brake line was cut, he looked at me like I was an unfrozen caveman. Like after he explained about car hacking, he'd have to break the news that Airbuses aren't big iron birds."

"Cutting a brake line just means puncturing it so the brake fluid leaks out," Kate said. "Usually done at night, obviously, so it puddles under the car and the driver doesn't notice. Thing is, spongy brakes are hard to miss in the city. The idea is, you're motoring at a fair clip on a lonely road when the brakes fail. In London, you're more likely to be in stand-still traffic."

"Could have been a jammed accelerator, I suppose," Paul said. "But I don't know how you'd pull it off in a modern car."

"But the Millennials are too frou-frou for a IED under the hood," Jackson said. He looked almost as disapproving as he'd been over Ford Fabian taking his wife's surname.

"I don't know if it's frou-frou so much as deniability," Paul said. "I read about car hacking in *Wired*. A small bomb might be a dud. A big one could kill extra people or take out an entire block. Hacking the car as it's being driven is precise, like a surgical strike. And if it's done right, it looks like suicide or an accident."

"I knew the practice of putting computers in cars would come to no good. I don't think they'll bother with kidnapping," Jackson said. "Hackers will just lock the doors, crank up the heat, and make you pay a Bitcoin ransom to get out. It'll take a while for CSIs to give us confirmation. But assuming this is proven to be murder-by-hacking, what was their point of entry? Did one of them break into the car, plug in a laptop, and reprogram something?"

"Wireless, Guv," Kate said. "Invisible signals transmitted through the air alongside the big iron birds."

"Are you calling me thick, Hetheridge?"

Kate tried to brazen it out with an enigmatic smile. Jackson looked at Paul. "Well? Is she saying I'm thick? While you stand there grinning like a great prat?"

Paul started clearing his throat and coughing up bits of denials. "No… you see… that is to say… I wouldn't…."

Kate, who hated to apologize, tried to say something mollifying. "Just a little humor. Joke. Mini-joke. I never meant, to, ah, cause offense."

Jackson glared at them for five more seconds, then burst out laughing. "Oi! Tossers, both of you. Grow a pair, why don't you? Now what was that about wireless?"

Paul tried to regain his dignity by behaving as if the previous exchange hadn't happened. "There are lots of possibilities. The most obvious is the little Bluetooth trackers that car insurance companies have started giving out. The idea is harmless. The device transmits data whenever the car is driven. Time of day, speed, and so on, so your next quarter's rates are figured according to actual mileage, not a woolly estimate. Hackers realized they could interface with some of those devices wirelessly. If I remember the article right, some cars are so computerized, hackers can wirelessly take full control of the accelerator and brake."

"Is this still theoretical? Or has it actually happened in the UK?" Kate asked.

"Not sure we'd really know. Possibly. It's hard to nail down," Paul said. "I know there's been a couple of incidents in the States. Single car, deserted road, and an unpopular driver dead before he can testify against a crime boss or publish an exposé."

"I don't care if it makes me thick to admit it," Jackson said. "I understand cars have computers that run the odometer and the satellite radio and the service reminders. I don't see how a computer can pump an accelerator or move a gear shift."

"That's because you're thinking of old school motors," Kate said, throwing in a belated, "sir. Used to be, it was all mechanical —a physical action to trigger a physical reaction. Pump the accelerator, squirt petrol in the carburetor. But in modern cars, pressing the pedal or moving the gearshift triggers a computer signal. It could all be done with buttons or voice commands, really."

"I see. We're doomed." Jackson sighed, pushing his reading glasses onto the top of his head and tossing the file aside. "Rise of the computers. I'll be dispatched straightaway for nonconformity. Maybe you two will make it as a robot's pet."

"I, for one, welcome our coming AI overlords," Kate said. "So back to Ford Fabian. Based on the assistant's statement, his boss either committed suicide in the most rash, unexpected way possible, or his vehicle was tampered with. Where do the Fabians live?"

"Knightsbridge. The posh side."

"Of course they do," Kate said. Public figures who railed against modern conveniences and unsustainable lifestyles often resided in well-appointed neighborhoods. If they'd dwelt in a yurt on Salisbury Plain, *that* would have been surprising. "Lots of CCTV cameras round there, public and private. Do I need to put someone on the acquisition of private footage?"

"Already requested," Jackson said. "The public footage will take eons. You know how those B of K people are. The private owners live for police requests. They'll probably have it to us by this afternoon."

"I don't suppose Mr. Fabian's assistant provided any suspects?" Paul asked. "He was standing for PM. Maybe Giant Elmo or Lord Buckethead bumped him off to improve their chances?"

Kate chuckled. Politics in the UK were many things, but unremittingly stodgy wasn't one of them. Every duly nominated party candidate was allowed to stand—literally stand—for Parliament, and the rules which governed parties permitted a wide range of free expression. For this reason, on the night of the most recent election, the future PM had stood onstage awaiting the returns next to a Darth Vader knockoff and a man dressed as a Muppet.

"The assistant has a long list," Jackson said. "To hear him tell it, his late lamented boss was a towering figure with mortal enemies all over Britain. I don't know about that, but he did have some friends. The Scottish Greens are up in arms, naturally. And someone claiming to represent the Celtic Gaia Society went on telly to demand Scotland Yard investigate Fabian's death not only as a homicide, but a hate crime."

"Why?" Kate asked.

Paul, ever-buoyed by the slightest whiff of absurdity, bounced on his toes in delight. "Oh! I'll bet I know. It's a hate crime against Mother Earth."

Jackson nodded. Kate told Paul, "This must feel like early Christmas for you."

"It does. I'm metaphorically rubbing my hands with glee. Nope. I'm literally rubbing my hands with glee." He demonstrated.

"Right. Well. As it happens...." Jackson cleared his throat. "DS Hetheridge, I want you to solo on the Fabian case. Take along TDC Gulls, obviously. If the case wraps quickly, more power to you. If it metastasizes, check back with me, and I'll help you build a bigger team. Keep allowing Gulls the longest lead she can handle. These interviews may involve the very toffee-nosed twits we're meant to specialize in. I'd like to know how she performs with the quality, as my old mum called them."

Jackson turned to Paul. "DS Bhar. Why should Hetheridge here have all the trainee fun? I mentioned PC Kincaid. Turns out he's interested in going the detective route, too. Can't let Gulls outshine him, I reckon. You need to show Kincaid how this unit cracks on. I don't care how you put him to use. Delegate some research. Let him fact-check or do phone interviews. Mostly just turn on the charm. Kincaid's a good prospect. We need all the new blood we can get."

"I don't understand," Paul said.

Jackson sighed. "Yesterday, for my sins, I sat through a two-hour lecture about mentorship. Now the, er, fruit of that meeting rolls downhill. Hetheridge will continue mentoring Gulls in the field. You'll begin mentoring Kincaid on the administrative side. Simple as that. You savvy?"

Paul looked shocked. Kate felt the same. Since joining the Toff

Squad, she'd worked every major case with Paul. Tony had been the guiding force, naturally, but Kate and Paul had collaborated on everything. Moreover, Paul had seniority. Not to mention a personnel file full of commendations from his Henden training center days. If a choice had to be made, he should have received the high-profile assignment. Kate should have been relegated to the back-burner, clearly.

Except that wasn't objectively true. Paul's early fieldwork had been distinguished, but after the triple murder case that ended in Sir Duncan Godington's acquittal, things had gone pear-shaped. Convinced he was a good detective in need of career rehabilitation, Tony had provided Paul with some cover. But Tony wasn't around to shield him anymore.

"Look, Bhar. I realize this was unexpected. But in the end it all comes down to marching orders, and you have yours," Jackson said. "Meantime, give Kincaid a ring. Take him out for an early lunch and sell him on the perks of the job. Off you go. I want a word with Hetheridge alone."

"Sure." Paul took a step toward the door. "But... this is only temporary, right? I'm not being downshifted. Am I?" As many times as he'd announced that his career was in the karzi, now that the moment arrived, he looked gutted.

Jackson, for his part, looked ready to blow. "Perhaps there's a language barrier. I realize you're accustomed to hobnobbing with a Peer of the Realm. I'm a lowly Mancunian who picked the job over the joint. So tell me. What did Tony mean when he employed the phrase, 'Marching orders?' Was he declaring a safe space for insubordination?"

"No, sir." Paul snapped to attention. "Thank you, sir. I'll ring Kincaid's guv and get permission for him to work under my supervision." He exited at top speed.

After the door closed, Jackson sighed again. He still looked irritated. Kate knew it wasn't wise to keep pushing, but she couldn't help herself. Of her many character defects, one that shone brightest was her compulsion to speak up in defense of her friends. "Sir...."

"Me first," he cut across her. "Did I cross a line?"

"When?"

"When I said grow a pair."

It took Kate a moment to recall what he was even talking about. "No. No, of course not." She grinned. "I assumed you meant Paul."

"Too right. Second question. I commended you about Gulls. Now that it's just you and me, I want to know. Will you formally recommend her to become a detective constable?"

"I think so," Kate said. "She's sharp. Dedicated. So far, my only worry is, she's too dedicated. She may burn out. But Guv." She looked Jackson in the eye. "What's happening to Paul? Are you reassigning him?"

Jackson looked pained. Standing up, he stretched, groaned softly, and dropped into his office chair with such force it admitted its own vinyl-and-plastic moan.

"Hear that? My old chair did the job for ten years. Never a squeak, never a rattle. That chair was on track to take me to retirement. But due to the move, it was seized over my objections. Dumped in a landfill or auctioned off to some charity. Then the boys upstairs, in their infinite wisdom, requisitioned me a brand-new chair. And it's already falling apart, isn't it? A metaphor for the move writ large, if you ask me."

"One of the boys upstairs is a girl."

"I know. I blame her, too." Jackson studied Kate speculatively. "Now tell me. If I confide in you, will it stay in this room?"

Kate didn't answer. One of her other character defects was the inability to glibly lie on the spot. She was more likely to blurt out the truth and be forced to endure the results.

"We may as well come to a reckoning now," Jackson said. "I doubt even Tony was an open book when you worked together. More often than not, I'll need to keep mum, too. But there will be times when I'd like to clue you in, as long as I know it won't become tomorrow's breakfast chatter at Pret."

"I don't want to spread it around. Or take it over your head in the form of a complaint," Kate said. "But Paul's my friend. I'd like to tell him where he stands. If the tables were turned—if I were sidelined, and he could find out if I needed to cut my losses and resign—I'd want him to do it." She sighed. "Full disclosure. I'll tell Tony, too. But you know how he is."

"Silent as the grave," Jackson said, plopping his feet on the desk again. "We had our ups and downs over the years. He knew a load of my secrets, and he never spilled them. Now. Bhar. Thing is, no one wants to sack him. But his last cockup—you remember —was the final straw. There was a memo to take immediate action...."

"...which in Met-time means four months later," Kate said.

"Precisely. Maybe he never said, but he's been on more or less constant probation since Sir Duncan's acquittal. Still. During his training, he was a star. We've sunk too much into him to give up now. Seems fairly obvious there's only one way to let him succeed. Put him back where he excels. The classroom."

Reluctantly, Kate digested that. She'd hoped Jackson would say something patently unfair, a half-truth or willful distortion she could pounce on and correct. This was all too reasonable. It might even be right.

"I've been asked to ease him into it," Jackson said. "Keep him out of the field. Give him trainees to mentor. With any luck, he'll start to enjoy it. So when we reassign him to Henden training center, he won't sue us for discrimination."

Kate made a rude noise.

He looked surprised. "I thought that's why you were asking. To be sure it wasn't a race thing."

"No. I was asking in case there was still something he could do to turn this around. I guess not. So you'd might as well tell me, is that why I'm with Gulls? Am I getting put out to the Henden pasture, too?"

The usually easy-to-read Jackson turned opaque.

"Oh, no. Please. *Me* teaching courses?" Kate cried. "Total nonstarter. Have a look at my transcripts if you don't believe me."

"I did," Jackson said. "Funny thing. Detectives who come up the hard way tend to look a certain way on paper. Middling scores. No glowing notes from instructors. Not ranked at the top, not ranked at the bottom—just sort of hovering in the flabby middle. Then they step into the real world and boom. They start breaking cases. Making arrests. Rocketing up. Because the real world isn't about acing an exam. It's about grabbing the bull by the tits and making a difference."

Kate stared at him in rising disbelief.

"Erm. Maybe not the best phrase in today's climate." Jackson cleared his throat. "Point is, I've seen it all before. A brash young PC becomes a DC. Then a DS. Next thing you know, she's nominated to be a Detective Inspector. She still has hoops to jump through. Interviews, a health assessment, all the usual bureaucratic buggery. But she will be a DI, and maybe sooner than she thinks."

"Yes, sir," Kate mumbled. It seemed like a dream. "Thank you, sir."

CHAPTER NINE

*T*ea and toast was surprisingly good at the Saint Benedict drop-in center on Arneway Street. Tony had known about the spread, which was put out for the homeless and hungry every day, including weekends and bank holidays. He'd heard such places mentioned many times, of course. Either during discussion of one of his many charities, or in official MPS reports, typically in a sentence like this:

"Suspect has no fixed residence but is known to the staff and regular clients of the Saint Benedict drop-in center, where he sometimes has tea and toast."

But today, the sixth day of his investigation into Mariah Keene's death and her twin brother's disappearance, Tony was at Saint Benedict, sampling the goods. Specifically, he was sitting at a beat-up table in a dark corner, sipping hot tea with lemon and contemplating the curious habits of Mark Keene.

As above, so below. That was Mark's motto. He'd blogged about it, bent his father and mother's ear about it, tried to convince his therapist the four words were the gateway to higher consciousness. He'd even taken to defacing private property with related signs and symbols. In another time, Mark probably would have been a wandering mystic, living off the kindness of those who found his message captivating, if ultimately inexplicable. From what Tony had pieced together, Mark's university career had cratered when he stopped taking his meds. Next, he'd fired his therapist. Then he'd began making the rounds in London, especially the City of Westminster, for which he seemed to have a particular affinity. Within the City's proud confines, the heir to the earldom of Brompton reputedly made the rounds every day, which included nibbling free biscuits, drinking free tea from paper cups, and carving designs into the Saint Benedict center's furniture.

Yet I keep missing him, Tony thought, tracing a fingertip along the table's dominant design. It wasn't actually carved so much as pressed into the synthetic wood by the repeated application of a ballpoint pen.

The design was a rectangle with numbers and a spiral inside. The spiral, small and tight at the beginning, grew larger and looser toward the end. Seeming to arise from the number 1, the spiral passed quickly through 2, 3, and 5, then swept around 8, 13, 21, and 34. Mark had drawn the design with great precision, using a straight edge to get the proportions correct. That was Mark, from what Tony had gathered: delusional off his meds, obsessive even when on them, but always correct with mathematics, even if he was using them to express, or attempt to express, eschatological truths.

This particular figure was called a Golden Rectangle. Mark's preoccupation with the symbol had led Tony to reacquaint himself with a curiosity from his boyhood: the mystical Fibonacci number sequence. He'd learned about it at age nine, during his religious training at Christ Church Mayfair. The priest had described the sequence as beginning with "seeds": zero and one. Zero plus one equals one; one plus one equals two. One plus two equals three. Two plus three equals five, and so on. Mark had carved them along the table's edge:

1, 2, 3, 5, 8, 13, 21, 34, 55, 89, 144...

Tony and the other boys in his Sunday school class had been captivated to learn about the number sequence, which was visually expressed in the form of a spiral. The priest explained how certain arrangements of atoms followed the Fibonacci spiral. So, too, did the corkscrew pattern of seeds inside a sunflower, and the structure of spiral galaxies. Like a wink from a mischievous supreme being, the Golden Spiral, as the priest called it, turned up repeatedly throughout nature. This included hurricanes, tornadoes, nautilus shells, and the cochlea of the human ear.

"It's God's arithmetic," the priest had said, encouraging his class to seek the Golden Spiral in the natural world. Once young Tony started looking, patterns that cropped up that didn't seem like coincidence. A lily had three petals; a larkspur, five; a delphinium, eight; a marigold, thirteen; an aster, twenty-one. Cut open a banana and find three segments; cut open an apple and find five. The Golden Spiral proved itself over and over again.

Except it didn't, Tony thought. *Because it isn't true.*

At Oxford, Tony had tried to impress a pretty undergrad by mentioning the Golden Spiral, only to have the woman laugh in his face. She'd referred him to the Mathematical Institute, where one of his mates had lectured him mercilessly about logarithmic spirals, growth under constraint, Archimedean spirals, Fermat numbers, Lucas numbers, and at least ten types of flowers with petals that didn't fit the Golden Spiral. The idea of Fibonacci numbers as scientifically approved mysticism was, in the parlance of the day, bunk.

Nine-year-old Tony would have been crushed, but grown-up Tony didn't mind. Nor did he feel compelled to try and debunk the views of his religious friends, of which there were many. He didn't find religion uncomfortable. In general, it offered a positive worldview, a series of ethical demands, and hope for the future, even after death. But a career in murder had cursed him with x-ray vision. He could no longer cast his eye upon human institutions without seeing all the way through, down to the inevitable dark side. Even the Church of England, in which he'd been baptized.

He envied those who'd found transcendence. And it didn't surprise him that people who liked the idea of the Fibonacci number sequence didn't care if it was a myth. The spiral of the chameleon's tail would always be mystical, in its way, even if that mysticism couldn't be boiled down to a series of numbers and anecdotes.

But not for Mark.

Tony had questioned two dozen people in and around the City of Westminster. According to them, their strange friend Mark considered the Fibonacci number sequence nothing less than incontrovertible proof that God was speaking to him.

He hadn't viewed this as a comfort. Quite the contrary, Mark had found it a torment. God was speaking to him via nature in repetitive yet incomprehensible clues that only he perceived, but could not decode.

Tony pushed back his chair to look at the numbers etched into the table's edge again. After 144, Mark had deviated from the Fibonacci number sequence with a combination of letters and numbers: RV2117.

Once again, Tony's Sunday school classes at Christ Church Mayfair returned to him. Book of Revelations, chapter twenty-one, verse seventeen.

He pulled a small Gideon New Testament out of his pocket. It was one of the first things he'd received while undercover as a homeless man, along with £4 2p tossed at him by passersby, a card with the picture and phone number of a working girl who specialized in older men, and a curt "Shove it!" from a thug in a cheap uniform with a plastic silver-tone badge. The verse Mark referenced read,

And he measured the wall thereof, a hundred and forty and four cubits, according to the measure of a man, that is, of the angel.

"Hiya," a woman with a chirpy voice said. "You must be Tony. I'm Gert."

Instinctively he stood up to greet her, frustrated by his own knee-jerk courtesy. He wasn't meant to be Tony Hetheridge, who had many faults, none of which involved etiquette. He was meant to be Tony the homeless man, searching for his pal Mark, who'd promised to help him.

"I'm Tony, yeah." He gave the young woman's hand more of a squishy touch than a shake. It had been eons since he'd had cause to go undercover, and in his eagerness to do it well, he'd over-loaded his character's backstory with details. Tony the homeless man had a soft Welsh accent, a long rap sheet, and severe arthritis in his hands. Unable to make his living any longer in what old-school cons called "the collection business," he was looking into the brave new world of cybercrime.

"I see you're looking at some of Mark Keene's handiwork," the woman chirruped. "Fibonacci numbers, that's what he told me. And a Bible verse about the number 144. He tried to explain, but to me it was all very woolly. I'm Gert, by the way. Did I say that already? Sorry."

She was perhaps fifty, but sounded childlike in her enthusi-asm. Her curly hair was highlighted red; her plastic-framed specs were big, bold, and lime green.

"I'm a social worker," she continued, hardly pausing between sentences. "Always on the go. Today it's Saint Benedict's. How are you today?"

"Ah, mustn't grumble," Tony said, pulling out a chair for Gert before reclaiming his own. If he'd accidentally revealed himself a polite old git, he might as well continue in that vein. Some of the more brutal fixers and enforcers he'd met over the years were surprisingly gentle with women and children. They only harmed the people they were paid to harm.

"Pleased to meet you, Gert," he said. "But how did you know my name? Did someone send you?"

"That would be me," said a short man with a low forehead and deep-set eyes. As he approached the table, the short man nodded at Gert, whom he clearly knew. "I'm Cedric. I assign beds and swab the decks. Full-service lackey of the Lord. I hope you don't mind, Tony, but I asked my mate here to have a word with you. You've been in three times now, looking for our Mark. Gert's looking for him, too."

Tony pushed up his white canvas bucket hat, bought for a pound in an Oxfam shop, and smiled at Cedric. Tony Hetheridge was congenitally incapable of wearing a hat indoors, but Tony the homeless man took a more pragmatic view: what he kept on his body was less likely to be nicked. The rest of his undercover garb, a torn T-shirt, paint-splattered jacket, and well-worn chinos, were castoffs of Harvey's. Overseeing the renovations at Wellegrave House was playing havoc with the manservant's wardrobe.

"Mark was going to explain all this to me, you know," Tony said, tracing the design, known as a Golden Rectangle. "How there are signs all around, if we have eyes to see. Messages from God and all that."

"Yes, well. One never knows," Cedric said lightly. "In my humble experience, the best place to receive divine messages is in church on Sunday. Puzzling out scratches on sticks of furniture can be confusing. But I admire Mark's enthusiasm. I miss him."

"We all do," Gert said. "He'd become a fixture in these parts. Sometimes he caused a little ruckus. The City doesn't look kindly on graffiti, and great financiers in their Homburgs don't take kindly to being asked if they understand the relationship between the Fibonacci numbers and the measure of a man."

"Or an angel," Cedric agreed. "Mark was different, but he was all right. Never stole, or shouted, or raised a hand to anyone. He just talked about things only he understood. So tell us, Tony. What was your relationship to Mark?"

Old cons tended to be suspicious. Therefore Tony made a

show of *harrumphing*, glancing around the quiet little shelter as if he might be under surveillance, before he spoke.

"I don't know about *relationship*," he said. "Boy's a bit of a queer bird. But I like him all the same. I didn't ken everything he said about divine messages and whatnot. But when it came to those ruddy computers, he was clever. Dead clever. I thought I couldn't work 'em, on account of my hands. Crippled up, even with pills from the clinic. Can't do much with a keyboard. But Mark taught me to use the voice interface. Damn thing could understand almost everything I said. Mark promised to teach this old dog a few more new tricks. Help me start a web business." He cleared his throat. "Legitimate business, mind you."

"Good for you," Gert said.

"Legitimate is the way to go," Cedric agreed, still in that light tone. He was looking closely at Tony. Had he slipped up? Gone from sounding like *Fools and Horses* to more like *Downton Abbey*?

"When did you last see Mark?" Gert asked.

"Around Christmas," Tony said. That seemed like the safest bet, to claim no contact beyond that last bitter row at the Keenes', the one in which Hannah had given her children the keys to the street, as Peter put it. "I saw him loitering about the City. Told me he'd left Uni and started doing a bit of hacking. I wonder if he didn't get himself into a spot of trouble."

Cedric gave Tony another sharp look. Was he playing it wrong, steering the conversation to a suggestion of foul play so early?

"Then again, maybe Mark ghosted you lot," Tony said, changing tacks. "That's what the kids call it these days."

"Mark wouldn't do that," Gert said earnestly. "He doesn't play games. Always tells the truth. As he sees it, I mean. He's not just a mystic, with visions the rest of us don't understand. He's sick, off his meds. He needs them to function, Tony." She reached out to clasp his hand, then seemed to recall his claim of crippling arthritis and touched his wrist instead. "I worry what might become of him. That's why if you know anything, anything at all, you must tell us."

Cedric, still hovering beside the table with his arms folded across his chest, asked, "Do you know about his twin sister?"

"Yeah. Deadenfall," Tony said. "Bad business. Never met the bird. Still, if she was from blue bloods, like Mark, what was she doing climbing a half-finished building in the middle of the night?"

"I knew her slightly, you know," Gert said. "Bright girl. Walked with her shoulders back and a spring in her step. She left Uni when Mark washed out. Followed him about Westminster to keep tabs. Poor Mark must feel lost without her."

"Are you only looking for him in Westminster?" Tony asked. "Maybe he moved on to Shoreditch or Barking. This can be unfriendly ground for rough sleepers."

Cedric chuckled. "Is that so? You telling me my business now, Tony, my mate?"

He sees through me, Tony thought. *Time to confirm if drug use is a factor and bugger off.*

"I only mean, if Mark couldn't buy what he wanted in Westminster, maybe he moved on to the next borough. Lad liked his gear, didn't he? So did his twin sis. Synthetic weed, people say."

"I never saw Mark use," Gert said.

"Yeah, well, you wouldn't, would you?" Cedric glared at Tony. "Is that what this is really about? You looking to sell Spice to Mark? Or collect on old debts?"

"Nothing like that. I'm looking for a lad who entered a dangerous world," Tony said. "Hackers, Spice dealers, maybe worse. His sis pushed her way in, trying to get him out, and now she's dead. I may be the only mate of Mark's who could go into that world and stay alive long enough to bring him out."

Gert and Cedric exchanged glances. Hope shone in their faces, though both took pains to conceal it.

Mark's lucky to have such devoted friends, Tony thought. *Then again, he inspired that loyalty. Maybe luck has nothing to do with it.*

"Give me a sec." Stepping away from the table, Cedric turned the WELCOME sign on Saint Benedict's front door and locked up. After a quiet word with a dormitory worker, he shut the door between the dorm and the dining room. That left the three of them alone.

"I think Mark did enter a dangerous world," Cedric said, returning to the table and pulling up a chair. "Every street person looks dodgy to those who aren't used to hustlers and rough sleepers. But Mark fell in with truly bad company. He had a home to go to. But he seemed to feel safer at Saint Benedict's. I told Mark he'd always be welcome. But not those friends of his."

"The No-Hopers," Gert said.

"The No-what now?"

"No-Hopers. That's what Mark's hacker friends call themselves."

"Thought they were BASE jumpers," Cedric said. " I suppose they can be hackers, too."

"I know a bit about BASE jumping," Tony said. "Was Mark the sort of person who might fling himself off a building of a Friday evening?"

"Maybe when he's off his meds," Gert said.

"And nattering on about angel dust," Cedric put in.

"The first time I saw Mark with the No-Hopers was in a café, last November," Gert said. "I waved at him, but he pretended not to know me. I suppose the No-Hopers don't like nosey social workers of a certain age. So I texted him, and he replied back. I never deleted the thread. Let's see...."

She dug into her bag, a crocheted monstrosity that looked like a handmade gift from someone who despised her. "Where is the blessed... sorry, Tony... I think that's... no, it's sanitizer." She laughed, tossing a mini-bottle of Purell on the table. "Can't be too careful. Germs everywhere."

"Maybe just tell us the gist of the text, Gertie, love," Cedric said impatiently.

"Why do I carry a compact? I've given up on makeup," Gert continued, tossing the silver disk onto the table. "Sorry, Cedric, I know you can't keep the doors locked for long in the middle of the day—oh! Here we are. Whoops! Didn't mean to do that," she said as the flash went off. "Every time I try and send a text, I take a picture. Scatterbrained! But here we are... just a second... here." She passed her smartphone, in a battered red and black ladybug-patterned case, to Cedric.

"Right. Yeah," he said after reading it, and handed the phone to Tony.

On November 13 of the previous year, at 4:42 pm, Gert Verger had sent the following text to Mark Keene:

> **Saw you in Anatolia but you didn't see me. You OK?**
> *Mark:* **No.**
> *Gert:* **What's up?**

There was no answer. At 5:08, Gert sent another query:

> **Who was that I saw you with?**
> *Mark:* **My mates. So they say.**
> *Gert:* **Mariah mentioned them. No-Hopers.**

No answer. At 6:19, Gert asked,

> **How did you meet them?**
> *Mark:* **Xuanzhang.**

Tony recognized the name as one of the dark web's many anonymous marketplaces. What he didn't know about the hunt for modern cyber criminals was a very thick book, but some of the larger illegal cohorts were familiar to almost everyone in law enforcement. It wasn't surprising that a gifted young programmer like Mark would sample the dark web. Even nine-year-old Henry had confessed to checking out the "deep web," that vast semi-private layer between the surface internet, accessible to anyone, and the dark web, the digital underworld hidden behind walls of encryption.

It seemed that Gert, despite her somewhat naïve manner, recognized the name Xuanzhang, too. She'd texted back,

> **I don't think working for the NH is a good idea.**
> *Mark:* **Mariah hates them. Says I have to choose.**
> *Gert:* **Are you in trouble?**

No answer. At 7:58, Gert asked,

> **Tell me. Are you in trouble?**
> *Mark:* **Mariah is. It's OK. I won't let anything happen to her.**

Tony passed the phone back to Gert, who tapped the screen, presumably to close her text messenger. The flash went off again.

"Sorry! I'm a bit nervous," she said, returning the mobile to her ugly crocheted bag. "I don't like those No-Hopers. I kept at Mark about them. He admitted they were dealing Spice and weed. That some of them traded credit card numbers and personal data as a sideline. But mostly they did contract work he wouldn't talk about. For companies. For private individuals, too."

"So they say. They act like low-rent hooligans," Cedric said. "I never saw them do much except shoplift and crash shelters for free snacks and Wi-Fi. I barred them from Saint Benedict's, full stop. Said if I caught them trying to conduct so-called business under this roof again, I'd ring the City of Westminster police. Or inform on them to somebody like you," he added, looking Tony in the eye.

Tony sighed. "Is it that obvious?"

Gert, who was squirting Purell on her hands for no apparent reason, looked up. "Did I miss something?"

Cedric attempted a modest shrug, but his smug grin gave him away. "I've served in shelters and soup kitchens for twenty years. Three kinds of homeless folks come through my doors. Those who are mentally ill and compelled to roam. Even if they have a place, they won't stay there. Then there are those who've been knocked down by life once too often. Maybe by drugs. Maybe the drink. Maybe by something so bad it blotted out part of their soul, like a total eclipse blots out the sun. Last but not least is the grifters. Grifters always got a story. Who wronged them, how much they've suffered, and how much it'll cost to get them out of your face.

"At first, I thought that was you," Cedric continued, still grinning. "But you don't have a sob story about the wicked old Council, or your kids stealing your pension, or how you need bus fare to Dunstable. And you carry yourself like a man who's unafraid. Walked into this place like you owned it. That makes you a copper, I reckon."

"Well done." Tony abandoned his put-on Welsh accent. "Former copper. Private detective, now."

"Oh! Dead posh, aren't you?" Gert sounded delighted. "Could you really infiltrate the No-Hopers? I mean, no offense, but have you seen them?"

"I've seen some blokes around, dressed in black. Girls, too, with dark makeup and a funereal aesthetic, as it were."

"Blue or purple hair. Lip rings, nose rings. Tongue studs," Gert said. "Not one of them older than thirty. Except for the leader, Aaron, and he dresses young."

"They favor the anarchy symbol," Cedric put in. "You'll see it painted on their coats or sewn on their messenger bags. The letter A with a circle around it."

"I'm familiar," Tony said. "And I understand your skepticism. But as for infiltrating them—you might be surprised. Sometimes a harmless old git can wander in where a more appropriate young person is taken far more seriously. And therefore, is at greater risk."

* * *

IT WAS PURE COINCIDENCE, not suspicion, that led to Tony's last clue of the day. He had departed Saint Benedict's with the intention of walking to the Leadenhall building. As Tony the homeless man, he would enter via the parking garage, take the stairs to the floor where his Lexus was parked, open the boot, chuck in bits of his costume—that risible bucket hat in particular—retrieve his coat and wingtips, and ride the lift up to the Hetheridges' sublet condo. He'd done this so many times, one could reasonably have expected someone on One-oh-One's security staff to have stopped him, especially on the long walk from the street up to the Lexus, and inquire what a homeless man was doing wandering about the garage. But despite what Tony assumed were active CCTV cameras with menacing red lights burning steadily, no one ever seemed to notice his questionable behavior. One-oh-One's management policed the semi-public atriums with religious zeal, but seemed less interested in secondary points of entry.

It was his thought about the CCTV cameras in One-oh-One's garage—were they cost-cutting dummies?—that caused Tony to halt and retrace his steps. Just because he'd taken the Keene case off Cecelia Wheelwright's hands didn't mean he should assume her agency had done a thorough job of requisitioning footage. The café Gert had mentioned in her text, Anatolia's, was familiar to him. Hadn't it been in the news around Christmas?

Yes, it had. Something about an armed robbery, or at least a violent altercation. The mention of Anatolia's and the timing of the disturbance was probably mere coincidence, but like Hannah Keene, Tony refused to believe coincidences existed. He decided to wander into Anatolia's and check the position of their CCTV cameras.

"I know, love. It's hard to trust. But at some point you'll have to." A familiar voice cut through the chatter of Londoners and tourists, most of whom were on their way out of the City. After the close of business, it would be a virtual ghost town until the financial markets opened the next day.

Tony spied Gert inside one of Britain's iconic red phone booths, the kind that still adorned everything in the tourist shops, from commemorative plates to men's boxers. Though pay phones had all but disappeared from modern life, the phone booths were too well-loved to give up. BT had repurposed several of them into Wi-Fi hotspots. Thus Gert was using her own mobile, but the booth provided both relative privacy and a signal boost.

"What about the photo?" she asked as Tony moved closer, pretending to examine a flyer advertising a flat to let. "Did you run it through FaceFinder?"

She paused to listen as Tony's eyes moved over the flat's details, unseeing. So Gert's genial incompetence while locating her mobile had been a put-on. And those accidental flashes had been a shrewd way of checking into Tony via facial recognition software, much of which was available for free online.

"See?" Gert's tone suggested she was pleased with the answer the person on the other end gave. "This could be your moment. He told me he'll keep turning up in Westminster, day after day. He's not giving up, kiddo."

Gert fell silent listening for so long, the words of the flat advertisement actually penetrated Tony's brain.

Lovely double bedsit, inclusive of all bills. Mattress and wardrobe provided. £300 per week. Deposit of £4500 required. No pets. No time-wasters.

With rates like that, Saint Benedict's won't be closing its doors anytime soon, he thought. The final insult, "No time-wasters," was so outrageous, it nearly made him miss Gert's parting words into her mobile.

"All right, love. Friday at the Horse Guards parade. Twelve sharp. Don't stand me up!"

Smiling, Tony inserted himself into an amorphous tour group, drifting along with them until he was halfway home. In a matter of days, unless he was very much mistaken, he'd finally meet Mark Keene in the flesh.

CHAPTER TEN

$\mathcal{P}$aul did take PC Kincaid out to an early lunch, not because he was in any mood to obey DCI Jackson, but because he didn't know what else to do. His alternate plan, writing a thermonuclear letter of resignation and posting it on Twitter for the world to see, was a little too final. Hadn't he told his mates this might happen? Hadn't he practically introduced himself to Kate, that very first day, by mentioning the career albatross around his neck?

Maybe I thought I could ward it off by talking about it. The way talking about what you want seems to guarantee it never comes to pass, he thought.

It was pushing two o'clock. PC Kincaid had long since returned to the Yard, eager to crack on with his first trainee assignment— tackling the phone calls on Paul's afternoon to-do list. That meant Paul could stay right where he was, a booth opposite the telly in a Weatherspoon's bar. They were doing two-for-one pints, the better to delight tourists and day-drinkers. He was on his fourth, which meant he'd seen the inside of the men's room more than once and his head was beginning to hurt. He'd never make a proper drunkard. He always started feeling poorly long before he got well and truly hammered. Which was too bad, because getting hammered was the only socially-approved masculine way to process disappointment—make that shame—of which he knew.

Kyla should be home tonight, he reminded himself. *Maybe I can cry on her shoulder.*

Except he wouldn't. She'd think him weak. He didn't like to admit that to himself, but it was true. Emmeline would have commiserated with him a bit before switching to tough love, which for her meant one of two things: taking positive action, or changing the subject. Emmeline would consider excessive moping weak, but she wouldn't judge him for failing to conquer within his chosen career. She'd tell him he gave it a shot, and that was more than most people did, when the going got tough. Whereas Kyla….

Truth is, I don't know what she'd say, Paul thought. *But I can't help thinking she'd see me as a loser from here out. If I leave the MPS, or accept whatever downshift I'm given, I'll have to convince her it was all my idea. That I'm in charge.*

The game on the telly was bollocks; the color commentary, colorless. As usual, when the TV screen failed him, Paul turned to the smaller one on his phone for comfort. He was scrolling through Twitter, watching animal vids and liking the pithier comments, when his phone buzzed. Incoming text.

Detective Bhar. A friend gave me your number. We've never met but I feel as if I know you. Something dangerous is happening. I want to tell the police, but must be discreet. Can't go the usual route. My friend said you're accustomed to delicate situations. Please call so we can arrange to meet.

The message came from an unknown number. Paul sighed. The trouble with being a smart-alecky piss-taker was that payback always lurked around the corner. Every day he said or did something that enraged a PC, DC, DS, or higher ranked officer who swore vengeance. Now that he was in career purgatory, the word was probably out. Knowing that no detective, especially one in need of a win, could resist the offer of a juicy tip, one of Paul's esteemed colleagues had no doubt sent him the text. If he bit, Mendelsohn would probably answer with, "Oi, Pepe Le Pew! You got Prince Albert in a can?"

He texted back one word—Crimestoppers—followed by the official tip line number.

Almost immediately came the reply:

One person died this morning. More will die if I can't find a way to pass on what I know without becoming a victim too. BTW it wasn't a car bomb. It was a group of hackers. The No-Hopers.

That reference to Ford Fabian's murder got his attention. None of his colleagues would use the privileged details of an ongoing investigation in a wind-up. He took a final sip of his lager, exited, and staked out a corner between the pub and a Waitrose. Then he rang the number, which picked up on the second ring. The caller didn't speak.

"Detective Sergeant Paul Bhar," he snapped. "You called me. What do you know about the death of Mr. Fabian?"

"Hi. Um. Listen." It was a woman with a posh accent. "Here's the thing. I need to talk to you in person."

"Why not now?"

"You could be recording this."

"I'm not."

"But how do I know? I have to take care. If you publish what I say and release the tape as proof, I'm dead. Full stop."

Paul sighed. The bloody lager had started his headache, and this phone call was exacerbating it fast. "You have me mixed up with the press. I'd need a warrant to record this call," he said, leaving out the fact that recording conversations for personal use was perfectly legal.

"It's not that I don't trust you," the woman said. "I know you worked with Lord Hetheridge and his new wife."

"Why not call one of them, then?" Paul asked, enabling an app. Now he *was* recording the call, just in case.

She sighed. "Look. I can't give you proof the No-Hopers killed Ford Fabian. But I can tell you how I know they did it. I can also tell you why. But I want to meet you face to face. If I'm risking my life, you owe me that much, don't you?"

The small hairs on the back of Paul's neck stood up. Ever since he'd first glimpsed a black dog—the dog that had turned out to be Sir Duncan's—he'd been jumpy, prone to letting himself get spooked over little or nothing. Unkind people suggested it was because of the knifing he'd suffered last October, a wound that could have been fatal. Kate had flat-out told him that until he faced down another physical threat in the field, he'd be oversensitive, fearing danger beneath every shrub.

"Where did you want to meet?" he asked. "Dark alley? Abandoned warehouse?"

She made a little sound of amusement. Clearly, her fear of being killed hadn't snuffed out her sense of humor. "I was thinking of somewhere very public. People, CCTV cameras, security guards. Like the V&A."

She meant the Victoria and Albert Museum, a huge, world-class repository of art that Paul, like many Londoners, hadn't visited in a dog's age. As far as safe spots to meet, the V&A certainly ticked the boxes. Admission was free, too. London was one of the most expensive cities in the world, but it made loads of art available to all.

"I can be there in twenty minutes by Tube," he said. As one final test, he added, "Just let me call this in to my guv. If you don't want me to bring DS Hetheridge for some reason, there's a trainee who'd love to take notes."

"Don't call it in. And don't bring anyone else. I mean it," the woman said firmly. "I'll freely give you the information. I can't go on if I don't tell someone. But I'm not ready to die. Hear me out, Detective. Give me five minutes. If you think I'm a liar, walk away."

"Fine. The museum is gargantuan," Paul pointed out. "Where will I find you?"

"Go to the café. Beyond the dining room, there's a courtyard. A bit of lawn where the artists and Uni kids congregate. I'll be there."

"Text me your picture so I'll know you."

"No. Just be there. I'll know you."

"At least tell me what you're wearing."

"Black," she said, and rang off.

* * *

THOUGH ADMITTANCE TO THE V&A was free, there was a suggested donation for patrons with means. Paul dropped a couple of coins into the Lucite collection box and headed for the café. During the short walk from the South Kensington station to the museum, his headache had eased. Maybe, just maybe, Ms. Posh Voice would turn out to be the real thing. A repentant hacker, or maybe one of the killer's ex-girlfriends. Past lovers with axes to grind made the best snouts.

"That will be 40*p*," the girl at the café cash stand said, looking at Paul as if he might be an alien. Everyone else in the queue had trays laden with sandwiches, slices of pie, and bags of crisps. He had a pint bottle of chocolate milk, which he fully intended to drink, once he was sure his lager had settled.

The V&A's dining room was full up. The crowd, unremark-able: pensioner couples; battalions of uniformed schoolchildren; mums and babies and toddlers.

Outside, in the sunny courtyard with its round reflecting pool and carpet of grass, the teens and young adults had self-segregated. Paul saw giggling girls, morose boys, artists with sketchpads, couples, loners, and a handful of mobile addicts who lurked in the shadows, the better to see their screens. He quickly realized he was the only adult male, which made him instantly uncomfortable. A lone man in business attire among scores of teens wasn't a good look. The only other grownup was a black-habited nun, seated on the reflecting pool's stone lip and sipping a bottle of water.

Can't be.

As if reading his mind, the nun's head turned. Even from where he was standing, he could tell she was fully made up, including carmine lips. In her extravagant black and white wimple, she looked like the understudy of Maria in an especially glitzy *Sound of Music* revival.

Might as well get this over with, Paul told himself, marching toward her. It was on his lips to greet her by saying, "You look ridiculous." Then he recognized the face inside the wimple and stopped dead.

"Oh, my," he said. Except he didn't say "my." And the word he did use, seemingly hurled in the face of a woman of God, made even the most jaded teens stop talking and stare.

"Hello, Detective," said Lady Isabel Bartlow, half-sister of Sir Duncan Godington.

CHAPTER ELEVEN

"*B*aiting me with a dog wasn't enough?" Paul demanded. "Now he's sending *you* to do his dirty work?"

"Oi! Mate! Shouldn't be shouting at a nun," one of the sullen teen boys said.

"Say the word and I'll report him for you," one of the girls added.

"I'm sure that won't be necessary." Lady Isabel gave the pair a resplendent smile. "This gentleman's a policeman. I've never felt more safe. I know it's a public courtyard. But would you and your friends mind giving me and the detective a little space? Even though I've no right to ask?"

The boy, spotty-faced with thick specs, looked dazzled. "Sure. Why not? C'mon," he told his friends. Grumbling a little, the teens obeyed their leader, relocating closer to the V&A's Victorian red brick edifice.

"Bless you," Lady Isabel called after the kids, the wooden beads of her crucifix rattling. When they were out of earshot, she told Paul, "I would have told you who I was over the phone, but I knew you'd tell me where to go. It's understandable. But I swear to you, Duncan isn't involved."

"How did you get my private number?"

"I stole it."

"From...?"

She sighed. "Duncan's mobile. I'm sorry. I don't know how he got it. He has a thing about you. And Kate and Tony Hetheridge, obviously."

"Dressing as a Catholic sister is a little over the top. Why rent a Halloween costume?"

"I didn't rent it. It came from my closet," Lady Isabel said. "My brother and I went through a costume party phase. Duncan was the priest. I was his girlfriend, the pregnant nun. Same outfit, I just left out the pillow padding."

"You people make me sick," Paul said in a soft, fervent whisper. He didn't believe she had any information to share, so he had nothing to lose by speaking his mind. This was another trick, another obscene parlor game for the homicidal rich. Lady Isabel's easy manners and tinkling laugh persuaded many to think her an innocent bystander in her brother's crimes, but Paul never had.

His hostility didn't seem to shake her. "I didn't ask you here so I could win you over. I have a story to tell, and I want you to hear it."

"Why not ask Kate? You've made her acquaintance," Paul said. "Or Tony. You've known him socially for years."

"Duncan is watching them closely. He would have noticed."

"But he's lost interest in me, is that it?"

"In a sense." She looked around the courtyard. Near the café's glass doors, a security guard had appeared. He was looking in their direction.

"Please. Sit down. Listen," Lady Isabel pleaded. "If the guard thinks we're disturbing the peace, he'll come over and recognize me right away."

"No, he won't. You're not famous like your brother."

"No, but I'm on the board of this museum. It's one of the reasons I chose it. That, and the fact Duncan has never willingly set foot in here. He finds art very dull. These days, I'd gladly live here, just to escape from him, if such a thing was possible."

"You expect me to believe that? You're on the outs with your half-brother, soulmate, and… whatever else he might be?"

"I don't expect you to believe, or disbelieve. I hope," Lady Isabel said, staring into Paul's eyes, "that you'll sit down and listen. That's all I ask. I swear."

He loathed her. Never in his life had he seriously contemplated attacking a woman, yet it crossed his mind that he could dig his fingers into the soft flesh of her neck and snap it long before any lovestruck teens or security guards could intervene.

But that wasn't him. He wasn't a killer. He was a copper. Even if he could overcome his deep respect for the rule of law, for its impartial application as symbolized by Lady Justice atop the Old Bailey, he knew killing Lady Isabel for her years of complicity would never please him as much as seeing her convicted and put away for life.

Besides, though he could scarcely admit it to himself, there was something brittle about her today, an almost glassy shine to her gaze. And the makeup didn't entirely conceal the shadows beneath her dark brown eyes. If her brother had put her up to this, she wasn't enjoying it.

He sat down. In his coat pocket, his iPhone recording app had been switched on since he entered the V&A. He didn't care if the digital audio file later proved inadmissible. There was no way he was listening to whatever she had to say without recording every word.

"Right. Now. I can do this," Lady Isabel said, offering him a weaker version of the brilliant smile she'd turned on her teen defender. "Would you believe I've never told my story to another living soul? Only myself, very late at night, when dawn is just around the corner. That's when I can look at the truth, and claim it. At least until it burns off by the light of day."

Taking a deep breath, she lifted her chin and began.

* * *

"DUNCAN IS MY HALF-BROTHER. He's twelve years my senior. Imagine it. He was a big, strapping boy, on the cusp of all those teenage hormones, when I was a newborn. Utterly helpless in my cot. It's astonishing I grew up at all. I think that's down to our father, Sir Raleigh. He was frightened to death of Duncan, and in the course of protecting himself, he accidentally protected me. But I can't begin with my birth, because it skips ahead. You need to understand the true history of our family. And to understand that, you need to know about psychopaths.

"I suppose as a policeman you must receive some training. Not just statistics and individual case studies, but broader scientific data. Or maybe you don't. I find most people throw the word around too easily. On chat shows, in newspapers, everywhere you look, people are accusing one another of being a sociopath or a psychopath without any idea of what they're saying. My amateur career, if you will, has been devoted to abnormal psychology. So allow me to dictate the rules of the road.

"First. The word 'sociopath.' Put it aside. It's an idea based upon the *tabula rasa* model. The notion that every human being is born a soft, blank slate. You, me, Albert Einstein, Adolf Hitler. We all start with malleable personalities that are completely shaped by nurture. The society we keep, our parents, our neighbors, the church, the government — they all combine to produce a normal person or a dangerous person. It's a squishy concept, impossible to strictly measure or test for. So forget it.

"Psychopathy is different. It can be quantified. Psychiatrists can test for it. MRIs and EEGs can corroborate those tests. So the term psychopath has no intrinsic baggage, at least when properly used. To be scientifically labeled a psychopath doesn't point to society, your upbringing, or even your own personal choices. It's simply a series of ticked boxes, mostly deficits. Lack of conscience, of course. And lack of empathy.

"I wonder if a policeman can accept that. Your sort—and I mean that respectfully, even if I, as you said, make you sick—tends to reject any theory of crime that doesn't revolve around selfishness as a matter of free will. Sometimes I wonder how much free will any of us really have. Did you know children who will become adult psychopaths begin showing signs at age two or three?

"If you don't believe me, ask the administrators of large schools or institutions. They know, because they've seen it. Parents have seen it, too, even if it's taboo to say so. There's a belief, a lovely belief, as far as I'm concerned, that all children are innocent until corrupted by bad people, or bad choices. To say otherwise is to risk a public shaming. So there's a tension, I think, between the truth that can be observed and the truth that can be spoken.

"Perhaps that's why so many horror movies seem to be about possessed children. Evil kiddies with dead eyes, plotting to kill anyone who crosses them. It's a safe way to process the tragedy of a psychopathic child. In most cinema, the evil can be driven out. But in horror movies, nothing is fair. Good people suffer for no reason. Just like real life.

"So psychopathy is inborn. It also seems to run in families. Look at the Godingtons. On paper, we should have risen higher and contributed more. Yet violent, heedless tendencies always held us back.

"During the reign of Henry VII, there was a Godington—Richard Ivey—who was the natural son of Arthur Tudor. On the strength of that connection, he inherited property and a title—Earl—but managed to lose it all within a year, plus his life. He feared nothing, including his own death. So he made a sorry end of it, convicted of murder and beheaded on Tower Green. Family historians liked to say his erratic behavior was caused by his blue blood. Because he was a bastard, he was denied his royal prerogative, and without his royal prerogative, his aristocratic nature drove him mad. Nowadays we can say with almost total certainty that Richard Ivey was a psychopath.

"He isn't the only one. It's amazing the Godington name survived at all, but here we are, shut out of the Peerage, possessing no historic estate or heroic forebears. My father, Sir Raleigh, who I must decline to call Papa, did very little with his life because he lived almost entirely in the moment. Which is true of most psychopaths.

"Sir Raleigh had three passions: racing cars, partying, and sleeping around. No woman who knew what he was would have had him. But the rest of the family was determined to see him married, so they chaperoned him, if you will, with a *nouveau riche* heiress named Opal Grissom. Sir Raleigh didn't want to tie himself down to her, or anyone, so his father bribed him with a yellow Testarossa. If Opal received a bribe, other than a lot of broken promises, I don't know what it was. It was hoped that a calm, conventional girl like her would settle Sir Raleigh down. She didn't.

"Opal had two boys, Eldon and Duncan. Eldon was the very worst sort of rich boy. Banknotes out his arse. No personality but a sneer. At least he wasn't a psychopath. How's that for damning a man with faint praise? He lived his whole life in fear of Sir Raleigh. But not Duncan.

"I never knew Opal—she died before I was born—but she kept a journal. A few days before she died, she posted it to a friend for safekeeping, and many years later, my mother obtained it. In the journal, Opal said that even as a wee boy, Duncan never backed down or said sorry, no matter the punishment. Sir Raleigh would shout, swear, break his favorite toy, it didn't matter. Even at two years old, Duncan never cried or moped after a correction. He took revenge. Quietly.

"I can see by your face, Detective, that you doubt this journal of Opal's even exists. It does, I promise. If the Crown prosecutors had discovered it, and read it aloud during Duncan's triple murder trial, perhaps the verdict would have been different. According to the journal, when Duncan was four, he gathered up the keys to Sir Raleigh's yellow Testarossa and tossed them in the lake. When he was five, he poured bleach in Sir Raleigh's decanter of Balvenie single barrel. Of course, one whiff kept Sir Raleigh from taking a drink and poisoning himself. But the fact that a small child could conceive of and execute such a plan is singular, to say the least.

"When Duncan was seven, he attended a pool party and got into a fight with another boy. Opal's journal says Duncan slammed the other boy's head against the lip of the pool. While he was semiconscious, Duncan pushed the boy's face under water and held it there. If the adults hadn't intervened, he would've committed his first murder.

"I wish Opal's journal still existed. If it did, I'd gladly hand it over as proof. After Duncan was arrested, my mother threw it in the fire. Not to cover for him. To protect herself, and me, from the necessity of turning it over to Scotland Yard, and from testifying in court against Duncan as he looked on. No one, and I mean no one, who truly knows Duncan would ever risk speaking negatively of him on the record.

"This doesn't mean everyone who interacts with Duncan comprehends the danger. He's always had his hangers-on. The Cult of Sir Duncan, I call them. The latest ones are those hackers I mentioned, the No-Hopers. And society is full of halfwits who view him as an exotic diversion. To them, hosting Duncan at their dinner party is a coup, like hosting a vampire—a charming, witty vampire who assures everyone he's not thirsty for blood. Not just yet.

"But inside the family, everyone's terrified of him. And by extension, they're terrified of me. My own mother holds me at arms-length. Just close enough to try and keep me happy. Just far enough not to become a blip on Duncan's radar.

"But where was I? Opal. Poor Opal. She was trapped in her

marriage to Sir Raleigh. Her greatest comfort, according to her journal, was his obsession with chasing other women. He didn't spend enough time at home to make her completely miserable. But after the swimming pool incident, she stopped telling herself her boys were thriving and nothing else mattered. She knew something was wrong with Duncan.

"So she made the rounds, taking him to see all the best child psychiatrists. A world-famous kiddie shrink in New York City diagnosed Duncan as a sociopath. In the mid-80s, that was the hot diagnosis. After declaring Opal a cold, unfeeling parent – which he in turn blamed on England, which he called a cold and unfeeling country – he suggested therapy to teach Duncan respect for interpersonal norms. Whether or not this would prevent him from attacking another child or spiking his father's whiskey with a less obvious poison, the world-famous kiddie shrink couldn't say.

"The next doctor, an ultra-spendy one on Harley Street, scoffed at the notion of a child sociopath. As he saw it, Duncan was delightful and highly cooperative boy. He'd simply let his emotions run away with him from time to time. Talk about a case study. The Harley Street emeritus, hoodwinked by an eight-year-old psychopath.

"The third expert, a Canadian who worked mostly with troubled adults, interviewed Duncan several times before giving his opinion. He told Opal he preferred not to label a child, but Duncan's impulsivity was high, his empathy was virtually nonexistent, and his utter disregard of punishment were all key indicators of someone who would spend most of his life in institutions. Opal believed the third expert. She said it was almost a relief to hear someone calmly, rationally confirm her own observations.

"Unfortunately, the Canadian offered no treatment. Only extrapolations based on his studies. He said Duncan was likely to become violent at school. He would never understand why rules and laws ought to be obeyed, so he'd have to be watched, constantly. The expert suggested Opal keep a log of Duncan's violent and antisocial behaviors. Then she could use that documentation to get him institutionalized as quickly as possible.

"I wish she'd done as he suggested. It's almost unfathomable, how different my life might've been if she had. But she loved Duncan. She lived for him. Sir Raleigh was selfish and heartless, and Eldon was his mini-me, vain and high-handed. But Duncan could be so charming. And he'd never taken revenge on Opal. He'd never tossed her keys in the lake or poisoned her drink. According to her journal, he was solicitous with her in a way he never was with others. If she looked sad, he noticed. If she wanted a hug or a kiss, he gave it, even though he shied away from displays of affection with others. Opal believed that he loved *her*, and that made her hope he could learn to love others.

"She took Duncan back to the famous kiddie shrink in New York City. He designed an immersive therapy to be administered by a team in London. For two years, Duncan had therapy seven days a week. And it seemed to work. Everyone was happy. Everyone, except Sir Raleigh.

"He was hitting middle age, and the change didn't agree with him. He'd worn out his welcome with his old mates. They'd become devoted to their families, kicked the booze and cocaine, started voting Tory. It infuriated Sir Raleigh, losing his place in society, so he decided to play man of the house. That's when he realized just how much time Duncan spent in the care of psychiatric professionals. He thought it reflected badly on the family. Other red-blooded lads were out playing football while his neurotic boy was lying on a fainting couch, talking about his feelings. He told Opal it had to end. For the first time, she stood up to him. Said Duncan had to keep up the therapy. Sir Raleigh beat her black and blue. She couldn't show her face out-of-doors for more than a month.

"You don't look shocked to hear that. Maybe you learned about Sir Raleigh during the course of the trial? You must have. He was on trial as much as Duncan, if not more so. His character was so repulsive, the defense counselor made reference to it as often as possible. It made Duncan look sympathetic by comparison.

"Sir Raleigh was violent with many women over the course of his life, but he developed a special viciousness toward Opal. After the first beating, he couldn't seem to stop hitting her. Opal chronicled it in her journal for a few months. Then she seemed to give up. She posted the journal to a friend with an enclosed note asking her to keep it safe. Two days later, she was dead. The official diagnosis, cerebral aneurysm. Supposedly it had gone undiagnosed. Popped off one day, nobody's fault, just one of those things.

"I'm sure you remember what happened next. Sir Raleigh hired a nanny to rear Eldon and Duncan. Soon after, he was shagging her, and soon after that, she was dead. Books by crime writers who've never met my brother always point to the death of the nanny, Marcy McNabb, as the beginning of Duncan's career in homicide. They think he killed her, probably in a fit of jealousy, and turned evil thereafter. Usually the theory goes like this: Duncan loved his mother in the Oedipal sense. Therefore, he was enraged when his father took up with another woman. Too young and weak to take on Sir Raleigh, he killed Marcy McNabb instead. Not a bad theory, but wrong.

"Early in his therapy, the clinicians gave Duncan a puppy. The idea was for him to form a relationship with the dog and acquire empathy. Everyone expected him to kill the poor thing, I think, but Duncan bucked the trend. I don't remember the breed, but I know he adored it. Plus, it was a never-ending source of filth, which he could use as a weapon against Sir Raleigh, Eldon, or anyone else who displeased him. Marcy McNabb, not being an animal lover, decided the household would be more hygienic without pets. She got rid of Duncan's dog. He got rid of her. Simple as that.

"There was an inquiry into her death. Sir Raleigh was the prime suspect, but of course it came to nothing. As I understand it, no one ever looked Duncan's way. He behaved carefully around the policeman. Two years of therapy hadn't given him a visceral fear of consequences — nothing could do that – but he did gain an intellectual appreciation of them. In therapy, Duncan learned to defer his impulses if they were likely to produce a punishment that curtailed his freedom. The expectation was to make him a better citizen. The actual result was to make him function smoothly in society and commit murders whenever he liked.

"After the McNabb inquiry was closed, Sir Raleigh decided it was time for another wife. He married my mum, Helen, and she gave birth to me seven months after she said 'I do.' Duncan was at Eton. Eldon was at Oxford. Apart from brief, obligatory phone calls, Sir Raleigh pretended they didn't exist. A state of affairs that suited them, I shouldn't wonder. They stayed at their dorms year-round. They weren't allowed to come home, even for Christmas.

"But when I was three and my baby sister, Pansy, was about six months old, Sir Raleigh had a heart attack. It happened on the twenty-fourth of December. Duncan and Eldon were permitted to come home so everyone could pray for a Christmas miracle— that Sir Raleigh would die, of course. He didn't, but he was too weak to order his sons out. Eldon went back to Oxford after a week, but Duncan stuck around.

"I have so many snaps of me and Duncan from that winter. Him carrying me on his shoulders. Playing Barbies with me. Helping me bake a cake. I don't know why he took to me. He was fifteen, I was three. And there was no whiff of interference, of ugliness. Perhaps I was his pet dog all over again. It was a happy time for me, but not Mama, because Pansy died. People called it a cot death. It wasn't, of course, and Mama suspected Duncan.

"She made a plan to leave Sir Raleigh. She had to be careful. If she told him straight out that she wanted a divorce, she might turn up dead, like Opal. So she secretly got her affairs in order. She hired a private detective to dig into the Godingtons in hopes of finding something to hold over Sir Raleigh's head. The PI turned out to be indispensable, not only to her, but to me. In her case, he discovered a juicy piece of leverage, one that sent Sir Raleigh's solicitors scurrying. He agreed to the divorce.

"For the next ten years, I saw Duncan not at all, and forgot him, truth be told. Mostly I forgot Sir Raleigh, too. Life was orderly and safe. Rather dull, really, until Duncan came back into my life. By then, I was thirteen years old and he was twenty-four.

"He'd just returned from Borneo. Fresh off his first expedition into the jungles and the handsomest man I'd ever seen. Hair bright from the sun. Tanned like an American. Charming and witty and an astonishing conversationalist. He knew everything and I knew nothing. Except I wanted more.

"Of course, Mama didn't arrange the visit. He turned up on her doorstep one evening and she was too quintessentially English to shut the door in his face. Can you imagine telling a family member to bugger off? It can't be done. Even if he might be a murderer. I mean, what's the mere possibility of being murdered in your home compared to the undying memory of your own rudeness?

"I enjoyed every second of the visit. But the moment Duncan left, Mama closed the door, shot the bolt, and said never again. I went to pieces. I think it shocked her to the bone. Not that I was a thirteen-year-old brat, but how quickly and completely I'd fallen under his spell. So she sat me down at the kitchen table, gave me a mug of Horlicks, and told me Duncan was sick in the head. Said his homicidal tendencies weren't just rumors. That as far as she was concerned, he'd killed Pansy.

"I pretended to listen. But in those days, I thought myself a sterling judge of character. There was nothing wrong with Duncan. There couldn't be. An exceptional man like him would never murder anyone, much less a helpless baby. I decided Mama hated Sir Raleigh so much, she irrationally hated his son, too.

"Duncan knew he wasn't welcome at Mama's, so he never came back. But one day, he walked past my school when my class was at recess. Now I know his 'accidental' appearance was by design. At the time, I thought it was fate.

"I was one of those nauseating children who believed in love that crosses oceans. In two hearts that beat as one. In lovers who must never be separated, never mind the disapproval of the unfeeling world. I'll never forget that day, talking to him through the chain-link fence, him in a gray wool jumper and me in my school uniform with my backpack sitting at my feet. I felt transformed by his attention, certain every girl in my class would have given anything to be me.

"After school, he took me out for ice cream. He said he wanted us to become friends, but it would have to be a secret. I told him right away I'd never tell. Nothing made me happier than to swear loyalty. I would've cut my wrists to mix my blood with his if he'd asked.

"That spring was the spring of Duncan. He picked me up twice a week after school, taking me here and there. Little fun outings. On my fourteenth birthday, he gave me a present: a flat within walking distance of my school, exclusively for us. So we could meet.

"Mama never knew. My school friends were only too happy to help me keep her in the dark, because they didn't know Duncan was my half-brother. I considered that beside the point. So what if we had the same father? The heart wants what it wants. People today would say he was grooming me.

"I settled into the apartment. Duncan and I became intimate in every way. If that shocks or disgusts you, it's not my intent. I don't apologize for my choices. Especially the ones I made when I was a little girl who thought she was all grown up.

"So. Though I won't apologize, I will explain. Because as I grew older, as I went to Uni and was exposed to new ideas, my relationship with Duncan did begin to trouble me. Not because of consanguinity, but the other blood. The blood he spilled."

CHAPTER TWELVE

*L*ady Isabel paused before continuing. She spoke softly but clearly, without self-consciousness, as if none of the young people lounging in the courtyard could overhear, or that it would matter if they did. Apart from the moral concerns, which were certain to alienate jurors and would be harped on any competent defense counsel, she'd make the ideal witness, Paul thought. If she could be persuaded to testify, her calm, matter-of-fact manner of speaking would make her impossible for jurors to dismiss. Ex-lovers with axes to grind made the best snouts, it was true, but shaky witnesses. Blood relatives with deep insight were a prosecutor's dream.

After taking a moment to collect herself, Lady Isabel resumed her story.

"Now I need to tell you about the murders. I wish I could say I never knew. But Duncan concealed nothing from me. I didn't participate, but I was beside him every step of the way. I've never considered him evil. But he does evil things.

"At some point in your life, I'm sure you've heard a religious person debate an atheist. Quite often the religious person will argue, even if there is no God, people must *believe* there is a God, because only fear of God holds society together. In other words, human beings would rape, steal, and murder all the time, but for the fear that God will strike them down or consign them to hell.

"The atheist will say, I don't believe in God, but I reject rape, theft, and murder. Not because of fear of supernatural punishment. Because of empathy. To atheists, this is the only life we'll ever get. Every minute of every life becomes all the more precious if there are no cosmic reparations after death.

"But Duncan *is* the religious person's rhetorical argument come to life. He doesn't respect laws. He doesn't fear God. And that's why he kills.

"Pansy was his second murder. Marcy McNabb was killed in anger. Pansy died because Duncan decided to test himself. Find out once and for all if he was as sick as his therapists assured him he was. So he slipped into baby Pansy's room and stood over her in her cot. I don't remember her, of course, but I can imagine it quite clearly. Pansy at six months old with rosy cheeks and bright eyes. A bit of downy dark hair. Maybe she laughed when she saw Duncan looking down at her. Made those squeaky little sounds of pleasure, kicking her legs and arms. What did she feel when Duncan pinched her nose and mouth shut? No one can say. But when it was done, Duncan didn't feel a thing.

"I was seventeen when Duncan admitted this to me. He'd already told me about Marcy McNabb, and I'd absolved him, because it's easy to demonize an adult. But a baby?

"For one lucid moment, Detective, I foresaw this moment. Not sitting in the V&A courtyard dressed as a nun, of course, but disillusioned and confessing every sordid detail to a police officer. Maybe Duncan's actions weren't his fault. Maybe he really wasn't human, in the sense we understand the word. But I am. I have a responsibility, don't I?

"But the lucid moment fluttered away. The impulse to do the right thing is small. Weak. Like a little baby in a cot, lying there in her fleece onesie, looking up at you with big bright eyes. If you don't swoop in and pull it to you, if you don't seize the moment, the impulse dies. And the next time it comes to you, it's even smaller, even weaker, and easier to ignore.

"So I made excuses for Duncan. I told myself it was just a mistake, a terrible mistake, made when he was only a boy. I promised Duncan it didn't matter, and I would never leave him.

"But we needed fig leaves, as it were, to keep from being shunned by polite society. That brings me to my marriage. Blink and you missed it. I married Mike Bartlow on a whim. I did it to hurt Duncan, because we'd had a terrific row over his insistence on disappearing into jungles for months at a time. What seemed adventurous and romantic when I was a schoolgirl had turned into a bloody inconvenience, now that I was grown up and expected a plus-one at fêtes. Duncan couldn't understand why I wouldn't just go with him. But the life of environmental missionary? Dodgy water, dodgy electric, and no creature comforts, just the pleasure of my own zealotry. I wouldn't do it, even for him.

"Looking back, this was my greatest sin. If there is a God, and he threw me into Duncan's path to redeem him, then refusing to accompany Duncan into the jungle is where I failed. I let him go off alone, to dwell among beings he *did* value—orangutans—and watch poachers slaughter them, sometimes for food, sometimes for fun. If he'd developed even a flicker of empathy for human beings, it died in Borneo. I don't know how many poachers he killed while he was there, but it freed something in him. Like the lion who gets a taste for man.

"Sorry—I forgot to finish my thought about Mike. It says something, doesn't it? Even when I specifically bring up my ex-husband, I end up nattering about Duncan. That was the marriage in a nutshell. So Mike walked out on me, I went back to Duncan, and all was right with the world. No spilt blood. But the next time we had a row and went off one another, Duncan went on another murder spree. Not overseas. Here at home.

"He was angry with me, so he planned it alone, with help from the Cult of Duncan. After he was arrested for killing Sir Raleigh, Eldon, and the family butler, Jergens, I kept my distance. Not because I disapproved. They were terrible people. No one denies that, not even the Crown prosecutors. And after you forgive a man for suffocating a baby girl, forgiving his other murders is just maths. No, I kept my distance because of the Cult of Duncan. Specifically, Tessa Chilcott.

"I loathed Tessa with every fiber of my being. We were of a similar type, physically, and Duncan seduced her very young, just like me. The mere sight of her made me green with envy. She shook my worldview.

"At fourteen, I chose to believe I was a special girl. My half-brother was dashing and dangerous and I had every right to break the rules, because I was the one girl in all the universe who could tame him. Who could transform the beast into the prince. But when he started sleeping with Tessa, it hit me. Maybe any slim brunette who was young and dumb was all he needed? Maybe there was nothing special about me at all.

"You know what happened next. Duncan was acquitted, Tessa lost her mind, and he returned to me. The killings stopped. Not only was I special again, I was more special than I'd fully realized. Unlike Tessa, I could walk through the fire without getting burned. I was his better angel, his emotional touchstone. How many women can say that their illicit romance is for the greater good? That it quite literally keeps other people alive?

"But last October, I noticed a change. You remember the double murder in Mayfair. Duncan was a person of interest, naturally, so Tony and Kate turned up at our yearly Halloween party, pretending the visit was purely social. I thought their RSVP would make Duncan laugh. Instead, it made him angry. He ended up confronting Kate and Tony, and nearly came to blows. It was so out of character. When I said so, Duncan blamed it on migraines.

"Then came the Michael Martin Hughes investigation.

Duncan was a person of interest again. I genuinely believed he was innocent. After all, Hughes was poisoned, and Duncan is nothing if not hands-on. After your lot made the big arrest, I told Duncan that after two strikes, Scotland Yard would think hard about harassing him again. That's when he admitted he'd done it. He had a new Cult of Duncan, younger kids with computer skills, who'd helped him beat the CCTV cameras and provide an alibi.

"I was shocked. He was ignoring me and spending untold hours with the young people. He was stalking you with the dog, Kaiser, and spying on Kate from afar. But the strangest thing was how he killed Hughes. I asked, why poison? He said it was just easier. Then he went to bed with another migraine and stayed there for a week.

"I wanted a look at Duncan's medical charts, but he'd always been secretive about that sort of thing. Remember the private detective my mum found? The one who'd dug up dirt on Sir Raleigh? I knew he'd do anything if the price was right, so I engaged him again. He brought me Duncan's childhood brain scans.

"When Duncan was ten, one of his doctors enrolled him in a pediatric neurology study. The hope was to prove that many troubled children have no biologic abnormalities. But in Duncan's case, the CT scan revealed a small mass in his frontal lobe.

"It was ruled inoperable. It also seemed to be inert. The doctors observed it, and for years it didn't grow. But it's growing now.

"I'd never been through cancer with someone I loved. But I've seen the soppy movies. I've read the tearjerker books. And heaven knows we have money. I was ready to be Duncan's rock, to advocate for him every step of the way. I came clean to Duncan. Said I knew about his brain tumor and I knew it was malignant. I showed him a list of spas and clinics we could try. You know the type. Available only to the richest and best-connected people in the world, the court of last resort for celebrities. But Duncan wouldn't have it.

"He said when he was a boy, the world had done its best to convince him he was damaged. They'd shown him a shape on a bit of x-ray film and said, see, you'll never be human. Since then, someone had given him a new perspective. Another inductee into the Cult of Duncan. Lord Brompton's son, Mark Keene.

"I met Mark, once or twice, when I was trying to make Duncan see sense. He was strange. Subnormal, I think. Can I say that? Sorry. I'm subnormal, too. At any rate, Mark always wanted to talk about sacred geometry and the number 144 and mystical equations that hold the universe together. I thought he was barking, but Duncan loved hearing Mark talk. They understood each other. Suddenly a man who used to laugh at religion was saying, 'As above, so below.' He and Mark could happily swap inanities like that all day.

"Mark was the strangest of the No-Hopers, but the others weren't much better. Duncan met them through one of his other girls. I turn a blind eye—as I said, our relationship isn't based on physical fidelity. Two or three of them are skinny brunettes with doe eyes. Mark's sister was, too. She's dead now, but I'm getting ahead of myself.

"Duncan and Mark came up with a new way to look at the tumor. They decided it was actually part of a transformation process. That he was not less than human, with a gap in his mind or heart. That he was more than human. Superior.

"Therefore, the tumor wasn't a malignant lesion. It was a second brain, a superior brain, enabling Duncan to think more clearly than ever before.

"Nothing I said could convince him to go back to his doctors. He didn't need me anymore. He had Mark, and his other girls, and the No-Hopers. They're the most radical Cult of Duncan yet. I feel certain they killed Ford Fabian, simply because Duncan went on a rant about him. I don't have proof, but surely if you know where to look, you can find what you need. There's an office building in Westminster that Duncan owns. It's between Cardinal and Victoria. That's where the No-Hopers used to go. They moved after Mariah Keene died, but you should be able to pick up the trail.

"I know it's counterintuitive about Ford Fabian. The Fabians love to announce that their blood runs green. They might seem like Duncan's allies rather than enemies. But Duncan's a very practical conservationist. He's of the opinion that if you insist ordinary people give up cheese, steak, cars, hot showers, and so on and so forth, they'll throw up their hands and do nothing. As far as he's concerned, people like the Fabians set the Green movement back by making it easy for people to dismiss. So he hates politicians like Ford Fabian, and I know in my heart the No-Hopers killed him. Mark had an idea about hacking cars. If he's still with them, maybe he did it.

"I don't know if Duncan killed Mariah Keene. First, I thought she was one of his girls. Then I thought she was cozying up to him just to get Mark out. Then one day I picked up my phone and there it was—she was dead. I can't explain why he would have pushed her off the top of a building, but nothing Duncan does makes sense anymore. He hears the music of the spheres, or sees a spider web in the shape of a rhombus, thinks it's a sign, and boom, he's off again.

"I haven't seen him in a couple of weeks. Have you? One look at him will tell you everything I've said is true. He's leaner. Sharper. But less defined, like a knife that's had too much grinding. He can't have much longer left. I hoped he would go back to Borneo and die there. That's always been his plan. To die in the jungle, in a deep green space with no human voices and no human faces. But the last time we spoke, he told me he'd stay in London until he dealt with our father.

"I asked what he meant. I thought perhaps he intended to desecrate Sir Raleigh's headstone. It's not like he could dig up the corpse and violate it—he only left bits and pieces the first time around. He said he was walking Kaiser in Mayfair and saw Sir Raleigh, who threatened to kill him. At first I was mystified. Then I knew. And what came to me next was another tiny impulse to do the right thing. This time, I didn't let it die.

"I used to think it was odd, how he seemed taken by your colleague, Kate. She's no skinny brunette with doe eyes and half a brain. Then I looked up a picture of Opal Grissom before she married Sir Raleigh and I understood. She was a pretty girl with wild blonde hair, just like Kate. Maybe that's why Duncan believes Sir Raleigh is alive and well and living at the Leadenhall building. He means to kill Tony Hetheridge. And the No-Hopers are helping him plan it."

CHAPTER THIRTEEN

"*T*ony! Oh my God! Tony!"

When Henry burst into a room shouting his name that way, Tony found there was no point berating the boy. He seemed to be going through a phase where anything that delighted him had to be trotted over for inspection and approval. Tony had decided the best way to temper this was to silently, unhurriedly finish whatever he was doing, then politely ask Henry to repeat himself. But in this instance, Tony was bench pressing 130 kilograms without a spotter, a somewhat risky act in itself. Unhurriedly finishing up was therefore his only course.

Henry's face, as round as his owlish specs, drifted into Tony's line of sight as he lifted the barbell back into the frame. "130? That's a lot."

"Yes, it is." Sitting up, Tony mopped his forehead with a flannel. The suite's fitness room had come equipped with an elliptical trainer, a stepper/climber, a treadmill, mirrored walls, and a pyramid of free weights. Tony and Kate had moved in their own equipment, including Tony's powerlifting bench and chain-suspended heavy bag. The rest of the generous space was used

163

either for Tony's favorite form of exercise, fencing, or for Kate's, mixed martial arts.

Henry said, "You're not meant to lift that much without a spotter."

"True."

"Not behaving responsibly, are you?"

"I suppose not."

Henry continued studying him minutely. "Your face is awfully red."

"I shouldn't wonder. You do have some reason, I hope, for bursting in this way and subjecting me to critique?"

Ignoring the question, Henry said, "You don't have to worry about bullies. Why do you care if you stay fit?"

"Because I have a young wife. Now. I see you have the phone. May I assume it's for me?"

"Oh! Yeah. Sorry." Henry passed it over. "It's Paul. He said it was a police emergency and I should put you on the line right away."

"Then start with that, next time, and leave off the personal questions." Tony put the phone to his ear. "All right, Paul. What's happened? It's not Kate, is it?"

He listened. And listened. And listened some more, all the while quietly going through the stretches that were now a non-negotiable part of his routine. It was all very well to prioritize strength and cardiovascular stamina, but let him pull a hamstring or tear a ligament and he'd be sleuthing in a motorized scooter.

It took Paul almost ten minutes to debrief himself, even without interruption. All the while, Henry hovered about the fitness room, transparently feigning disinterest. It was curious, how easily Tony could balance three tasks in the moment: listening to Paul, performing his stretches, and keeping an eye on the boy. Perhaps nothing focused the mind like a credible death threat.

"Hang on, Paul," he said when the younger man finally paused for breath. "Henry! I don't suppose you have any homework for me to look over?"

The boy had the nerve to look blank. *What is this homework of which you speak?*

"I thought I could suit up and do some fencing practice," Henry ventured.

"Your teachers expect no papers from you tomorrow?"

"Maths," Henry muttered. "And a book report."

"Have you read the book?"

"Mostly."

"Off you go," Tony said.

Henry tried his wounded expression, the one that occasionally worked on Kate. Tony was stone.

Sighing, Henry trudged toward the door. He turned back at the threshold. "Will it be on the news? Paul wouldn't tell me. Is it bad?"

Tony put his hand over the receiver. "Office politics. People are losing their jobs. Paul wants advice on how to weather the storm."

Henry's shoulders slumped. "Crikey. I thought it was another terrorist attack." He left without further complaint.

Tony waited to hear the lift *ding* on the next floor up before closing the fitness room door and sitting down on the weight bench.

"Sorry, Paul. Had to bundle off the boy. Too clever by half, that one. Now." He took a deep breath. "Where are you?"

"Men's room, fourth floor of the new HQ," Paul said. "AKA the dead zone. I wanted to tell you everything before I told Jackson."

"Well done. Did Lady Isabel tell you where she was going after you spoke?"

"She said she was getting out of London for good. No details."

"Did she say which Godington residence Sir Duncan lives in now?"

"I asked. She said she didn't know."

"Did you get a sense if she might ever be persuaded to go on the record?"

"She won't," Paul said. "Maybe when we have her brother in custody. Maybe not."

"If your taped conversation is ruled admissible, it may be enough. Find Vic. Put the wheels in motion from your end," Tony said. "I'll go to work on mine."

* * *

ALTHOUGH RITCHIE DIDN'T OBSERVE boundaries, Tony still knocked on his open door before entering his room. "How was dinner?"

The plate on the unmade bed was empty, but for a couple of crusts. There was a reason Kate rarely ordered pizza. She saved it for times she wanted to immobilize Ritchie and Henry into food-induced ecstasy. Ritchie, a bit of tomato sauce dried on his chin, had plowed through the unexpected treat. Now he sat cross-legged on the floor, putting together a Batman-themed Lego set. He didn't answer Tony's query, or even look up.

"Word is, there may be Mr. Kipling cakes later," Tony said, popping into the room's en suite and returning to Ritchie with a damp flannel. "But you and Henry need to earn it by staying up here. Which should be no sacrifice. Lift your chin."

Ritchie paid no attention.

Tony put a hand on the younger man's shoulder. In the beginning, Ritchie had screeched in alarm when Tony touched him. Now he flinched, but didn't seem frightened. While he didn't welcome interruptions, and perhaps never would, he now trusted Tony enough to let him get close.

"Here we are." With one quick motion, Tony wiped the dried tomato sauce off his brother-in-law's chin. Kate could do absolutely anything to Ritchie, including spoon-feed him during a meltdown and give him a sponge bath when he felt poorly, but mere mortals like Tony had to attempt violations of Ritchie's personal space like a surgical strike. One quick move, a yelp of dismay, and that was it. You got what you got and moved on.

"Hey." Ritchie rubbed peevishly at his now-clean face. "Don't touch me."

"Sorry. Remember, there's a Mr. Kipling cake with your name on it, if you stay upstairs," Tony said lightly, dropping the flannel back in the en suite. "Keep up the good work with Batman."

"I want a Death Star," Ritchie said. "A classic Lego Death Star play-set with Harrods-exclusive Darth Vader figure and collectible trading card."

It was no good reminding Ritchie that he'd been assembling precisely that item when he'd burnt down half of Wellegrave House. Nor was Tony surprised that his often uncommunicative brother-in-law could recite the precise name of the toy as listed on the Harrods website. For three weeks, Ritchie had been making this demand daily to anyone who would listen: his paid daytime carer, random people in One-oh-One's lobby, and the man who sold candied almonds near Westminster tube station. All Tony could do was fall back on Kate's standard response, "Something to ask Father Christmas about," before going to check on Henry.

"Come in," the boy called cheerfully when Tony knocked. Like Ritchie, he'd abandoned his empty dinner plate on the bed and set up camp in the middle of the floor. Both Wakefield males seem philosophically opposed to chairs.

"Is it time for Mr. Kipling cakes?"

"Not yet," Tony said. "Finished reading, I take it?"

Henry, immersed in one of his comic books, closed it reluctantly and opened the assigned book, *Island of the Blue Dolphins* by Scott O'Dell.

"It's about a girl. That's it. One girl. There was a boy, and I thought I might care what happened to him, but he died straight away."

"Keep at it," Tony said. "I read that years ago. A tale of survival against all odds. As I recall, the girl befriends a wild dog."

Henry perked up. "But she just tried to kill Rontu, the leader of the pack."

"Then you're not far. I'll check back in a couple of hours. With the promised Mr. Kipling cake, so long as you stay up here without complaint."

"Any news about when the Internet router will be fixed?"

"A man will see to it first thing tomorrow," Tony lied. In truth, specialists from the MPS Cyber Crimes unit were engaging in a bit of digital sleight-of-hand that might take forty-eight hours to complete. From the outside, the Hetheridge family's IP address and DNS server would appear unchanged, the better to tempt hackers. But from now on, it would be continuously monitored until the No-Hopers were arrested. Meantime, a secondary closed system, fully secure, would provide the family slower, safer web access, once it was up and running. Cyber Crimes did their job well, but fast was another story.

"Kate said you're having people over. It's not a party, is it?" Henry asked.

"Good Lord, no."

"Who, then?"

"Our interior designer, the head of construction, and a conservation officer from Historic England. Kate and I will be going over samples of reclaimed wood, negotiating about the sort of oil-based paint permitted on the ground floor, and examining vintage wallpaper swatches."

The boy groaned. "*Boring*. I don't know how grownups stand it."

"Boring, indeed."

Smiling, Tony closed the door. Within the condo, he usually took the stairs—too much reliance on the lift, and his arthritic left knee would take it as a form of capitulation—but this time, he bowed to technology. Before exiting to the living room, he used the car's internal keypad to disable it. Then, for good measure, he locked the stairwell door. Now there was no way Henry or Ritchie could slip downstairs, and if they obeyed him, they'd never know the difference. Ritchie was less of an issue, though one never knew what he might absorb and repeat at the wrong moment. But Henry noticed too much, drew astute conclusions, and would recognize Assistant Commander Michael Deaver and DCI Vic Jackson on sight.

It *did* look like a party in the living room—a hanging party, perhaps, or a wake. Everyone was dressed in black or gray, the colorless tones of men and women with access to secrets. The liaison from the Home Secretary was working quietly on his laptop. Tony's friend and ex-boss AC Deaver, his long face longer than ever, was on the receiving end of a phone conversation which required him to do no more than murmur, "I see," from time to time. Vic Jackson, who looked like a man with a rash in an unmentionable place, was thumbing through a thick hardcopy file from his personal collection. In the kitchen, a Cyber Crimes specialist was going over the specs for both of Tony's cars, the silver Lexus and the classic Bentley. Neither contained the proper computer interface to be hackable, which was one benefit of driving cars until the doors fell off.

As Tony entered the living room the MPS specialist, a young blonde with specs and a jaunty ponytail, looked up from her work. She'd taken over the coffee table, which was now piled with tech debris: empty boxes, torn plastic bags, and bits of paper.

"Your new mobiles are all set," she told Tony.

"Sir," AC Deaver corrected the specialist.

"Sir," she repeated, inflectionless. Apparently her blonde ponytail was the sprightliest thing about her. Tony didn't care. Like Kate, he'd surrendered his iPhone as a potentially hackable item. If Box 500, as people generally referred to MI5 in mixed company, could give him and Kate more secure mobile phones to use during this crisis, the specialist's brusque manner troubled him not at all.

"Same number?" he asked as Kate drifted to his side.

"Yes." The ponytailed specialist handed an identical mobile to Kate.

"We're restricted to calls only, I take it?" she asked.

"For maximum security, yes. So you won't forget, I didn't install an Internet browser or text messenger," the specialist replied. "For those functions, you'll have a secure PC. See those laptops, charging on the bar top? They're downloading the last bits of firmware now."

"Perfect," Kate said, sliding an arm around Tony. Before the meeting, she'd been slightly agitated, concerned that Henry or Ritchie might choose this night to misbehave in a way that would reveal the truth. Now that both Wakefield males were happily bribed with take-out pizza and the promise of Mr. Kipling cakes, Kate was perfectly composed.

"Does this have a brand name?" Paul asked, fiddling with his heavy, distinctly unsexy new phone. His iPhone had been entered into evidence hours ago.

"It's a Blackberry variant. Made for us alone," the specialist said. "Good news. You hold in your hands the most exclusive, limited-edition mobile you'll probably ever own."

"Lucky me. Cheers." Smiling at Tony, Paul slipped the secure mobile into his coat pocket. "So. Where are we?"

Tony looked toward AC Deaver, who'd quietly concluded his call, an emergency briefing from his counterpart at MI6. This sort of off-the-record coordination between services, bypassing labyrinthine processes in favor of speed and accuracy, was Deaver's specialty.

Strictly speaking, Tony had no right to any information about the new investigation of Sir Duncan. Hearsay death threats of current and former civil servants were taken seriously, of course, but they were literally daily occurrences. SIS had the resources to pinpoint the whereabouts of a public figure like Sir Duncan, who carried a BTS mobile, paid for everything with chip and pin credit cards, and traveled in and out of London on his Syberjet Sj30. What SIS couldn't do, on the basis of a hearsay threat, was pass on that critical data to a retired policeman. And neither, in his official capacity, could Deaver.

"Tony, you have an office one floor down, do you not?" Deaver looked to him for confirmation. "Excellent. Gentlemen. And lady," he added, nodding at the ponytailed specialist. "Thank you for all your help. Now, if you please, give us the room. We'll call you back after we've had time to confer."

After the MI5 agents and Cyber Crimes techs had filed down-stairs—a comfortable space where they couldn't overhear anything that would make them a party to improper or illegal actions—only Deaver, Jackson, and Paul remained. Kate sat down. Tony stayed on his feet. It was easier to project calm that way, and above all, calm was essential.

"First," Deaver said. "The bad news. The No-Hopers aren't on our radar to any significant degree. They don't appear to traffic in the drugs or sex trade. One or two people associated with them have been arrested in the last twenty-four months, but in both cases, the charge was aggravated trespass for BASE jump-ing. Neither stuck in criminal court, and both were reduced to simple trespass in civil court. The No-Hopers are classified as an Urbex group. A nuisance."

Tony took that in. Perhaps Mariah Keene's death *had* been an accident, the unintended consequence of climbing a half-completed high rise for the fun of it. Moreover, perhaps Mark Keene's influence had not only transformed Sir Duncan's outlook, but the No-Hopers' mission, too.

"Second," Deaver said. "Regarding Lady Isabel Bartlow. She's liquidating her London real state at what can only be called fire sale prices. She also appears to have purchased a cottage in St. Ives via a shell company. These actions don't prove she's in fear for her life, of course, but they indicate her desire to give up the social butterfly routine and go incognito, at least for a time."

"I don't think she was playing mind games with me," Paul said.

"I don't think you're capable of discerning, one way or the other," Deaver retorted. "At the close of this meeting, you will disassociate yourself from the Sir Duncan and Lady Isabel matter altogether. Rest assured, DCI Jackson will keep you occupied with other concerns."

As if responding to some telepathic baton pass, Jackson cleared his throat. "You know the drill, Bhar. The less you're involved, the fewer excuses Godington's defense brief can make as he stands in the dock. If Lady Isabel leaves you a message, bring it to me. If she calls, use your new mobile's record option. If something unexpected happens, don't act alone. Come to me for guidance. Until the situation is resolved, you're not to visit your mates here, or at Wellegrave House. Even at the office, I'll ask you to strictly limit any conversations with DS Hetheridge to unrelated professional matters. Am I clear?"

Tony needed no telepathy to perceive Paul's frustration, but he was pleased when his former subordinate agreed to Jackson's order swiftly and with due respect. Paul's desire to redeem himself was perfectly understandable. But if he gave in to that desire, Sir Duncan and his complicit half-sister might once again get away with murder.

"Now comes the good news," Deaver said, reclaiming the floor. "Our friends at SIS tell us Sir Duncan Godington flew out of Heathrow on his private jet three days ago. London to Brunei. No stops, no tricks. Godington ticked all the requisite security boxes. Heathrow provided CCTV images. See for yourself."

On his secure laptop, he pulled up the pictures for Tony, Kate, Paul, and Jackson to review. As Tony expected, they had been passed on via an anonymous email account, which signaled the origin was someone in SIS. Although the black and white stills were light on detail, they clearly depicted a tall, well-dressed man with bright blond hair. Judging by the faces of the airport employees, many of whom were beaming, England's most charming eco-warrior hadn't lost his touch.

"Lady Isabel told me he was sick," Paul said. "That one look at him would prove it."

"Yeah, and she said Godington wouldn't leave London until he'd settled his score with Tony," Jackson said. "She's a liar, mate. Just like her brother."

"Lady Isabel's manner is nothing if not sincere," Tony said. "I've never seen her appear dishonest, even when she was almost certainly putting on a show. If Sir Duncan hatched a plan that requires us to look in the wrong direction, she'd be the natural choice to bait the trap."

"That's my view," Deaver agreed. "Classic misdirection. Purpose unknown."

"For now," Tony said. "So. It seems our friends from Box 500 have covered the bases as far as a hacking threat. We have new mobiles, a secure CPS interface, and absolute certainty that my Bentley can't be controlled via wireless, since it was manufactured in 1960. We also know Sir Duncan is out of the country. Can we get a definitive heads up, day or night, the moment he sets foot back in England?"

"Yes. I give you my personal assurance," Deaver said gravely.

Tony looked at Kate. Their chosen profession was dangerous, without respect for the sanctity of the home. If they still resided in Wellegrave House, he wasn't sure how he'd view their situation. But high above London in the Leadenhall building, he felt secure.

"In the interest of wrapping the Ford Fabian case as soon as possible," Jackson said, "I'll assign additional detectives to DS Hetheridge's team. If the No-Hopers killed Fabian, we'll pin them down fast with MI5's help. If they're a red herring, it's further proof Lady Isabel is a liar."

"Well?" Tony prompted Kate. "I feel cleared to proceed on the Keene case. What about you?"

"Same. I'm ready to crack on with the Fabian case. And to deliver Mr. Kipling cakes to the boys upstairs."

* * *

TONY ALWAYS SHOWERED BEFORE BED. Early in his career he'd formed the habit and at this point it was a ritual, a way to slough off the cares of the day and prepare for sleep. Five percent of the activity was literally getting clean; the other ninety-five, standing under a spray of hot water as thoughts drifted in and out of his mind. When he emerged from the master bedroom's en suite, towel around his waist, he was pleased to find Kate already in bed. She had her own ritual before sleep, applying lilac-scented skin crème. Sometimes he helped.

"Did Henry finish his book report?"

"Hmnh? Oh. No," Kate said, still absently massaging a forearm. "He finished the book, but didn't write a report. He wants to turn up late to school tomorrow, quote-unquote accidentally, so he can get it done before arrival."

"That's a non-starter."

Kate chuckled. "So I said. He wasn't best pleased when I said he should wake up earlier and achieve the same result."

"I'll get him up." Tony pulled off the towel, used it to give his steel-gray hair one last bracing rub, and got into bed. No matter how late he retired, he almost never slept past half-five. He liked waking in darkness, brewing strong coffee, and watching the sun rise. While at the Yard, he'd been known to sneak in a power nap in the office of an afternoon, a fact many had suspected but no one could prove. Now that he could nap any time he pleased, he found he didn't enjoy it as much. Human beings were a contradictory lot.

"Why are you smiling?" Kate slid closer, folding herself against him.

"I was thinking people are endlessly perverse. You've had insomnia since the fire. Now, after Paul's news, which would keep most people awake for years, you look ready to curl up and sleep."

"I can handle that kind of danger. If I couldn't, I'd be in the wrong business. Besides, AC Deaver brought the heavy firepower."

"Michael will do anything to protect his officers," Tony agreed. "Knowing Sir Duncan has returned to Brunei gives us breathing room. I wonder, though—do you suppose anything Lady Isabel told Paul was true? Sir Duncan seemed healthy and rational the last time I saw him."

"Healthy, rational, and murderous, eh? I guess that's healthy for him," Kate said. "Sometimes I wish you'd killed him."

"Sometimes I do, too." He didn't have to say the rest—that crossing such a bright line would have carried a cost. Probably that cost was different for every person, but without a doubt, the bill would come due. As a bachelor, he'd suffered occasional periods of loneliness or ennui, and the prospect of a psychological penalty might have seemed like no great risk. But as a husband and surrogate father, he'd discovered a well of unexpected joy; fresh waters he didn't dare poison. Thus he'd chosen not to proactively eliminate Sir Duncan. He hoped he never had cause to regret that choice, even if the other path would have been murder.

"Shall I turn off the lights?" he asked Kate, playing with a lock of her hair.

"If you want. I hope I can sleep, but I keep thinking about Lady Isabel's story. It was revolting. But a little sad, too."

"And quite possibly all an invention. Time to put it out of your mind. Pass me your ereader."

"I thought you were reading *The Guns of August*."

"So I am. Thank you. Ah, here you are, in the middle of *Persuasion*." Putting on his reading glasses, he said, "Dim lights by 75%."

The bedroom lamps obeyed. Kate smiled. "Lord Hetheridge, bending the very appliances to his will."

He ignored that. "'Chapter Five. On the morning appointed for Admiral and Mrs. Croft's seeing Kellynch Hall, Anne found it most natural to take her almost daily walk to Lady Russell's....'"

"Mmm." Kate closed her eyes. "The very first thing I ever loved about you was the sound of your voice."

"Hush," he said with mock severity, and read on.

CHAPTER FOURTEEN

$\mathcal{K}$ ate emerged in One-oh-One's lobby at half-nine, a full hour later than planned. For once, it wasn't because things had gone wrong. She'd awakened at the same time as Tony. Cuddling up to him, she'd found incontrovertible evidence he wanted more than a predawn embrace. Afterward, he'd gone off in search of coffee and she'd fallen deeply asleep on his side of the bed, contained within the impression of her husband's body like hot wax poured in a mold. It was the best sleep she'd had since before Wellegrave House burned.

Kate had expected her new secure mobile to wake her. She'd set her preferred ringtone, the obnoxious bell of an old school telephone, a sound that she couldn't ignore no matter what she was doing. The previous night, she'd ordered TDC Amelia Gulls to ring her as soon as the appointment time to interview Ms. Alfalfa Fabian was confirmed. Instead of receiving a call between six and seven a.m., she'd awakened on her own at half-eight to a text from Gulls that read,

AF's solicitor says she is a late riser and won't see us until one'o clock. Shall I meet you at HQ around noon to prep?

TDC Gulls dictated her texts via voice, which meant they were always in comprehensible full sentences. Kate, an early adopter of texting when 2 meant to and 4 meant for and a mere glance at text exchanges made language purists despair, was retraining herself to use voice-to-text. Alas, her new phone didn't offer such a program. Inconvenience was, of course, a small price to pay for safety. But Kate hoped Lady Isabel hadn't been lying about Sir Duncan's ill health. He was devilish slippery when it came to the law. Maybe the brain tumor, if it existed, would take him down first. Then London would be safer, his victims would receive at least symbolic justice, and she'd have her iPhone back, stat.

To Gulls, Kate replied,

C U @ 12

The best thing about a Blackberry variant was that good old-fashioned Blackberry keyboard. Funny how her thumbs hadn't forgot.

After a quick shower, Kate threw on a skirted suit—dark and somber for the Fabian interview—and wrestled her hair into a high bun. At some point it would fall down, and she would pin it up again. Instead of applying makeup, she tossed a cosmetics pouch containing her beauty trinity, red lipstick, black mascara, and extra hold hairspray, into the tote which held her gym kit. As she stepped into heels, low and dark to match the suit, she rang up Paul.

"You've reached the mobile of DS Bhar, how may I fail you?"

She groaned. "This is a training date, not a pity party. Are you at the gym?" she asked, meaning the fitness center down the street from his building.

"Not yet. Having a late brekkie with Kyla. She'll be off to Milan for the weekend, so we're lingering. When will you be here?"

"Can't I just meet you at the gym?" While Paul had dated both Kyla and Emmeline, Kate had felt free to offer unkind comments about the former. Now that Paul had made what she considered the wrong choice, Kate was obliged to be kind and loyal. But sustained insincerity had never been her strong suit. Even brief, necessary, I-get-paid-for-this bouts of insincerity tended to go off the rails if she didn't coach herself beforehand.

"C'mon, Kate," Paul said softly. "I decided to tell Kyla a little about what's happening. She practically lives with me. I couldn't leave her completely in the dark. Suppose you-know-who tries to contact her?"

That possibility had crossed Kate's mind, too. Kyla had severed all contact with her elder sister Tessa Chilcott, who remained in a secure psychiatric center and would probably never emerge. She'd also renounced her brief connection to Sir Duncan as youthful foolishness. He'd made a few introductions for Kyla in the fashion world, and she'd lied for him to Scotland Yard. Paul had forgiven her instantly, and Tony clearly wasn't bothered, but Kate still held it against her. Kyla was stylishly emaciated, high-cheekboned, and good-haired. She'd get along just fine without Kate's approval. But if Paul was asking Kate as a friend….

"So she's bricking it and you need backup?" Kate asked.

"Yeah. If she sees you're calm, she'll be easier in her mind."

Kate sighed. "Fine. If you're still eating, stop. I don't want you getting sick all over me when I kick your arse in the gym."

Before leaving, she queued up for her usual, a double espresso latte. As she waited, she watched the French concierge bustle here and there, nostrils flaring. He passed a gleaming brass dust bin, noted a bit of rubbish on the floor nearby, and made a beeline for the cleaner on the lobby's opposite end. Dutifully, the woman put down her flannel and furniture polish, left her cart sitting beside a half-polished table, picked up the wadded rubbish and dropped it in the bin. This, Kate reckoned, was world-class hotel management on display.

"Here you are, love," said the barista with the afro ponytail, handing Kate her drink. "Please tell me you bought that man his classic Lego Death Star play-set."

"With Harrods-exclusive Darth Vader figure," added the barista at the cash stand.

"*And* collectible trading card." Kate grinned. One-oh-One wasn't all bad. For every despotic concierge, there were three regular people just doing their jobs, and doing them pleasantly. "Sorry. Sometimes Ritchie talks in an endless loop."

"Does it work?" the barista with the afro ponytail asked.

"More often than not," Kate admitted.

"Might as well get it for him, then."

She's probably right, Kate thought.

She had a sip of her double espresso latte. It tasted like pure energy. As she headed for the revolving doors, the concierge swept past her, packaged sandwich and juice bottle in hand. He was making for a scarecrow figure in a dirty coat and balaclava. Another day at One-oh-One. Kate was growing used to it, but she hoped never to become too used to it.

* * *

PAUL's little flat in Lambeth overlooked Streatham Common. It was absurdly small for one person, and outrageously small for two, like an episode of *Black Mirror* in which future Londoners were required to dwell in lockers at Paddington Station. Still, Kate approved. It was clean, neat as a pin, the bog flushed, the kitchen came with a hotplate and mini fridge, and the Murphy bed folded back into the wall when not in use. There was no tub, only a shower stall with the approximate dimensions of a vertical coffin. But Paul could afford it, and he was proud of it. If he asked Kyla to move in with him, he'd need something larger, but until then, Kate thought it suited him fine.

"Hiya," she said when Paul let her in. "Good morning, Kyla. Lovely day." Why was she trying to be chirpy-cheery, like Gulls? You had to mean it with every fiber of your being or you sounded barking.

Kyla was sitting at Paul's postage-stamp kitchen table, which was only big enough for two chairs. In a white silk wrap over matching nightgown, she looked pale, frail, and older than her years. Stylish emaciation? Check. Couture cheekbones? Check. Good hair? Not even close. It was a rat's nest, held together with clips and dyed an unflattering shade of chestnut.

She must rely on wigs or extensions. How thick can I be?

"Hello." Kyla offered her a cool smile. Her late breakfast, a cup of low-carb yogurt, sat unopened before her. "I'm having detox tea. Would you like some?"

Judging by the size of the mug in Kyla's hands, this detox was one for the ages. It was one of those giant gift mugs usually sold wrapped in cellophane, along with chocolates and a pink teddy bear. Patterned with red hearts, the mug read, **FOREVER YOURS**. Who knew Paul had a soppy side?

"Sit yourself down," Paul said, removing his breakfast plate from the tiny table so Kate could occupy the other chair. "I was just telling Ky that Godington made no specific threats against me. And while our unnamed informant is well-placed, other evidence suggests they may be lying."

"These things happen," Kate agreed, trotting out the standard reassurance patter she'd developed over the years. "I know if you watch telly at night, it seems like every detective ends up in a shootout with a suspect who also just happens to be a criminal mastermind. But the truth is, most of the bad guys are all mouth and no action. They lie, they threaten—half their stock-in-trade is pure intimidation. Maybe our informant," she said, pleased that Paul had declined to name Lady Isabel, whom Kyla had surely met, "had a beef against the Met and decided to wind us up, that's all."

Kyla sipped from her ridiculous mug, watching Kate over its rim with her big, sad eyes. Then she said in a small voice, "It's just that we know what he's capable of."

"Yes," Paul agreed earnestly, turning away from the sink, where he was applying hot water and Fairy liquid to the dirty dishes. "We know Godington kills poachers and people who do terrible things to the environment. We know he kills family members for fun and profit. We know he stalked me all over London with a big black dog just for kicks. What he hasn't done is go after the police. Or their friends and family."

Kyla, silent, stared straight ahead as if unmoved. Was she on the brink of tears, or just practicing a fashion advert look? Kate thought she looked like one of those supposedly cursed pop-art paintings the *Sun* used to write about, the ones with a crying lad that were rumored to magically burn down houses. She wanted to grab Paul, spin him around, and shake out the stupid. But he had a right, she supposed, to be attracted to a waifish nonentity, just as homeowners had a right to hang rubbish "art" near fireplaces that hadn't seen a chimney sweep in forty years.

"So if I'm not meant to be upset, why did you tell me?" Kyla put down the mug. Her hands were shaking. "Why poison my peace of mind for a windup?"

Kate turned to Paul. He looked like he wanted to stick the fork he'd been washing into his eye.

"I only wanted to be honest," he said. "Share what's happening, even if the risk to us is purely theoretical."

"This is why people don't like cops," Kyla said.

Paul groaned.

"Wait. What?" Kate snapped.

"It's true," Kyla said, those big eyes achingly earnest. All they lacked was glued-on lashes. "You stick your noses into everything. You stir up the public against Sir Duncan. Then you muff the prosecution so he gets off. Then you stir him up again in Mayfair," she continued, referring to the case that had introduced her to Paul. "I'm not taking his side. But the truth is, cops make everything worse, don't they? Now *she* gets a death threat, her and her millionaire baron husband," Kyla pointed a trembling finger at Kate, "and suddenly I'm told over breakfast that maybe I'll be hacked to pieces in my bed or slashed to death in the street?"

The last few words were a sob. With a sweeping gesture, Kyla knocked the mug off the table. Then she retreated to the tiny flat's only private space, the loo. The bolt shot home with a resounding click.

"Sorry," Paul murmured. "She didn't...."

"Didn't mean to bring up the so-called muffed prosecution?" Kate asked loudly, determined that Kyla would hear, unless she was sitting on the bog with her fingers in her ears. "That sounded like a cut against you, love. Even though *her bloody sister* is the one who betrayed you and *her bloody sister* is the one who got nicked for slashing someone to death in the street!"

Pulling a dishcloth off the hook, Kate knelt to wipe up the spilled tea. The FOREVER YOURS mug, apparently made from some diabolical space age polymer, was intact.

"Would you look at that?" Kate picked it up and slammed it down. The handle snapped off. "Broken. Sorry. I'll buy you another, promise. The next time I'm in hell shopping for eyesores." She chucked the pieces in the bin.

Paul looked like he was in agony. He obviously didn't want Kate to say or do anything more to antagonize Kyla. Snatching up his keys and coat, he hurried to the front door and opened it wide.

"We're going," he shouted toward the locked loo, and ushered Kate out.

* * *

THERE WAS NO BETTER Close Quarter Battle training session than the one that came after an ugly row. Fortunately, Kate and Paul had plenty of room and no other gym rats offering advice or tapping their watches. That morning, the gym's other clients skewed to the machines—elliptical, Pilates, treadmill, or rowing. Kate and Paul had the far corner, bare except for a stack of orange and purple mats, to themselves.

Perhaps for the first time, Kate had an eager student. Usually Paul had to do something silly, like pretend the stacked mats were mattresses and he was a princess troubled by a pea, before he could get down to business. This time, he put on his gel gloves, took thirty seconds to center himself, and came out fighting with a judo throw.

Kate blocked it with her hip. Not because she'd expected such an attack, but because her muscles knew all the moves. Paul, however, was determined to bring her down. Keeping his hold on her despite the block, he refused to release his grip. In a real confrontation, Kate would have kneed his groin, broken his fingers, or both. In a training session, she needed to make a less agonizing point he'd remember.

She shifted her hip as if to wriggle free. This changed her center of gravity, allowing Paul to throw her. No sooner had she hit the mat on her back then he was pressing the advantage, trying to pin her. She kicked wildly. He took the bait, freezing her leg by digging his fingers into the fabric of her leggings. That made an opening between his body and the crook of his arm. With cool precision, she slipped an arm through, leveraged the grip with her other hand, and pulled the elbow until he groaned. Blindly, he tried to escape, allowing her to pin him in a classic judo submission.

"Crikey," Paul muttered when she let him up. "I just don't have the killer instinct."

"It's not about that. At least, not this time." She waited for him to ask for explication—in general, frustrated students listened more closely to advice they themselves requested—but he was too stubborn to speak.

"Look. Your blood's up. Let's do strikes and takedowns. Krav Maga, baby."

"Is that the one where if I can't pull your arm off and beat you to death with it, I'm allowed to run away?"

Kate chuckled. "You're always allowed to run away. Sometimes anything else is suicide. C'mon. Roundhouse kicks. I brought a padded vest so you can really show me what you've got."

Paul did far better when permitted to wear himself out attacking her. She didn't take it personally, even if some of his ire really was directed toward her. She had far more respect for anger sublimated into martial arts practice than she did for whinging and pouting. After almost an hour, they were both sweat-drenched and in need of tea. So they hit the showers, switched from gym kit to professional garb, and popped into the nearest café.

The waitress seated them by the window. She passed over two paper menus. "Tea?"

"Yes, please," Kate said. "Is there a lunch special?"

"Soup and sandwich. All veg on gluten-free bread or turkey and provolone on wheat. Comes with tea. Cake is extra." She indicated the café's glass case, which was loaded with a seductive variety of slices: yellow, angel food, devil's food, German chocolate, orange crème, and coconut with red maraschino cherries crowning each piece. Funny how you could spend an hour practicing deadly hand-to-hand and make up the caloric balance with one dessert.

"We'll get to cake soon enough," Kate assured the waitress. Her wardrobe from her twenties was gone; as long as she could still do up the zips of her current crop of trousers, the occasional slice of double chocolate or toffee spice would be hers. "I'll take the turkey sandwich with tomato soup."

"Same," Paul said.

They sat without speaking until the tea pot arrived. "I'll be Mum," Paul muttered, and poured for them both.

"Those roundhouse kicks looked good today," Kate said, accepting her cup. "If another tosser with a knife crosses you, he'll be sorry."

"Not sure I could do it under pressure." Paul placed the teapot back on its trivet. "When I got knifed, I wasn't thinking clearly. Instead of kicking the weapon away or knocking him down, I probably would have fallen on my arse. Had my leg grabbed in mid-kick or something." He sipped his tea. "Can that happen? You go for a big kick and the guy just catches your ankle and drops you?"

"Sure. Tough enough guy or a weak enough kick, absolutely." Kate shrugged. "It's an all-or-nothing move. Good to have in the arsenal. Not foolproof. Even a shooter isn't foolproof."

"Yeah. I guess that's why Kyla's so afraid. I raised the idea that I'm potentially in danger, without any assurances for her to cling to."

Kate said nothing.

"It makes sense."

Kate once again allowed herself to contemplate the many cake slices on offer.

"What? Geez. Just say it."

"Next you'll be telling me my mother has a smooth forehead." Kate smiled at Paul, who looked thoroughly miserable. "Listen. Mostly I have no opinion. I *will* correct you on one factual point. Kyla didn't ask for an assurance that you'd be okay. She was talking about herself. She's afraid for herself. And considering how she got in bed with Sir Duncan once, metaphorically speaking, maybe she has good reason. Who knows what he shows you once you're in the inner circle."

Paul made an exasperated sound. "You don't like her. You want to think the worst of her."

"Maybe." Kate shrugged. "Anyway. If I was out of bounds with her back at your flat, I'm sorry. Consider me contrite. While you're in a bad mood, I might as well crank it up to eleven. I talked to the guv after he assigned you Kincaid."

"Oh." Paul blinked. "Go on."

"The top brass doesn't think you have a future in field work. Since you were a golden boy in training, they want to send you back to Henden as an instructor."

"Right. Well. It could be worse."

Kate steeled herself, then said all in one breath, "And I'm on track to be promoted to DI."

Paul's face split in a grin. "Hah! Well. They're not all asleep at the wheel upstairs, are they? Good on you! Wait till I tell my mum. She loves to hear about women succeeding in a man's world."

Kate took a moment to soak that in. She wanted to tell him he was her best friend in the world, and she'd do anything for him. She even wanted to beg his forgiveness for shouting through the loo door at Kyla, who in Kate's opinion was a bony piece of work who deserved far worse. But she couldn't slobber all over Paul in a café. If she did, it would be a complete break with the traditional rhythm of their friendship: insults, one-upmanship, and encouraging one another's rebellious impulses.

"So anyway, as your friendly neighborhood future DI," she said, "I'll give you a scoop. AC Deaver was serious about protecting us. He's already put a team on dissecting Lady Isabel's story, word by word, and fact-checking every claim. Her accusation about the No-Hopers killing Ford Fabian falls under my purview. So. Of course, you're not meant to dig into anything regarding Sir Duncan. But how do you fancy helping me by digging into the No-Hopers? In a very appropriate, supervising TDC Kincaid, fully-deniable-if-it-touches-on-Sir-Duncan way?"

CHAPTER FIFTEEN

*T*he morning had started in the best possible way, in Tony's view. How could the rest of the day fail to follow suit?

He began by giving the tireless Mrs. Snell the day off. The poor woman was tormented by her position as his agency's sole employee, which currently consisted of dusting, rearranging office furniture, and wishing the phone would ring. Mrs. Snell wasn't designed for sloth.

Seating himself behind her impressive Louis XV-style writing desk, surrounded by unread English classics chosen by the condo's owner to attractively fill the built-in bookshelves, he opened his secure laptop and checked his emails. As he'd hoped, several of his pending queries had at last borne fruit.

The email from his daughter Jules's boyfriend, an IT consultant and hacker named Steve Zhao, was written in bullet points. As he read, Tony found himself seeing Steve's cheeky grin and hearing the words in Steve's bass voice.

Hiya, Lord H.,

- **Mariah Keene was seen in the company of some**

fringe cracktivists, i.e., hackers who pick a cause and cyberattack it, last year. But based on her digital footprint, her skill level was never higher than a script kiddie, if that. Must have had a boyfriend there, or just been looking after her twin.

- Mark Keene is the real deal. I knew him from chat rooms as "Rain Man" and "Sheldon Britannia." He never said or did anything to make me think of him as a "black hat," i.e., a cybercriminal. He also seemed agnostic about ethical behavior and would probably commit crimes if he saw a good reason. One of those people who flails around in real life and soars online. He went dark when his sister died.

- Peter Keene's IT guru "Dr. Optics" is Aaron Ajax. As hackers go, he's a bit of a joke. If you recognize his real name, it's because he trespassed on the roof of the Shard a few years back and parachuted off the top. Got off with a warning. Tried to arrange other Urbex stunts but no luck. You're the sleuth, not me, but I can't help but wonder: do you think Mariah was doing some kind of stunt rehearsal for AA when she died?

- I can't prove it in a court of law, so don't ask me how I know, but Peter Keene was being blackmailed last year. I would never dig into encrypted private financial records, but it came to me in a dream that PK made no strange payouts, created no shell companies, and liquidated no assets. I think the blackmailer may have been AA, and maybe his price was the "Dr. Optics" gig. Should this email go astray, I trust any law enforcement official will realize I am a notorious deceiver and will be of no use in any future investigation.

xoxo
SZ

Tony smiled. Like many digital wizards, Steve was in love with his own cleverness. Despite the inherent danger of sending the information by email, he apparently couldn't resist, phrasing the dodgy bits in ways that would sound ridiculous if read aloud in court. To give Steve his due, it would probably work, if push came to shove. But if he didn't learn to control his ego, someday he was sure to overstep. In the meantime, Steve's willingness to ferret out information had once again proved invaluable.

The next email he opened was from an old friend now working in Specialist Crime & Operations. Unlike Steve Zhao, the man providing the information was a humorless lawman who didn't entrust his career to a cheeky disclaimer. It came from ed7389403@gmail and contained only the barest answers to questions Tony had asked in person. Perhaps it was arrogance, but they'd served in the trenches long enough to believe they understood the rules well enough to occasionally break them. There was no greeting and no signature, only the following:

-Possession of pornographic materials featuring minors
-Solicitation of pornographic photos from minors online
-Charges never brought, caution expunged

There it is, Tony thought. *What Peter Keene was holding back. Criminal accusations of pedophilic behavior. I did warn him I'd find out. If he'd simply told me he was being blackmailed around the time he introduced his children to Sir Duncan, I might not have gone so deep.*

Pushing away from the desk, Tony leaned back on the chair's back legs. Part of being a detective was hammering raw facts into a sort of vessel, then filling up the vessel to see if it held water. What stories could he weave from what he'd learned thus far? Which, if any, had the ring of truth?

After a time, he eased forward again, front chair legs thumping against the parquet floor. Something, some essential piece, was still missing. Probably only Mark Keene could supply it, if Tony could convince him to talk.

I still have a little time before I'm due at the Horse Guards parade, Tony thought. *Perhaps Gert and Mark will be there. In the meantime, I can look into Aaron Ajax.*

According to the enhanced public records searches that Tony, as a newly-minted PI, was permitted to access, Aaron Ajax was thirty-eight years old. His mug shot after parachuting off the Shard was boyishly exuberant; the moment Tony saw it, he remembered the news reports, most of which had been openly sympathetic to BASE jumpers. Ajax was thirty-five at the time, but looked younger, with tousled brown hair, blue eyes, and a lopsided grin. Or as *Bright Star's* headline had declared, **Shard Scamp Sparks Sympathy: Brave Brit Thrills the World.**

Ajax had clearly enjoyed his fifteen minutes. The tourists in and around the Shard had cheered as he drifted to earth, his parachute cheekily emblazoned with the white, red, and blue of the Union Jack. The image had proved irresistible in the court of public opinion. Although the City police dutifully brought charges, the trial amounted to a gentle slap on the wrist. Ajax was merely cautioned against future stunts and complimented on his patriotic parachute.

Further digging provided Tony with a thumbnail sketch of Ajax. A lifelong Londoner, he'd left school at age sixteen to marry his teenage girlfriend, who was pregnant. Two years later, they divorced. Mrs. Ajax had died of breast cancer before the age of thirty, and her obituary made no mention of an ex-husband or child. In *Bright Star's* profile, Aaron Ajax had lied about his age, claiming he was thirty, said he'd never been married, and opined that he couldn't imagine bringing children into an overpopulated, inequitable, polluted world.

Did Mrs. Ajax lose the baby? Did they surrender it for adoption? Tony wondered. It probably didn't matter. That was the trouble with prying into private lives; every new bit of data felt relevant, but often amounted to mere gossip.

Having concluded the "Shard Scamp" portion of his life, Aaron Ajax had disappeared from public view, and indeed, the public records search, for a few years. He'd never held a job, so far as Tony could tell, nor had he returned to school via a route like Open University. He wasn't registered as disabled or caring for a relative, and had drawn jobseeker's benefits for the last decade.

Until Peter Keene took him on as Dr. Optics, the IT image guru, Tony thought.

For his first real job, Ajax had physically transformed himself. While Peter Keene's reelection website made no mention of him, Tony spied Ajax in a staged photo taken at Peter's campaign headquarters. As Dr. Optics, his hair was cropped short and he wore the obligatory loud suit and outré specs of an image consultant. He was also grinning, just like in his mug shot.

Yet Steve said in his email that as hackers go, Ajax is a bit of a joke. To all appearances, he's simply drifted about, having adventures, since his teens. Why suddenly give up his benefits and his open schedule for a day job? And one with a politician's long hours and life-in-a-fishbowl quality.

In the staged photo, Peter's hand was lifted benevolently; the kindly young Earl, working for the good of the people. His reelection staffers looked more or less insanely pleased to be involved in the campaign, waving at the camera or giving the thumbs-up. Ajax wasn't waving, but his left hand was held close to his body, thumb and inner fingers curled, pinky and forefinger sticking out. Most coppers had at least a nodding acquaintance with certain hand signals. This one, often used to indicate "respect" between rappers and rockers, had another common meaning: Anarchy.

Tony pondered that, then checked his watch. Not enough time to research the No-Hopers, assuming he could dig up anything. He'd expected Steve to provide more, a sort of gang profile, as it were, but perhaps things didn't work that way anymore. The members favored black, displayed the anarchy sign, and squatted wherever Wi-Fi could be found until the shopkeeper kicked them and their laptops out into the street. Probably any collective of people that truly believed in anarchy didn't have bylaws, official literature, or a website that laid out a cohesive worldview for the public to contemplate.

He looked over the rest of his email, searching for anything relating to Sir Duncan. Sure enough, AC Deaver had sent a link to Heathrow security camera photos. As a former detective and current consultant, Tony still had access to parts of the MPS database. He logged in, offered his PIN and security token, and studied the images.

Is it glare from the screen?

Blinking, he angled the laptop differently and looked again.

Perhaps I need my specs.

He fished them out of a pocket. Half-glasses on his nose, he worked his way through ten of the hundred-plus images provided. Then he rang the assistant commander's personal mobile.

"Is that Tony?" Deaver sounded surprised.

"Michael. The man at Heathrow isn't Godington."

"Beg pardon?"

"I'm reviewing the CCTV images of a man passing from a VIP lounge to his private aircraft. He's the correct height, right sort of hair, right sort of clothes and manner. Sir Duncan is always gracious to his fans. But this isn't Sir Duncan," Tony said firmly. "His upper lip is too full. His hairline is too low. No widow's peak."

Deaver sighed. "I don't suppose there's any room for doubt?"

"No."

"Very well. I'll speak to McGrath at MI5. He'll obtain the necessary warrants. Only…."

Tony waited. The silence stretched out for several seconds.

"If you're wrong about this, and we enact intrusive searches, only to find that *was* Godington and he *is* in Brunei…."

"I'm not wrong," Tony said. "But I understand it's your neck on the block, not mine. Perhaps Box 500 has an agent in Brunei? Someone who can confirm that the man visiting under Sir Duncan's name is a double?"

"Yes. Shouldn't take more than twenty-four hours. That would be more prudent," Deaver said. "I should tell you, Truro's chief hasn't located Lady Isabel. She booked a first class rail ticket to St. Ives but never boarded. That means Godington may be in London and she probably is, too. You need to be careful when out and about, Tony. And so should Kate."

"No worries on that score." He strove to sound casual. In truth, he was angry—angry with Deaver, for his solemn and believable assurances, angry with Heathrow's security for failing to see the difference between a lookalike and one of Britain's most famous faces, and angry with himself for not demanding a look at the images the night before. When he felt this sort of anger bubbling up, there was fear beneath it—real fear. An emotion that had to be contained carefully, lest it become the biggest danger of all.

"I have one last thing on my schedule," he told Deaver. "Then I can spend the weekend up in the clouds awaiting the all-clear."

* * *

TONY ARRIVED in Whitehall about thirty minutes early, hoping to find Gert waiting near the area she'd named, the formal entrance to St. James and Buckingham Palace. The Horse Guards parade area was where the world-famous changing of the guard took place, which meant it was always packed with tourists, but especially on a sunny, mild day like this. No sane Londoner would propose meeting anyone in such a crush of holiday-makers, so

Tony assumed Gert had actually meant within sight of the area, perhaps on the lawn not far from the colossal white monument to Queen Victoria.

Once again in his Tony the homeless man costume, floppy bucket hat on his head, he staked out a place in the shadow of Victoria Regina and scanned the people on the green. Say what you will about London damp and cold, it made the residents truly grateful for a whiff of Spring. There were Uni students on blankets, mums and kiddies in canvas lawn chairs, Frisbee games, boys and girls chasing one another, and a football getting kicked around. When the wind picked up, these hearty souls zipped their hoodies and put on their gloves. They were enjoying the blue skies and sunshine, cold breeze be damned.

He was thinking about Sir Duncan's smiling double shaking hands in Heathrow when he noticed the woman loitering about. It wasn't Gert with her springy red curls and big lime specs. This woman was much younger; tall with dark hair cropped very short, a long calico dress, denim jacket, knitted scarf and matching fingerless gloves. Her back was to him. Yet as she paced, clearly waiting for someone, he noticed her confident bearing—head up, shoulders back.

Mark identified Mariah's body. Peter and Hannah asked him to do it by phone, didn't they? And never saw him again, except in photos around Westminster. No one's seen or spoken to Mark since last December. He'd be gone without a trace, except for the times he stands near a CCTV camera. Like a living reminder. A rebuke.

Tony strode toward the young woman, nearly pushing aside a tourist in his haste. Gert the social worker was heading in from the other direction, a worried look on her face, but Tony got there first.

"Mariah Keene. How wonderful to meet you at last."

CHAPTER SIXTEEN

*M*ariah didn't flinch. If anything, she seemed relieved to hear her name spoken aloud.

"You don't look like I expected." Her eyes raked over Tony, from his paint-splattered trousers to his shapeless Oxfam bucket hat. "Investigators usually wear suits and sunglasses. You crept up on me."

Gert reached them at last, curls windswept, lime glasses slipping. "Oh, my. What're you doing here, Tony? This is my client. She has a right to privacy. You have to respect that."

"I do," Tony said mildly. "I was retained by Lord and Lady Brompton to locate their son, Mark. But he was buried under your name, wasn't he, Mariah?"

She nodded.

"We can't talk about this out in the open," Gert whispered, looking about nervously. "Mariah's life is still in danger."

"We can't go back to my place. I don't have one, really," Mariah said. "I'm sleeping on the floor at a friend's flat. She doesn't know who I really am."

"My office is about as private as Paddington," Gert said.

"Never fear. I know just the place," Tony said. Amused by Gert and Mariah's dubious expressions, he added, "Trust me."

* * *

THE BLACK HORSE & Bridle was a crumbling hole in the wall that looked like it had survived the Blitz, but actually dated back to 1982. It billed itself as "Westminster's Most Authentic Pub," which was problematic on several levels, not the least of which was, it was actually in Clerkenwell. Owned and operated by an old B&E man who'd served his time in HM Prison Wandsworth and come out willing to inform on all his former associates, the Black Horse & Bridle catered to serious drinkers. It had a short bar with four stools crammed together, a hearth with a little table and two chairs, and a single wooden booth. On the rare occasions when its clientele needed elbow room, they spilled into the courtyard out back.

"Hiya, Frankie," Tony called to the proprietor, a bald seventyish man who sat behind the bar reading the *Daily Mail*.

"That's Mr. Tucker to—oi! Lord Hetheridge in the flesh," Frankie said. "I didn't recognize you. Undercover for Scotland Yard?"

Mariah and Gert must have looked astonished, because Frankie immediately tried to paper over his mistake.

"Oh, ladies, don't listen to me, teasing this old rascal. He's my mate from the joint, where everyone called him 'Lord' on account of his manners. So what'll it be, milord? Single malt? Dom Perignon in cut crystal?"

"Two glasses of cider for the ladies. Lager for me," Tony said. "And private use of your beer garden, if you don't mind."

Frankie snorted. "Private's not a problem. Bloody cold out there. Stay inside and I'll switch on the electric fire. Don't worry about me listening in, I'll be minding my own business. Reading my newspaper, hearing nothing. Oblivious, as it were."

It wasn't hard to see how Frankie's threadbare lies had ended his breaking and entering career. It was harder to see how he acquired enough information to serve as a Met snout when he denied eavesdropping before anyone accused him.

"The beer garden is a must," Tony said. From the inner lining of his hat, he withdrew a couple of notes—three times the cost of the alcohol—and placed them on the bar with a smile. "Have one for yourself. I'll show the ladies out and return to collect the drinks."

"I'll bring them." The cash disappeared from the bar top, secreted somewhere in the vicinity of Frankie's many-pocketed apron. "Just go and take the air. I'm not bothered. Happy to provide privacy. More peace and solitude for me."

"He'll be listening at the door," Gert whispered as Tony led them into the beer garden. It consisted of two tables, four benches, and a view of grim brick walls with gray shuttered windows.

"Which is why we'll speak quietly." Tony indicated the nearest table, remaining on his feet until Mariah and Gert had seated themselves. "My name is Tony Hetheridge. Retired from Scotland Yard and working with a private investigator called Cecelia Wheelwright."

"Dad's still searching for Mark," Mariah said. She didn't sound pleased.

"Your mother, too." Tony studied Mariah, who in person was more attractive than her family photos had suggested. Her ultra-short hair emphasized her eyes and cheekbones; her frank gaze made her look like a woman to be reckoned with.

"I saw her on TV. The appeal is on YouTube for anyone to watch." Mariah's voice, like Hannah's, was quite low, verging on mannish. "All she does is sit there. Dad's the one who actually begs Mark to come home."

"Yes, well, having met your mother, I suspect she didn't trust herself to speak on camera without breaking down," Tony said.

EMMA JAMESON

"Hannah fears for your brother. She told me he was fragile. Even likened him to your grandfather, who committed suicide. She believed *you* were murdered, because she insisted you'd never take your own life."

"Mark wasn't fragile," Mariah said hotly. "He didn't top himself. He sacrificed himself. And I *did* want to die. Mum always gets it wrong. She sees nothing. I pity those children with leukemia she's meant to help. She couldn't find a cure. She couldn't find her own arse with Google Earth."

"Here we are, don't mind me, don't let me interrupt," said Frankie, entering the beer garden with three pints. "Cider for madam." He placed a glass in front of Gert. "Cider for madam." He placed another in front of Mariah. "And lager for a geezer that doesn't deserve such beauty." He put the final pint in front of Tony. "Can I bring you something else? We have peanuts, pig snacks...."

"Privacy," Tony said.

"I find nothing goes with a bit of solitude like a salty...."

"Privacy." Tony looked Frankie in the eye. The old B&E man went away grumbling, but he went away.

"I think I should say sorry for lying to you, Tony, back at the shelter." Gert curled her fingers around her glass of cider, but didn't seem interested in drinking it. "I first met the Keenes years ago. When I did in-home therapy for troubled children, Mark was one of my clients. I knew he was dead. I've known for weeks."

"She saw a picture of 'Mark' in *Bright Star* and thought he looked odd," Mariah said. "Funny old world, isn't it? Trained investigators accepted me as Mark. Mum and Dad accepted me as Mark. Then Gert took one look at a photo and said, 'Nope, not right, I don't believe it.' So she came to the City and walked around every day asking questions. Made an arse of herself until I gave up and appeared in front of her, dressed as Mark. She threw her arms around me and said, 'Mariah, you're alive, thank

God.'" Mariah sniffed, blinking back tears. "She knew me. My brother's old therapist is the best friend I've got."

"I only wish you'd let me do more," Gert said.

"And end up dead? Like Ford Fabian? Like Jennie Concord?"

"An informant told me Sir Duncan wanted Fabian killed," Tony said. "And he asked the No-Hopers to make it happen. Do you know if that's true?"

Mariah shook her head. "I really am dead to them. If I nosed around at all, I'd be back on Duncan's radar. I'm surprised he hasn't made more of an effort to find Mark. For weeks, he and my brother were like this." She held up crossed fingers. "Probably the No-Hopers are waiting for Mark to surface online, and pin him down that way."

"Why does the name Jennie Concord have a familiar ring?" Tony asked. "Is she with the Scottish Greens, or some other eco —" He stopped. "Ah. I was used to thinking of her as Jennifer Lane Concord. One of Sir Duncan's friends from before the trial." He didn't add that prosecutors had believed, but never succeeded in proving, that Jennie Concord was an accomplice in the triple murder. Tony could recall her sitting in the witness box, blonde hair in a French twist, dressed in the good-girl costume suggested by her counsel: white blouse buttoned all the way up, floral skirt, cardigan with shiny brass buttons. She'd lied unwaveringly for Sir Duncan with an eerie calm, just like the rest of her cultish friends.

"What happened to Ms. Concord?" Tony asked.

"She fell out with Duncan." Mariah shivered as the wind kicked up, rattling gray shutters above the little courtyard. "The No-Hopers treat him like a god. And Aaron Ajax and his girl-friend, Kay, like the high priest and priestess. It's bizarre, full stop. But since Jennie knew him from Uni or whatever, she talked to Duncan however she liked. She accused him of being sick."

This dovetailed with what Lady Isabel had told Paul. Tony asked, "Sick in what way?"

"Ill. With something he picked up in the jungle, maybe. Or cancer," Mariah said. "He'd gone skin and bones. Never worked out anymore. Dark smudges under his eyes. Jennie said, this is bollocks, you're going to see someone, you look like death. And Duncan went off on one of his speeches about the number 144 being the measure of both a man and an angel and when you die as one, you're reborn as the other."

Gert sighed. "When was this?"

"First of December," Mariah said. "I'll never forget that day. We were in Jekyll House. It's five minutes from here, around Cardinal and Victoria. An office building, four stories, with a furnished IT room for the No-Hopers to work and a top-floor flat for people to crash.

"Anyway, Jennie and Duncan were up in the flat, screaming at each other. Mark was frightened. Everyone was frightened, except Aaron and Kay. They're addicted to drama. So Jennie asked Duncan point-blank, 'Are you saying you won't see a doctor because you want to die? That you think you'll transform into something better?'

"He slapped her," Mariah continued. "Hard enough to put her on the floor next to the hearth. Then he kicked her. Over and over. He just kept kicking her." Her voice broke but she struggled on, blinking back tears. "It was… endless. I wanted to do something, but I was too afraid. I think I could have tackled Duncan. He was breathless, trembling, overheated. But Aaron and Kay were right there watching. Having the time of their bloody lives, the sick pair. I couldn't make a stand against all three.

"When he was exhausted, he got down on the Turkish carpet beside her and lay there to rest. Jennie wasn't moving," Mariah said. "I couldn't tell if she was breathing or not, her face was— well. Hardly a face. Next thing I knew, Aaron and Kay were carrying her body out of Jekyll House, rolled up in that carpet.

"I wonder why you didn't choose that moment to run away," Tony said.

"Haven't you heard of PTSD?" Gert snapped. "She'd been in an abusive environment for months."

"Yeah. No. Cheers, Gert, but that wasn't it," Mariah said, giving the social worker a sad smile. "I could have slipped away. But there was Mark. He was in deep with the No-Hopers. They're like any other gang with the initiations. New blood has to prove themselves by committing a crime. So Mark wrote some ransom code to lock a hospital staff out of their database. They had to pay several thousand pounds in Bitcoins to get their lab tests and x-rays back. Aaron videoed the whole thing. Insurance in case Mark decided he wanted out."

"If you had gone, would they have hurt Mark?" Tony asked.

Mariah shook her head. "Can I start over? I began in the middle, really, with Duncan killing Jennie."

"By all means," Tony said. "Begin at the beginning."

Mariah took a sip of cider. "It's always been Mark and me. Even now, I feel like it's still the two of us against the world. He's been dead for four months, yet he's not quite dead to me. Maybe he never will be.

"Have you heard that theory of family dynamics? That every child has a fixed role to play? In ours, I was the hero," Mariah said. "Good manners, top marks, cheery, never sulked or grumbled."

"Whereas poor Mark was the scapegoat," Gert said. "Labeled anti-social. An embarrassment to his father and a project for his mum. But the diagnosis and the meds made a difference."

"Except he wouldn't stay on them," Mariah said. "He kept quitting them for stuff he heard about online. Like Spice. And Spice made Uni a disaster for Mark. He kept having meltdowns. Wouldn't go to class. One day he was so high, he decided to get physically high, too. So he broke into the school's clock tower, climbed to the top, and sat by the bells until the cops removed him. That was it for Uni. But after the climb, he wanted more. Urbex, BASE jumping, that sort of thing. So he looked up Aaron Ajax and joined the No-Hopers."

"Did your parents know?" Tony asked.

"They should have done. I told them. But they don't listen. Mum was always at the lab, and Dad changed the subject."

"I had the impression Lord Brompton was wholly devoted to you. That your wellbeing was his top priority," Tony said, hoping to prod out the truth.

Mariah's upper lip curled. "Bloody hell."

"He appears quite distraught," Tony went on. "Your old bedroom has become a shrine of sorts. Most of your current possessions are gone. Replaced with toys. A crystal constellation on the ceiling. A princess canopy over the bed."

Gert placed a hand over Mariah's. "Do you want me to tell him?"

"No." Mariah met Tony's gaze. "You know he's a paedo, don't you?"

Tony nodded.

"Did you hear he was caught with kiddie porn on his government computer?"

"Yes. Though I've no idea how he managed to keep a lid on the scandal. Forgive me for speaking plainly, but your family's finances have been lean for some time. He couldn't have paid off the investigators."

"He didn't. He's a solicitor, you know, as well as a politician. He threatened to sue the government for discrimination if they didn't allow him to seek help," Mariah said.

"Was he sincere?"

"I don't know. I doubt he knows," Mariah said contemptuously. "But he's good at seeming sincere when his back's against the wall, just like any politician. In the government, a minister with a drink or drugs problem can get help. Same with gambling or sex addiction. It's all very discreet, no revelations to the constituents.

"Dad swore he'd been fighting his obsession all his life, and he wanted to be cured. Then he accepted everything they offered. Aversion therapy, psychiatric meds, talk therapy…."

"I'm astonished your father confessed all this to you."

"He didn't. Aaron discovered it when he was hacking into the DEFRA mainframe for Duncan," Mariah said. "Duncan wanted to know about the government's long term plans to fight climate change, internal memos about the Paris Accords, etc. Aaron did one better—he blackmailed my dad and got himself access to Parliament through dad's campaign."

"For information?" Tony asked.

"The No-Hopers were already providing that," Mariah said. "I think Duncan needed a mole for something else. Probably something more hands-on. Anyway. I was trying to explain about Mark and me. Until I was ten, I was Daddy's girl. I adored him. He was my best friend. I don't count Mark, because Mark was like the other half of me. One soul in two bodies.

"Then one night, when it was time for bed, my father came to tuck me in. I'd had a bad day at school. I was teary, in need of a kind word. He climbed into bed with me. I fought but—" She stared hard at Tony. "Do I have to say it?"

"No," he said quietly.

"He swore me to secrecy. I said yes. I would have said anything to drive him away. Once he went to Mum's bed, I slipped into my brother's room.

"Mark wasn't asleep. I knew he wouldn't be. He could always feel it when something was really wrong with me," Mariah said. "I had to tell him. You can't keep a secret from yourself. I fell asleep in his bed. While I slept, Mark got up, took the silver letter opener off Mum's writing desk, and crept into the master bedroom.

"Dad woke up screaming. Mark only stabbed him once, but he

made it count." Mariah smiled slightly. "Dad came back from hospital missing one of the family jewels. Mark got in-home therapy, which is how we met Gert. And I wasn't the hero anymore. Dad insisted his bedtime visit to me never happened. That I was a nasty little liar. And Mum believed him."

"I see. Well. I can't say for certain," Tony said, "but I suspect your mother has come to regret that with all her heart. Perhaps the heaviness of guilt is why she insists you didn't take your own life. If she thought you did, knowing how she failed you in childhood, her guilt would be unbearable."

Mariah shrugged, staring into her mostly-full pint as if it were suddenly fascinating.

"You're almost there, love. I'll fill in what I know," Gert said, patting Mariah's hand. "Mark and I reconnected when he started hanging around the No-Hopers. He dressed like them, all in black, and carried a backpack with the Urbex gear. Duct tape, lock picks, binoculars, an *axe*…." She laughed nervously. "I asked what in the world he carried an axe for. He said, in case you get stuck in a tight place. It was brand-new. Purple silicone blade cover. Never used, like most of his gear. Poor lad thought he'd be looking down on London like an eagle every day. But once the hackers realized he was the best of them, they kept him busy."

"He went in headfirst," Mariah agreed. "He loved Duncan's mysticism, and he loved thinking about Fibonacci spirals and secret messages from the Universe. I was afraid he'd never emerge, so I went in after him.

"It wasn't hard to make nice with Duncan. In the beginning, he was handsome and charming and I liked him." Mariah sighed. "Thought he'd been stitched up by the cops, too, I guess it goes without saying. Maybe all that wank about karma is real. I watched him kill Jennie. Pretty cosmic payback, if you ask me.

"I didn't sleep the night she died. Not only because it was a ghastly sight I'll never forget, and I was a bloody coward who did nothing to help her," Mariah said. "But because I'd fallen out with

Duncan over his nonsense, just like Jennie. He'd become so doolally on the notion of rebirth and the galactic brain, I couldn't bear to listen anymore. I'd already tried to leave once, Gert. It wasn't PTSD that stopped me. It was Aaron and his girlfriend, Kay. They said if I left, Mark would leave, and if Mark left, Duncan would be angry. If I died, Mark would be sad for awhile, but then he'd get over it. So Kay took me out for drinks, Miss Pretty Princess with her lavender hair and her zero body fat, and told me very sweetly that I *could* leave, but only in the way that wouldn't anger Duncan."

"Tell Tony about the phone hacking and the car hacking," Gert urged. "All the things the No-Hopers could do without setting foot within ten meters of you."

"I'm all too familiar," Tony said. "My wife is working on the Ford Fabian case. This Kay you mentioned—is she an Urbex celebrity, as it were? Like Ajax?"

"No," Mariah said. "I don't even know her surname. Just another nutter who worships Duncan. When she threatened my life, I believed her. I thought maybe I could plead with Aaron, or even Duncan, if his mood was right. But not her. She's a zealot.

"I asked Mark to meet me at the Rookery. It's a little boutique hotel, one people forget about. We ordered up room service and two bottles of wine. Over dinner, I told him everything. How Jennie died. How Aaron and Kay seemed to revel in the sight of it. How Kay threatened me. I said maybe death was the only way out. I wasn't being melodramatic. I meant it.

"I fell asleep around midnight. Passed out, really, since I'd drank most of the wine. I woke up in my bra and knickers on top of the duvet. Mark must have undressed me. My bag and ID were gone. My clothes were gone, but his were spread out next to me. He'd taken my phone and given me his. There was a video message for me. He said…." Mariah's voice caught. "He said if he fell from a great height, the remains would be almost impossible to identify. And if I dressed as him, and identified the body, that would probably be the end of it. The last thing he told me was not to worry. That Duncan was right. As above, so below. The measure of a man is the measure of an angel."

She dissolved into silent weeping, face in her hands. Tony, despite his unanswered questions, allowed her to cry without interruption. He'd felt no particular emotion when her mother, Hannah, had wept. But his throat constricted as he watched Mariah grieve for the brother who'd valued her life so far above his own.

CHAPTER SEVENTEEN

"Knackered" was the word that perfectly fitted Kate's mood. In bygone times, the knackerman had slaughtered horses that were injured or too old to work, often by knocking them on the head with a ball peen hammer. Or so people said. Kate found the image repulsive, but sometimes it came to her nonetheless, especially after long, tedious interviews with people like Mrs. Alfalfa Fabian.

"What a day," Kate said, settling into the Bentley as she might have settled into a warm bath. "You look ridiculous."

"Thanks for that." Tony grinned. "Typically I cast off my homeless costume, shower, and dress appropriately before you get home. But today was a marathon. In the end, I didn't care to walk back to One-oh-One, so I asked Harvey to bring the Bentley round. I thought you might like a ride, too, the sight of me notwithstanding."

"You're right. Sorry." She kissed him. "Oh, and cheers, Harvey," she added, waving at the manservant in his rearview mirror. "You're a sight for sore eyes. How's the renovation going?"

"Dante got it wrong. The ninth circle isn't Satan eternally

chewing on Judas Iscariot," Harvey said. "It's restoring a Grade II listed home to legal specs."

"Crikey. Stay for dinner? We'll crack open a bottle of wine and listen to your tale of woe."

"I have to go back," Harvey said. "The dining room wallpaper's going up. We're paying a fortune for after-hours labor. I will take John Alastair Hetheridge's cavalry sword off the wall and draw blood before I let the paper hangers leave without seeing this nasty, brutish matter concluded to my satisfaction."

Chuckling, Kate asked Tony, "Which one of your ancestors is John Alastair?"

"No idea whatever."

"Born in 1792. Fought in the Battle of Waterloo," Harvey replied. "Died of typhus soon after. Only the sword came home."

"Of course, John Alastair, my heroic forbearer." Tony shrugged. "Traffic isn't moving. Might as well settle in. I take it Mrs. Fabian was unpleasant?"

"A bitter old bird who lies as easily as she breathes," Kate said. "I let Gulls conduct most of the interview. Turned out to be the right strategy. Mrs. Fabian has been a politician for so long, she's used to saying whatever pops into her head. She told Gulls she doesn't own a computer. But she pays BT for Internet service. She said the last couple of weeks have been business as usual, just the staff in and out of the house, nothing to report. But her neighbors told me young people visited her house the night before Ford Fabian died. Emo-looking, all in black, No-Hoper types. It may take a few days to nail down a connection, but I like my odds."

Tony looked intrigued. "So perhaps Lady Isabel's belief that Sir Duncan targeted Ford Fabian was wrong?"

"Going purely on instinct, I'd say he and Mrs. Fabian joined forces to bump off her hubby. Heaven knows why," Kate said. "As we dig into the No-Hopers, we may find several roads that lead back to Sir Duncan."

"On that topic, I have a name for you. Jennifer Lane Concord. Called Jennie." Tony put his head back and closed his eyes. He sounded as tired as Kate felt. "Mariah Keene witnessed Sir Duncan kill her in a rage. She'll testify against him."

"Mariah? But isn't she ... Oh. So someone else jumped off Deadenfall?"

"Mark."

Kate paused to take this in. "So that's why you just happened to be on the Embankment this afternoon?"

"Arranging protective custody for Mariah, yes."

"Her parents must be in absolute shock."

"They don't know yet. No one will know until we have Sir Duncan in custody. As for Lord Brompton, he does have a shock coming. He'll be arrested tomorrow on charges of sexually abusing his daughter. Makes me rather proud to be an English-man," Tony said. "No statute of limitations for rape."

"I never did understand putting an expiry date on serious crimes," Kate said. "So did Mariah take on Mark's identity? Dress in his clothes and make appearances in the City?"

"She did. Once a week, she'd pick a CCTV camera and stand nearby. Or pass a shop where Mark was known, and leg it when someone called his name," Tony said.

"Why?"

"To torment her parents. Her father violated her. Her mother refused to believe it happened. So she stayed 'dead,' as it were, to hurt her father, and appeared as Mark to haunt her mother."

Kate let herself digest that. "Mariah sounds a little diabolical. Maybe I am, too. Because I sort of get it."

"As do I," Tony said. "And she isn't consumed with rancor. Rather, by pain and justice too long delayed. When she sees Sir Duncan standing in the dock—when she hears his sentence pronounced—she'll begin to heal."

"I hope so. What a piece of work he is, sending a body double to Brunei," Kate said. "I don't care what anyone says about Lady

Isabel. I believe her. The man's lost his mind." The climate-controlled, plush-seated Bentley was too soothing; such comfort wouldn't allow her to get properly torqued up, like a good copper should.

"According to Mariah, his illness is all too real. Perhaps he has business in Brunei that's best conducted in person, necessitating a proxy." Opening his eyes, Tony took off his bucket hat, running his fingers through his steel-gray hair. "Or perhaps he's deliberately confusing the Met as to his whereabouts. Which concerns us, because I consider the Leadenhall building inadequately secured."

"Wonderful. Can't say I'm surprised." Kicking off her pumps, Kate massaged her right foot, which was throbbing. "Henry creeps here and there and no one ever seems to question him. I've seen security doors propped open for event staff. Little infractions can add up."

"According to Mariah, urban explorers rely on little infractions. The No-Hopers started as BASE jumpers," Tony said. "Aaron Ajax parachuted off the Shard and created a twenty-four-hour news sensation. He was tried, got off, and has been trying to top himself ever since. Just last week, he tried to lead a group into 20 Fenchurch but failed. The street access doors had been upgraded."

"I should hope so," Kate said. "The Walkie-Talkie building is an icon. That makes it a target. I'm always shocked when a place like that leaves doors and windows unsecured."

"Another sin chalked up to convenience," Tony said. "While Mariah was being processed, I rang One-oh-One's general manager. Came over as aristocratic as I could, but still couldn't convince him to meet us over dinner. Friday night plans, I suppose. Perhaps if we were owners and not subletting we'd receive greater consideration. At any rate, I have a meeting with him and his head of security tomorrow morning, seven o'clock sharp."

"To read them the riot act?"

"More than that. With their permission, I'll have Cecelia's people in. Her corporate espionage team and her security squad are willing to work on Saturday if I pay their overtime. One Hundred and One Leadenhall has done a fine job of making their atrium impenetrable to the homeless. Not to mention girls on the game. Unfortunately, we can't be certain anyone coming to harm us will be badly dressed."

"Women," Kate said. She was trying to push her feet back into her pumps, but they were swollen and didn't want to go.

"Beg pardon?"

"Women on the game. Not girls. Now called sex workers, actually."

"Oh. I don't care for 'sex worker,'" Tony said. "Sounds like some poor beggar relegated to an unsavory farm chore. Like peering at the dribbly end of baby chicks to sort the boys from the girls."

"'Dribbly-End Peerer' sounds accurate to me," Kate said. "But you mentioned Cecelia's espionage team. You don't think secure mobiles and computers are enough?"

"It's a start," Tony said. "But the No-Hopers might send up a maid or appliance repairman to bug us the old-fashioned way. Even try a home invasion."

"Right," Kate said. "So after I check the fire pulls and the smoke detectors, I should settle down for a night of staring at the ceiling and listening for intruders." She sighed. Then she remembered One-oh-One's resident-only lifts.

"Even if someone slips into the building, they'll be stuck on the public floors until security chases them out," Kate said. "The private lifts need a key card. A visitor without a key card has to call upstairs for the resident to buzz them in."

"True."

"What about the security cameras? Are they manned 24/7?"

"No idea. I couldn't get a straight answer from the general manager on that topic."

"Which doesn't bode well. What about the stairs?" Kate asked. It was no good telling herself to calm down. That was impossible until she'd reassured herself as much as she could.

"The stairs look acceptable, at least on paper," Tony said. "There are different locks on every floor, each specific to a manager or a resident. To reach the roof, an intruder would need over forty separate key cards. But I'll sleep better once Cecelia's crew evaluates the reality."

"I feel like I should contribute to this discussion in some way," Harvey said. "Other than to announce the fact I'm absolutely terrified."

"Sorry, love." Kate felt a little guilty; she'd forgotten all about Harvey up front, listening to them talk shop about rape, surveillance, and murder. "Just trying to brainstorm all points of access. Usually if I think up a million horrible possibilities and fixate on them hard enough, they don't come true."

"Funny how that works. Forgive us, Harvey," Tony said soothingly. "It's worth noting that while urban exploring does happen at night, it's usually in buildings that are abandoned. BASE jumpers penetrate landmarks properties like the Leadenhall building, but during peak hours, for ease of entry. It would be outside the No-Hopers' skillset to breach One-oh-One on a Friday night with extra security in the lobby and a gala in every ballroom."

He was right. Willing herself to relax, Kate forced her still-aching feet back into her pumps. When they reached the Leadenhall building at last, Harvey, always courtly, helped her disembark. For the first time, she looked on One-oh-One with genuine pleasure. The acres of polished brass, the big tinted windows, and even that gigantic snail-slow revolving door—it was becoming home to her. As they entered, Tony slipped an arm about her waist, and that felt like home, too.

The residents' private lifts were tucked between the management offices and a row of Corinthian columns. There, a mixed bag of Friday night revelers waited to travel from earth to sky. Someone was throwing a party with an eclectic guest list. This was lucky for Tony, Kate thought, whose homeless costume wasn't quite so jarring beside punk rock types with dyed black hair and pierced lips. When the bell dinged and the doors whooshed, Tony and Kate crowded into a lift along with two men in dreadlocks and Armani suits, three young ladies in shimmery dresses, and a white-haired man with a whiskey sour.

The white-haired man edged close to Tony. "I'm Warner. What about you? Sony or Universal?" The man had an American accent, which explained why he was accosting a total stranger in an enclosed space.

"Virgin," Tony said. The trio of young ladies looked impressed.

The doors whooshed open on the thirty-third floor. There, a ballroom pulsed with canned electronica, the kind that made Kate feel old. The white-haired man disembarked, as did the men in Armani suits. Two of the young ladies departed, but one lingered on the lift's threshold.

"Aren't you coming, Mr. Virgin Records?" one of them asked Tony. If she was aware of Kate's existence, she gave no sign.

"I fear not."

"I'm Desiree. Room 7575," she said, batting her eyelashes. "Call me tonight on the house phone. I'll buzz you in."

The doors closed. Kate was too stunned to laugh. Tony looked like the cat who got the canary.

"What can I say? Animal magnetism. Oxfam bucket hat not withstanding."

"I've half a mind to go back to that ballroom and arrest *Desiree*, if that's her real name."

"On what charge?"

"Inflating your ego."

He chuckled as the lift deposited them on their own floor. "You're jealous because I took in the visual cues. Dreadlocks, a girl with a treble cleft tattooed on her ankle, and an American mentioning music corporations. With that information, I chose to pass myself off as a Virgin executive."

"Aren't you Sherlock Holmes?" Kate asked tartly as they approached their front door.

"As the great detective said, 'You see, but you do not observe,'" Tony quoted shamelessly. "Take that black scuff on our door, just there. By the jamb. When did it first appear?"

"Today." Kate groaned. "Three guesses how it happened. Henry probably locked Ritchie out, or the other way round. This is what I've been talking about. In the old flat, they treated property with respect. Appreciated what they had. This place is giving them the notion everything is disposable."

She fit her key card into the lock. There was no click. After two tries, she realized the little circle was already green.

"*And* they've left the bleeding door unlocked." She clenched her fists. "I swear to God, Tony, when I get my hands on Henry—"

"My fault," said Sir Duncan Godington, filling up the doorway.

Purple smudges stood out under his eyes. His face was thinner, the lines deeper. He was dressed like a yachtsman or a dockhand—loafers, chinos, navy wind-cheater, and a knit beanie covering his hair. In his hand was something long and black.

"Gun!" Kate cried.

She tried to knock it aside, but Sir Duncan was at point-blank range, with the element of surprise. Something struck her chest with such almighty force, it seemed to at once toss her into the air and hammer her into the floor.

Things went from light to black to light again, like a jump-cut in an old movie. The carpet pattern was *right there*. An inch away from Kate's eyes. And Ritchie was right, it looked like woven Legos: rectangles, raised discs, and divots.

Am I shot?

Probably. It hurt less than she'd imagined. But her limbs didn't work at all.

A loud sizzling sound, like a cartoon electric surge. Something fell heavily onto Kate. It groaned. Only then did she realize that heavy something was Tony.

"Henry," she croaked. Fighting to lift her head, she got no higher than the cuffs of Sir Duncan's chinos.

"I'm afraid your lad gave me a bit of trouble." Sir Duncan sounded disembodied. His voice drifted above her like the whisper of a malevolent spirit. "Buzzed me up like a good little soldier when I said I was Assistant Commander Deaver. But when he saw it wasn't, the little sod slammed the door in my face. Tried, at any rate. I wedged in my foot and zap! Gave him a dose of current."

Kate made a horrified sound.

"You'd call that barbaric? I don't know. 5000 volts is all very well and good for cattle. Since I acquired this Hot Shot model, I've discovered human beings don't bear up very well to the sort of abuse they routinely visit upon helpless animals."

Not shot. Get up, Kate. Get up.

She got up on her knees somehow. Her arms trembled uncontrollably; it felt like she'd been beaten all over with a bag of oranges. She still couldn't see around Sir Duncan's legs, nor could she force out the question, *Is Henry alive?*

"Makes a pretty picture, doesn't it? You on your knees." Sir Duncan sounded jovial, as he almost always did. "And no, I didn't kill the boy. He's a part to play in all this. I rather suspect you'll do as I say so long as I leave him untouched. Same with your brother. I don't want to hurt him. He's like an ape, isn't he? Perfectly lovely. Entranced by my offering."

As he spoke, Sir Duncan stepped aside, opening the door

wide. Kate saw a crumpled Harrods bag, discarded gift wrap, and a box with LEGO on the side. It was the Death Star set Ritchie had asked for, over and over and over again.

The thought of Sir Duncan giving a *gift* to her brother sent a jolt of galvanizing rage through Kate. Her muscles stopped tremoring. She willed herself to stand, and her legs obeyed.

"Oh, pull the other one," Sir Duncan said, watching her rise.

Kate tottered in her heels. It was everything she could do to keep from falling. She balled up a fist to swing. Then the cattle prod touched her throat, blotting out the world with one loud *bzzzrt.*

CHAPTER EIGHTEEN

*P*aul had spent the better part of his minicab ride telling himself he was cracked. Per Kate's request, he'd used the resources of the Met to peer deeply into the No-Hopers, with an emphasis on garnering the legal names of as many members as possible. Cyber Crimes had matched a couple of screen names with legal names, allowing them to decode conversations discovered via the dark web hub Xuanzhang. This had included a first name—Kay—and a BT mobile number he knew. He recognized it because it was stored in his phone, and he used it several times a week.

Maybe CC got it wrong. Or the person sharing the number hit a wrong key. I'm overreacting.

Underreacting, the contrary voice in his head replied.

I'm paranoid after what happened with Tessa. Any coincidence seems like a smoking gun.

The mobile number alone could be a coincidence. But "Kay" could be "K"—as in Kyla, the contrary voice said. *How much more smoke do you need?*

The contrary voice had a point. Hence the minicab ride to the Dolphin. This morning, Kyla had kissed Paul goodbye and left the flat with her suitcase, ostensibly headed to Heathrow, then Milan. At the time, it hadn't crossed his mind to doubt her. Yet today, after seeing the name of Aaron Ajax's girlfriend, "Kay," attached to his girlfriend's mobile number, he'd been over-whelmed with feelings of impending doom. Nothing had helped except to do something unethical: to use his position as a detec-tive sergeant to get BT to tell him, based on GPS, where Kyla's phone was. The answer wasn't Milan. It was a ritzy Westminster hotel called the Dolphin.

Maybe she's cheating on me. That would be mortifying, to burst into a suite ready to accuse her of criminal activities and find her in bed with some bastard.

If you find her in bed with Aaron Ajax, the contrary voice said, *she's deep into something sinister. Full stop.*

"Sorry this is taking so long, mate," the cabdriver said. "Too many closed streets and no regard for the working man."

Paul made a noncommittal sound. The minicab's slug-like progress suited him. He'd never stalked a girlfriend before, not for any reason. A man with half a brain would ring Kate and ask her to do it.

Kate would jump to the conclusion Kyla's guilty.

Kate has better instincts than you, mate, the contrary voice said.

"This time of night it ought to be easy-peasy to get you to the Dolphin," the cabdriver said. "Or the Leadenhall building, 30 St. Mary Axe, the Walkie-Talkie, the bleeding Shard, even, if you got more money than sense. But you're a native, innit? More sophis-ticated, aren't you, than tourists clamoring to pay God knows what to ride the London Eye for God knows why.

"Oh, pardon me. The Coca-Cola London Eye. That's what they call it now," the cabdriver continued, apparently encouraged by Paul's total silence. "Commercialization will take down this city long after we beat back the terrorists and tell Brussels where they can stick it. The *Coca-Cola* London Eye! I don't know, mate, maybe you'd be better off. It's past nine o'clock. Nothing at the

Dolphin past nine o'clock but pissers, tarts, and rent boys." He paused for an amen. When one didn't come, he added, "Not that there's anything wrong with that."

A woman exited the Dolphin's Moor Street entrance. Long lavender hair, blown straight. Newsboy cap, thigh-high boots, and a carmine duster coat. Under that coat, a white sheath that wrapped her angular body so tightly, it almost invented curves. In any other city in the world, apart from New York or Paris, a woman like that couldn't walk a hundred yards without attracting attention, and everyone would remember her. But London was accustomed to stylish people: fashionistas, movie stars, and princes. Runway models on the hoof of a Friday night was no stunner. Paul noticed only because she looked exactly like Kyla, apart from the hair.

"Let me out," he ordered.

"City of London regulations prohibit it, mate. I'll let you off around the corner. There's a designated drop off point for—"

"I'm not your mate. Official business. Scotland Yard." Holding his warrant card up against the Plexiglas barrier, Paul shoved banknotes through the slot. But the minicab was still creeping forward, and when he tried his door, it was locked.

"I said police business. Let me out now!"

The driver hit his brakes hard. The door lock popped. Bursting out of the cab, Paul ran full-tilt after Kyla. He didn't stop to think how it might look to the casual observer. Kyla's cry of alarm as she fled caught the attention of the Dolphin's uniformed doorman.

"Oi! What's this then?"

Paul, who'd seized Kyla by her upper arm, said, "Mind yours, mate."

"Grabby sod. I'll have the Met on you, sharpish." The doorman reached for his mobile.

"Let me go," Kyla shrieked.

Paul didn't. Eyes on the doorman, he tried to pass his warrant card, still gripped in his left hand, over for inspection. But Kyla was surprisingly strong. In her swim and archery days, she'd been a force to be reckoned with. But even whittled down to her *haute couture* weight, she managed to break Paul's grip, forcing him to use both hands to subdue her. The warrant card went flying.

The doorman, a great brick of a man, retrieved the warrant card and studied it laboriously. Kyla bucked; Paul held on with both hands.

"I don't know," he muttered. "Easy to fake documents these days."

"It *is* fake," Kyla cried. "This is my ex. Tell him to let me go! He's a stalker. I got my rights, don't I?"

"That warrant card is genuine," Paul barked at the doorman. "This is a CID matter. I have reason to believe this woman, Kyla Sloane, is a person of interest in a cybercrimes investigation. I'm detaining her for the purpose of a conversation. It's possible that some of her associates, also persons of interest in a criminal inquiry, are in your hotel. Will you ring your head of security, please?"

The doorman appeared to ponder that, blinking tiny eyes in the middle of a broad, boulder-like face. "Er... cybercrimes? Maybe you're thinking of Def Con UK. It's not at the Dolphin. It kicks off next week at the Walkie-Talkie. Why do you need my head of security?"

Emboldened by his waffling, Kyla screamed at a posh couple alighting from a black cab, "Help! He's stalking me! *Help!*"

"Get me your head of security or you're under arrest," Paul shouted.

That penetrated the guard's granite skull. "All right, all right, whatever you say. Mr. Cochran is head of security, but he's on vacation, see? Ms. Darden is his deputy, but it's her dinner hour. How about I give you the Concierge's waiting room?" he asked, tucking Paul's warrant card into his coat pocket as he held on to

Kyla. "We keep it open 24/7 for residents, but no one uses it at this hour. There you can have a chat with this young lady while you await Ms. Darden's return."

"Cheers." Forcing Kyla ahead of him, Paul propelled them into the Dolphin's lobby. Beneath its soaring ceiling and gigantic, many-colored Chihuly chandelier, he murmured in her ear, "You're not under arrest. Not yet. You *are* a person of interest, but I can clear that up if you tell me the truth." That was a lie, and one that didn't trouble Paul's conscience in the least. Was she vain enough to believe it?

Apparently, because she relaxed in his grip. Perhaps she'd been banking on that all long: that his weakness for Tessa would translate into a get-out-of-jail free card for her, even if he caught her mixed up with Sir Duncan again.

Mr. Thickie Doorman led them through the lobby, past the concierge stand, through a door marked Platinum Club, and into an impossibly luxe salon done in shades of aqua and ultraviolet. In an antiseptic hearth, a fire burned, yet exuded no heat, only genteel flames.

Gas? Paul wondered.

Digital, Mr. Thickie Detective, the contrary voice said. *About as real as your so-called love affair.*

As Paul steered Kyla toward a velvet sofa, the doorman lingered in the open doorway. "I have to get back to my post. Should I send in one of the lobby security guards?"

"Ask them to stand just outside, please. By the concierge stand," Paul said. "If Ms. Sloane does a legger, I'd appreciate help running her down."

"Right. Shall I call the City of London Police?" asked the doorman.

"No. This is MPS business. When I'm ready, I'll call it in."

Paul waited until the big man shambled out, then turned to Kyla. She'd arranged herself amid the sofa's velvet cushions as if they were on a date.

"Don't look so comfortable." Paul remained on his feet. He didn't trust himself to sit beside her, not with his adrenaline surging. "Your life's going straight in the karzi. You'll be tried, convicted, and spend your best modeling years reenacting *Orange is the New Black*. So you'd better bare your soul right here, right now, and give me something to shield you with."

"How did you know I was here? Are you using police surveillance on me? Would you really do that?" Kyla displayed extraordinary poise under pressure, just as she had during the French-Parsons case. Part of her success in modeling stemmed from her ability to emote whatever a photographer required: coquettishness, sophistication, or a blank slate. Apparently, she believed this situation called for bewildered innocence.

"Why did you tell me you were in Milan?"

"To get away from you. You're sick, Paul. I feel sorry for you, but this has to end. I won't let you stifle me anymore."

"That purple wig," he said, swallowing his fury. "Do you always wear it for Ajax?"

She didn't answer.

"Does he only know you as Kay?"

Her nostrils flared. "You *are* stalking me. This is abuse of power. Look. It was wrong of me to string you along, but you were so needy and clingy, I didn't know what else to do. That's why I didn't tell you I was seeing Aaron."

Her tone, as if she occupied the moral high ground, was more than he could take.

"I know about the No-Hopers," he said. "I know Ajax is their leader. They're the new cult of Sir Duncan. Are you the one who made the introduction?"

Kyla looked pained. "Paul. Your obsession with Duncan is out of control. You're sure to get the sack. Especially if...."

"Especially if what?"

"If you arrest me. My agency's counsel is top-drawer. Do you think they'll let me spend a minute behind bars? I'll be released straightaway and you'll be humiliated. Then I'll hold a press conference and tell the world your obsession has driven you mad.

"I don't want to expose you. I really don't," she said sweetly as he clenched his fists at his sides. "But you never loved me. You came on to me because I look like Tessa. In bed, you called me by Tessa's name—"

"Once," Paul cut across her, voice breaking. "None of that matters now. And I don't think you bothered pretending to fly out of the country just to give me the slip. Did you come here to meet Ajax? Or is Godington living in the Dolphin's penthouse?"

"None of your business." Kyla leapt to her feet. "Now let me go. If I so much as look over my shoulder and see your face again, I'll get an injunction against you for stalking, I swear it."

Someone coughed. It was the uniformed security guard the Dolphin's doorman had promised, standing in the open doorway.

"Sorry. I thought this was a CID matter. But it's getting loud and sounds, er, domestic...?"

"He's my ex," Kyla said, dropping back into that groove again. "A stalker."

"Right," Paul snapped. "I caught you leaving the Dolphin by a side door. I say you were trespassing. If you have an excuse, let's hear it. Prove me wrong."

Kyla looked flummoxed. Had she been too sure of herself to bother dreaming up a cover story? That, or being intercepted by him had shaken it right out of her bewigged head.

"Off you go," Paul insisted. "Do you live here? If so, tell the man which unit. Do you work here? Which office? Show the man your employee ID."

"I—I came for drinks."

"Perfect. This place surely has several bars. Tell us which one so the bartender can corroborate your story."

She glowered at him. The security guard looked persuaded by her inability to answer.

"I reckon this is CID after all." He turned to go.

"I was in the North tower. The Pickwick room," Kyla said, hurrying to the guard's side. "The private party. Nikoly Pavel-ishchev is the host."

"Er. Yeah. Bespoke security brought in for that one. Bespoke catering, too. The night manager wasn't best pleased." The guard frowned. "If you were here for the party, show me your invite, please."

"I don't have it. But I didn't crash. Word-of-mouth is how it works for the beautiful and the tragically hip, am I right?" Kyla smiled enticingly at the security guard, who was young and rather handsome.

He didn't seem to notice. "The Pickwick party weren't word-of-mouth. Nothing here is. My mate was stood on the 55th floor for two solid hours, scanning barcodes. You got a barcode?" He pointed to her wristlet, a zippered leather bauble only large enough for a mobile and a tube of lipstick. "It would be in there, wouldn't it? On your phone?"

"So it should be. But. Well. I'm a bit of a brainless bird, some-times." To Paul's chagrin, Kyla started doing that thing she did: deliberately mussing her hair with her long red fingernails, a sexy-awkward move many photographers had memorialized. "I hate to admit this. But I dropped my phone in the bog. Wasn't about to go in after it. That's why God gave us accident replace-ment, hey?"

"So you're too good to touch a little bog water?" the security guard asked.

Kyla pulled an adorable face. "Please, Mr. Officer. Don't make me say I did a poo and the phone fell in with it. Just take it on faith. I had my reasons."

"Right, right. Could happen to anybody." He seemed to soften. "Tell you what. Give me your full name. I'll check it against the authorized guests my mate scanned in. Prove you're legit in a flash."

"Her name's Kyla Sloane," Paul said. "And if you find that on the list of authorized guests, your next pint's on me."

"Fair play. I'll ring the North tower and find the bloke with the database. In the meantime," the security guard told Kyla, "why not sit your bony arse down and do as the policeman says? Can't flirt your way out of everything, love."

"Bloody queer," Kyla shouted at his back.

"Nice. Now," Paul said firmly. "If you want out of this, you have to be honest. Tell me why you're really here."

"Nicky Pavelishchev's party."

"Where's your mobile?"

"In the bog."

"Bollocks. You'd pluck that phone out of raw sewage with your teeth before you'd go twenty-four hours without it."

Kyla sighed. "You know what? I get it. You want an excuse to strip-search me. Spank me for going astray." A little taller than Paul in her thigh-high boots, she looked down at him speculatively. "Where do you think I have my iPhone stashed, love?"

Paul studied her clinically, like a man contemplating a fat, shiny worm. Her attempt to seduce the security guard into letting her off had failed, so now she was turning her superpower on him. How desperate was she? This last-ditch stab at seduction amounted to a drowning woman flailing for a rope.

He'd throw her some. Hopefully just enough to hang herself.

"Look. If you want one final grudge match, I'm up for it," he lied, making no effort to conceal his disgust. "But first, I need an admission. I've stuck my neck out with these rent-a-cops. I'll be in a spot Monday morning if I don't have you down for something—trespass, vandalism, petty theft—when the hotel manager rings my guv."

"Fine. It's trespass. I confess." Kyla's big dark eyes registered relief. She believed in her power over him, even now.

"Why were you trespassing?"

"Ever heard of BASE jumping?"

He nodded.

"You've discovered my dirty little secret. Urban exploring. Once you start, you can't stop. Aaron's famous for it. He's planning a day jump tomorrow from the Dolphin's North tower. 700 feet in broad daylight."

"Aren't the upper floors secured?"

"Of course. Manned cameras, too. Some of the boys tried a dry run, stairs to roof, and got busted," Kyla said. "So they broke out their laptops, figured out how the key cards work, and cloned a master. They reckoned they got collared because they dress like emo clowns. So Aaron sent me in because I look like I belong here. I crashed the party, took the express guest lift up as far as I could, and used the cloned key for the last few floors. I made it all the way to the roof."

"Why?"

"To drop off my handbag. It's sitting behind a water tower with Aaron's chute inside, waiting for him. Backpacks in plain sight are a no-go these days. The easiest way for a jumper to move through the lower half of the building, where all the security is concentrated, is by being unencumbered. Tomorrow, Aaron will slip in dressed like a maintenance man, empty handed."

"When you decide to confess, you go all the way, don't you?"

"You threatened to bang me up for life if I didn't. Besides, trespass is a misdemeanor, isn't it? People love BASE jumping. Aaron's new chute says GOD SAVE THE QUEEN."

"Fine. I still need to see your mobile."

"Good luck with that. I left it on the roof, too. Shows what you know about me being willing to give up my phone."

"Why?"

"It's in a filming bracket, clamped to a pipe. Tomorrow, Aaron will stand in front of it to broadcast his intro, then take it with him to record the drop itself," Kyla said, voice still husky with apparent desire, never breaking eye contact.

She's determined to be perceived as truthful, Paul thought. *If I asked, she'd probably go to bed with me. Just to make sure I bought the story.*

Perfect alibi, the usually contrary voice agreed. *If a crime more serious than a BASE jump occurs, she can say she was making love to a policeman at the time.*

"Right," Paul said. "One last thing. Take me up to the roof and prove you're telling the truth."

* * *

"Oi!" The security guard called to Paul as he and Kyla passed by. "I'm still trying to get my mate to get me that guest list. Where are you off to?"

"North tower. Floor 55. The Pavelishchev soirée," Paul said. "This one insists her phone's up there. Once I verify it, I can let her off with a caution."

"You're going the wrong way. You want those lifts, by the gift shop. Follow me."

When the car arrived, he leaned inside, sticking a plastic card emblazoned with the Dolphin logo into the VIP slot. The wall of buttons lit up. He pushed the one labeled PICKWICK.

"Ta. The MPS is hiring, you know," Paul said.

"Do me a favor," the guard scoffed. Then the polished gold doors closed and the lift began its swift, smooth ascent.

"So this party. What's the occasion?"

"MPs and lobbyists."

"Hope the dress code is business casual," Paul muttered, straightening his tie.

"It doesn't matter. When I left, the Grey Goose was flowing like water and people were wandering in and out of the ballroom. Hooking up behind the potted plants. We'll fit right in. You look like a gloomy ministry drone and I look like *vatrushka*."

"Which is…?"

"Dessert. Russian and luscious."

The lift *binged* discreetly on the 55th floor, PICKWICK. Striding confidently off the lift, Kyla led Paul into the quintessential posh hotel venue. Patterned carpet, tasteful wallpaper, and those narrow cherry wood tables that had no function on Earth except to support oversized floral arrangements. All the ballroom's doors were open, revealing three bars, a circulating wait staff, and what sounded like a swing band.

No one was dancing. The men did look like government drones, in gray suits with blue or black ties. Several of the women rivaled Kyla in youth and beauty. A handful of other females, in skirted suits and sensible heels, stood on the sidelines looking on, murmuring to one another. It didn't look like a Friday night frolic. It looked like a state function, minus the usual pomp. Something else was missing, too.

"Hang on," Paul said. Kyla's stride was so long, he had to work to keep up. "If those are ministers, where's RaSP?" he asked, meaning Royalty and Specialty Protection.

"At home or down the pub, I expect," she tossed over her shoulder. "I never said this was official. Not everything the MPs get up to with potential donors is approved by the PM. Now smile, you prat. We're meant to look like a randy pair in search of a dark corner."

Finding the express maintenance lift, they took it up through the North tower's uninhabited service and equipment floors. It deposited them into a long white corridor with florescent lights triggered by motion sensors. CCTV cameras were mounted near the lift, but no one challenged them via the PA speaker. Perhaps it wasn't surprising. Paul knew from experience that no modern building skimped on camera installation, but plenty cut corners when it came to hiring people to monitor those usually unremarkable feeds in real time.

"This way." Kyla started toward an unmarked door at the end

of the corridor. It was a two-and-a-quarter-inch security door with a serious-looking electronic lockset.

Kyla unzipped her wristlet. Withdrawing a plain white key card, she inserted it into the lockset's slot and punched in five numbers. Paul groaned at the sequence.

"1, 2, 3, 4, 5," Kyla agreed. "Convenience over cryptography. The BASE jumper's best friend."

Beyond the heavy door was a clean white stairwell, revealed as another automatic florescent light kicked on.

"I think we're good," she told Paul, starting up the stairs. "Still. Better chop-chop, in case someone playing eye in the sky called the cops."

"If they turn up, I'll show them my warrant card." Paul struggled to match Kyla's pace. Clearly, she wasn't concerned with stealth; the stairwell rang with the pounding of her boot heels. "How much farther?"

"Six flights. Cardio," she cried with strange gaiety, taking the stairs even faster.

After five, Paul's heart was beating itself against his ribcage, perhaps to break free and seek a better-conditioned body. The situation was strange, but Kyla's demeanor was stranger.

She's manic. Not with fear. Glee.

At the top of the sixth flight was another door. This had no impressive lock, only a metal push bar that Kyla struck with both hands, throwing the door wide. Paul stopped on the landing as the night air rushed in to meet him. A feeling struck him. Was it the feeling you had just before you got yourself killed?

I should've called for backup. Aaron Ajax could be up there. Or Sir Duncan. Or both of them and all of the No-Hopers, too.

He didn't have to step onto the roof. He could turn around. Run for it. He wouldn't have to make it down to the public levels. All he needed to find was a spot to hole up in and enough bars from bloody BT to call the MPS switchboard. But he'd have to choose that spot well. There was no way to lock or block the roof's access door. Who knew how many friends of Kyla's would pour down the stairs in pursuit?

"What are you waiting for, you great nancy?" she asked between gasping breaths, grinning down at him from the rooftop. "Don't you want to prove me a liar? Maybe there's no phone up here. No chute, either. Don't you want to slap me around when you see I've made a fool of you all over again?"

That jab at his pride meant nothing. But before he could turn to run, a woman cried, "Help! We're up here. Help! Please!"

The small hairs on the back of his neck lifted. Kyla's grin didn't falter. She looked like Tessa had the last time he'd seen her: stark, staring mad.

What he did next wasn't a conscious decision to gamble his life. He simply heard what sounded like the cry of a woman who needed his help and ran toward it, pushing past Kyla to emerge on the roof, under a handful of stars.

A gust of wind almost knocked him off his feet. The North tower's roof wasn't one of those tricked-out urban party zones. There were no built-in tables and chairs, no bandstand, no strands of multicolored fairy lights. This was a Cubist landscape of electrical boxes, rain reservoirs, and air conditioning units. Pipes ran here and there, stenciled with acronyms he didn't understand. Exhaust ports belched smoke; visibility was only fair. Most light came from the slightly taller, infinitely brighter skyscraper just east of the Dolphin.

Deadenfall, Paul thought, but he wasn't looking toward it. He was looking at the three individuals, sitting quite strangely in the shadow of a mammoth air conditioner unit.

CHAPTER NINETEEN

*L*ined up in hotel ballroom chairs, the ones that snapped together for perfect event spacing, the trio looked surreal, like something out of a dream. They were dressed as if they'd come from the Pickwick event. The pair of men, one pensioner-age, the other thirty-five or forty, wore suits and wingtips; the woman, young and pretty, wore a skirted suit, torn stockings, and one high-heeled shoe. Judging by the bloody scrapes on her legs and the clumps of hair matted with blood, she'd fought her captors and lost. The men's mouths were gagged with duct tape, but the woman's gag had fallen into her lap. It looked to Paul like she'd chewed through it.

"We're sitting on a bomb," she told him. "We—*watch out!*"

Paul spun around. His body automatically assumed the basic stance Kate had drilled into him: Left foot forward. Weight evenly distributed on both legs. Left hand raised to protect his face. Right hand a bit lower, to protect his body.

Kyla came at him. Perhaps it was the flood of adrenaline that made her seem to move in slow motion. The weapon she pulled from inside her boot, a spring-assisted survival knife, revealed its long, thick blade with the flick of a thumb. She knew his body well enough to go for his shoulder. Part of his mind saw it happen—Kyla reopening the old wound, yanking the knife free as he fell, and then slashing his throat. But his muscles remembered what to do. Stronger and faster, he blocked her with ease.

"No!" Kyla cried, clinging desperately to her knife.

He squeezed her wrist until she screamed. The knife dropped. From far away, he seemed to hear Kate saying, "Never leave your opponent upright."

"Damn straight," he muttered, balling up his fist and punching Kyla so hard, he split his knuckles on her teeth.

She hit the rooftop and lay sprawled on her back, unmoving.

His hand didn't pain him. His conscience didn't pain him, either, even though he'd never hit a woman before, outside of CQB practice. His adrenal dump narrowed his focus to the three hostages.

"Did you say *bomb?*"

The woman nodded. She seemed less frantic, now that Kyla was down, but her dark eyes were still wide with terror.

"Where is it?"

"Under us. The man called it Super-Semtex."

"There's no such—oh. Right." Vaguely Paul recalled a Met in-service on "designer" explosives, which had begun appearing in black markets alongside designer drugs. Many times more potent than PE-4, more commonly called C-4, Super-Semtex was sold in much smaller bricks, making it easier to smuggle across borders. Just last month, terrorists in Italy had used a duffel bag of Super-Semtex to blow up a Carabineri base, killing twenty-four and wounding scores of others.

Paul knelt to get a look at the bomb. Using Kyla's knife, he sawed through the duct tape wrapped around the woman hostage's ankles as he studied the neat pile of plain, deceptively innocuous-looking gray bricks.

That's way more than the contents of a duffel bag.

Just as his muscles remembered his training, some part of his policeman's brain remembered all those seminars on improvised explosive devices. He didn't see, or at least recognize, the IED's detonator, but he saw cords and wires connected to a cheap plastic clock.

"Did he say when it's meant to go off," Paul's gaze shifted to the woman's sticky name badge, "er... Neera?"

"No. At least not that I heard," she replied. "I fought back until he punched me in the stomach. I wouldn't give him the satisfaction of seeing me get sick, but it was touch and go for awhile there. By the time I was a hundred percent, he'd bound me to this chair. Said I'd better keep dead still. That even a tiny shift in pressure would make it detonate."

"He's a liar. C-4 is very stable. Super-Semtex is, too."

Neera's arms were folded behind her chair back. Dreading what he might see, Paul ventured a look. As he'd feared, Aaron Ajax and the No-Hopers had used standard police-issue cuffs, the kind with chain-linked steel bracelets. Neera's right wrist was cuffed to the chair. Her left was cuffed to the right wrist of the man beside her.

"Can you free my hands with your knife?" she asked.

"Sorry. No." Paul moved to the next hostage. Positioned in the middle, the younger minister wore a sticky name badge that read JEREMY PILKERTON. His pale moon face was wet with sweat and tears. His trousers were wet, too. Paul didn't find that unreasonable, considering the bomb beneath him could go off at any second.

"The bad news," Paul said, sawing through the duct tape wrapped around Jeremy's ankles, "is you're stuck in place for the moment. The good news is, you don't have to worry about keeping dead still. This stuff is stable. You could beat it with a cricket bat and it wouldn't go boom. Takes a surge from a detonator—a mini-explosion, really—to make it kick off." The words came out slowly because he was running mental scenarios so fast. As Paul tried to guesstimate variables like explosive poundage, blast radius, and minimum safe distance, he unthinkingly jerked the duct tape off Jeremy's face. The man shrieked.

"Your knife! Try it on our handcuffs," Jeremy babbled as Paul moved on to the pensioner-aged man. Under the spotty lighting, he looked like Father Time, gray-faced and trembling. His name tag read, The Rt. Hon. Edwin Jacoby. This time, Paul started with the duct tape gag, thinking it might be impeding the old man's air intake.

"First time," Edwin quavered as the gag came out. "This bloody gala. First time I've ever taken part in any kind of financial impropriety. I was chair of the ethics committee, three years running." Tears shone in his blue eyes. "Decades of service and nothing to show for it, not even a thank-you. Can you blame me for wanting a payoff?"

"Enough of that, Ed," Neera said. "We fouled up. Now we're paying for it. Save your confession for Sunday."

"Who says we'll live till Sunday?" Jeremy sounded close to hysterical. "Somewhere, the clock's ticking. We could be down to one minute for all we know." To Paul he said, "For God's sake, man, at least try to get us out of these cuffs."

Paul pretended not to hear. His adrenaline-fueled tunnel vision had pushed him to one inescapable conclusion. Folding up the knife, he stuck it in his waistband. Feeling in his coat pockets, he sought the only tool that stood a snowball's chance of saving him, the ministers, and possibly dozens of people in the Dolphin's North tower.

"What are you doing?" Jeremy cried as Paul pulled out his mobile.

"Calling 999, you great prat," Neera said.

"The clock's ticking! Free us first!"

"It doesn't matter. We're being punished. We deserve this," Edwin said shakily.

"Shut it, both of you," Neera said. "Or after we make it out alive, I'll kill you both myself, I swear I will."

"Name?" said the Met operator in Paul's ear. Her preternaturally calm voice, like the mobile's cool surface against his feverish skin, made him suddenly hope he was dreaming. But if this was a dream, why could he smell exhaust from the HVAC pipes, hear Edwin's raspy breathing, and feel the fresh wound across his knuckles?

"I'm the Parliamentary Undersecretary of State," Jeremy shouted. "Department for Environment, Food, and Rural Affairs. We need PaDP. We need RaSP—"

Paul walked away from the trio, towards the roof's edge, which was bordered with a waist-high concrete wall. "This is Detective Sergeant Deepal Bhar. I'm calling from the Dolphin hotel, Westminster. North tower. I'm on the roof. There's a big IED up here. There are hostages handcuffed on the IED and unknown numbers of people in the building," he heard himself inform the operator with surprising composure. If only Tony or Kate were around to hear. "Explosive capability unknown. Up to ten thousand pounds, if I'm looking at Super-Semtex. Enough to kill the hostages, if I'm looking at ordinary C-4."

"SO19 is being contacted," the operator said, still in that preternaturally serene voice. "Do you have backup?"

"No."

"Status of the perpetrator or suspect?"

"At large. I subdued an accomplice. As far as neutralizing the device—"

"Do *not* attempt—"

"I won't. But the Dolphin's night manager should activate the hotel's evacuation plan. Don't have his name, but the deputy head of security is called—"

"Is that DS Bhar?"

The interrupting male voice sounded bluff and self-assured: a specialist cop or a soldier patched through from SO19, no doubt. "You have visual on the IED? The detonator and timer, too?"

"Yeah. Got an iPhone? We could FaceTime it."

"Good God, you sound like a bleeding Millennial. Never mind. Think you can get the hostages off the roof and down to the street?"

"I'm an MP," Jeremy shouted. "There's three of us. From DEFRA!"

"Ministers." The man with the bluff voice sighed. "Crikey hell."

"I can't get them down," Paul said. "They're cuffed to chairs and to each other. Then again, the hardware's standard issue. Maybe if you got a handyman to fling up a hacksaw...?"

"Never mind that, Deepal. It *is* Deepal, right?"

"Just Paul." Now that the real prospect of rescue had been raised, he felt himself beginning to tremble. But that was no good. He needed his adrenaline-armor, his survival tunnel vision, if he was going to live through this, or at least die like a man.

"What else do you need to know?" he asked, turning back toward the hostages. "Um, yeah, the clock. It's old-school. Big hand, little hand. Plastic, like an ASDA special. Not sure about the detonator, but the wires—"

"Right-o, just Paul," the bluff voice cut across him. "We could swap maybes and whatsits all night, but let's leave it to the experts. I have three BMW X5s en route. My mate's on another line with the Dolphin's night manager. SO19 is scrambling. Keep your ears peeled for NPAS. You'll hear the rotors of *India 97* and *India 98* before you know it. You've done what you can for the hostages. It's time to leave them in our care. Propel your arse down the stairs and out to the street."

Paul looked at the trio of DEFRA officials sitting atop a homemade, military-grade demolition block. Edwin was weeping silently. Jeremy was twisting against his handcuffs. Neera, who'd brightened when Paul started talking, was watching him warily. The hope was sliding off her face like stage makeup under hot lights.

"I'm not going anywhere," he said, loud enough for all three to hear.

"Paul." The man sighed. "Mate. Think it over."

"I don't have to. I'm all in."

"Fair play. Don't suppose you have a weapon?"

"I do. A knife. Took it off the perp."

"And where's that perp now?"

Kyla. How in the world had he forgotten her? Adrenal tunnel-vision had its downside. Paul turned, expecting to see her coming at him all over again, another spring-assisted black blade in hand. To his relief, he found she was still down. Sitting on her knees with an unnerving look on her face, but down all the same.

"A few yards away. If she says boo, I'll put her down harder."

"Good man. Oh—someone passed me a note. Evacuation of the Dolphin's North tower is underway. Surrounding hotels are being notified, too. Alarm bells must be going off everywhere. Hear them, Paul?"

He could, faintly. Odd how this reassuring Met voice kept calling him by his given name. No doubt it was a calming psychological technique, and a successful one at that.

"Paul. Still with me? Here's another note. Apparently I need to dot my *I*s and cross my *T*s. Is Mrs. Sharada Bhar still your preferred contact? Shall I ring her for you?"

Usually his mum was in bed by this hour. He didn't want anyone waking her to say, "Beastly luck, Mrs. B. Your one and only son is what coppers call pink mist. Turn on the Beeb and catch the replay as little Paulie goes out in a blaze of glory."

Worse, the Met switchboard might patch her through to me for some mutual abasement before it all goes boom.

That was a non-starter. If he had any final words, he'd give them to Kate. Or better still, his old guv.

"I don't suppose you could ring Chief Superintendent—that is, Lord Anthony Hetheridge?"

"He can't," Kyla said from behind him. She sounded oddly triumphant. "But I can."

A chill went through him, scalp to toes. "Hang on."

As he placed his mobile on the rooftop, the bluff voice commanded,

"Paul! Stay on the line! Paul!" But he was already walking toward her.

"What did you say?"

"You heard me." Kyla's dark eyes stood out in her pale face. She'd bitten her lip during the fall. Blood dribbled down her chin; grit from the rooftop was ground into her coat's satiny fabric. Without trying to rise, she continued,

"We've put so much planning into this. Aaron and his team intercepted emails about the Russian party weeks ago. You want to know why there was no Parliamentary security present? DEFRA didn't want them.

"This was all supposed to be hush-hush, lobbyists and oligarchs. A secret summit about killing the EU's green policies rather than continuing them," Kyla continued. "When Duncan found out, he was livid. Aaron wanted to lure ten ministers away from the Russian charm offensive, but only three were greedy enough to take the bait. Those three," she said, pointing at the trio of hostages, "are greedy little buggers. A £5000 payoff, upfront and in cash, was all they needed to sell out the human race."

"We were wrong." Jeremy's gaze pleaded with Kyla. "We should be sacked. Maybe even brought up on charges. But we don't deserve the death penalty."

"Yes, you do." Kyla flashed him a red smile. "And when you go, the top of this tower will go, too. Look around. Not a single solar panel. *Boom*," she cried, loud enough to make the hostages flinch. "Duncan's been issuing warnings to England—to the world—for years. This is the one that will finally penetrate."

"But what about Hetheridge?" Paul snapped. "What did you mean, only you could call him?"

"Can't explain without my mobile," she said, still grinning. "It's just there. Stuck in the bracket, like I told you. Fetch it to me and I'll spill."

Following the direction of her gaze, he spied her mobile, still in its pink Swarovski crystal-studded case. As she'd described, it was fitted into a recording stabilizer clamped to a pipe.

Could be a backup detonator. Or the actual one, if the bargain-bin clock is a misdirect.

"Lord, you're so transparent. It's not a detonator," Kyla said. "Simple time bombs succeed for a reason. They can't be nullified by radio signals or microwaves or whatever else the government uses. You place them, get to the minimum safe distance, rinse and repeat."

Despite her assurances, or perhaps because of them, Paul approached her blinged-out mobile with caution. The iPhone's screensaver had been disabled, so the first thing he saw was himself, looking wide-eyed and frightened. When he stepped aside, he saw the hostages sitting on the IED.

"You're running a live feed?"

"Of course. People pay in Bitcoin to see this stuff happen in real time. Besides, if Aaron can't show proof, his mates on Xuanzhang will never believe he did it."

Revolted, Paul hit the home button. That minimized the video live feed and brought up another app. It was a digital stopwatch. The counter read 00:07.

"Seven minutes?" Paul burst out.

"Oh, God," Edwin cried. Jeremy looked petrified.

"Calm down," Neera ordered the men. "At least we know. Seven minutes is better than one. SO19 will arrive before we know it."

"Bring me my mobile," Kyla repeated.

He wasn't willing to touch it, which seemed to amuse her.

241

"Aww. Poor Paulie. Too much of a big girl's blouse to risk it. Fine. Bring me yours and we'll do it that way."

He retrieved it. The man from the Met was still calling him by name, urging him to pick up, but Paul hit the red button. The digital clock now read 00:06. Having once laid eyes on it, he found it difficult to focus on anything else.

"Find your torch app," Kyla instructed. "Turn it on. Now face the Leadenhall building. See the spires? There's a strip of roof just beneath. It's not too visible at night, but it's there. Flash your torch in that direction."

He obeyed. The Leadenhall building's quadruple spire glowed emerald green that night, an ironic color in light of the DEFRA murders Sir Duncan planned. Otherwise, it was dark.

"How many times do I—"

He broke off. There it was: a tiny flash of light in response. As Paul watched, it flashed again.

"Is that Aaron?"

"Please." Kyla's voice vibrated with the smugness of one no longer obligated to feign affection for a man she loathed. "This is Duncan's final statement to England and the world. You don't think he'd accept anything less than a ringside seat?"

Her pink crystal-studded mobile started chiming "Silk."

"That's him, wanting to know what's wrong," Kyla said. "Why I'm up here signaling again. Aaron and the boys are already home. I should be stepping off the Tube in Clapham South about now."

Paul wrenched her mobile out of the bracket and hit the button.

"Kyla, my love. Why are you still on the roof?"

"SO19 is en route." Paul enunciated his syllables clearly, hoping each one penetrated Sir Duncan's cheery carapace like bits of white-hot shrapnel. "The North tower has been evacuated. The DEFRA ministers are being freed. Next thing you know, you'll be squatting over a mirror in HM Prison Wakefield, spreading them wide for guards who enjoy their job a little too much."

Silence.

"Cat got your tongue?"

"The No-Hopers gave me a countdown clock," Sir Duncan said. "Let me check it."

The ambient noise—wind, traffic, distant alarms—suddenly seemed to be coming in stereo. Paul realized he was hearing half from the North tower, half through the mobile. Sir Duncan had put his device on speakerphone.

"Kate. Be a dear and read that number out to your friend Paul Bhar."

He's a liar, Paul told himself desperately. *It's another trick. Like stalking me with that big black dog.*

No one spoke.

"I said be a dear!"

Somebody grunted as if struck. Then Paul heard Kate say, "Five minutes."

"Five minutes," Sir Duncan repeated. "Did you hear that, *Lord Hetheridge?* Clever *nom de guerre,* isn't it, Paul? As if I don't see through it. Go on, milord. Tell your friend you're up here, too, or I'll kick Kate's teeth in."

Tony, faintly: "I'm here."

"Right." Sir Duncan sounded obscenely pleased with himself. "You know what I think, Paulie my lad?" He didn't wait for Paul to ask. "I think five minutes is plenty of time to kill Lord and Lady Hetheridge before a Met helicopter trains a single spotlight on Deadenfall. And who knows, maybe there'll still be fireworks."

CHAPTER TWENTY

A familiar smell awakened Kate. It reminded her of D&T in her secondary school: specifically, the Year 7 ritual of introducing eleven and twelve-year-olds to carpentry or metalwork. She'd chosen the latter. Even now, two odors had the power to transport her back to the days of tin can roses and cigar box ukuleles. One was hot metal. The other was burnt flesh.

She opened her eyes. It was dark. Her head weighed three stone and her upper chest throbbed like she'd been flayed. Then the sound came back to her: *bzzzzt.*

Cattle prod. God in heaven. No wonder the bloody beasts stampede.

She lifted her head. Perspiration rolled into her eyes, yet she was cold, so cold she was shivering. When she tried to rise, the world lurched. Up became down; she tasted bile. All she could do was close her eyes and wait for her equilibrium to return.

Toughen up, Kate. It's not like you're shot. But where's Tony?

Taking a deep breath, Kate sat up slowly. Her vision cleared after a few blinks and she saw where she was: a narrow catwalk under the stars.

She'd collapsed, or more likely been dumped, in the middle of a maintenance bridge between ventilation ports and electrical units. Her stockings were shredded; the diamond-patterned steel bit into her bare knees. Her heels and handbag were gone, or her eyes hadn't yet adjusted enough for her to pick them out. One Hundred and One Leadenhall's roof was mostly unlit, apart from a couple of florescent boxes. Still, the City of London's gaggle of skyscrapers provided plenty of light. So did One-oh-One's four-pointed spire, illuminated in emerald green in honor of World Environment Day.

Gripping the catwalk's cold metal railing, Kate hauled herself up. Her reward was more pain in her shoulders and a second wave of nausea. Flashes of memory came back to her. Coming around in a lift. Being urged through a narrow vertical passage, possibly an air vent, with a reminder that Henry's safety hinged on her cooperation. Maybe she'd tried something that made Sir Duncan electrocute her again. Maybe she'd just passed out. But judging by the ache in her arm sockets, she'd been dragged much of the way.

Where's Tony?

Kate looked around. The maintenance bridge was apparently the highest point a person without a line and harness could achieve atop the Leadenhall building. Above her loomed the spire; before her, steep metal stairs, eight steps down, and a narrow spit of rooftop.

Sir Duncan wasn't there. Neither was Tony.

She saw two massive electrical units and a stunted wall, no more than eighteen inches, separating the roof from thin air. She was alone.

Kate's heart leapt. Alone was almost as good as free, if she kept her wits. She looked a second time for her bag, but like her shoes, it was gone. Inside were two items she never left home without: her Met-issued tear gas spray and her mobile.

So much for calling for backup. There has to be something up here I can use as a weapon.

Descending those eight steps wasn't easy, even while clinging to the handrail. Every step sent a peculiar vibration up her legs, ankles to glutes. Not quite like pins and needles. More like light-bulbs flickering just before a power cut.

On the final step, her ankle turned. Her usual agility was gone; she fell gracelessly, like an old lady slipping in the bath. The roof's gritty surface cut her palms like ground glass. It abraded her chin, too. But that was nothing compared to the pain of biting her tongue.

Spitting out blood, Kate blinked away tears. Staggering upright, she lurched toward one of the electrical units; slowly, so as not to fall on her face again. The skyscrapers leaned in absurdly close, a knot of titans bearing down on one tiny woman.

Wind battered her, sharp and cold. Still unsteady on her bare feet, Kate didn't dare veer too close to the short wall separating the roof from a fifty story drop. The vantage point allowed her to survey the surrounding high-rises. Atop Hotel Nonpareil, she saw the helipad recently installed for the convenience of VIP guests. Over at the Dolphin's East tower, she saw blinking red lights. They marked the start of a quickie zip line strung between the East and West towers. And over at the Walkie-Talkie build-ing, the entire penthouse had been converted to a nightspot with floor-to-ceiling windows and a 360° view of London. It was infu-riating to be almost within hailing distance of so many luxury hotels, yet unable to leverage one for a rescue.

Hang on. What's that?

Sitting innocuously in the shadow of an electrical unit was something that looked like a gym bag. Kate moved carefully toward it.

Were her legs becoming more reliable? Perhaps. That weird buzzing from her ankles to her glutes had intensified, but she ignored it. The twice-shocked spot where her throat met her clavicle hurt like hell, so she refused to look at it or touch it with her fingertips. She didn't care if she had a great gaping hole in her chest. She only cared about Tony, Ritchie, and Henry.

The gym bag, black canvas with unobtrusive gray piping, blended in nicely with the roofscape. Heart speeding up, she unzipped it and dug inside. Only after she plunged her hands inside did it occur to Kate that it might contain a bomb.

Nice going. Two zaps and all my training's out the window.

Fortunately, she withdrew nothing resembling an IED. First came a digital camera on a neck strap, its long lens already attached. Next, blueprints and maintenance schematics, printed on copy paper and held with a binder clip. Then an Android mobile phone.

"Oh, thank God," she babbled. It was charged and functioning. But the lock screen wanted a ten-digit passcode and didn't display the word EMERGENCY. Nor did it respond when she mashed the buttons that should have triggered a wipe/reset.

"Bollocks!" She dumped the bag's remaining contents. Out spilled a mini Maglite, a pair of police-issue metal handcuffs, a roll of duct tape, and a fourteen-inch camp axe with a green plastic handle and matching blade guard.

"Yes!" She snatched up the axe.

"The No-Hopers pack an intriguing overnight bag," said someone in a familiar arch tone.

Kate turned. Sir Duncan stood on the maintenance bridge. Tony was in front of him, on his feet but only half-conscious from the look of him. An angry red welt stood out on his cheek. Sir Duncan had the cattle prod he'd called a Hot Shot positioned beside Tony's right eye.

"Bloody hell. You look a mess, Kate. Hard to believe I once found you mildly attractive. The old man's sucking the life out of you, no?" Sir Duncan waved the cattle prod like a magic wand. "Funny how the fight went out of him when I zapped him in the face. I wonder, if I tried the eye, would it induce a stroke?" He shook Tony, hard. "What do you think, Chief? Will I trigger a fit of apoplexy, as people of your generation used to say, if I send 10,000 volts to your brain by way of the optic nerve?"

Kate didn't need to be told to put down the axe. She placed it in front of her feet. Then she rose, keeping her eyes on Tony. Was he playing possum? Maybe. Sir Duncan was twenty years younger and half a foot taller, but maybe, just maybe....

"Good girl," Sir Duncan said. "Ordinarily, I find disobedience more interesting. But if you come over as the hard-charging heroine, it will play havoc with my scenario. Take five, Tony."

Only when Sir Duncan released him did Kate realize he'd been holding her husband up. The metal catwalk rang dully as Tony hit it, knees first.

Kate went for the axe. Before she could raise it, Sir Duncan closed the distance and yanked it out of her hands. Dropping it behind his back, he put the cattle prod level with her nose.

"Think this would burn a hole in your face if I held it against you long enough?"

Another gust of wind barreled through, rattling the big antennas on the lighted spire. An updraft caught the Leadenhall building's specs in their binder clip and carried them over the side. Kate, seeing Sir Duncan's eyes flick toward the unexpected movement, knew this was the moment. She threw all her strength in a 360-degree roundhouse kick.

He caught her right leg, twisting her in midair. Kate's scream was silenced only by her agonizing impact with the roof.

The pain was too immense to scream again. It was all she could do to keep breathing. Her knee bulged in the wrong place; her lower leg was at an angle.

"Slow. Soft." Looming over her, Sir Duncan sounded impressed with himself. "Either that, or I can add superhuman speed to my list of remarkable personal attributes." He glanced toward the maintenance bridge. "See that, did you?"

"I did," Tony said, rising as she had earlier, pulling himself up courtesy of the catwalk's guardrail. "A fit man took down a beat-up woman. If only your mother were alive to see it."

Sir Duncan folded his arms and put his head to one side. In

his blue jacket, white shirt, chinos, and boat shoes, he might've just popped round to St. Katharine Docks for a Friday night yacht cruise.

"Is a bit of pop psychology the best you can do, Baron Wellegrave? A dig about Mummy in hopes of sending me over the edge? Literally." He glanced theatrically toward the roof's short barrier wall and the dizzying depths just beyond. "Wouldn't you be better off telling me I need to make a deal? That perhaps I can negotiate a helicopter to some extradition treaty-less banana republic, if only I take you as my hostage and spare dear Kate?"

Tony appeared intent on descending the metal stairs. He didn't make eye contact with Kate, which she took as a good sign. Perhaps her husband's lurching gait and trembling hands were manufactured for Sir Duncan's benefit. If not, they were both going to die on this rooftop. Approximately five seconds after Sir Duncan tired of toying with them.

Tony made it down the first step. "Why don't you tell me what we're doing up here, Godington?"

Sir Duncan grinned. "That's right. Put me in my place. I'm only a baronet. You'll always be better than me, even if I hack you up with my Day-Glo hatchet and rain bits of you on the City like beads during Mardi Gras. What are we doing up here? We're about to witness my greatness made manifest."

Kate surreptitiously tried to move her injured leg. The stabbing pain brought tears to her eyes. Maybe Tony's plan was to tempt Sir Duncan into bloviating. It was a good idea—except she was thirty feet from the camp axe and able to get to it only if she crawled.

"Isn't your greatness already manifest?" Tony asked. He eased onto the second step. "Just last week you blew up a fringe candidate for prime minister courtesy of some low-rent hackers."

"Yes, well, that's nothing compared to blowing up DEFRA's corrupt Secretary of State and her two equally corrupt ministers. Not to mention a good chunk of the Dolphin." Sir Duncan pointed at the neighboring skyscraper's tallest tower. "I no longer care if this country is globalist or nationalist. All this talk of Whitehall versus Brussels? It means nothing to me. But the UK must continue adhering to the EU environmental regulations. And DEFRA was poised to betray us. Whinging that it was all too difficult, too bloody *hard*, for Britain to continue its green commitments after the next Great Divorce." He grew visibly angrier as he spoke. "Do you realize, do you have the slightest idea, what our elected public servants were up to tonight?"

Tony, on the third stair, shook his head. Kate was glad Sir Duncan seemed especially intent on making his point to her husband and not to her. The camp axe might be too far to reach without losing the element of surprise, but the gym bag's dumped contents were mere inches away. She'd go for the handcuffs. Could she do anything with them?

Maybe. Clamping them on his wrists would require springing up, attacking, and generally being stronger and faster than she'd been before Sir Duncan shattered her kneecap. Snapping them around his ankles was something Bugs Bunny might try on Elmer Fudd. It would seem desperate if she succeeded and barking mad if she failed. But humiliation was preferable to meek submission.

Sir Duncan was still complaining about DEFRA. "They were drinking vodka and eating caviar with their friends from the Russian Embassy. Diplomats, spies, escorts, and fossil fuel robber barons."

"Wish I were there now," Tony said, easing down to the fourth step like a man who might topple at any moment.

"I don't doubt it. There's plenty of money, power, and prestige for those who understand this is a once-in-a-lifetime opportunity to do something for the Kremlin," Sir Duncan said. "The Russians are *counting* on climate change. No ice makes for easier oil drilling. As for Ms. Neera Nausherwani and her ilk, they have no one to blame but themselves. They let themselves be separated from the pack, and for any prey animal, that invites certain death."

"And killing them will change things, you imagine?" Tony asked as if considering the practicality of Sir Duncan's approach. "I'll admit it will put the spotlight on the environment for a week. Perhaps two." He descended another step. "Is there really a bomb at the Dolphin?"

"Oh, yes. Gunpowder, treason, and plot, old man." Sir Duncan smiled. "I told the kiddies I wanted one of your cars blown up, just like they blew up Ford Fabian for his wife. What a disappointment when you started using the Bentley. Still, it must have hurt you to park the Lamborghini and that ghastly yellow Testarossa. One of the happiest days of my boyhood was sabotaging your petrol-wasting cars."

Lady Isabel was right. He's gone round the bend, Kate thought. *He thinks Tony's Sir Raleigh.*

"I fear I must remind you of your father," Tony said. "But I'm not. Look at me, Godington. I'm Tony Hetheridge. I may have retired from Scotland Yard, but I still have plenty of influence. I can help you disentangle this knot. Let me help you. If not for your own sake, for your sister's."

"Ah. Yes. Dear Izzy," Sir Duncan said. "You needn't concern yourself with her any longer. You were never a father to her, except in name. I intended to be gentle, but she woke just as I dripped the first bit of superglue into her nostrils. That hardened fast, which was lucky, because sealing her lips was a beast. Then she clawed at her face so much I had to sit on her chest. Dead in a quarter-hour. Cheeks red and bloody. Didn't feel a thing."

"Is that how you'll live with yourself?" Tony asked, stepping onto the roof at last but still clinging to the handrail. "Imagining she felt no pain?"

Sir Duncan giggled. Once, he'd been deceptively handsome. Now there was no other word for him but ugly.

"Oh, Izzy surely felt pain. Superglue in the nostrils must burn.

My knees pinning down her flat chest probably wasn't a day at the fun fair, either. I meant, *I* felt nothing."

Tony straightened his back. When he spoke, it was with a strength and authority that gave Kate new hope.

"Sir Duncan Forgive me for saying so, but you're not the man you were. You need a way out. Only imagine. Wouldn't your trial be a sensation? A worldwide event. The entire planet would tune in to hear your manifesto on climate change. The DEFRA ministers would be publicly shamed for their lack of ethics. And showing mercy would give you the moral high ground, which will cement your legacy. You know I'm right."

Sir Duncan's lip curled. "*Daddy* doesn't dictate to me," he spat, lunging for Tony. In the same instant, Kate surged.

She got vertical by pushing off with her arms and her uninjured leg. It hurt like hell, but pain was meaningless. All she felt was desperation. A groin kick would be ideal but impossible. A groin punch was possible, but dangerous. It would expose the back of her neck to Sir Duncan, putting her center mass within his grasp. So she went for a throat rip, knowing she would fall in the process and hoping to take him down with her.

"Kate!"

Bzzzzt

She screamed as the Hot Shot touched her jaw. Its sizzling jolt knocked her back on her heels, one of which couldn't support her. She fell with no idea which way she was falling. Would she land in front of Sir Duncan, near the gym bag? Or behind Sir Duncan, near the camp axe?

At her back was a chilling updraft. She hit something short and hard—the stunted wall at the roof's edge—and heard something she'd never heard before: her husband's scream.

Sir Duncan caught her by the blouse front. As his fingers dug in, her blouse tore at the seams with a soft, dreamlike *riiiiip*. She felt herself propelled backward.

This can't be happening. As she stared into Sir Duncan's mad bulging eyes, Kate prayed wordlessly, *Please God, save him.* "Him" meant Tony, meant Ritchie, meant Henry. Her three loves; the three lives she would trade her own to protect.

Sir Duncan released his grip on the cattle prod. Kate didn't hear it collide with the roof; that was because it went over. Right hand freed, he seized Kate's jacket. Hauling her back from the brink, he flung her down beside the camp axe. She tried to seize it, but her grip was feeble. He took it away.

"Not a machete," he said, smiling at the weapon before turning to Tony. "Still, it will do."

CHAPTER TWENTY-ONE

"There we are, old boy." With the snap of a metal bracelet, Sir Duncan seemed restored to the glib good humor that had once been his trademark. "Too tight?"

Tony pulled hard against the cuff connecting him to the maintenance bridge's handrail. Sir Duncan had fastened it exactly right, damn him. The handrail was secure, too, welded seamlessly into the metal catwalk. A sledgehammer wouldn't have loosened the railing. But that wasn't necessarily a disadvantage.

An avalanche of things had gone wrong that night. But since Tony regained consciousness on the Leadenhall building's roof, three things had gone right. One: Kate was still alive. Two: he was still alive. And three: he'd discouraged Sir Duncan from cuffing his hands behind his back.

Sir Duncan's ease in handling the cuffs made it clear this wasn't his first go-round. Hoping he knew that if a captive balled their fists and squared their shoulders, it would cause the cuffs to be applied too loosely, Tony made a show of immediately putting his hands behind his back when Sir Duncan approached him. Taking a deep breath, he made himself as big as he could.

Fortunately, Sir Duncan noticed. Tutting, he'd seized Tony's wrist, saying, "I think I'll feel better with you attached to an immovable object." So Tony's right hand was cuffed, but his left was free.

The cuffs were the classic style, metal bracelets joined by two steel links. Irrespective of manufacturer, most relied on the same inner mechanism. Therefore, any random pair could be opened by almost any random key. They were easy to pick, too. Dozens of items would do the trick: paperclips, ballpoint pens, safety pins, a bloody seafood fork. But Tony had visually scoured every millimeter of the roof within reach and spied nothing that fit the bill. Only a dog-end and a butane lighter.

Not that he wasn't capable of overlooking something in his present state. The cattle prod had been rougher on him than on Kate. Perhaps it was the difference in their ages. Perhaps it was because he took his initial jolt to the face. But despite shambling the last hundred yards to the roof, Tony hadn't regained his wits until he saw Kate try her Taekwondo kick and fail. Only then did he realize the full peril of their situation.

"I've no idea why the No-Hopers included handcuffs," Sir Duncan told him. "They're not part of the standard Urbex gear. Unless they're for rooftop sex games. Those kids are degenerates."

Watching Tony carefully, as if angling for a specific response, he continued, "Tell me, did you ever use restraints on any of your women? Was that how it went wrong between you and my mother?"

Before Tony could decide how to reply, Sir Duncan waved his question away. "Never mind. Evolved as I've become, I don't need to know. There was a time when it used to torture me, imagining what you did to her. No longer."

"Perhaps I've always misunderstood you," Tony said. It was standard advice within the Met never to challenge an assailant's delusion. Playing along or redirecting was safer. Trying to drag the individual into the here-and-now could provoke a fatal attack. "Tell me about this evolution."

"Yes, you'd like that, wouldn't you? You still think you can talk your way out of this. Bluster, bully, and run right over me." Sir Duncan's cannibal grin, long celebrated by the tabloids, flashed green as the Leadenhall building's four-pointed spire pulsed far above. "You know why you're still alive? Why she's still alive?"

Turning, Sir Duncan gazed upon Kate like an artist studying his half-finished landscape. She remained where he'd left her after taking away the axe. Tony allowed himself to meet his wife's eyes for only a split-second. She looked scared, pained, and mad as hell.

"I'll tell you why," Sir Duncan said. "Because no triumph is complete without an audience. Our friends from DEFRA can't have much time left. Not more than... Oh, bugger."

He was looking out at the city, apparently at nothing. Was the man hallucinating? Then Tony saw it, faintly. A flash of light from one of the Dolphin's towers.

"Now what?" Pulling a mobile from his wind-cheater, Sir Duncan speed-dialed someone. When the line engaged, he said, "Kyla, my love. Why are you on the roof again?"

Kyla Sloane, Tony thought. *Kate never liked her. I hope she gets the chance to say 'I told you so.'*

Sir Duncan listened to the response, idly twirling the camp axe and pacing. Each time the man turned his back, Tony rotated his shackled wrist clockwise, pulling with all his might. The handrail held; his bracelet left a hairline scrape on its metal surface.

"The No-Hopers gave me a countdown clock," Sir Duncan said into his mobile. "Let me have a look." He advanced in Kate's direction, turning his back again.

Twisting himself counterclockwise, Tony threw all his weight behind an even harder pull, exerting so much force he thought his wrist might dislocate.

The mobile *beep-booped* as Sir Duncan tapped the screen. Then he stooped in front of Kate, thrusting his mobile in her face. "Kate. Be a dear and read that number out to your mate."

She glared up at him, not answering. Sir Duncan's back was still turned. Tony rotated his wrist clockwise again, straining his biceps and triceps enough to elicit an involuntary grunt of pain. Sir Duncan should have heard him, but clearly, Kate's defiance held his attention.

"I said be a dear!" he shouted, kicking Kate's injured leg.

Tony closed his eyes. As Kate answered, "Five minutes now," he made one last desperate pull.

"Five minutes. Hear that, *Lord Hetheridge?*" Sir Duncan asked, spinning on his heel to point at Tony. "Clever *nom de guerre*, isn't it, Paul? As if I don't see through it. Go on, milord. Tell your friend you're up here, too, or I'll kick Kate's teeth in."

Tony's eyes flicked to Kate. She looked pale with shock, worse than when Sir Duncan had pulled her back from the brink. That kick to her dislocated knee had done its work. As well as the news Paul was mixed up in this; that he might die tonight, too.

"I'm here," Tony said. He didn't know enough about Sir Raleigh Godington to impersonate him with assured accuracy. However, he, Tony Hetheridge, had something in common with Sir Duncan. They were both the second sons of difficult men. That alone might allow him to speak with Sir Raleigh's voice, cutting through Sir Duncan's cold good humor to bring forth the deranged, thoughtless beast.

"I think five minutes is plenty of time to kill Lord and Lady Hetheridge before a Met helicopter trains a single spotlight on Deadenfall," Sir Duncan was telling Paul. "And who knows, maybe there'll still be fireworks."

"I wish you would kill me, Duncan," Tony said, imitating the cold, uppercrust tones of his own father.

Sir Duncan's back straightened. Leo Hetheridge and Sir Raleigh Godington hadn't looked much alike, but they'd shared a near-identical manner of speaking. In channeling Leo/Sir Raleigh, he'd apparently succeeded.

"At first, I thought I'd die of mortification, but no such luck," Tony said. For years, he'd tried to forget these words, delivered by Leo on the occasion of his twenty-sixth birthday, but they remained etched upon his memory. Now they fell from his lips with remarkable ease.

"This grand career of yours is a sham. Such a little man, scampering about with ludicrous self-importance. The do-gooder out to save the world. Everyone's laughing at you."

Sir Duncan dropped his mobile and picked up the camp axe.

"Your brother never would've done this. Your brother knew what was expected of him. I was proud of him. I was proud to think of one day giving him my title. But you. You—"

Sir Duncan was upon him, axe raised high. Tony brought both hands up, the right encircled by a silver bracelet with a broken chain. As the axe came down, he could have blocked it, but he didn't. Instead, he grabbed the open collar of Sir Duncan's windcheater.

A thunderous blow landed on his face. Maybe it hurt too much for his nerves to register. He felt no pain, only a shattering impact from skull to heels. But his double grip on Sir Duncan's collar only intensified. As he fell, he brought the other man crashing down with him. Something was in his eyes – blood – but Tony ignored that, viciously twisting the wind-cheater.

Sir Duncan flailed. The camp axe flew out of his grip. Seeing a flash of Day-Glo green, Tony realized he'd been hit with the blade guard still in place. No wonder there wasn't a hatchet sticking out of his face. But strangling the bigger, taller man with his own jacket wasn't working. Worse, Tony was positioned at a disadvantage: below his opponent and reaching up. He needed to reverse that. All chips to the center of the table.

Tony let go of the collar. Sir Duncan drew in a desperate breath. As he shook free of the fabric bunched around his throat,

Tony sprang to his feet. Seizing Sir Duncan's head with both hands, he twisted with all his strength, as far as the neck would allow, and then up, up, *up* until something snapped. Maybe in his enemy. Maybe in him.

Duncan slumped and went still. The sudden loss of tension made Tony overbalance. He staggered backward, calf hitting a low barrier.

"No!" Kate screamed. "The edge!"

Somehow, he righted himself. The wind ruffled his hair as he looked out over London. It was immense; ancient; his. When he turned, his left eye saw nothing, but his right saw his wife clearly enough. She was trying to come to him, but there were no hand-holds within reach and her injured leg wouldn't support her.

Something primal swept through him. He heard an animal sound, a guttural roar that belonged in the jungle but came from within. Seizing Sir Duncan's body, he lifted it over his head and pitched it into the darkness.

Knees... hurt....

Of course they did. He'd fallen to them, the better to gasp for breath. Rage had given him the strength to cast down his enemy, the man who'd hurt Kate. Perhaps love would give him the strength to crawl to her side. He wanted to say goodbye to her before the top of the Dolphin's North tower exploded.

The sound announced the helicopter before he saw it: a black and yellow NPAD EC145 passing overhead. It hovered above the Dolphin, its spotlight picking out one person standing on the roof of its tallest tower, and a row of what must've been the DEFRA hostages near an air conditioner unit. As the ops commander barked instructions at the people on the roof, another helicopter swooped in from the south. To Tony, the EC145 was a marvel, as heart-stoppingly beautiful as only *deus ex machina* could be. It was quieter than the Met's original air support unit, with a big cabin capable of delivering a nine-man team, or rescuing a handful of people all at once.

A lightly kitted-out officer descended from copter to roof via fast rope. The moment he touched down, he ran toward the hostages—and the bomb. To Tony, it seemed like a lifetime had passed between breaking out of the handcuffs to tossing Sir Duncan's corpse off the roof. Had the IED failed to detonate? Or was the timer still counting down?

CHAPTER TWENTY-TWO

"*G*ive me the key to the handcuffs." Paul thought he sounded remarkably rational. He was only barking orders at Kyla. What he really wanted to do would get him banged up for GBH. Or murder. "If you help me free the hostages, I'll let you go when we reach the street. You can do a runner, I swear."

"You're lying. Besides. I don't have it. Aaron or one of the boys took it with them when they legged it." Rising, Kyla smiled as if her lip wasn't bleeding and her front tooth wasn't chipped. Always poised, right down to her marrow.

"Fine. But you're not going back down those stairs," Paul warned. "You'll stay right here with me and the hostages and we'll go to kingdom come together."

Kyla's smile didn't flag.

"Is that what you want? Is that how you really want this to end?"

"Angels don't die. Heaven is deathless. As above, so below."

"That's gibberish."

"To you. I'm among the initiated." Sliding her hands into her lavender wig, Kyla pulled it off, dropping it onto the gritty rooftop. The mesh cap over her real hair made her skull look bumpy. "Do you know how a caterpillar becomes a butterfly?"

Paul looked at her iPhone's countdown clock. 00:04. Did he hear the throaty *whirr* of NPAD helicopters? Or was that just wishful thinking?

"The caterpillar," Kyla said louder, apparently determined to have her say whether he cared to listen or not, "wraps itself in a cocoon. Inside the cocoon, it liquefies. That's the only way to attain a superior form. Complete destruction. Duncan has to die. If not tonight, soon. He'll go above and return below. Elegant. Terrestrial to winged to terrestrial again."

She reached into one of her thigh-high boots. Paul dropped into his ready stance. Laughing, she peeled off the boot and tossed it aside.

"Believe me, if I had another knife, or maybe a gun, you'd already be dead." Peeling off the other boot, she dropped it near its deflated twin. "I was a champion, you know. But I never did it in boots."

Before Paul could puzzle out what she meant, Kyla spun on her heel and sprinted away. He was too shocked to cry out, and too stunned to go after her. At least, that's how he told the story afterward, to himself and to others.

Kyla reached the tower's waist-high concrete ledge. Vaulting it, she balanced atop it for a split-second. Then she executed a straight forward dive into thin air, hands folded for a splashless entry.

"Look!" Neera cried.

"Helicopter," Jeremy said. "Helicopter!"

The spotlight from *India 98* fell upon Paul, momentarily washing out his vision. As the EC145's yellow landing skids and black fuselage became visible, a thick braided rope was tossed from the open cabin. Sliding down via gloved hands and feet, an operative descended with astonishing speed. Behind him came three more men. They were dressed in light gear, just fatigues and side arms.

Paul had expected Kevlar-armored, hooded-suit-wearing Explosive Ordinance Disposal techs. On telly, EODs were slow-moving blobs who advanced deliberately toward the bomb while others ran the other way. Then again, fictional EODs rarely dropped out of the sky via fast rope. Besides, the words "pink mist" were no exaggeration. If the Super-Semtex IED was as potent as he feared, body armor would be about as effective as sunblock.

"Saw the girl go over. Some geezer got pitched off Leadenhall, too," the lead operative shouted at Paul.

Did he say geezer?

Paul convinced himself he'd heard the operative wrong. The *whir* of helicopter blades was thunderous. And Tony couldn't have died that way, he just couldn't.

"You're Paul, yeah? Fancy a flight?" The man's kit looked like Army, not MPS, but with SO19, the lines blurred.

"I promised the hostages I'd stay till the end."

"Soppy tosser." The operative pulled a pair of compact, heavy-duty snips from his belt. "I'll free them. Stay planted."

India 98 was on the move. Less than fifty feet above them, its pilot seemed to be assessing the North tower's roofscape, searching for a place to set down. The copter's whirring blades drew up clouds of rooftop grit. Paul threw up an arm to shield his eyes as a hot gust of particulate blew into his face. When he dared look, the operative with metal snips was freeing Neera.

She leapt up the moment her handcuffs were severed. Next came Jeremy, flexing arms that must have been stiff and sore, and Edwin, who clung to Jeremy like he might faint.

The two EODs closed in on the bomb. One had a hand-held device that reminded Paul of a *Star Trek* tricorder; the other, some kind of tablet. They didn't seem to be in a particular hurry.

He knew EODs were methodical and cautious–the living ones, anyway—but why drop in like superheroes only to stand there?

"Paul!" Neera threw her arms around him. Closing his eyes, he held her tight. He felt absurdly that she understood him.

Overhead, the copter wheeled, apparently unable to land. For an aircraft that could carry roughly ten people, its fuselage was remarkably compact. But the jutting tail boom and tail rotors extended too far for the copter to land without smacking into a water reservoir or one of the tower's bulky antennae.

How much time?

The air was still thick with grit. Fanning it away, Paul advanced only a few steps—enough to make out 00:02 on the timer—when the operative who'd used the metal snips shouted, "Okay, ladies and gents, this is how we're doing it. One at a time." Seizing Neera's upper arm, he jerked her away from Paul.

The EC145 dipped low beside the very stretch of roof off which Kyla had thrown herself. Defying the wind, the pilot kept the copter hovering with admirable steadiness, the aircraft bobbing gently as she adjusted and readjusted. The cabin door was wide open. The bright yellow landing skids, though in constant motion, remained just a few inches above the concrete guardrail, forming approximate steps.

"Your chariot awaits," the operative shouted at Neera. "Don't you worry, that bird'll stay put. My CO's at the stick and she's dead brill. See that great prat holding out his arms? That's my mate, Devin. Run to him!"

Neera shot a glance at Paul. Then she was running full-tilt at *India 98*, jumping onto the guardrail and tripping on the lower landing skid.

"No!" Paul cried.

But Devin wasn't having it. Catching her under the arms, he pulled Neera into the copter with ease.

Jeremy made a better job of the jump, clambering aboard *India 98* mostly under his own steam. Then Edwin ran for it, lost his nerve before the jump, and had to be half-coaxed, half-dragged inside the aircraft.

Paul glanced at the EODs. Two were still consulting the tablet-sized device. The one who'd approached the bomb put down something and backed away.

The operative swatted Paul between the shoulder blades, shouting, "Go! *Go!*"

Then Paul was running, legs pumping, eyes locked on Devin. He didn't imagine the jump. He imagined the concussion, the scorching heat and blinding light that would inevitably vaporize him seconds before he reached safety. Wasn't that how his luck always ran?

Not this time. His right foot bounded off the lower landing skid, propelling him up. Devin didn't catch him so much as Paul caught him, latching onto his fatigues like a tick jumping onto a spaniel. Pivoting, Devin flung Paul against a solid object that turned out to be Neera.

I'm alive. I'm still alive.

Before he could come to grips with that, the lead operative collided with him, courtesy of another Devin pivot. All three EODs followed, rocking the EC145 like a ferry taking on extra passengers.

"Countercharge!" one of the EODs told the pilot.

"Roger that."

The copter shot up. Then it banked sharply as something exploded below.

No one spoke. One EOD, leaning slightly out the cabin door as his fellows kept him anchored, seemed to be counting under his breath. After what felt like an interminable interval, but was probably only thirty seconds, he addressed the pilot.

"IED null, ma'am."

"The bomb exploded?" Edwin looked wrung out, long past tears.

"They blew up the detonator," Neera told him.

"But that would have set the bomb off."

"No, Edwin, the *detonator* would have set the bomb off. Take away the detonator and the bomb's inert." She turned to Paul. "Right?"

He had no business answering. Most of his training regarding IEDs could be summarized in two words: consult SO19. He hadn't mentally worked it out like Neera. Maybe she'd contemplated her career history of bomb threat in-services while handcuffed to that pile of explosives. Or maybe her Netflix queue was nothing but thrillers.

The lead operative poked Paul in the ribs. Apparently, that was his cue to agree.

"Yes. Countercharge nullified the detonator," he told Neera. "Well done, you."

"Scotland Yard knows his stuff," the operative said humbly. Talk about a good bloke. Not only did he play angel of deliverance, he played wingman, too.

"What're you called?" Paul asked him.

"Me? Oscar."

"Oscar. Thanks for saving my life." He looked at Neera, Jeremy, and Edwin. "Our lives."

CHAPTER TWENTY-THREE

"*N*PAD loaded them all," Tony told Kate. "I'd need field glasses to swear it, but Paul must have been with them."

He'd made it to his wife's side just as the air rescue began. A smart man would have tried to drag her toward shelter from the coming blast, if such a thing existed. But Tony lacked the strength. His face hurt, his head hurt—everything hurt, really. And a creeping fuzziness made any action seem impossible.

"Can they reach minimum safe distance?" Kate asked. Sitting up with her injured leg straight out, she couldn't see over the low wall.

"Let's see." *India 97* looked good. But *India 98*, weighed down with its human payload, was still close to the North tower when something went *boom* and a cloud of white smoke came up.

"Oh, God! Was that it?"

"No. It must have been a countercharge. SO19." He tried to think of a phrase profound enough to express his gratitude to that command, but the creeping fuzziness was clogging up his brain. All he could do was repeat the name of the antiterrorist branch more slowly, pronouncing the designation like a benediction. "SO19."

The *whirr* of copter blades went from loud to near-deafening. Brilliant white light flooded the roof as *India 97* appeared overhead, training its spotlight on Tony and Kate. From the external speaker a voice boomed, "GODINGTON! HANDS UP!"

Tony's hands were already high in the air. That required the same effort he usually exerted to bench 130kg. He'd drawn on something primitive to lift Sir Duncan. Now the adrenaline had fled. Only the consequences remained.

"Do I look like Duncan Godington?" he shouted into the blinding light, well aware that no one in the copter could hear a word. "It's Hetheridge! Scotland Yard. Sent packing six months ago!" He wasn't sure why he added that last, except that it struck him as funny.

"CHIEF?" the PA boomed.

"Well-spotted! Lovely weather, eh?" he laughed.

"Tony, they can't hear you," Kate said.

"WAS THAT GODINGTON WHO WENT OVER?"

He gave *India 97* the thumbs-up.

"PARAMEDICS EN ROUTE. STANDBY."

That news earned a double thumbs-up. "No hurry, old man. Wouldn't want to be a bother."

"*Tony,*" Kate said sharply. "Sit down before you fall down."

His wife had a point, as usual. He tried to kneel beside her, but his arthritic left knee took that as permission to give way. The impact of his body against the rooftop sent a bolt of agony through his skull.

"Come here." Kate drew him close. Her warm breath against his throat was simple. Miraculous. Like a small girl, she whispered, "Are you sure we're alive?"

"If it hurts this much, I'd say yes."

"And he's dead?" she asked, meaning Sir Duncan.

"Twice over."

"Henry — Ritchie—" Her voice shot into its highest register.

"They're fine." He gave her a gentle shake. "They're absolutely fine, I promise."

"What about you?" Her gaze lingered over his injuries. She lifted her hand, but seemed afraid to touch his face.

"Do I still have an eye in there?"

"I think so. It's swollen shut. Oh, Tony."

"PARAMEDICS CLEARED TO ENTER THE BUILDING. ETA TO ROOF, THREE MINUTES."

"Rather like getting updates from God, isn't it?"

"The big guy's a little late on the scene," Kate said.

"No. He came through," Tony said, tightening his embrace. "I still have everything I ever wanted."

CHAPTER TWENTY-FOUR

By Monday, Paul had acquired a second phone, an off-the-rack burner, to handle his truly personal calls. He'd already appeared on morning telly, radio shows, and American cable news. Now the calls were metastasizing into financial offers, many of them dodgy. Would he like a Hollywood agent? Possibly a Bollywood agent? Amazon Films had called him directly, no middleman, about a biopic. Several traditional publishers wanted to ghostwrite his autobiography on an accelerated schedule. Every tabloid he'd ever seen wanted to discuss his love life, his fashion sense, his favorite restaurant, and his iPod playlist. They all wanted exclusive photoshoots, too. He was getting scared to listen to his voicemail. Hence, the second phone.

His mum, Sharada, was holding up well. Who knew the woman who threatened to call the paramedics when he burned his thumb on the cooker would behave like Marcus Aurelius the stoic when summoned to St. Thomas's Hospital? In the A&E, Paul's checks had been perfunctory, of course, but he'd refused to leave until Kate came out of surgery. Sharada had accepted this with perfect equanimity, despite the fact they were stuck in the waiting room until three o'clock in the morning. Then she took him home—his childhood home—and made him palak paneer.

Emmeline had done interviews over the weekend, too. Television programs, especially cable news, wanted to know about Kyla Sloane, the up-and-coming model with a dark side: what she'd been like, if there'd been signs, and on and on. Emmeline was good on camera, and she didn't mince words about Sir Duncan and the public's adoration for a serial killer. Even now, conspiracy theories were proliferating online. Maybe he'd been murdered by the Met and posthumously framed. Or maybe the real Sir Duncan was safe in Brunei, and an imposter had died in his place. Or the Met had been right about him, but in the end he'd pulled the wool over their eyes again, staging an epic faked demise straight out of the popular show *Sherlock*. Paul didn't know how to combat group fantasies or militant suspension of disbelief. He only hoped the people who accepted objective reality continued to outnumber the ones who did not.

When Paul ran into Emmeline in a BBC1 green room, she didn't mince words with him, either. She called him a tosser, a wanker, and a gormless git. She also told him she loved him, and they needed to get back together because he wasn't safe out on his own. He tended to agree with her.

DCI Jackson had met with Paul twice, once alone in his office, again in a Scotland Yard conference room with those stone-faced worthies they called "the top brass" or, more cosmically, the Powers that Be. No one mentioned the press's characterization of him as "the heroic face of today's modern police service." Nor did procedural infractions come up. He was starting over, *tabula rasa*. He would continue under DCI Jackson's supervision on the Toff Squad, with one change. His rank would be Detective Inspector.

Mates and casual acquaintances kept asking him how he was holding up. He always smiled, laughed a little, and said something meaningless. If only he was an American who could weep in the arms of strangers and spill his deepest fears in a tweetstorm. But he wasn't, and he couldn't. In the aftermath of the crisis, he'd never felt more English.

Alone in his bed at night, he relived it all, sometimes in flashes, sometimes from start to finish. When it got bad, he pushed away the worst moments, focusing instead on the time after his rescue.

India 98 had set him and the hostages down on Leadenhall Street. Neera, Jeremy, and Edwin were loaded into yellow and blue ambulances and taken to St. Thomas's Hospital with an MPS escort following to debrief them. Ordinarily the City was lightly traveled after dark, but that night the streets around the Dolphin and One-oh-One were crowded with people, many pushing against the red police barriers. Some were evacuated residents, impatient to know what was happening. Others were curious Londoners drawn by cable breaking news.

At first, the media presence was ordinary. Then someone found out the shattered body under a foil thermal blanket was Sir Duncan Godington. Fifteen minutes after word got out, plastic barriers weren't enough. In their place was a line of bonnet-to-boot police cars to keep out the cameramen, producers, and trench coat-clad correspondents.

The wait for the paramedics to bring down Tony and Kate seemed to last forever. Chatter on police radio kept mentioning a bloody axe found on the roof. The very idea of Sir Duncan with a machete-like weapon gave Paul, who'd disembarked from *India 98* already shivering, a violent case of the shakes. Since he refused to take an ambulance ride until he'd seen his friends, he, too, ended up draped in a foil blanket, just like Sir Duncan.

Finally, the sliding glass door beside One-oh-One's big revolving door *whooshed* open. Out came Tony, on a gurney and wearing an oxygen mask. He was whisked out of the Leadenhall building and loaded into an ambulance with such dispatch, Paul had no chance to speak to him. But his old guv nevertheless gave him something to cling to by waving at Paul before the doors closed. Thus Paul knew two things for sure: Tony was conscious, and at least one limb was still attached.

About ten minutes later, the paramedics brought down Kate. This coincided with the time a separate ambulance crew blocked the street to collect Sir Duncan's corpse from the point of impact. The operation was so gruesome, the City of London police formed a human shield inside the MPS vehicle barrier to further confound the paparazzi. That meant the dead man's bits wouldn't be plastered all over YouTube in real time. But one of the career photogs would get a picture for the tabloids. They always did.

Paul cast off his foil blanket to watch the crew work. He wasn't immune to human carnage. Had Tony come down in pieces like the corpse of Sir Raleigh Godington, the sight would have put Paul on his knees. But as he watched the technicians collect Sir Duncan, a process of scraping and bagging, all he felt was detached relief. On a parallel street, of course, another biohazard-suited crew was probably doing the same with Kyla. But he stuck his feelings about that in a deep, dark, emotionally subterranean compartment and shot the bolt.

"Hey," Kate said weakly. Like Tony, she was on a gurney and wearing an oxygen mask. Despite her distress, the blocked street gave the paramedics no choice but to wait in the street until it was clear to pass.

Paul went to her side. She had an angry red welt on her chin, a bigger one in the well of her throat, bruises on her forearms, and a stabilizer brace on her right leg. He grinned down at her. "You look beautiful."

She had two words for him. They were music to his ears.

"Now I know you'll live. They were so bloody long bringing you down, I was bricking it."

"I went a little mental. Made them stop the lift on our floor and prove to me that Henry and Ritchie were okay," Kate said. "They only did it was because I kept screaming I was Baroness Hetheridge."

One of the paramedics, positioned beside the gurney to monitor Kate's vital signs and until that moment discreetly feigning deafness, said, "That wasn't why."

"Was it because you're a mum?" Paul asked.

"Because I'm a human being," the paramedic shot back. "Thank God the boys were okay. If it had been bad news, I would've knocked you out with Versed and let someone else break it to you later."

"Who's with them?" Paul asked.

"My intern. She's the cuddly type. Kiddies love her," the paramedic said.

"That's a start," Kate said, clearly making an effort to sound grateful. "Paul. I need you to call someone. I can't remember the number. She's ex-directory, so you might need to use a little black magic to get it. My sister." Kate's voice broke. "Maura."

"Er... Really? Is that smart when she's suing for full custody of Henry? On the premise that you and Tony's work is too dangerous?"

"She's right." Kate sobbed weakly. "Tell Maura to bring all the court papers guaranteeing her right to visitation. She'll need them to reassume custody."

"Lady Hetheridge." The paramedic's tone was no-nonsense. "You're emotional. This isn't the time to make decisions that can't be undone."

Ignoring her, Kate blinked away tears and addressed Paul. "Sir Duncan got Henry to buzz him onto the floor. He was *in* the apartment. Gave Ritchie that Lego thingie to keep him quiet. Told me—" She took a moment to collect herself. "Told me he used the cattle prod on Henry. 5,000 volts."

"But he didn't," the paramedic said. "I checked that boy myself. He wasn't best pleased to have been locked in his room. But once he saw his uncle was A-OK and heard his parents were all right, he stuck his chin out. Grew an inch taller right before my eyes."

"Tony and I aren't his parents," Kate said miserably.

"That's not what he told me." The paramedic smiled down at Kate. "He said, 'Tony Hetheridge is my dad. His wife, Kate, is my mum.'"

Kate stared at her. "Did he really?" she whispered.

"Ask him if you don't believe me."

"I'm glad Sir Duncan didn't hurt Henry or Ritchie," Paul said. "Surprised, if I'm being honest. But glad."

"I guess some part of his old persona was still in there," Kate said. "He liked animals because they were simple, and pure. Maybe Ritchie and Henry both fell under the same category."

"Maybe. Does your hand hurt?"

"No."

"Good." He squeezed it gently. "What happened to your leg?"

"Remember that all-or-nothing roundhouse kick? I tried it. Got nothing."

"Tell me the bastard didn't really come after you with an axe."

"Not me. Tony. Hit him in the face. Thank God the plastic safety thingie was still on the blade."

Paul felt nauseous again. Now his old guv's wave was even more significant. "So is that how Sir Duncan fell? Swinging the axe like a maniac?"

"No. Tony killed him. Then threw his body off the roof."

"Oh. What did he kill him with?"

"His hands."

Paul glanced at the paramedic. Eyes wide, she'd mouthed, "Hands?"

The mix of City of London police and MPS officers were still buzzing—"The chief did for Sir Duncan with his bare hands" — long after Kate had been loaded into an ambulance to join Tony at St. Thomas's. For some reason, the memory of that gossip making the rounds always made Paul smile. Score one for the Toff Squad. It would be a long time before anyone accused them of being unwilling to get their hands dirty.

CHAPTER TWENTY-FIVE

*B*riarshaw, drowsy and golden in summer, had become Kate's favorite place in the world. Rehabilitation after her knee surgery meant moving about, and lots of it, first with a scooter, of all things. After a full patellectomy and ACL repair, she'd been forbidden to put the slightest weight on her knee for four full weeks. Fortunately, Briarshaw, like Wellegrave House, had a Gilded Age-era lift to trundle Kate from floor to floor. The house's low-pile vintage carpets didn't slow down her scooter, or the Zimmer frame that followed. Great country homes like Briarshaw, built in the eighteenth century in the Palladian style, seemed to contain a secret around every corner. Kate had spent the month of May nursing Tony, nursing herself, and soaking in the house's endless eccentricities. But now it was mid-June. The days were hotter and dryer, she'd been issued a pair of crutches, and every day was an adventure out-of-doors.

Briarshaw was two parts farm and one part garden—the rustic sort, not one of those excessively manicured showplaces Kate associated with France. The trees were old, their massive roots making the lawn difficult to cut, except by non-motorized, bladed mower. The groundskeeper thought that was too much trouble, so with Tony's blessing, he simply allowed the nannies and kids to graze there twice a week. Sometimes they got into the Queen Anne's Lace and had to be lured away with sweetfeed. Kate enjoyed helping wrangle the goats, especially the babies. She would have let them pick the shrubberies clean, but the groundskeeper wouldn't stand for it.

Kate started most mornings by exploring the garden. It was slow going on crutches. The paths weren't concrete or earth, but rather loosely-packed pebbles, which could be tricky. Twice she'd fallen and had to shout for assistance. It was no fun lying on the ground awaiting rescue, but she was beginning to accept the idea of physical limits. The NHS doctors had declined to speculate on whether or not she'd do roundhouse kicks again, but the private orthopedic specialist had given it to her straight. Her titanium knee and transplanted ligaments would allow her to walk, run for short bursts, and traverse some stairs. But it would never be as flexible as the original, nor would it be as stable.

She spent a long time in the garden, drifting from flower to flower. Once her physical therapist allowed her to kneel, or at least stoop, she planned to start weeding. Briarshaw's decorative areas were too large for one man to care for properly, and nowhere did it show more than the garden, where "natural" had become an excuse for weedy and overgrown. Lifelong Londoner and proud urbanite Kate had even learned, with the help of a botany manual from Briarshaw's dusty old library, the names of the flowers she visited daily: cornflowers, dahlias, daisies, freesia, gardenias, and lisianthuses. The yellow hyacinths and purple larkspurs were in particularly fine form that day. The smell was heavenly. How had she gone so many years taking the green bits of this earth for granted?

Sometimes lunch was big and communal, but most often it was private, in the solarium with Tony. They'd become one of those couples some people didn't get, the sort who frequently ate together in silence. Most of the meals at Briarshaw were farm to table, simple but delicious. Even egg salad sandwiches for lunch meant this morning's eggs, yesterday's loaf of bread, and December's canned pickles. Food that good was meant to be savored. Besides, Tony liked to read while he ate. Kate liked to stare out the window, watching the black and white cows on green rolling hills. Sometimes she watched her husband, too.

He'd had three surgeries since the fight with Sir Duncan—one to repair the small bones between his nose and ocular orbit, one to remove the traumatic cataract in his left eye, and another to remove the age-related cataract in his right eye. The unexpected news that his right eye was "ripe" for cataract surgery, and that such a thing was still called a "senile" cataract by some, had seemed to bother him far more than the trauma to his left eye.

His gaze flicked up from his ereader, catching her in the act. "Hmm?"

"Nothing." The ophthalmologist, a private specialist, had worked her magic, as had the oculoplastic surgeon, the NHS doctor who'd repaired the facial fractures. Two days after events on "the roof," as they euphemistically referred to the event so as not to upset Ritchie, Tony's ocular swelling had gone down enough for Kate to see the damage. She'd immediately assumed he'd be scheduled for a prosthetic, or at least a swashbuckler's eyepatch.

Temporarily blinded by the traumatic cataract, which had formed within hours of the direct blow, Tony's left eye had drifted to the wall. At the time, just forty-eight hours after her own surgery, Kate had been angry, weepy, grateful to be alive and enraged by the unfairness of life. She'd always thought of her husband's eyes as ice blue. To see one with a frozen white center, drifting away from its rightful place like a chunk of glacier broken off from the floe, had made her want to gather Sir Duncan's ashes, resurrect him, and kill him all over again.

But now Tony looked like himself again. The cataracts, traumatic and age-related, were gone, and the vision in both eyes was restored, thanks to microscopic silicone lens implants. It was one of those everyday miracles of the modern age that people took for granted. Kate was overjoyed. Though if he'd been forced to wear a black leather eye patch, she had no doubt he would've made it sexy, just as he made reading sexy.

"Will you visit the lake this afternoon?" he asked, putting the ereader aside.

"Yes. Edith will be out with the cygnets. I've decided to call them Charlotte, Emily, and Anne." She'd named the white swan and her fluffy gray chicks after famous English authors.

"How do you know some of them aren't male?"

"I don't. Unless you want to play dribbly-end peerer."

"No, thank you. I'm sure the pen knows if they're boys or girls, and has named them accordingly." He smiled. "I came down there yesterday, you know. About four o'clock, to see if you wanted a late tea. You were asleep in a chaise with the most deliciously satisfied look on your face. I crept away without disturbing you. I couldn't help but think you'd turned a corner."

He was right. When she'd arrived at Briarshaw for their healing sabbatical, she'd been so prone to fits of emotion, she'd wondered if knee surgery had poisoned her blood, or watered it down to the strength of a damp Kleenex. When she woke up after surgery in a comfortable ward with Henry and Maura smiling down at her, she'd cried. When Harvey brought her a Starbucks Toffee latte and a slice of lemon pound cake, she'd cried. When Lady Margaret and Lady Vivian turned up for a visit and promptly got into a row over whether or not Lady Vivian's lollipop bouquet was at all appropriate, she'd cried, and when Lady Margaret told her to stop, she'd cried even harder. And when Paul visited with DCI Jackson in tow—a man who looked about as natural offering sympathy as a hedgehog teleported to Mars—it had taken every ounce of Kate's strength to hold back her tears until they departed. Even her mother Louise's phone call, never quite getting to "I love you" but going as far as "take care," had thrust a knife through that wet Kleenex and into her soul.

But perhaps what didn't kill you really did make you stronger. The first time she'd come to Briarshaw, she'd been overawed by the estate, worried about saying the wrong thing to the staff and afraid Ritchie might fall in the lake. This time, with nothing else to do and the necessity of moving slowly, she'd made friends with the house, farm, and garden. It was hers now, as much as Tony's, for as long as he lived. And Ritchie had a local carer named Tabitha who performed many indispensable tasks, including keeping him from falling in the lake.

"I wonder how Henry's doing?"

"Call him." Tony picked up his ereader again.

She felt in her tweed coat—another vintage find in a house that hadn't been redone since 1945—and pulled out her iPhone. Aaron Ajax and the No-Hopers were all in remand, awaiting trial. Therefore she'd traded that Met-issued secure mobile for her preferred handheld distraction.

When Henry answered, she put the call on speaker so Tony could hear.

"What?"

"Did you just answer, 'What?' Cheeky monkey," Kate said.

"I knew it was you. I'm polite to strangers."

"Oh, well, in that case. How's tricks?"

"Okay. Maura's smoking."

"I had one fag. Half a fag, before this nosy parker made me stub it out," Maura called from nearby. "Six months clean and sober. Six months! And our Henry reads me the riot act for a puff of tobacco."

"Cancer, Maura! God!" Henry shouted.

"Don't shout at Maura," Tony said without looking up from his book.

"Sorry," Henry muttered. "What are you doing?"

"Finishing lunch," Kate said. "You?"

"Birdwatching. Up on the roof." He paused. "You wouldn't want to come up, would you?"

"Thought you'd never ask."

* * *

SOMETHING ABOUT SURVIVING a major trauma made people want to issue proclamations and swear vows. At least, that's how it was for Kate. In the time between discharge from the hospital and her arrival at Briarshaw, she'd determined the following:

First, none of them were returning to One Hundred and One Leadenhall. A moving company was dispatched to pack up all their possessions. They would stay in Briarshaw until Wellegrave House was ready in August. Kate initially hoped she wouldn't be away from the Yard that long, but her absence was allowing DI Paul Bhar to shine. And when she returned as DI Kate Hetheridge, she was determined to be at one hundred percent.

Second, she was issuing amnesty to her mother, Louise, and her sister, Maura. The past was the past. She hadn't survived being dangled fifty-two stories above London to whinge about who burned breakfast twenty-five years ago. Bang. Amnesty.

Third: at some point, when she was back in London, she'd visit Lady Isabel's grave. Perhaps even lay a wreath. Kate didn't condone Lady Isabel's choices, but then again, Kate hadn't come under Sir Duncan's influence in her formative years. Perhaps the family's explanation for their violent members, the blue blood of a king's bastard denied his royal prerogative, was a load of wank. But Lady Isabel had told Paul the unvarnished truth, as near as Scotland Yard could reconstruct, and saved many lives in the bargain. She'd died horribly, staring into the face of her half-brother, and her love. Surely that balanced the cosmic scales a bit.

Fourth: the little matter of rooftops. They'd be easy enough to avoid. Except Kate had already spent a magical evening with Tony on the roof of Briarshaw. It was the sort of roof made for small parties or family gatherings, adorned with three mysterious female statues and overlooking the Devon hills. So being afraid of rooftops was not an option. Only the stairs had kept Kate from visiting until now. With her crutches, and considerable care, she made it up to where Henry and Maura awaited her. The breeze felt lovely.

Maura had arranged herself in a canvas deck chair. Her arms and face were greased up with sunblock. In her lap was a paperback copy of *Sweet Savage Love* by Rosemary Rogers. Maura didn't like ereaders, and she wasn't much for modern romances, either. She was old school.

"Well, look at you," she said as Kate *thump, thump, thumped* to her side. "Little miss unstoppable. How's that knee?"

"So-so. See anything good, Henry?" Kate bellowed at the boy.

"I'm watching a blackcap. Now shut it. You're too loud!" he roared at her, not bothering to tear his eyes away from his new binoculars.

"He lacks what you'd call a sense of irony," Maura said. "Stay where you are and I'll get you a seat."

Kate forced herself to wait patiently as her elder sister heaved herself up, found a bookmark, marked her place, had a sip of fizzy soda, and ambled across the roof to the bracket securing three other deck chairs. Maura was new to being helpful, and Kate was new to being helped. It would be awhile before the wheels turned smoothly.

Once they were both settled in deck chairs, Maura felt around in the satchel which doubled as her handbag, withdrawing a spiral-bound notebook. "So I mentioned I have six months, right?"

"You did. I'm proud of you."

"Yeah. I thought I could rest on my laurels. But my sponsor won't let up. Makes me call every day. Emails me homework, too."

"Seems like it works."

"I guess." Maura seemed to be working up to something, trying out words and replacing them with others. "She said... after I... you know I have to be honest with... it's just... I'm meant to tell you directly how grateful I am. And I am. Grateful, I mean. Truly."

For a second Kate feared she'd turn back into a soppy Kleenex. "Oh, come on. We've been through all that, haven't we?"

"No," Maura said. "The fact is, I'm glad you're adopting Henry. I want him to have the best of everything. I always did. I just didn't want to be shut out. And now... I never dreamed... I can't believe you...."

"It was Tony's idea," Kate reminded her sister truthfully. "He's the one that pointed out we have more than enough rooms here, and at Wellegrave House. Most of them stand empty all year round."

Maura nodded. She, too, appeared to be fighting back tears. "I love it here. It's so cozy. The food. The bed. Everything. But I don't belong. It's—what do you call it? A double-edged sword. The villagers stare at me. The staff doesn't know what to make of me. I broke a vase just by walking past it. It's like you invited a bull to live in your china shop."

Kate smiled. Maura wasn't exaggerating. Briarshaw's staff transparently found her foibles and missteps exasperating. The village of Shawbridge, population 250, shunned her like a leper. Fortunately for Maura, there was a chapter of Alcoholics Anonymous in Shawbridge that met twice a week. It had three members —with Maura, four.

"I mean it," Maura said. "Fine, I'm not a bull. I'm a dozy doped-up cow."

"And I'm a gobshite detective with a bum knee. Nothing's perfect. You said you were willing to do anything for Henry. Suffer for him," Kate said. "Well. Here we are. He'll be Henry Hetheridge and you'll live where he lives and be part of his life.

There will be times when it makes you feel like a bug under a microscope. That's what you have to suffer to make this work."

Maura seemed to absorb that. Then she turned in the deck chair to observe the child she'd given birth to and Kate had claimed as a son. "He's better," she whispered.

"I know."

"He still sleeps with his phone. Just in case—you know."

"I think that's okay for now." Kate didn't want to say that she, too, slept with her phone. Someday she'd fully process that Sir Duncan Godington was dead and gone. Henry would, too. But it would take time. Neither of them was like Ritchie, able to forget completely when he chose. He'd even forgotten his old fear of Maura. By the time they returned to Wellegrave House—which would surely elicit a string of meltdowns—he'd be expecting Maura to comfort him, same as he expected Kate to.

"Okay, so, mission accomplished." Opening her spiral notebook, Maura scribbled something inside before tucking it back in her tote bag. "Funny old life."

"What do you mean?"

"Just, if you'd told me a year ago that I'd be sitting on the roof of a posh country manor with my little sis, I'd have laughed myself sick. You have an amazing life. What set you down this path?"

"That's easy," Kate said. "Meeting Tony."

"Oh. Right. Dead sexy, he is. I even like the way he reads."

"I seem to remember you calling him a wrinkly."

Maura grinned. "That was before I met him."

"Don't so much as look at my husband." Kate kept a straight face for a good five seconds before breaking up. It felt good to laugh, full-throated and fearless, on a sunny rooftop at Briarshaw, her favorite place in the world.

THE END

FROM THE AUTHOR

I hope you've enjoyed this latest story about Tony, Kate, Paul, and the ever-growing supporting cast of my *Lord & Lady Hetheridge Mystery Series*. As always, I must thank my readers for their boundless patience, enthusiasm, and kind words. Let me also answer the question I'm most frequently asked: "Will there be another Blue book?"

The answer is, there will *always* be another Blue book. Some of them will take longer to arrive than others, but I adore these characters and never plan to say goodbye.

Having said that, it's clear by the end of this one that the Hetheridges need a long holiday. So my next story will be set in Dr. Bones's wartime Cornwall. There, it's 1940, and I feel sure that year will be a momentous one for Ben, Lady Juliet, and the village of Birdswing. Also England, Europe, and the world.

Thanks again for reading. I'm more grateful to you, dear reader, than I can ever say.

Emma Jameson
February 2018

ALSO BY EMMA JAMESON

Ice Blue (Lord & Lady Hetheridge, Book #1)
Blue Murder (Lord & Lady Hetheridge, Book #2)
Something Blue (Lord & Lady Hetheridge, Book #3)
Black & Blue (Lord & Lady Hetheridge, Book #4)
Blue Blooded (Lord & Lady Hetheridge, Book #5)

Marriage Can Be Murder (Dr. Bones #1)
Divorce Can Be Deadly (Dr. Bones #2)

Dr. Bones and the Christmas Wish (Magic of Cornwall)
Dr. Bones and the Lost Love Letter (Magic of Cornwall)

Made in the USA
Middletown, DE
19 October 2023

41106491R00177